SALT LAKE
DREAMS

PAIGE WINSHIP DOOLY

D0063432

BARBOUR
PUBLISHING

Cover design: Kirk DouPonce, DogEared Design

Published by Barbour Publishing, Inc., P.O. Box 719, Uhrichsville, Ohio 44683,
www.barbourbooks.com

*Our mission is to publish and distribute inspirational products offering exceptional
value and biblical encouragement to the masses.*

Member of the
Evangelical Christian
Publishers Association

Printed in the United States of America.

Dear Reader,

Thank you for picking up a copy of *Salt Lake Dreams*! I hope you enjoy reading about the characters and their stories as much as I enjoyed writing them. Utah has a history that is rich in adventure, exploration, and outlaws. I situated each story in a setting that would best suit the characters' journey.

Join Jake and his band of misfits as they rescue Abbie from outlaws in *The Petticoat Doctor*. Through Jake, Abbie learns to trust God for her safety and her needs. In *Carousel Dreams*, Ellie Lyn finds out that she doesn't have to stand alone while running her resort and raising her precocious young daughter. As Ellie and Bascom grow closer to the Lord, they also grow closer to each other. And in the final story, *The Greatest Find*, independent Tabitha meets her match in Hunter as they compete in a dinosaur dig competition. When things get dangerous, Tabitha learns to lean on Hunter and to put her faith in God.

Though these stories are meant to entertain, I hope you'll also walk away with a stronger trust and faith in God and with a renewed desire to pursue a deeper relationship with Him.

Enjoy the Adventure!
Paige Dooly

The Petticoat Doctor

Dedication

In memory of my precious grandma, Mary Ellen.
You will be missed, Gram! I love you.

Chapter 1

Train travel wasn't at all what Abigail had hoped it to be. After years of continuous study, the twenty-four-year-old was ready for a change, ready to explore the world outside the walls of her school and even ready, perhaps, to have an adventure. Instead she sat in an overly warm, crowded train car where her nose stung with the disagreeable odor of coal smoke. Soot clung to the windows, walls, her hair, and even her wrinkled traveling dress. Nothing seemed immune to the sticky substance. Though the maroon seats were sufficiently comfortable, her muscles screamed for a chance to stretch for a longer period of time than their rapid stops allowed.

The stench of unwashed bodies, sweaty from travel and too-close quarters, filled the air around her. Abigail glanced out the window. Even the birds had it better. They were able to settle on the roof during stops where they could feel the wind upon their faces instead of sitting in a smelly, confined car like her. Granted, the smoke and soot would be even worse up there, but the birds could always take flight on a whim for some uninterrupted fresh air as the train sped up.

But she had to admit, the view outside more than made up for her discomfort. Though the window was dirty, it didn't hide the beauty that surrounded them. Tall, majestic mountains stretched high above, bumping up against a brilliant blue sky, some of them even taller than her eyes could see. Vivid green pine trees climbed the sides of the mountain, and once in a while their glorious scent wafted through the air around her. She savored the moment, knowing from her research that the view in central Utah Territory, while beautiful in its own rugged way, would be nothing like that of the Rocky Mountains that momentarily surrounded her.

The train careened around a curve, and even after several days of travel, Abigail found herself clutching her jacket in fear.

"Are you all right?"

Abigail glanced at her most current seatmate. Thin and regal, the white-haired woman had settled in beside her at the last stop, and though they had sat next to each other for the better part of an hour, the dignified woman hadn't spoken more than a few obligatory words until now.

"I am all right. Thank you." Abigail forced herself to relax. "I can't seem to get used to these ridiculously fast speeds. I've heard at times the train can go up to forty miles per hour! And some can even go sixty. Why, if the train jumps the track, I can only imagine what will happen to us!"

The woman patted Abigail's hand, her maternal touch reassuring. "I know how you feel. But I've ridden the rails many, many times, and I have never run into a problem. Ever since my husband passed away, I've traveled back and forth between my two daughters' homes. And as for speed, with all these twists and turns, I doubt we'll top fifteen miles per hour. By the way, I'm Hattie McPherson."

"I'm Abigail Hayes. And you simply cannot imagine how relieved I am to hear that you've never had a problem." Abigail took a deep breath and pointed at the newspaper beside her reticule. "I've been reading about the area since my last stop. The articles are unnerving to say the least. One mentioned the most recent train derailment, and the story covered the entire front page. The inner pages weren't any better. There are stories of outlaws and villains. Stagecoach and bank robberies. One article even talked about travelers who were cut off from their journey by a wall of rocks. And I'm traveling to that very area! Well, actually, slightly north of the area. . .as a matter of fact, central Utah Territory but still. . ." She stopped, embarrassed. "I'm sorry. I'm rambling. I tend to do that when I'm nervous."

Her new friend laughed. "I have nowhere to go. Do continue. How ever did the travelers get through? Or did they turn back?"

Abigail suspected the older woman only encouraged her as a distraction, a gesture she very much appreciated. "They had to blast their way through the mountainside. They dubbed the area Hole-in-the-Rock. It was a very interesting article. But the thought of the train derailing is what really unnerves me. I guess these articles aren't the best choice of reading material when traveling by the very same mode of transportation into the very same area."

"Never fear, nothing like that should happen to us. As I said, in all my travels, I've not once run into any of those situations."

"Good, because the thought alone has made me quite jumpy."

As soon as the words left her lips, the brakes squealed, and the train suddenly slowed to a stop. Abigail's hand returned to her chest, this time to clutch at the cross she wore on a thin chain around her neck. Her parents passed away soon after she began medical school, and she'd sold most of their belongings to pay her tuition. The small gold ornament was all she had left from her mother.

Hattie again patted her hand and gave her a kind smile. "I'm sure it's another routine stop, dear. I've not traveled this direction often enough to be sure—I'm on my way to visit my sister this trip—but most likely we'll join the masses in trying to get a quick bite to eat before the train takes off again, and that will be the most exciting aspect of our stop."

Abigail shook her head. "I've managed to evade that particular experience other than buying a boxed lunch here and there. It's pure chaos at the stations. I brought along enough provisions to last for the journey and then some. As a matter of fact, I have extra if you'd like to join me for lunch. Here, let me show you what I have." She opened her bag and began to dig around inside.

When her new friend didn't immediately answer, Abigail glanced at her. She noticed Hattie's thin face had gone pale as she stared past Abigail and out the dusty window.

"Ma'am?"

Still Hattie didn't speak; she just lifted a shaky hand and pointed outside.

Abigail shifted in her seat, lifting her heavy skirts as she moved around for a better view. She searched through the murky glass for a moment before her eyes lit on the subject of the other woman's focus.

"Oh my." Abigail's voice came out as a whisper, but in the sudden silence of the car it sounded to her like she'd bellowed. She pushed back the curls that escaped her fancy hat, but the view remained the same. "We're in the middle of a train robbery? But you just told me. . ."

"There's a first time for everything, I suppose."

Fear mingled with dismay in Abigail's chest as she glanced down at the newspaper beside her. Would this potentially harrowing adventure make the next front page? She couldn't even imagine such horrible things happening, let alone ever desire to read about them in the future. Yet here she sat, on a train entering Utah, to live with her older brother, while a band of train robbers held them up.

Because the track ahead curved gently to the right, Abbie could see the entire scene as it played out before her eyes. The front gunman moved forward. He spoke to the conductors and motioned toward the cars. Their conductor stepped inside. Abbie watched people begin filing out of the train, and several minutes later the conductor arrived in their car.

His voice wavered as he spoke, and he leaned against the wall for support. "I need to request that all passengers calmly leave the car and line up outside in a row."

A large man in the front seat loudly refused. "You can't make me go out there. We're safer if we stay put."

"He's right. I'm not going out, either. My children are dependent on me for their safety." The speaker, a plump woman, hugged her children—a boy and a girl—close.

"If we don't do as they say, the outlaws will enter the cars and escort you out," the conductor explained.

Panicked wails erupted from the children.

The conductor's face paled, and drops of sweat beaded on his forehead. "They made it clear that anyone who refuses to obey their commands will be singled out as examples."

His words had the passengers shoving for the doorway. Abigail watched as mixed emotions ranging from anger to fear moved across the faces of people sitting nearby. The conductor, his expression now sympathetic, aided each passenger as they stepped to the ground. She and Hattie, whose seats were in the middle of the car, slipped into line and moved slowly down the aisle.

They exited into the suffocating midmorning air and lined up with the others as the gunmen had requested. A pile of dynamite blocked the track. Irrationally, Abigail registered the slight breeze that blew past—the only good so far to come of this experience—which momentarily cooled her overheated skin. She found her legs were shaking and stiffened them. Anger gradually replaced her initial shock. Hattie wavered beside her, and Abigail took hold of her arm.

"We're going to be fine, Mrs. McPherson. We'll do exactly as asked, and I'm sure they'll send us safely on our way. They won't want to stay around too long and risk capture." Even as she said the words, she took hold of her necklace and slipped it beneath her collar. Though she had money and valuables in her reticule, which she'd tucked under the seat as she exited, the necklace would be far more painful to lose.

The outlaws rode closer, guiding their horses as they slowly moved along the line of dozens of travelers. A couple of them jumped down to leer into the passengers' faces.

Abigail's breath hitched as they neared. Hattie's shaking grew stronger. Inhaling deeply, Abigail forced herself to remain calm. She'd learned to keep her wits about her during medical school back in Philadelphia and would keep her wits about her now. Though fainting would be a welcome respite from the ordeal, it would also single her out and render her helpless.

The leader neared, and Abigail stared him fully in the face. His beady eyes met hers, and she released the full venom of her anger into her glower.

He pointed in her direction. "You. The lady in the fancy hat. Step forward."

Abigail glanced around her at all the women in fancy hats, and they all stared back at her. Realization set in as she slowly returned her attention to the vile man.

"Me?" Her voice squeaked, hardly depicting the ferocious image she'd meant to portray only moments earlier.

"Yes, you. Step forward." The despicable man leaned forward on his horse, his gums pulling back into a leering grin to reveal yellowed teeth. His other men fanned out along the line of people, their rifles held at the ready. Hattie gasped audibly and grabbed for Abigail's arm, frantic to hold her back, but Abigail gently pulled from her grasp. Somehow their brief friendship had gone from Hattie being the encourager to Abigail being the protector.

"What do you have for me, little lady?" The man's raspy voice caused a shiver of repulsion to run down her back.

Abigail noted with distaste that his stringy red beard was caked with what looked to be dried tobacco juice.

"I have nothing." At least her voice had grown stronger. She squared her shoulders and looked directly at him, trying not to retch at the putrid odor emanating from his unwashed body.

"Oh, I'm *sure* you have *somethin'* you can offer. Is your life worth nothin'?"

"Only when it comes to you." The words came from deep inside her, but why her lips let them escape she didn't know.

"Is that so?" The man's eyes hardened, and he motioned for one of his men to move forward. "We'll be taking you along with us. You'll regret your insolent words." He motioned to the others. "Search the passengers."

The second man, just as disgusting as the first, grabbed Abigail roughly by the arm and dragged her toward his horse. Abigail heard Hattie's panicked voice call out for someone to do something. A moment later, looking over her shoulder, Abigail saw that the woman had dropped to her knees and bowed her head in petition to God for Abigail's life. Hattie prayed loudly for God to intervene.

Just as the leader stalked forward to silence her, a shout from the far end of the line distracted him. The man holding Abigail loosened his grip as he tried to see what the commotion was about. A moment later he shoved Abigail roughly to the ground and ran for his horse. The leader and the other bandits did the same, then turned their mounts and headed for the nearby hills.

As the men scurried away, shouts of relief rang forth from the crowd as the passengers worked their way back toward their various cars. Abigail pushed to her knees, and a handsome older man with a black mustache and derby hat held out his hand to assist her. Dust swirled around them from the hasty dismount from his horse.

"Are you all right, ma'am?"

The man steadied her, but it was his quiet, gentle voice that soothed her rapidly beating heart.

"I think so. Thank you." Though he was older than she by at least a few years, if she had dreamt up a hero, this kind and thoughtful man would define him.

"You get on back to your seat then. I'm sure my friends have chased the bandits far away by now. You won't have to give them another moment's thought."

She couldn't prevent the slight quake in her words. "Perhaps I'll not give further thought to those men, but how many others like them are out there?"

"Are you traveling far?"

"Not far from here, I don't think. I'm heading for Salt Lake City, then on to Nephi."

His mouth quirked up into a brief smile. "In that case, I can pretty well assure you that no other outlaw will prevent you from reaching your destination."

"I surely hope not." She steadied her hat on her head with all the dignity she could muster. Her breath caught as she choked back the sob that threatened to escape now that the danger was past. "Are you after those men?"

"No. I chased my share of their sort in the past, though. For now I'm just a writer passing through. We saw them holding up the train and stopped to help. I hope the rest of your journey is uneventful." He tipped his hat and swung up onto his ride.

Abigail shakily returned to the train's steps where an awestruck conductor helped her aboard.

As she glanced back, the rider had already slipped into the trees at the base of the hill. She hurried to her seat, and Hattie, frantic, pulled her into a firm hug.

"Do you realize who just assisted you?"

"He only said that he's a writer."

"That, my dear, was the infamous Bat Masterson."

"Really?" Abigail raised an eyebrow and glanced back through the window. "I had no idea."

Obviously she'd had no idea about anything this dreadful trip would entail. She appreciated that the former lawman had intervened and saved her life. But at this point, she simply wanted this frightful excursion to be over. With her parents deceased and her estranged brother, Caleb, as her only family, she suddenly wanted nothing more than to reach the end of her journey and settle in at his ranch in central Utah. She'd decidedly had enough surprises and ordeals to last her a lifetime.

Chapter 2

Hank feels 'slightly irregular'?" Jake jumped down from the cumbersome wagon and jerked his worn gloves from his hands. He didn't have time for this. He'd purposely left early to tend to business in town. At the rate they were going, they'd barely meet her train, business notwithstanding. They'd already lost valuable time leaving the ranch due to Hank's sour stomach several days earlier. Now he felt "slightly irregular"?

"What on earth does 'slightly irregular' mean?" Jake glared at his men who cowered in light of his rage. He should have left the newcomer behind.

"He's sick, boss. He ate something bad, and it's doing terrible things to his stomach. He needs to make pretty frequent runs for the bushes, as you've noticed."

"For the love of—" Jake bit off the rest of the words. He'd made a conscious effort not to swear, and he wouldn't mess that up in a moment of frustration.

"God?" Scrappy, the youngest member of his group, his watery blue eyes huge, interjected the word with reverence. Tall and thin, the young man had a propensity for getting into skirmishes, hence his nickname. Jake had peeled him off the ground in an alleyway a few months earlier, where he'd been abandoned after losing a fight.

Somewhere along the line, Jake had begun the practice of collecting strays as his ranch hands.

"Jake wouldn't use the Lord's name in vain, Scrap. It's Pete, right, boss?" Grub pulled his worn hat from his large balding head, slapped Scrappy across his shoulder with it, and slammed it back in place. The cook's huge jowls jiggled as he chewed a piece of hardtack.

"Pete?" Jake echoed, confused. As usual, he had no clue what the men were talking about with their wandering conversation.

"No, a good woman." Red nudged Jake suggestively in the ribs. "You were about to say, 'for the love of a good woman.' Right?"

"Sorry to disappoint you, Red. I wasn't going to say anything of the sort. I just...," Jake shook his head. "Never mind. The point is we need to get back on the trail. Caleb trusted me to get Miss Hayes safely back to the ranch. Scrappy, go over and see what we can do to nudge Hank along."

Scrappy paled and gulped air like a dying fish. "Go over...there?" He looked toward Hank's horse with pronounced dread. All traces of humor disappeared. "I

13

can't, boss. Sick people make me. . ." He gagged dramatically without finishing the thought.

"You can't be serious."

Scrappy gagged again.

"All right." Jake sighed, looked around, and focused on his cook. The man made a living by killing animals with his bare hands and then turning them into delectable meals. Surely he wasn't squeamish. "Grub?"

Grub froze where he leaned against the wagon, biscuit halfway to his mouth, and gulped convulsively. He stared at Jake in horror. "Me?"

"Yes, you."

"Can't. It ain't good for my digestion. I've only just eaten and wouldn't want to mess up my constitution."

When *wasn't* the man eating?

Jake shook off the irritating thought and turned to the third man in their group, Red. Red's name defied him. Yellow-bellied would have been a more apt description, but since Jake wouldn't call a man such a thing to his face, the name Red was blurted out and stuck. The man was small and wiry, but women appeared to consider him handsome with his dark auburn hair and roving blue eyes. More than once his nature had gotten him into trouble when he was caught flirting with the wrong woman. Off he'd go, full speed out of town when a husband caught wind of his behavior, leaving Jake and the others to clear up the mess. Red considered himself to be the ultimate ladies' man, and he was—if a person overlooked the fact that his natural tendency made him run from all stressful situations.

"Huh-uh." Red raised his hands up in front of him and backed away. "I'm not goin' over there. From the sounds of things, he's half dead anyway. Maybe we should just leave him."

"We aren't going to leave him. I'll check on him myself. Scrappy, take care of the horses." Jake stalked off in the direction Hank had taken after pulling away from the group. His horse waited near a stand of scrubs, and from the sounds on the other side of the bush, Hank wasn't going to feel better any time soon.

Jake had a gut of lead, and the noises from behind that bush weren't welcoming no matter how tough a person might be. He froze in his tracks, spun on his heels, and hurried back to his motley band of misfits.

"Problems, boss?" Scrappy snickered.

Jake silenced him with a look. Somehow his men had it in their heads that if they provoked Jake too thoroughly, his temper would boil over. He came from mixed Irish and Mexican roots, and while his father had lived up to his Irish heritage in temper, Jake liked to think he favored his Mexican mother, who had the sweetest nature Jake had ever seen. He let the men believe their illusion. The Maverick men of the past had a history of temper, and apparently it was his father's Irish blood that the men feared.

He began to pace. He didn't have many options and made a quick decision. "If we don't pick up our pace, Miss Hayes will be waiting at the station before we can make it into town. I'll take the wagon along with Scrappy and Grub and head on in to collect her. Red, you stick around and wait for Hank to feel better, and then you both can join us."

"We'll be dead before we get there. You've heard the rumors of Injun attacks in this area."

"They're only rumors, Red. You can't put stock in such a thing. You know the Indians have moved to reservations."

"Well, there are always the stragglers—the way I heard, not all of 'em wanted to go. And what about renegades? There's something behind the stories. I've heard of several attacks."

Scrappy scratched his head, and his face contorted—a sure sign that he was deeply contemplating their dilemma. "I say we dump Hank in the wagon and tie his horse to the side."

"Very thoughtful, Scrap. I'm sure Hank will appreciate your sentiment when he feels better."

Scrappy's eyes widened briefly, and he clamped his mouth shut. One run-in with the mouthy greenhorn had apparently been enough for him.

"The boy's got a point, boss." Grub popped in the final morsel and spoke with his mouth full. Crumbs spewed out with his next words. "Maybe we don't dump him in, but we could make him a pallet and move on even if he has to balance over the side of the wagon to do his deed."

Jake tried to get his mind past that image and contemplated the rest of the idea. He didn't have a better one, and they did need to move on. "Prepare to pull out then. I'll go tell Hank the plan and secure his mount." He started in that direction.

"Boss?"

"What is it, Red?"

"How we gonna know what Miss Hayes looks like?"

Jake hesitated. "Caleb said she has long blond hair; a lively, inquisitive personality; a ready smile; and a gentle, soft-spoken nature."

"She sounds like a true angel." Red's awe was palpable.

"She sounds like nothing but trouble." Jake narrowed his eyes in warning. "And you'll do well to keep that in mind." The last thing he needed was Red—or any of the other hands—flirting with the woman. He hurried off to round up Hank.

❧

Abigail sat on her trunk at the train depot waiting for her brother and wondered why it was such a surprise that he wasn't there to meet her. After the eventful trip she'd just experienced, nothing should shock her.

The station had bustled with activity when she'd first descended the stairs of the train, but now only a few stragglers remained. A man and child eagerly embraced a well-dressed woman who had traveled in Abigail's car, and Abigail felt a wistful smile twist her mouth as she watched them. The lines at the ticket window had long ago disappeared, and only a wagon here and there passed by on the nearby road. Abigail suddenly felt very alone.

She carefully studied the face of each passerby, but no one remotely resembled her older brother. Thinking of the years that had passed since she'd last seen him, Abigail's heart thumped in eagerness for their reunion. Thankfully, she'd been able to clean up from the trip before greeting him. She tried to smooth the wrinkles from her dress, but when that proved fruitless, she settled with splashing some water on her smudged face from the nearby hand pump.

She found herself missing Hattie and wished her new friend had continued to Salt Lake City. Instead the woman departed the train a few stops earlier, and now Abigail waited alone while tamping down a growing panic that stemmed from not knowing a single person in town.

A well-dressed man approached. After looking about the now empty platform, he politely inquired about her escort. When she mentioned she was expecting one momentarily, his face wrinkled into a frown. "Might I accompany you over to the hotel and help you secure a room? It isn't safe for a woman to wait alone."

Though not nearly as handsome as her rescuer during the train robbery and not nearly as muscular or tall, this man had kind eyes and his own type of charm. He wore a crisp white shirt and neatly creased gray pants—so perfect that they looked ready-made and straight off the store shelf. His hair lay meticulously pressed into place under his pristine black hat. His apparent care in choosing his attire showed an attention to detail, which Abigail could appreciate. And which made her feel dowdy in comparison.

"I appreciate the offer, but my brother will be along shortly." She frowned. The fact that she'd missed a connecting train due to the attempted train robbery unnerved her. Then several other delays had put her into town way behind schedule, causing her to miss her connecting train into Nephi. And while she could take another train down to Nephi, she wouldn't be able to get one until the next day. She didn't want to leave and miss her brother in passing. Even after that wretched experience with the train robbers, safety concerns about sitting here alone hadn't entered her mind until now. She'd felt perfectly secure waiting for her brother, but what if she had a false security? Her stomach clenched in fear, and she sat up straighter in an effort to hide the tremble that rolled through her body.

What if Caleb had arrived earlier and, not finding her, had headed back home? Earlier in the day, when she'd first realized she was behind schedule, she'd sent a telegram to Nephi, informing Caleb about the delay. When she arrived at Salt Lake City, she found a return telegram telling her to stay put because Caleb would meet her there. Why hadn't she thought to have him leave more specific word so she'd know more clearly what to do? She had no idea when Caleb would arrive or how long she should wait before heading over to the hotel.

Surely he'd wait and check several trains first. But if so, wouldn't he already be at the station? Again she fought back her panic. She'd made it through school at the Women's Medical College back in Philadelphia—a difficult but satisfying achievement—and she would make it through this final leg of her journey. It wouldn't do to fall apart now. Most likely Caleb had stepped across the street for a late noon meal and would return shortly to collect her.

"Is there anything I can assist you with? You look most unhappy. I hope it wasn't something I said."

She started to shake her head, but was distracted when she saw movement out of the corner of her eye. Eagerly, she peered around the friendly man as another male hurried along the rough hewn sidewall of the station. She looked up at him with hope. Her heart plummeted, though, when he glanced her way. The handsome but dangerous looking man most assuredly wasn't her brother. Though she hadn't seen Caleb since she was fourteen, his fair coloring and playful nature wouldn't have changed into this scowling, brooding man even in the decade that had passed. Nor would this be the type of man that the Caleb she remembered would ever associate with.

Though she knew it wasn't polite, she couldn't help but study him with errant fascination. For the first time since disembarking the train, she felt she'd really arrived in the Wild West. A low-slung belt around his waist held two pistols, one on either side of his slim hips, and a lethally sharp knife lay sheathed next to one of the pistols. His form-fitting tan pants outlined sturdy leg muscles as he stalked along the walkway, and he wore his shirtsleeves rolled up far above his elbow, which highlighted his sun-kissed arms and accentuated strong biceps. As an avid student of anatomy, Abigail couldn't help but appreciate the years necessary to hone the man's muscles into such an enticing package. The men she'd known back in the city were all pale and thin with no muscle tone to speak of.

She forced herself to move her perusal on to his face and froze in mortification.

His dark brown eyes bore into hers, and for a long moment she forgot to breathe. He'd stopped walking sometime in the last minute and now stared back at her with raised eyebrows. Long black hair dusted against his collar and framed his strikingly handsome features, perfectly balanced by high cheekbones. He deepened his scowl, which marred his classic features into a most unapproachable and disgruntled grimace. Abigail shivered. Thank goodness for her innate ability to judge character. She'd do well to avoid the likes of him and to warmly embrace the protection offered by the kind gentleman at her side.

The well-dressed man beside her turned his back on the newcomer and stepped protectively close. Abigail sent him her most charming, grateful smile. At this moment, more than ever, Abigail welcomed his reassuring presence.

℘

Jake bit his lower lip in frustration. He knew he should have been on time, but situations happened and he couldn't change that now. He'd arrived in Nephi, only to find a telegram stating that Abigail wouldn't make the connecting train from Salt Lake City. They'd left the wagon there, sent a return telegram telling her to stay put, arranged passage for the men and their horses on the train, and had just arrived in Salt Lake City.

His men were still unhappy with the decision.

"I still don't see why we had to ride in, boss, instead of waiting for her to arrive in Nephi in the morning," Red had grumbled.

"After Bert beat up Caleb and left him for dead, he told Caleb his final revenge would be to kidnap Caleb's sister."

"But how would he know she was in Salt Lake City, especially if her train's late?" Scrappy's confusion had shown on his face.

"He might not know, but if he's here waiting, hoping to intercept her, this would give him the perfect opportunity. We can't afford to risk it. I have a bad feeling about the whole situation. If Bert gets to her first, I'll need each of you and our horses to go after them."

But the only woman in sight rested on a large trunk and didn't begin to match Caleb's description. Her dress, though tousled, spoke of money and class, and she wore her hair pulled back severely and tucked beneath a huge frilly hat. The woman's cool green eyes studied Jake with blatant interest, much longer than propriety allowed, before suddenly dismissing him with disdain. She obviously belonged with the man who stood intimately close to her side. Jake didn't envy him. He certainly wouldn't want to be saddled with such a disloyal woman. She returned her attention to her oblivious companion, and Jake backtracked to his waiting men.

"Just as I expected, she isn't here." He sighed, wondering if the day could possibly get any worse. A rumble of thunder in the distance proved that it could. "Scrappy, Grub, go check the restaurant across the street. She might have decided to eat dinner while she waits." He hesitated. If Grub stepped into an eating establishment he'd surely want to taste all that was offered. "On second thought, Red, you go with Scrappy. Grub, you'll come with me, and we'll check the nearest hotel and boardinghouse."

Hank, who had made a miraculous recovery once they resumed their trip, offered to go and talk to the stationmaster. "I'll see if he remembers anyone with her unique description."

Jake nodded and stalked away, Grub's heavy legs double-stepping to keep up.

Chapter 3

I simply cannot let you sit here alone a moment longer. Allow me to escort you to lunch, and then we'll set about finding you a decent place to stay while waiting for your...," he paused, "brother, did you say?"

"Yes. My brother Caleb. And how very kind of you to look out for my best interests in this way." She hesitated. Back home she'd never have spoken to a strange man, let alone let him escort her anywhere. But maybe things were different out West. And what choice did she really have? Besides, a restaurant sat just across the road. How much trouble could she get into on such a short walk? After seeing the arrogant man who had rounded the corner last, she had no idea what the next scoundrel's arrival might bring.

The dapper man held out his hand, and she allowed him to assist her to her feet. Her legs were tired from the long wait, and despair coursed through her. How would Caleb find her if she left? And how would she transport her trunk?

"What is it?" The man dipped his knees to peer directly into her eyes. "If you'd feel better, I can find some people to vouch for my character."

"It's not that. If I leave, I don't know how my brother will find me. And what about my trunk? I can't just leave it here."

"Sure you can. Stationmasters look after people's belongings all the time. And we'll leave a message for your brother. He'll ask about your arrival at the window, will he not?"

"I suppose. If you're sure." Thoroughly disconcerted, Abigail suddenly felt as if this man were her lifeline. If he were to leave, she'd be terrified. All her brave aspirations that had brought her thus far now deserted her. The enthusiasm that accompanied her from Philadelphia had seeped from her bones with her energy. She hadn't had a solid meal in days. And she didn't know where to go even if she had the courage to do such a thing alone.

A sudden realization hit her. "Wait!"

He stopped and spun on his heels, anxiety creeping across his features. "Is there a problem?"

"Only in that I've agreed to accompany you to dinner, and I don't even know your name."

A strange mix of relief and annoyance battled across his face before he smiled and hurried back to her side. "Please forgive my complete lack of manners. I was so distraught to see you here alone that I forgot the most basic rule of etiquette." He pulled his hat from his head and gave her a slight bow. "Allow me to introduce myself. I'm Robert Sanchez. At your service."

"Abigail Hayes. And all is forgiven. I'm so tired I'm not thinking clearly myself. I'm sure that once I have a nice meal and locate a safe hotel room, I'll feel much better. I can have my trunk brought over as soon as I have a place to stay."

"Sounds like a good plan."

His eyes surveyed her oddly, almost in question, and Abigail felt a peculiar anxiety form in the pit of her stomach as he sauntered over to the stationmaster.

She glanced across the street and saw a large family enter the eating establishment. No harm could come from one meal with a stranger—a kind stranger at that—could it?

Robert hurried back to her side, led her along the boardwalk to the front of the station, and gestured for her to move ahead of him toward the steps that led down to the road. She carried her valise along. Surprisingly, he didn't offer to carry the large bag for her. So much for chivalry. As she paused at the edge of the road to check for errant wagons before she began to cross the street, he put his hand to her back and guided her instead toward a cluster of horses.

"Oh." She stopped on the spot. "I thought we'd eat over there, somewhere close where I can see my brother if he arrives."

Robert leaned closer than propriety allowed. "Change of plans. If and when you eat, it will be far away from here. I can assure you that your brother won't be showing up to surprise you."

Abigail stared at him in stunned silence before looking around for someone who might offer her aid. Though the street bustled with activity, no one was near enough to do her any good. Maybe if she screamed...

"Don't even think about it."

She felt a small cylindrical object press against her side. She glanced down. He had a *gun*? Her pulse raced, and she struggled to breathe, her breaths coming in rapid gasps. "But why?"

"Let's just say you're the payment for a little debt your brother had to settle with me."

"My brother? Why would he ever associate with the likes of you?" Her own inability to trust her instincts rested heavy upon her heart. She'd fallen for the deceitful man's trap. Why wouldn't her brother? Gullibility apparently ran in the family. From this side of the situation, even the rough-looking man at the station might have been a better choice of company.

Robert pushed the gun harder into her side. "Get up on the horse and don't bother trying to make a scene. I've shot more than one man dead in the street and rode away to tell about it. It won't bother me a bit to try the same with you."

He smirked at her, his eyes suddenly cold.

She did as he asked, but stepped hard on his foot with her pointy heel as she stalked by him.

He grunted in response and shoved her.

The horse loomed above, and she struggled to mount him. The horse danced in irritation, and Abigail clutched at the saddle horn.

"Leave the bag behind."

"I will not. It contains things I need."

"Fine. It's your choice, but don't expect any of us to carry it for you."

He grabbed her waist and shoved her up and almost over the other side of the huge beast. She clasped the saddle horn with one hand and her large bag with the other and dangled precariously toward the far side before righting herself. She sent him her most haughty glare as his words sank in.

"Us?"

"My men or myself."

He had men? What on earth had she gotten herself into? All her life she'd been sheltered and pampered. Not until her parents died had she ever been alone. And by then she'd been deeply enmeshed in her education, and her school responsibilities carried her through the grief. Only now, for the first time, did she have an inkling of how utterly alone in the world she'd become. "What have you done to my brother?"

He made a hard sound. "You don't have to worry about him. Your brother turned me in on gambling charges. He agreed for me to take you as my bride in exchange for the debt."

"He'd never agree to such a thing."

The man had the audacity to laugh. "Well, maybe he didn't exactly agree, but he wasn't in any shape to disagree when I left him. I figure if I have you along, I'll have a little leverage in the event the law catches up with me. Suffice it to say, you won't have to fret about him coming after you. He's been taken care of."

"Taken care of?" As a physician she'd promised to do everything in her means to protect the life of her fellow man. This man made her want to betray that promise. "Did you hurt him? Because if you did. . ."

He leaned close. "If I did. . .then what?"

He trailed a dirty finger along her cheek, and she fought off a shudder. How had she missed the obvious signs of the disreputable man who now blocked her path? She refused to let him know how much he disgusted her.

"You'll be sorry."

He looked at the man who had watched the horses and grinned, sarcasm dripping from his raised eyebrows. "Did you hear that? I'll be sorry."

He suddenly swung back around and grabbed her by the arm, almost yanking her from her mount. "You listen to me. If you don't do as I say, *you'll* be the one who's sorry. Your brother is dead. Now shut up and move along." He squeezed her arm hard before releasing her, and she grappled with balance once again. Tears formed, but she furiously blinked them back.

Terrified, she did as he said. Abigail remained silent as she rode up the street alongside her captor. If it was true and her brother was dead. . .she had nowhere to go. But if he was dead, who had sent the telegram from Nephi? At least someone out there knew of her arrival. She could only hope they'd come after her. She'd worry about her future when she was safe.

Part of her felt it would be better to make a scene and let the dust settle as it may. But another part of her insisted upon staying safely in the saddle. She somehow knew she'd get away. Even if her intuition had failed her, surely her intellect would prevail. It had to.

They met up with his gang outside of town, and he didn't even bother to introduce her. She felt grateful for that fact. As far as she was concerned, the less contact she had with the ruffians the better. The dirty, unkempt men brandished a variety of sidearms and looked as dangerous as the men who'd held up the train.

Abigail hadn't been in a saddle for years, and it took all her concentration not to bounce off while juggling her large bag. According to the sun's location, they were heading south at a fast pace.

Robert moved ahead as they neared a small cabin and called back over his shoulder. "Stay with her, Boggs. We'll check things out."

"Sure, Bert. I got her covered." Boggs, a burly looking man, dropped back to ride beside her.

"I don't need to be 'covered.' I'm not going anywhere." Abigail wasn't foolish enough to try to escape. At least not yet. But *Bert's* intentions at the farmhouse had her more than a little concerned. Though the last thing she wanted in the world was to speak to the vile man beside her, she couldn't help asking. "What are they going to do?"

He leaned forward in the saddle. "Do you want the graphic version or the watered-down one?"

Abigail gulped. "Watered-down, please."

"They're going to get supplies."

"Will they hurt the people who live there?"

"I thought you wanted it watered down."

She shuddered. "Never mind."

Against her will, tears began to course down her cheeks. Though she wasn't familiar with prayer, she tried to recall Hattie's prayer back at the train robbery. Maybe if she could find the right words, God would watch out for the people inside.

Dear God, I don't know You real well. Actually, I don't know You at all. But I saw how Hattie's prayers were answered at the train, and I'm wondering if You could consider doing the same for me. I'm willing to read up on how all this works in that book of Yours, but I can only do that if I survive long enough to get away from these awful men. And please, if I can put in a special request for the people who live at this cabin, could You somehow keep them safe?

"What're you muttering about over there?" Boggs pulled his horse closer.

Abigail sighed. "Nothing." Most likely it *was* nothing. She didn't feel any different or better, and the sky didn't split open and release a lightning bolt to strike down the miscreants. As a matter of fact, the storm that had brewed on the horizon all afternoon still lingered there.

Bert kicked through the front door, and the men filed inside the homestead. A few moments later they exited, looking disgruntled. Abigail's heart picked up speed. Bert motioned for Boggs and Abigail to move forward.

"What's the problem?"

"No one's here. Ruins all the fun."

Sick, despicable man. Abigail felt a scowl pass over her face even as she felt a jolt of excitement that her prayer had been answered. Or had it? The people hadn't been here in the first place, so did that really count as an answer to prayer? She didn't begin to know. She did know she felt happy that a family wouldn't be hurt. At least, not if the gang resumed their journey before the occupants returned.

"So, how far behind us do you think anyone chasing us might be?" Her innocently phrased question had the desired effect.

"Let's get a move on." Bert directed a couple of guys to ransack the house, and he headed toward the barn. Abigail tried to relax in the saddle, but the sound of gunfire and a panicked squeal from the barn had her swinging down and running to the open door.

She raced through the opening, anger making her careless. Bert whirled and turned the gun on her. At this point, she didn't care. Dying by his bullet was preferable to whatever else he might have planned for her.

"What have you done?" She glanced around and tried to identify the victim. She saw a large pink shape in the dusky interior and stepped closer for a better view.

Apparently Bert decided to let her have a look because he lowered his weapon and motioned her forward.

"You shot a pig?" she asked in disbelief. She surveyed the animal before them. A tiny piglet squealed and clambered around Abigail's skirt, tripping over her boots. The rest of the litter huddled in a far corner. She bent down and scooped the panicky piglet up into her arms. "Why?"

"Why not? There's nothing else here to shoot."

Abigail heard snickers behind her at the door and glanced back to see the other men gathered there.

" 'Sides. We gotta eat, don't we?"

The piglet had calmed in her arms. Abigail stalked past the vile men and headed for the barn door. No way would she eat the piglet's mother in front of him. She'd starve first.

"I'll take you along with me, but you have to behave." Abigail had a feeling if she left the piglet, Bert would shoot it, too. Most likely he'd still shoot it, but she had to try to protect the innocent creature. Her own inability to protect herself drove her to it. If she had something to care for, she wouldn't feel so vulnerable. "I'll call you Hamm, but we'll work hard to make sure you don't become one."

Abigail realized the men were focused at the moment on planning the best way to remove the larger pig to a place where they could cook a meal. She quickly headed for her horse. Wrapping the piglet in a soft cloth, she secured him on top of her open valise. With newly practiced ease, she balanced her bag on the saddle and swung up to sit behind it.

Tufts of dust rose up from the north, and she prayed it was a rescue team sent to retrieve her, not the owners returning home. She lost valuable moments debating her next move. If she rode toward the dust and ran into the homesteaders, she'd lead the gang straight to them. She couldn't live with that thought so turned the horse around to head the other way. She could always double back.

"Where do you think you're going?" Bert had exited the barn and walked her way.

Abigail couldn't resist one more glance toward the north.

Bert followed her motion with his eyes.

"Come on out here," he bellowed to the others while climbing on his mount. "We gotta get going."

Disappointed, Abigail consoled herself with the knowledge that at least no one else would be hurt because of her poor decision-making skills.

A loud squeal burst forth from her bag. Well, no one would be hurt unless Hamm met his demise due to her rescue attempt.

"What was that?" Bert rode closer.

"What was what?"

The squeal resumed as the piglet head butted the interior. The bag shifted, and Abigail had to grab for it so it didn't fall to the ground. "Lay still, Hamm."

She held her head high and continued forward.

"You brought the piglet along?"

Abigail shrugged. "I'll make sure I give restitution to the owners as soon as I'm able."

"He's the runt. He's already been ostracized by the rest of the litter. The owners will likely shoot him." He stared hard at her. "You know he's not going to make it."

"I know I'm not likely to make it, either." Abigail turned to look him fully in the eyes. "But I'll do my best for us both in the meantime."

Bert momentarily stared at her in shock and then let loose a sinister laugh. "Yes, you do that. You'll each fill a specific appetite when you fail."

Chapter 4

Jake looked around. His chest tightened with anxiety, and he felt each passing moment weigh heavily upon him. They'd lost a lot of time looking for Miss Hayes. Though he'd peeked into the boardinghouse's dining room earlier, he thought he'd check one more time in case he'd missed her. This was the most likely place for her to wait if she'd indeed arrived. The commerce area was mostly silent, with townsfolk likely home preparing for their evening meal, but a few couples strolled along the boardwalk here and there.

Jake stepped into the rough-hewn building, and his mouth watered as the pungent aroma of baked chicken teased his nose. He glanced around, taking note of each diner that lined either side of the sturdy wood table, but none of them fit Abigail's description. A woman bustled through a doorway on the far side of the kitchen and waved him to a seat.

"Just pick a place and make yourself comfortable. I'll bring you a plate in a moment."

Jake waved her away. "I won't be staying. I'm looking for a friend. A female friend."

The woman hesitated, wiping her hands on her apron. "Tell me what she looks like, and I'll tell you if she's been through here today."

"She came in on the train, or at least she was supposed to." He described Abigail to the best of his ability, but the friendly woman shook her head before he finished.

"No one matching that description dined with us today." She hesitated a moment, and her expression turned thoughtful. "There was a lady across the street. . . ."

"Did she match the description?" Jake hoped he'd found a clue to Abigail's whereabouts.

"Well, she was far away, and it was hectic, but I glanced out and saw a couple across the way a couple of hours back." She frowned again, contemplating her words. "I was able to see her clearly enough to see her confident smile as she started across the street toward our establishment. She appeared to be escorted by the man, but when she moved in this direction, he stepped close and said something to her. Suddenly her entire countenance changed. She glanced around, and her expression turned to panic." The woman twisted her apron in her hands. "I figured perhaps she'd taken ill because she glanced down and the man took hold of her and guided her the other way. I lost track after that because things became hectic again. I'm afraid from there I don't know what happened to her. I'm really sorry I can't be of more help."

Jake asked for a description of the woman's attire, and his heart sank. She matched the description of the woman at the train depot. Surely she hadn't been Caleb's sister! If so, who was the gentleman with her? *Please, Lord, don't let it be Bert.* Caleb hadn't mentioned Abigail having a travel companion. "You said she looked distraught?"

"Yes, she did. I'm so sorry. I got busy and didn't give it another thought until now. I do hope she didn't fall in with the wrong person. It's generally safe around this area, but you never know."

"No, you never do." Jake thanked her and headed out the door. He saw Scrappy and Red heading his way and met them in front of the train station. "Any news?"

"No, boss. We didn't find out a thing. No one saw hide nor hair of anyone matching Miss Hayes's description." Red rubbed his chin. "What about you?"

Jake shared his information, and both men's faces reflected his own concern. "Where's Hank? Maybe he found out something new."

As if his words called forth the man, Hank rounded the corner of the train station and jogged down the steps to join them. "I hate to tell you this, but a woman matching Miss Hayes's description arrived on the last train and left with a man awhile back."

"How long ago?" Jake bit out the words, now more sure than ever that the woman on the trunk must have been Abigail.

"Not more than two hours. He said she waited alone for a bit before a man came up and made conversation with her. The only reason he remembered her was because she left a trunk with him."

"Has she returned to fetch it?"

Hank shrugged. "I didn't think to ask."

Jake bit back his retort and instead took the steps two at a time and hurried to the ticket window. The man checked a pocket watch, stuck it in the pocket of his pin-striped vest, and stepped Jake's way. "May I help you, sir?"

Jake didn't waste words. "I need to see the trunk the woman passenger left behind."

"I'm afraid I can't do that, sir. I can only release the trunk to her or her escort upon her return."

"That's just the thing. I *am* her escort. And I think she's fallen into the wrong hands. I need to verify that the trunk belongs to the woman I'm here to pick up."

"I can read you her name." He ruffled through some papers and picked up a note. "Abigail Hayes."

"Send the trunk on to Nephi."

A frown of concern furrowed the man's forehead. "Has she met up with foul play?"

"I sure hope not, but it appears that way. I'll head over to alert the sheriff before I start out of town."

❧

Abigail watched with horrified fascination as the drunken men who held her captive staggered around their makeshift camp and waved their loaded weapons brazenly in the air. They'd traveled hard for two days, and Abigail had lost hope that anyone would come to rescue her. If she were to get away, it would be at her own hand.

She jumped as gunfire went off nearby. The acrid stench of gunpowder drifted through the air and made her sneeze. The low fire offered little light, and she stayed in the shadows, hoping the despicable men would leave her alone. Boggs, who had apparently assigned himself her temporary protector, was the only man not drinking. Bert, her husband-to-be, drank slower than the others, but still he'd had more than his share.

No sooner had she thought his name when he dropped to sit beside her in a fluff of dust. "Well, bride. I see that you're staying awake to watch the festivities?"

"If you consider the suicidal acts of imbeciles festive, then yes, I guess I am. Though it's a tad hard to sleep when wondering if a stray bullet will cause my demise at any moment."

He reached out and ran a calloused finger up the sleeve of her blouse. "Well, after tomorrow you'll worry no more."

A prickle of fear coursed up Abigail's back. She asked the question she knew she didn't want answered. "Why is that?"

"Because tomorrow night you'll become my bride." His sinister laugh repulsed her. Everything about him repulsed her.

"I can't. I won't." She scrambled backward, tufts of dust encircling her boots. "I won't become your wife tomorrow or ever." She waved the dust away from her face, but the force of her words was weakened by the dust-induced sneeze that followed.

Bert clutched her skirt and yanked her forward in the dirt, her backside dragging through the dusty soil, and pulled her hard against him. He grasped her hair, wound his fingers into her curls, and pulled her face up against his. "You can marry me, and you will. Do you understand?"

Her eyes blurred at the pain his tight grasp caused her tender scalp. More than once during the past two days, he'd reacted in the same violent way. Most of her hairpins had come loose and were lost due to his rough handling. She knew she'd die before she ever became his wife. His terse words and hard eyes dared her to defy him. Before her lips could form the sharp retort in rebuttal, another loud crack filled the air, and this time a scream of pain quickly followed.

"You *shot* me, you idiot!"

"Only 'cause you jumped in front of my grun. . .gurn. . .um. . .gun, you imbecile."

Bert released his tight hold, and Abigail sank back from him. She watched as the two men staggered dangerously close to the fire before the shooting victim fell to the ground. Though she'd still not been introduced to the men, she knew from hearing them talk that the gunman, Walter, had shot the meeker man, Bill.

She didn't want to get involved, but she'd taken an oath and felt compelled to honor it. "I can help him." She spat the words through clenched teeth.

"Oh yeah? What are you going to do. . .shoot him again?" Bert glanced at Boggs and laughed. Boggs didn't respond. Instead he nodded and directed Abigail to move forward.

"Boggs, could you bring me my bag?" Abigail hurried to the fallen man's side and tried to see the severity of his wound in the dim firelight. Boggs arrived at her side with the bag and took hold of Bill's healthy arm and dragged him closer to the fire. He then hurried off to grab some kindling to throw on the blaze, allowing Abigail more light to work with.

The bullet had entered the front of his upper arm, but hadn't come out the back. "I'll need to remove the bullet before packing his wound."

"You ain't touchin' his arm." Bert had moved close behind her, and she jumped at his nearness.

"If I don't he'll get an infection and die." She dug through her bag and lined the necessary items alongside her on a clean towel. "Boggs, I'll need some water boiled over the fire."

Boggs hurried off to do as she directed.

"Wait a minute." Bert's words were slurred as he watched her movements. "How do you know how to do this?"

"I'm a physician." For the first time, she stared him hard in the eyes. "I'm trained to do this."

"A fish-ish-ion? Like, a doctor?"

She nodded and registered the look of respect that momentarily passed over his features.

"Well how d'ya like that? I'm marrying a lady doctor."

"No, you're not."

"Yesh, I am." His eyes rolled up, and he fell backward.

Boggs returned with the water and set it to boil. He grasped Bert by the heels and slid him from the area. Again the dust tickled her nose and made her sneeze. A coarse laugh behind her made her glance away from her ministrations to Bill's arm.

Boggs squatted nearby, ready to help if needed. "You'd best get ahold of yourself with those sneezes. If you're sensitive to the conditions now, you'll be miserable as summer progresses."

A small smile shaped Abigail's mouth. "I can't stop myself from sneezing, now can I? Apparently there are a lot of unknowns on this trip I hadn't expected." She tore Bill's sleeve off, and he moaned.

"And I'm right sorry, Doc, that things are working out this way for you."

Abigail stilled her hands and looked over at him. "Then why are you going along with it? Why don't you stand up to Bert or help me get away?"

Boggs sent her a sympathetic frown. "I would if I could. But Bert has a way of finding folks' weak spots. With you, it's your brother. With me, it's my wife and child. He knows where they are, and he's threatened that if I don't do his bidding, he'll make them pay for my foolishness in getting involved with him."

"So you'll let him control you forever? When does it end? Your wife and child are alone while you're out here with him, miserable. I can see it in your eyes."

"Aye, I am miserable, but at least they're safe."

Abigail placed a hand on his arm. "Boggs, you need to get away. If you go now, he'll let you leave. He's too focused on me to change plans. You go get your wife and child and take them away from here to safety."

He sighed. "And leave you behind? I can't do that when you've been so thoughtful. Look. I deserve to be with the gang. You don't. I voluntarily rode with them before I realized just how corrupt they were. We'd fallen on hard times, and I thought some easy money would be nice. But you came along and suddenly I'm thinking of my wife and her spunk and I'm missing her. She'd want me to help you. You leave, and I'll hold them off. I'll figure out a way to lose them later."

Abigail glanced down at Bill's silent form. "If I leave, he'll die. I need to remove the bullet and stop the bleeding. He'll need watching for the next couple of days." She remembered Hattie's prayer and her immediate answer. Though Abigail's own later prayer had gone largely unanswered, she felt in her heart that if she did the right thing—if she stayed to save the rotten life of the big oaf before her—she'd somehow be all right.

❧

Jake pulled back on the reins and slowed his mount. "I don't understand. Why haven't we caught up with them? We know the direction they headed. We talked to the people whose homestead was ransacked. We've followed their tracks this far."

"They have to be running their horses hard." Hank rode up alongside him.

"We can't keep up the same pace. The mounts are tired, and the men need to rest."

"We'll continue on as long as the moon is bright enough to travel by. I won't lose any more time. I have no idea what the man's intentions are, and I won't have Caleb's sister terrorized when I'm supposed to be watching out for her."

They rode in silence. The moon shone down to highlight the landscape into eerie shapes. Jake's neck prickled in response. He sent up a prayer for protection. Something evil was afoot, and he wasn't sure what.

Hank broke the silence. "Jake?"

"What?"

"The stationmaster told me Miss Hayes apparently went willingly with the gentleman. He said they appeared to be friendly."

"And what do you make of that? She didn't come in on the train with the man. She never wrote to tell her brother of a chaperone or male companion who would meet her when she arrived. What is it you're getting at?"

"I don't know exactly, other than those are the facts as I know them. Something isn't right, and I just figured you'd want to know. She might not be the sweet little sister Caleb remembers her to be."

"Did the stationmaster mention the man's name? The one that she left with?"

"Robert. Robert Sanchez."

Jake's stomach did a slow dive. "Robert Sanchez? Are you sure?"

"Positive." Hank looked at him from under his hat. "Why, do you know him?"

"He's the man who intended to send Caleb to his deathbed. Caleb helped the sheriff capture Bert for gambling charges. Bert got away, and Caleb paid a price. If I hadn't found him when I did, he'd be dead right now. The fact that Bert left his real name at the station means he intended to send a message to me. . .or more likely to Caleb. I'm sure Bert figured Caleb would pick her up if he survived the attack."

"But where does his sister fit in?" Hank persisted. "If she knew Bert, do you suppose she had something to do with Caleb's attack?"

"I have no idea, but for now I think we should keep quiet about our connection to Caleb when we meet up with her. I need to find out more about this Abigail Hayes before taking her to see Caleb. I won't have him hurt again."

☙

Morning dawned with the beautiful sky painted in hues of pink, orange, and lavender. The day—her *wedding day*—so perfectly bright and sunny, mocked her panic over the passing of time. She needed a miracle. She could feel her hair arc out in a halo of wild curls after the restless night she'd spent caring for Bill. He'd pulled through and didn't show any sign of fever, much to Abigail's relief.

She sat up and stretched, taking in the location of each of the men around her. They'd passed out in various sections of the camp. She smiled when she realized Boggs had disappeared at some point during the night. Perhaps he'd heeded her suggestion and had left to take his wife and child to safety. She hoped so. If that were the case, at least one good thing would have come out of this sorry mess.

Abigail checked Bill's wound and leaned back on her heels. Today would be a turning point; she could feel it. She wouldn't "marry" Bert tonight as he planned. With no reverend around, there'd be no proper wedding, and she refused to act and accept anything less when her time came.

Since she'd stabilized Bill, she had the perfect opportunity to slip away while the others slept. God willing, she'd escape and find help before the gang caught up with her. The thought gave her pause. She had no experience with the rugged landscape and from what she saw, nothing but mountains and scrub bushes and dry landscape surrounded them. She had no idea how to get food, or how to find water, once she left the men. After securing Hamm in her bag, she snuck over and quietly worked to loosen her mount's ropes as her mind raced through her options. She could backtrack and try to follow their previous trail and the landmarks she'd noted as they rode by on the previous days, which would allow her to find water and possibly even food. Or she could continue south and hope to find another ranch or homestead, though the area appeared to be pretty barren.

Lord, I tried this before and it didn't go so well. I don't feel like You heard my prayer. But if possible, I need a miracle. I need out of this situation. Please don't make me marry Bert. I don't have many options, but maybe You could help me find the best one.

As she contemplated her choices, a chilling scream filled the air. Her horse reared and pulled from her grasp and took off at a frantic run. The hair on the back of Abigail's neck stood up, and she watched as the men stumbled to their feet, disoriented.

The horrendous scream sounded again, and the men jumped into action. Bert snatched up his rifle and jumped onto his mount in one fluid motion. He never once looked around for Abigail or anyone else. Walter's horse left him behind, so he began to run on foot, carrying his boots. Bill lurched sideways, stumbling weakly away from the commotion. Abigail stood rooted to the spot, not knowing what was happening. After a moment she followed the men's lead and grabbed her bag and, without her mount to escape on, ran toward a large boulder. She ducked behind it as the men fled the area.

More screams filled the air and, petrified, she watched between cracks of the large piece of stone as a band of fierce Indians surrounded her captors and struck them down with their weapons. Bert never made it to the trees. Walter lay facedown, his boots still clutched in his hand. Bill lay a few yards away from him. Abigail gulped for air, trying to quiet the terror that tried to force a scream from her own throat. She knew her life depended upon her silence. She rocked back and forth on her knees, hugging Hamm close against her chest, willing him to stay quiet.

The chaos died down along with the men who'd captured her. The savages stood and surveyed their handiwork. Abigail began to shake. Though the gang of men was despicable, no one deserved to die at the Indians' hands as these men just had. The dust settled over the area, and Abigail's panic increased as she felt a tickle in her nose. If she sneezed, they'd know she was there. She dropped her head and prayed as she'd seen Hattie do during the train robbery. She threw herself forward, facedown, and muffled her face in the folds of her skirt. But try as she might, she couldn't contain the sneeze that burst forth. She peeked through the crack between the rocks and watched in horror as a tall Indian, dressed in black leggings and a black shirt and who wore his long hair in beaded braids, began to walk in her direction. She felt faint, but instead of giving in to her fear, she gave in to her anger.

"That's *it!*" Abigail screeched. She jumped to her feet in a complete rage. At the same time, she held Hamm close and cuddled him protectively against her breast.

The approaching Indian stopped in his tracks. His face registered a look of complete shock.

Abigail felt the fury seethe out from her eyes as she surveyed the sickening massacre before her. Never in her life had she felt such a pure, unbridled wrath. She stomped her foot, hard, and shrieked again—the sound foreign to her ears— before stepping methodically forward. As she walked with slow, steady steps, she flipped back the mass of blond hair that had tumbled loose the day before when she'd lost her hat.

The Indian looked over his shoulder, but the other braves had retreated at her first scream. With a look of trepidation, sprinkled with confusion, he also took a step backward.

Abigail's chest heaved with each deep breath of air she forced into her lungs.

"In the past seventy-two hours," she hissed through clenched teeth, "I've been held up in a train robbery, kidnapped by an outlaw and his gang, and attacked by Indians—*you*." She spat the word and poked the surprised man in the chest with her finger. "I've watched my friends *die*. Well, maybe they weren't my friends and maybe they were more like enemies, but still, they *didn't* deserve to die!"

She continued to punch her finger into his chest as she enunciated to underscore each of her words. She paused, panting and trying to catch her breath as the anger coursed through her. "So, if you have it in your minds to do something awful to me and Hamm, then by all means," she spat at the man's chest and released the last of her rage in a scream that defied definition, "get it over with *now!*"

Hamm's reaction to her pitch was immediate. With a loud squeal, he poked his head from the blanket and stared into the native's face. The man, after seeing the pig's head pop out from beneath the blanket, backed up so quickly that he tripped and went head over heels. Without missing a beat, he flew to his feet and retreated, motioning for the others to flee, while repeating the same foreign word over and over.

Abigail tipped her head back and let out an anguished cry as she dropped to her knees. She knew without checking that all the men were dead. Her inexperienced prayer had caused their deaths. She hugged Hamm close and curled up into a ball. She hoped the Indians came back. She didn't deserve to live.

She crawled back behind the boulder to shut out the gruesome sight before her. The terror of the moment caught up with her, and in shock she fell into a deep sleep.

Chapter 5

W hoa." Jake pulled back on Steadfast's reins and motioned for his men to stop. He remained in the saddle, surveying the landscape in front of them. They had headed south toward Provo, and he was sure this would be the day they caught up with Abigail and her companions.

"What's up, boss?" Red rode up beside him.

"I'm not sure." Jake hid the anxiety he felt and tried to appear nonchalant as he settled back in the saddle. "See the smoke over there? It's midmorning. If the smoke is from Miss Hayes's campfire, why would they still be here at this late hour after running so hard the past few days? Seems to me they'd have packed up and left at dawn's first light if that were the case."

"Maybe one of 'em's sick. Or maybe we took a wrong turn and we've been trailing someone else."

The other men pulled up to join them.

"I guess it's possible one of them can be under the weather. Miss Hayes isn't used to traveling in these conditions or the climate. But I know we're following the right trail. We didn't divert off to follow the wrong group."

"So we gonna sit here all day or are we gonna go check things out?"

Hank's words grated on Jake's last nerve. Something about him rubbed Jake wrong. As soon as they returned to the ranch, Jake planned to settle up what he owed the man and send him on his way.

Jake chewed a piece of grass and took his time answering. "I suppose we might as well check things out." He spat the stalk to the ground, wishing he could rid himself of the troublesome ranch hand as easily.

He led the other men and followed the valley as it wound along the base of the hills. The smoke grew clearer in the distance, and they could smell the acrid scent of burning wood. The aroma made Jake long for the ranch. He wished he were sitting in front of a roaring fire at home instead of chasing after his friend's errant sister. The spring air was crisp and hadn't yet reached the full intensity of midday. The setting felt contradictory to the chill that ran up Jake's back as they neared the camp.

The men remained quiet as they entered the area. Not a person or creature moved, yet they could see at least one horse huddled up against a stand of trees.

"Somethin's not right for sure." Scrappy pulled his horse close to Jake's.

"What do you make of this, boss?"

Jake didn't answer. Instead he chose to continue forward. As he rounded a cluster of rocks, his heart sank as he took in the scene before him. The kidnappers from the train station, as far as he could tell, Bert and his men, lay scattered about on the ground before them. Reluctantly, while fighting his churning stomach, he rode Steadfast closer, checking each man for a sign of life. Their wounds proved without question that no one had survived the attack.

Scrappy took in big gulps of air from his place behind Jake, while Grub rode to a nearby bush and lost his breakfast. Red sat motionless on his mount, while Hank suddenly moved faster than Jake had ever seen him move. He rode until he reached Bert's crumpled form and dropped to his knees.

His anguished cry took Jake by surprise. He exchanged startled glances with the other men and rode closer, trying to make out the man's words.

"It wasn't supposed to be like this. It wasn't."

"What wasn't?" Jake dropped down beside Hank, keeping a tight hold on his horse. The horse, skittish, fought at the reins.

Hank didn't answer.

Jake placed his hand on Hank's shoulder. "Hank?"

Hank reacted violently, jerking backward and splaying his arms around in the air. "Leave me alone!" He shoved Jake backward, hopped on his horse, and rode out of sight.

The rest of the men remained rooted in place.

"Hank, get back here. It's not safe!" Jake called after him, but Hank continued on as if death itself were on his heels.

"What was that all about?" Grub seemed to have semi-recovered, though he remained pale, as did all the hands.

"I have no idea." Jake glanced back at the emptiness where Hank had disappeared from sight and stared, trying to decipher the man's actions. "I mean, this isn't easy for any of us. But that seemed to be a strange reaction no matter how you look at it. And the last thing he should do is ride out of here alone."

"Something's up." Though Red's words stated the obvious, the men nodded in agreement.

Scrappy kept his eyes on the hills, refusing to look around. "I thought the Indians had left this area. Didn't they sign a treaty a few years back?"

Jake nodded. "They did. But a band of Utes tried to kill their chief after the signing. They weren't all happy with his actions. As we said the other day, I suppose it makes sense that not all of them rode willingly onto the reservation with him. And there have been rumors of other bands of Indians getting permits to go off the reservations to find deer. In the process, they've also shot cattle and had altercations with the ranchers. But the attackers could be from anywhere, possibly just passing through."

Grub's voice, much quieter than his usual robust exuberance, echoed from behind them. "And that doesn't mean other tribes don't have rogue bands in the area."

Jake forced his attention back to the grisly scene that surrounded them. He didn't relish the thought of informing Caleb that his sister had been involved in an Indian attack. But now that he forced his thoughts in that direction, he realized he hadn't seen any sign of Caleb's sister.

"Where's Miss Hayes?"

"Where's Miss Hayes, indeed," Grub repeated. "Maybe they took her with them?"

"I don't think so. She'd be a liability to them. From the violence here I think they'd—," he cleared his throat, "—do the same to her."

"Oh no. Not Caleb's sister." Scrappy shook his head. "He won't take that very well. We need to locate her."

"Sorry, boys, but there's no way she survived an attack of this magnitude. Look around. They didn't have a chance. That one over there was half dressed, still putting on his boots. Bert was hit from behind." His throat constricted as he fought off the urge to follow Grub's lead and run for the bushes.

"Then where is she?" Red rode forward, suddenly the brave one as he searched out Caleb's sister's remains.

"Fan out and look for her." Jake heard the hard edge in his voice, but he couldn't help it. This wasn't how the trip was supposed to go. Abigail was his responsibility. He'd let her, and Caleb, down.

God, why would You allow something like this to happen? I just got Caleb on his feet. He's still weak. Bert wasn't much of a loss, and I can't mourn him completely because of what he did to Caleb and to Abigail. But even he didn't deserve an attack like this.

He swung up onto Steadfast's back and rode with purpose away from the others. The least he could do would be to gather Abigail's belongings for her brother and to give her a decent burial, which wouldn't be easy in the hard-packed dirt at his feet.

A thorough investigation of the area turned up no sign of Abigail.

"She isn't here. Are you sure they wouldn't have taken her?"

Jake wasn't sure of anything anymore. "It doesn't make sense, but maybe they took her somewhere else to. . ." He refused to voice the thoughts that passed through his head. "Maybe they had other plans for her."

Before the others could register what that meant, Scrappy leaped from his mount. "Over here!"

He lifted up a lone piece of paper.

"What is it?" Jake joined him.

"I dunno. It looks to be some type of scientific paper."

Jake reached out to take it from him. The paper was smudged with dirt. "It's handwritten notes from a medical journal."

"A medical journal?" Grub scratched his head. "Why would they have something like that?"

"According to Caleb, his sister had some type of medical training. She's here. Look harder."

They spread out and began to search behind brush and rocks and scrub.

Jake heard a moan from behind a pile of rocks and hurried over to check the area. Abigail lay on the ground, her blond hair fanned around her. She looked nothing like she had in town. Her face lay hidden under the long locks of hair. Hesitantly, he moved forward and lifted a soft strand, afraid of what he might find beneath.

With a shriek of terror, she bolted backward. Jake tumbled the opposite direction, startled by the transformation.

"You're alive!" Though she'd just taken ten years off his life, he couldn't hold back his laugh of relief. "You survived the attack!"

He could hear his words echo behind him as his men spread the word that she'd been found alive.

He watched as she buried her face in her hands. He slowly moved forward. "Abigail. Miss Hayes?"

She didn't respond.

Again he pushed back some strands of hair that hid her face.

She reacted violently, her hands scratching at him like a wildcat. "Noooo!"

"Miss Hayes!" He grabbed her arms. He felt blood run down his cheek from her attack. "My name is Jake. We're here to help. Listen to me." He gently shook her, and her eyes vacantly sought his.

When they met, the cloudiness evaporated.

"You." She whispered the words. "The ruffian from the train station."

"I don't think I turned out to be the ruffian you expected. I'm here to help you, remember?"

"But you looked so threatening."

"Looks can be deceiving, as I'm sure you figured out by now. Obviously your kind friend Bert wasn't quite what he appeared." The moment the words left his mouth he regretted them. The cloud returned to her eyes, and they filled with tears.

"I killed him."

"You killed him?" Jake looked around. "I don't see how you could be capable of something like this."

"I prayed him dead."

Before he could further question her, the others surrounded them.

"Is she hurt?" Scrappy knelt gingerly down beside them. "Miss Hayes, I'm so sorry for what you've endured. Are you all right?"

Scrappy talked to her as if she were royalty. Though Jake had to admit the man probably hadn't ever been so close to such a lady in all his years.

Jake hadn't even thought to ask. "Are you hurt?"

Abigail shook her head and frowned, her forehead crinkling with confusion. "I don't think so."

She sent Jake, then Scrappy, a small smile. "Thanks for asking."

Scrappy sat inches taller at her words.

Jake watched as she put a shaky hand to her forehead. "I'm so sorry. I think I have a touch of shock." She glanced at the ground around her. "Hamm? Where are you? Hamm!"

The men exchanged bewildered looks.

Red leaned close to Jake's ear. "Who do you reckon Hamm is? One of Bert's men?"

"Not that I've ever heard. The only one I can see who's unaccounted for is Boggs."

"Do you think he has the capability to do this?"

"No way. I've only run into him a couple of times, and each time I came away wondering why a man like him would run with a gang like Bert's."

Abigail pushed to her feet and swooned. Jake jumped up to stabilize her. "Ma'am, it's probably best if you sit for a moment and get your bearings."

"I have to find Hamm." Her voice rose in pitch. Jake knew she was at the edge of hysteria.

"Can you describe him for us? We'll help you look."

She looked at Jake like he'd grown a second head. "He's small and pink, with a snout."

"A snout? As in a pig snout?"

"Yes."

"Boss, do you think she's hallucinatin'?" Grub watched her in fascination.

"I don't know."

Jake supported her full weight, and when she made note of that fact she pushed him gently away. She slowly spun in a circle, surveying the rocks. "There you are." Relief softened her words.

A small pink pig nestled securely in the rocks beside them, sound asleep. Abigail moved forward on shaky legs and gathered him into her arms. The piglet nuzzled the soft skin of Abigail's neck, and she gave a short laugh as tears flowed from her eyes. "You survived." A sob replaced the smile. "You survived and I survived, and no one else did."

"Miss Hayes." Jake kept his voice quiet, not wanting to send her further into her grief. "Please." He took her arm, not sure of how she'd react, but instead of fighting him this time she turned and burrowed her face against his chest.

After a moment's hesitation, he wrapped his arms around her quivering body. He looked over her shoulder at his men for help, but they all scattered in the other direction.

"We'll get to work digging a grave, boss."

It shouldn't surprise him that they deserted him in his time of need. After all, since he'd found them all in various forms of avoidance, why would they suddenly grow backbones now?

Her sobs turned to convulsive, heartrending cries of pain.

Words escaped him, but he tightened his hold and let her cry. She felt so right in his arms. Her soft form molded to his, and he pushed her hair back from her face, this time savoring the feel of the silky strands. After several minutes, he found his tongue. "There, there, Miss Hayes. It's going to be all right. We're here with you now. We'll get you safely far away from here."

She pulled away, her green eyes searching his as if seeing him for the first time. "And how can you guarantee me that?" She motioned around them. "They seemed to think we were safe, too. But look how that turned out."

"It turned out with my standing here, that's how. They didn't get us in the attack. They didn't get you. Perhaps you had a Divine intervention on your part. I have no clue how you survived, but you did." Jake was surprised to see a look of guilt flash across her face. Now that he really looked at her, he had no idea how he could ever think of her as severe as he had at the station. She had beautiful, delicate features.

After resting her head against his chest for a moment more, she stepped back. "Thank you. I'm sorry I fell apart like that."

"I think you had good reason."

Her body trembled with a shaky sigh. "I've seen as much and worse in hospitals during my training. But I guess the difference is back home I'd have been in charge of the situation. I didn't expect. . .this. Not out here."

"Your training?"

"I'm a physician. I trained in medicine."

That surprised Jake. Caleb had said she trained in medicine, but Jake thought he'd referred to nurse training or something of that sort. He thought it best not to show his surprise. He didn't think she'd take too kindly to that type of reaction. "It's the West, Abigail. You can't predict anything. You can't let down your guard, ever." Nothing like a few words of comfort to make a person feel better, but she needed to know what she was up against. He tucked his thumbs in the waistband of his pants. "It's not civilized out here like it is back East. And the farther we head south, the more risky the terrain becomes. Outlaws hide in the rugged land out this way."

"Thanks for the encouragement." Her sharp retort inspired him. At least she wasn't the simpering female type he'd pegged her to be at first glance. "But I beg to differ on your assessment of the East. I treated stab wounds, gunshot wounds, and wounds from broken bottles used during bar fights. Human depravity exists everywhere, not just here."

"I stand corrected."

They stood and assessed each other silently.

"I'm a horrible judge of character." She sighed.

"Is that so? Why would you ever think that?" He tried to keep the sarcasm at bay, but it crept in anyway.

"You saw Bert at the station. He looked kind and showed concern. How was I to know it was a farce?"

He didn't respond.

"And you." She looked him up and down. "You came barreling up the walkway looking dangerous with your dark scowl and all those weapons fastened around your waist."

"Weapons that would have prevented this attack had I been here." He crossed his arms in challenge. The woman had transformed from needy to annoying.

"So you say." She tightened her grip on Hamm. "You didn't see it happen. One minute things were quiet. And the next, things went crazy. The men were all running, and I didn't know what was happening. By the time I saw the Indians…" Her throat convulsed. "Before anyone could react…" Again her words drifted away. She cleared her throat. "Before anyone could react, the men were all dead."

"I'm so sorry you had to experience that. I'm sorry we weren't here sooner."

Suspicion laced her features. "Why are you here?"

"Excuse me?"

"Why should I trust you?" She backed away. "I saw you at the station and now here you are, out in the middle of nowhere, playing Knight in Shining Armor. How do I know you don't have ulterior motives? Or maybe you even knew about the attack or planned it."

"Ouch." Jake accentuated his wince. "Or maybe I was sent to help you."

"How would you know I needed help?"

"Because you left town with Robert, and nothing he ever does is on the up-and-up."

"For all I know, my brother also owed you a debt and you called it in, same as Bert."

"Same as Bert? What'd he tell you?"

He studied her as she turned a shoulder his way and looked far off into the distance. She bit the corner of her lip before uttering carefully calculated words that were laced with pain. "Apparently, my brother traded me in marriage to pay off a debt to Bert. Bert blackmailed him because Caleb turned him in for gambling. Tonight was to be our wedding night." She shuddered.

Her words and obvious repulsion brought a whole new wave of anger to Jake. Somehow the attack didn't seem as vicious after she spoke. The man deserved his fate. He felt immediate guilt at his reaction but brushed it away.

"Your brother would never have traded you off for anything. Bert lied. He took you to get even."

How typical of Bert to add to her trauma by making her dread the passing days, knowing what awaited her.

"Abigail, there's something you should know. Caleb didn't—"

"Boss, Hank's back."

Jake scowled at Red's interruption, but sure enough, Hank lurked just outside the clearing, hovering suspiciously behind the trees.

Chapter 6

Distracted, Abbie looked over at the edge of the trees where the men were all staring. A man rode from the shadows and headed their way.

Jake stood tall, hands fisted on his hips, and waited for the man to come closer. A slight breeze stirred and blew his dark hair around his face. Absently, he pushed it away. "You doin' all right, Hank?"

"I'm fine." Hank bit off each word, his response anything but friendly.

In fluid movements, Jake stepped over and caught hold of Hank's horse's bridle. Though his actions appeared to be casual, Abbie had the feeling they were anything but. "What did you mean by 'it wasn't supposed to be this way'?"

Hank scowled, looked away, and answered vaguely. "What do you think? We were supposed to pick up Miss Hayes and return to the ranch. Seeing the aftereffect of a massacre wasn't in the plans. Not that I was aware of anyway."

"You sure?" Jake stared him down for a long moment. "You seemed to take an extra interest in Bert."

"What interest would I have in the man?" Hank ran his hand through his messy hair, and his eyes darted to the man's still form.

"I don't know. That's what I'm trying to figure out."

Abigail ran her fingers through her own tangled tresses and watched the men with interest. She'd been trained to watch for signs and signals when treating her patients, and it was more than obvious there were undercurrents here she didn't understand.

Hank glanced her way. "Miss Hayes?" Ignoring Jake, he headed toward her. "How interesting that you alone survived." He took her wrist and pulled her around, forcing her to look over at the massacred men.

She pulled from his tight grasp. His forwardness and cold tone unnerved her.

She noticed that Jake was watching their interaction with interest. He scowled when he met her gaze. His brown eyes bore into hers. Her chin raised a notch, and she refused to look away. Her reaction spurred him into action.

"We need to finish up here and move on. It's not safe to linger." He grabbed a small shovel from his saddle and joined the others in digging a shallow pit.

Abigail turned her head, not needing to see the rest. She peeked a few times and saw them move the bodies and then place stones they'd gathered from the area over the mound. Scrappy checked her wayward horse after leading him from the trees and readied the saddle before heading her way.

"Do you have everything you need?" Jake's voice, coming from behind her, made her jump.

Her fingers stuck on a tangled strand of hair. "I have all my things gathered up if that's what you mean. I only had the one valise. They made me leave my trunk at the station."

"I know. We checked there first. They're sending the trunk on to Nephi where we'll retrieve it."

He assisted her to her feet and up onto her mount.

"Thank you." She caressed the horse's mane. Other than Hamm, he was the only thing familiar to her. She didn't know what else to say.

Jake stood below her, staring. He, too, raised his hand to pet the stallion. "What's his name?"

"I'm not sure. They," she glanced at the mound of earth and winced, "had him waiting at the station and weren't much for small talk."

"Better pick out a name then. He's yours now."

Before she could say anything else, Jake stalked off and swung onto his own horse.

❧

Hank stayed near her side the entire afternoon. Though he didn't say a lot, his angry glances made her increasingly uneasy as the day passed. Jake took the lead most of the time, which kept him to himself.

As the shock of the day wore off, Abigail began to wonder about their destination.

"Excuse me. I need to speak with Jake." Hank looked at her in surprise, but made no move to stop her as she rode forward and came alongside the man in charge. Jake's eyebrows rose as he surveyed her, then narrowed into a scowl. She had no idea what she'd done to turn him from rescuer to disgruntled guide.

"I have some questions." She noticed he made no effort to slow their pace in response, which was fine. Though a tad sore, she'd become a pretty adept horse-woman during the past few days.

"I don't guarantee I'll answer them."

Surprised at his tart response, she could only stare. They rode on in silence while Abigail formulated her words. "If you're trying to intimidate me, it won't work."

Her comment brought a slight smile to his lips. "It won't?"

"No, it won't." The trail narrowed, and she let her horse drop back as they diverted around shrubs and strange-looking brush. Large mountains loomed in the distance.

"What is this?" She rode back up beside him and pointed to the plant in question.

"Sagebrush."

"Really? I read about it! The Indians use it for medicinal purposes."

"Is that right?"

His comment, somewhat sarcastic, caught her off guard.

"I've somehow offended you." She pulled her attention from the landscape and focused back on him.

"No."

"You talk even less than Bert and his men."

"I'm not here to talk. I'm here to keep you safe and to take you to the ranch."

"But I told you, I have questions."

His chest heaved in exasperation. "What are they?"

"Where are we going?"

"To the ranch. It's south of Provo, near Mount Pleasant."

"Why you?"

"Your brother sent me. He was in bad shape and in no condition to travel. I said I'd fetch you and bring you back."

Her heart lurched as she recalled Bert's words. She couldn't even begin to think about what her future held without Caleb. She didn't want to discuss it with this distant stranger. She'd sort everything out after they arrived at the ranch.

"But is he. . . ?"

"Boss, someone's trailing us." Red rode up to the front of the line and edged Abbie out of the way. "Want me to ride back and check it out?"

Jake worried his bottom lip with his teeth. "No, let's pick up the pace and see what happens. We'll skirt Provo and make camp on Utah Lake."

He dismissed Abbie with a nod and spurred his own mount to a faster pace. Abbie mimicked his actions and kept her place at his heels. She studied him as he sat in his saddle. Though he'd originally looked menacing from her city girl point of view, she'd quickly learned the value of traveling fully loaded with weapons. She'd seen him use his knife earlier as they journeyed, and now he reached down and grasped the handle of his gun, checked it for bullets, and slipped it securely back into its holster.

They didn't speak for the larger part of an hour. Abigail noted a town to the west, but they stayed clear of it. Finally, Red moved back in place alongside Jake and stated that their followers had either disappeared or had dropped far enough back that they weren't leaving any dust by which to track them.

"Let's continue the pace for another hour or so, and then we'll pull off and make camp. Red, you and Hank drop back and see if you can find any sign of our pursuers. Most likely it was someone bound for Provo, and they turned off at the road into town."

Red tipped his hat at Abigail, and she found herself responding to his warm smile. A glare from Jake sent him scurrying down the line. After he and Hank turned the other way, Grub fell into place behind Abbie, and Scrappy brought up the tail.

Abigail sneezed as Jake's horse kicked up a pouf of dust, but not nearly as bad as she'd sneezed while riding with Bert.

Jake turned his sour expression on her. "Are you ill? Do we need to seek medical care in Provo?"

"No." *Achoo!* Abbie dug a handkerchief out from her valise. Her movements disturbed Hamm, and he began to squeal. Another sneeze followed.

"Why do you keep sneezing? I heard you awhile back and thought you'd sneeze yourself off your mount. And by the way, have you named him yet?"

"The dust affects me, as do many of the plants in the area. This is why I keep sneezing. And if I were to need medical care, I'm more than capable to treat myself. I'm trained as a physician, remember?"

"Ah yes, Doc, I do seem to remember a conversation about medical school."

"And I've not yet had a chance to think up a name for the horse. I'll make sure that's a top priority in the near future."

"See that you do. It isn't right for a creature as magnificent as yours to go nameless."

"He's not mine."

"I told you, he is now. His owner is gone. Consider it your pay for the trauma you endured at Bert's hands."

Her voice dropped to a whisper. "I'd rather not have endured the trauma at all."

His eyes hardened as he stared at her. "I know."

So that was it. He somehow knew she was to blame for the men's deaths. She'd prayed to God for a way out, and their demise was His answer.

❧

Jake winced as she paled and speared him with pain-filled eyes. He turned to hide his reaction.

She blamed him for the whole Bert disaster, he could tell. Once he brought it up, her eyes had widened and then narrowed, and now she rode in silence. He could kick himself for leaving her at the station. He knew the thought wasn't rational; she hadn't matched Caleb's description and Bert had thrown him off, but Jake was the one sent to collect her, and he'd messed up. She had every reason to be upset with him.

He cut west and headed for the lake. They'd make camp and set out early in the morning for the ranch. Another few days, barring any more problems, and they'd be there.

"Where are we going?"

"I thought we'd stop at Utah Lake for the night. You can clean up and relax, and the men can fish and catch us some dinner."

Her features tightened with apprehension.

"You don't like the idea?"

"I don't like much of anything since getting here, to be honest."

"I'm sorry."

"It isn't exactly your fault."

So maybe she didn't hold him responsible. But it didn't matter. He held himself responsible. "But it is. If I'd collected you from the train station at the beginning, you'd not have suffered at Bert's hand."

She surprised him when her mouth widened into a grin and her green eyes twinkled in amusement. "And what about the train robbery on the way out? Do you want to take responsibility for that, too?"

He pulled his horse to a stop, momentarily stunned. "You were involved in a train robbery?"

She grimaced and nodded. " 'Fraid so. It's not been the relaxing journey I'd hoped for."

They prodded their horses to move on.

"I guess not. And then you arrived at the station only to find out that Caleb—"

"Yes." She interrupted him, not allowing him to finish.

She looked away but not before he saw the tears that filled her eyes. The fact that Caleb had been laid up and couldn't meet the train must have really upset her. If that were the case, he'd do well to avoid the subject until they got to the ranch and she and Caleb settled up their relationship. He'd do well to change the subject right now as a matter of fact.

"And the horse's name is. . . ?"

She tucked a strand of hair behind her delicate ear. "No name. Not yet."

"No Name. That suits him."

"I didn't mean. . ." Her voice drifted off, and she looked contemplative. She reached out and ruffled the stallion's mane. "You know. . .I think it does suit him. His new name is No Name."

Jake reined in Steadfast and jumped down to the ground, ready to stretch his legs. "Whoa, No Name." He reached up to assist Abbie. "Let me help you down, Doc. We'll set up over there."

಄

Abigail followed the direction of his finger and saw a beautiful lake just ahead. She released Hamm from her valise and set him loose on the hard-packed dirt. He rutted around and snorted as he began to chew on strands of plants at their feet.

THE PETTICOAT DOCTOR

Scrappy and Grub came up behind them, and in the distance she could see Hank and Red turn their way.

Abbie felt at odds while they set up camp. She didn't know how to help, so she tried to stay out of the way. She called for Hamm and walked to the water's edge. It looked shallow enough, and she hoped there'd be a way for her to bathe. Her hair was a mass of tangled strands. Though they'd passed several streams and creeks while she was with Bert, she hadn't dared ask to bathe with them around. For some strange reason, she felt she could trust Jake and his men.

The sun sat low on the horizon when Jake headed her way. "Okay, Doc, why don't you head on over and relax in the water, and I'll watch over our things. I can make sure you're safe from here, and the men are heading down around the bend to another area to fish."

Abbie hesitated. *Could* she trust him? She reached up and touched her hair. She had no choice. She couldn't leave it in such a condition a moment longer. And she refused to arrive at her brother's ranch in such a state. The hands and staff would think her a mess.

She gathered a bar of lye soap from her bag. She'd wash her outfit as best she could while in the water. Hamm trailed her to the water's edge and hesitantly dipped his front leg into the surface. When he made contact with the water, he squealed and backed away. Two more tries assured him that water wasn't something he wanted to mess with, and he curled up on the ground a short distance from shore.

Abigail looked around and couldn't see anyone other than Jake, and even he was only a tiny figure near the campfire. She waded into the water, relieved to find it a pleasant temperature. Tiny fish darted around her ankles, and she swished them away before they could nibble on her skin. Once she'd reached waist depth, she lowered herself to the surface and, holding her breath, submerged herself. She slipped out of her outer garments and used friction to clean them as well as possible. The lye soap clouded the water, but she didn't care. It would feel delightful to be clean once again. She waded out and after wringing her dress as well as she could, she draped it over some stones at the water's edge.

She returned to the water and lathered up her hair. She scrubbed it, running her fingers through the tangled tresses. She wouldn't be able to do much without her brush. She wished she'd brought it to the water's edge, but she was too lazy to get out of the lake and retrieve it. She floated on her back and swam underwater, and before she knew it, the sky had darkened further and she knew it was time to head to the campfire.

The water smelled fresh and stars studded the sky. She kicked and moved toward shore, but when she stood, her dress wasn't where she'd left it. A shiver coursed through her. Perhaps she had been wrong to trust the men after all.

Her underclothes weren't proper attire to wear while sitting around a fire with a bunch of men.

"I took your clothes." Jake's voice broke through the silence, and she lowered herself into the water. "I put them near the fire so they'd dry."

"And what am I to do—sit here in the water until they do?"

"Of course not. I brought you a blanket to wrap in. It will be completely proper until your clothes are dry."

"But the men. . ."

"Have been instructed to sit tight at the other campfire until dinner is ready and we head over their way." He motioned to a fire in the distance. "I'll join them as soon as I know you're safely sitting in front of this fire."

"Drop the blanket and move away."

"As you say, Doc."

He did as she asked and moved into the shadows, keeping his back to her. She stepped out of the water and hurried over to grab the wool coverlet. It felt heavenly as it warded off the shivers that had enveloped her as soon as she stepped from the water.

"I'm all set."

He returned to her side and picked up her valise.

"Would you mind getting Hamm for me, too?" She motioned to his huddled form on the hard-packed beach. "It would be awkward to try to carry him and hold the blanket together."

"I can imagine."

She hurried forward, not wanting to know what else he might be imagining. She stepped into the circle of light from the fire and quickly settled down on a boulder near the warmth. Her thin underclothes would dry quickly in the heat of the fire.

Jake stepped beside her, looking dangerous in a new way. She hadn't realized exactly how handsome he was until now. His presence filled the area until she felt she couldn't breathe. His dark brown eyes sought hers, but she avoided them, looking toward the fire instead.

"Do you need anything else?" His warm chuckle surrounded her, making her feel even warmer.

"No, I'll be fine." She reached forward and pulled her brush from her bag and began to pull it through the tangles. They were in such a mess that she couldn't make any progress.

"Here, let me."

"No!" She hugged her brush against the blanket covering her chest.

"Doc, I have three younger sisters. I'm not a stranger to brushing tangles out of snarled hair."

"It wouldn't be proper. And thank you so much for painting me in such an attractive way with your words. Every woman dreams of being referred to as having snarled tangles."

He chuckled again, this time his breath warm on her cheek as he settled down behind her on the boulder. "Give me the brush."

"I won't."

"You're a physician, correct?"

She huffed out her exasperation. "You know I am."

"And aren't there times when you cross the boundaries of propriety when dealing with patients?"

"Well, of course. But that's different."

She felt gooseflesh prickle her skin at his nearness. Her heart began to beat faster, and she wondered if she'd have some type of episode if it continued at such a pace.

"It's not different. This is a unique situation. I promise to behave as a complete gentleman. But I'm a starving gentleman, and if we all have to wait for you to get this brush through that hair before we can settle down for dinner, it won't be pretty."

"No one's asking you to hold off your meal. By all means, go join the others and eat your fill."

Her traitorous stomach growled loudly at the thought of food.

This time Jake laughed out loud. "Your stomach seems to have a difference of opinion from the words that escape through your mouth. Now stop being so stubborn and let me have your brush."

Before she could refuse him again, he reached around and snatched the brush from her hands. His arm bumped against hers, and her skin tingled at his nearness. She clenched her teeth in consternation, but if they didn't want to die of hunger while battling the issue, she needed to give in and let him help her.

As she expected, her clothes dried quickly in the heat. And she had to admit, it felt wonderful to relax beside the fire while its warmth spread through her. The scent of burning wood enveloped them into their own private world, and she let her eyes drift closed. She hadn't slept well since her arrival days earlier, worried to let down her guard.

With Jake she felt safe and protected. She didn't realize she'd fallen asleep until Jake cleared his throat and said in a tight voice, "There you go. I'll let you finish up, but I think I got the worst of the tangles out."

Abbie's eyes popped open, and she found that she rested against Jake's firm chest. She didn't want to move. She glanced upward and found Jake's face inches away from her own. His dark eyes bore into hers. The fire reflected in their depths. Her mouth opened, but no words came out. They studied each other silently for a moment before Jake pushed her gently upright and moved several feet away.

"Thank you." Heat filled Abbie's face, and she lowered her chin to her chest. She pulled the blanket more securely around her. "I'm sorry. I guess I drifted off. I'll dress and be over at the other fire shortly."

"Doc." Jake squatted at her side and pushed a few errant strands of hair from her face. She regretted it. The curtain of hair shielded her from his gaze, and now she felt exposed. She refused to meet his eyes.

He reached out a finger and lifted her chin, forcing her to look up at him. His solemn face transformed into a delightful smile. "You didn't do anything wrong. I'm honored that you felt safe enough in my presence to sleep. Wouldn't you want the same for any of your patients?"

"Yes. But..."

"But nothing. I doubt you've slept at all the past few nights. You're safe with us. You're safe with me. Now, I want you to get dressed and join us at the other fire. We'll have your dinner ready. As soon as we've eaten, I want you to go to sleep. We'll take turns with the watch, but we've chosen a safe place for a reason. No one can move in on us from the water, and we can see well in advance if anyone comes the other way. Tonight you'll sleep soundly."

Abbie doubted it. She doubted she'd sleep a wink with the handsome, enigmatic man anywhere nearby.

Chapter 7

A bbie dressed quickly, not wanting to keep the men waiting, and hurried over to the other campfire. Jake stood at the outskirts of the little group, looking out toward the mountains in the east. Red, Scrappy, and Grub saw her coming and yanked their hats from their heads as they hurried to their feet. Hank remained seated, reclining on a couple of large boulders with legs crossed at the ankles. Jake moved their way and scowled at him. With a look of impudence toward his boss and a grimace at Abbie, he leisurely stood to his feet.

"Don't bother with formalities." Abbie waved them back toward their various rocks. "From everything I've seen we're far from the civility of town."

Jake stepped into the circle of firelight. "I disagree, Doc. I expect the men to continue to show respect for each lady they come across, whether they are in town or at a dusty, remote campfire. It doesn't do to let down on the manners."

"I stand corrected." Abbie walked to the boulder near Scrappy and sat primly on the edge. Whatever good mood Jake had when he left her, he'd lost on his way over here.

Grub neared the skillet over the fire and began to plate up servings of fish. He seemed to favor his right hand. Abbie looked closer and noticed fiery red skin on his right appendage.

"Grub? What happened to you? Let me see your hand."

Abbie moved closer to him, and he backed away. His eyes moved from Abigail to Jake and back.

"No offense, ma'am, but I ain't lettin' no petticoat doctor do any medical tinkering with me or my hand."

Jake fisted his hands on his hips and glared. "Oh, Grub, c'mon. I thought we discussed this before she headed our way. You agreed to let her take a look at the irritated skin and at least give her professional opinion."

"I didn't agree to any such thing. Did I agree to let her look at my hand?" His eyes moved over each of his friends' faces, who respectively shrugged their shoulders in response. "I ain't never had a lady doc messin' with me in the past, and I don't aim to start that nonsense now. As a matter of fact, I'm not real big on any kind of doctor messin' with me."

He reached for the spatula and moved another piece of fish onto the nearest tin plate.

"Grub." Jake's jaw set in a firm line, and he glared down at his cook. "I didn't suggest you let Doc look at your hand. I ordered you to do so."

"The fish are gonna burn if'n you make me leave the fire right now."

"I'll take over." Scrappy hurried to Grub's side and pulled the utensil from the heavier man's hand. Grub looked as if he'd like to slam it into the side of Scrappy's face.

Abbie intervened before they could come to blows. "My bag's over at the other fire. Grub, why don't we head over that way, and I'll look at the hand while the men here finish cooking dinner. If we hurry, we'll be back before they can eat the first bite."

"I ain't happy about this."

"Guess what?" She lowered her voice, tucked her hand reassuringly around his arm, and leaned close. Her mouth formed into a conspiratorial smile. "I can tell."

He muttered under his breath, but allowed her to lead him to the other camp. The fire, not having been replenished, burned a deep red. Abbie stoked it with some more brush, and it flared. She motioned Grub to sit on a nearby rock and went to collect her bag.

"This is all a lot of nonsense. I've burned my hand many times before."

Though he blustered at her ministrations, Abbie didn't miss the fact that sweat beaded upon his forehead. He was in more pain than he admitted. The night air was brisk, and he'd been away from the cook fire long enough to cool down.

She gingerly opened his fingers, and he paled.

"How'd you do this?" Abbie kept her voice low and her tonality gentle, a method she'd perfected to set her patients' minds at ease.

"I always keep a cloth close by when I'm workin', in case I need to lift a pan from the fire. Tonight I got distracted watchin'. . ." His eyes darted to her and away. "Um. . .I mean, I wasn't payin' attention, and the pan slipped. I reached out and grabbed for it without havin' time to grab my cloth." He stopped talking as she gently wiped his palm. His breath came faster. "I couldn't afford to lose our dinner to the fire."

"I see." She opened a tin of salve and began to dab it on the inflamed skin. "Though I imagine we'd all have given up a night's meal in order for your hand to be unscathed."

"Maybe you would have, but I'd have never heard the end of it from the others. Especially Hank."

She glanced up at him and smiled. "Hank gets your dander up, does he?"

He seemed to be warming up to her and smiled back. "Hank seems to get all our danders up."

"So I've noticed." She kept him talking as she wrapped the wound in clean white fabric.

Grub looked down at his hand in surprise. "You're finished already? That wasn't so bad after all."

"So my doctoring skills pass muster with you?"

"I suppose you'll do." He gazed off over the top of the fire and then back at her. "I didn't mean nothin' by my reluctance. You seem like a nice enough lady. . . but. . ."

"I know. But therein lies the problem. I'm a lady. A woman doctor. Believe it or not, I've done enough doctoring of men to understand how you all think."

Grub wrung his hat in his hands. If he twisted it any harder, he'd tear it in two. "I've offended you. That wasn't my intent, either."

Abbie raised her eyebrows and gave him a moment.

He shuffled his feet, sighed, and looked up at the starlit sky. His lips moved as he talked to himself. He looked back down at her, his large face flushing, this time in embarrassment, not pain. "What I meant to say is, you done did a fine job of fixin' my hand, and I sure do appreciate your ministrations."

She laughed and settled her hand back into his arm. "Well then, if I meet your approval, what do you say we head back over to dinner? I heard the chef is masterful with his creations."

Grub puffed out his large chest in pride and, beaming, escorted her to the other men.

Jake surveyed them both with a scowl. His disposition had soured further in the short time it had taken Grub's to sweeten. "From the look on Grub's face, I can assume everything's all right with his hand?"

"Of course everything's all right," Grub chided, interrupting. "Miss Hayes is a wonderful doctor, Jake."

Red snickered from the far side of the fire, and Jake sent him a warning look. Scrappy looked at both in confusion, but when Abbie looked at Hank, he sent her a look of challenge.

He stood and sauntered over. "Well, Doc, if that's the case, I have this skin irritation I'd like you to look at."

Scrappy elbowed him out of the way. "I have an infected toe. It's all scaly and sore, looks right awful."

Not to be left out, Red hurried over. "And I have a cut that's not looking so good. I tore my side on a thorn a few days back, and it's festering."

Hank shouldered through the men. "Wait your turns. I got to her first."

"Well, maybe Doc would like to see who she'll treat first." Scrappy looked at her expectantly.

Abbie stood rooted in place. Earlier her apparent new nickname had been uttered with distaste. Now they stated the title almost reverently.

"How about *I* tell you what is going to happen?" Jake's frustrated tone didn't brook any arguments. "We're all gonna sit down and eat a good supper here around the fire. After we eat, if any of you have any life threatening injuries, I'm sure Doc will be glad to look them over. In the meantime, you're all gonna step away from her and let her sit down a spell."

He took Abbie by the arm and led her none too gently to the nearest boulder. "Sit."

Abbie sat, looking up at him in surprise. He scowled at her, picked up a plate, and shoved it into her hands. "Eat."

She didn't move. The hands stood around on the far side of the fire, as if afraid to come near Jake, Abbie, or the food. She glanced back up at her rescuer. "Is it all right if my patients sit, too?"

"They aren't your patients," Jake snapped. "They're vying for your attention. I've never seen such a needy gaggle of men in my entire life."

He snatched his plate and sat beside her. Abbie didn't know what to say. He was thoroughly disgruntled, and she had no idea why.

"If they all have various ailments, it isn't a bad thing to have me look them over. Perhaps they've held back because you seem. . .well. . .rather overbearing when it comes to this topic." His hand rested on the boulder between them, and she gently placed her hand on top of his. "Jake? Did you have a bad experience with a physician sometime in your past?"

He jerked his hand free as if she'd burned him. "A bad experience? No!" He glanced over at his men and snarled, "Why are you all just standing there? Don't you have something better to do than stare at us? Eat!"

The men scrambled to oblige. All except Hank, who narrowed his eyes and folded his arms over his chest. Jake engaged in a silent stare out with him for a few moments and then dismissed him by turning his back.

"Doc, these are my ranch hands. The whole lot of them." He sighed and maneuvered himself to face her. "Since we found you, they've turned into a blathering group of idiots. It's annoying to say the least."

Abbie fought back a grin and lost. She lowered her voice. "Jake, I hate to say it, but I'm not sure these men have changed all that much since my arrival. I know I'm new to the area, but I was sort of under the impression that most cowboy types are rough and ready—mean, focused, and independent. These men don't quite seem to fit that description."

She glanced at his crew. Scrappy lifted his plate from the edge of the fire where it had been set to stay warm. He carried it by the hot end, which caused him to quickly shift it to his other hand, and he lost his piece of fish in the process. He picked it up from the ground, dusted it on his pant leg, and placed it back on the piece of tin in his hand. Red winked at her as he sat down—missing the boulder completely in the process—and sprawled awkwardly onto the hard-packed dirt. Grub just stared at her with a silly grin on his face and waved his bandaged hand. Hank paced around the perimeter, sending venom-filled glares at Jake.

She felt like a specimen on display at one of the local museums back home. Jake laughed quietly from beside her. "I kind of see what you mean."

Abbie settled back. "May I ask how you collected them?"

Jake chewed a bite of food and then dipped his head to look at her. His hair had pulled loose from its band during the long afternoon and now curled enticingly at his neck. Humor danced in his dark eyes as he explained how each man had come to be in his service, and Abbie felt her heart soften toward the gruff man. He might prefer to put on a brusque exterior, but deep inside he had a heart that cared about people.

"That's really sweet."

He winced. "Sweet. Just the way a rancher wants to be described."

"It isn't a bad thing, you know."

"It is if any of the hands get wind of it. I'd never get anything done around the land."

She raised an eyebrow and skimmed the men with her eyes again before looking his way. "I'm not sure it will make much of a difference either way." She giggled.

He fought a laugh, but it followed hers anyway. "Well you can't blame a fellow for trying."

"True enough."

They ate in silence for a few minutes, Abbie constantly aware that she had a continuous audience from across the campfire. She held up her fork. "You all caught some good fish here. I've not eaten this well since I left Philadelphia."

"Aw, it weren't nothin'." Scrappy's face glowed in the firelight.

"I used my special spices," Grub inserted. "I bring 'em in 'specially for trips like this."

Red leaned around with disbelief written on his face. "You grow 'em on the ranch. They're basic herbs. Why are you tellin' her things like that?"

"I still bring 'em in 'specially for the trips. Not everyone can grow something like that."

"You're right, Grub, and I really appreciate the fine cooking." Abbie tried to diffuse the situation.

Scrappy appeared at her side. "Miss Hayes? Doc? Would you allow me to escort you back to the other site? I'm sure you're ready to retire by now."

Jake answered for her. "I'm sure she's more ready to finish her meal, Scrappy. Why don't you stop fussing over Doc and settle down to your own plate? We'll all walk over together after we finish our meal."

Abbie wondered how much longer it would be until they reached their destination. Never one to enjoy being the center of attention, she didn't like the feeling any better out here in the wilderness. "I'm sure I can find my own way over after I finish eating, but thank you for offering, Scrappy. It's very sweet of you."

"I had no doubt you'd find your way, Doc, but I was more worried about your running up against a coyote or such in the dark."

A chill passed through Abbie. "Coyote prowl out here?"

"Yes'm. They're all over the place at night. I thought you might sleep better if you avoided a run-in with one or more."

"I'm sure I would. I'll take you up on the offer as soon as we've finished eating."

She glanced at Jake, but he'd bent his head over his plate and didn't respond further. The man was a puzzle for sure. But Abbie didn't mind. She enjoyed a good mystery and the challenge to solve it. She'd find out in time what made Jake act the way he did.

So far she knew only that he kept his distance with his men—and apparently with her—yet he was gentle and caring under that harsh exterior. He looked up and caught her studying him. Her heart sped up, her hands went clammy, and her bones turned to liquid. She pressed her hand firmly against the rock for balance. The physician in her tallied her unfamiliar symptoms as his brown eyes pierced hers with a questioning stare she didn't understand.

Abruptly, she stood on shaky legs and hurried over to Scrappy. "I believe I am ready to head back after all. I'm not feeling so well and a good night's sleep will surely put things back in order."

Scrappy offered his arm, and Abbie dared one more glance Jake's way. He hadn't moved. He leaned casually against the rock, fork relaxed in his hand, and continued to study her as she quickly hurried away.

Chapter 8

Jake stayed at the fire's side long after the others bedded down for the night. Doc Hayes was a source of constant frustration to him. Since her arrival—or should he say rescue—the men had become like toddlers vying for a mother's loving attention. Though he didn't expect much out of them—other than hard work when they were on the ranch, which they did with a passion—he didn't understand their obsession with the doctor.

He kicked at a rock with his dusty boot. Who was he kidding? He completely understood their reaction. He had the same instinct; he just kept tamping it down. The woman wasn't just smart, having her doctoring degree and all, but she was beautiful, too. When she stared at him with her guileless green eyes, she truly had no clue what she did to his insides. She didn't fawn all over the men, waiting for their adoration. She naturally brought out that reaction in them. And didn't seem to notice when she did.

Assisting with her hair had been a bad idea. Necessary because it was such a mess she'd never have been able to brush through it on her own, but a bad idea all the same. As usual he saw something that needed to be done and barged right in to handle the task. He'd helped his little sisters many a time and didn't even think of the act as an intimate one. But the moment he'd touched Abigail's silky tresses, something akin to a lightning bolt had passed through his fingers and straight into his hardened heart. The act shattered something deep inside that had kept him frozen and away from kindness for years. The only other time he'd even briefly allowed himself to care for someone was when he'd ministered to Caleb and perhaps when he salvaged each of the men from their various predicaments.

The thought disturbed him, and he hurried to his feet and stalked off into the darkness. "She's nothing but a botheration anyway." The moon lit his path, and he walked toward the water's edge. Moonlight rippled where it reflected on the surface, mimicking the ripples Abigail Hayes sent through his body.

And the worst thing was that he didn't feel he could trust her. She'd escaped an Indian massacre. A massacre that was unusual—although not unheard of—in this area. Hank had been sure she'd left willingly with Bert from the train station, yet what purpose would she have to leave with him and then lose them all at the attack with hardly a backward glance? Granted, the massacre had affected her. She'd been pale, and the look of devastation on her face couldn't have been faked.

But was the devastation over losing Bert? Or over the attack itself? Yet Hank was the one who caused his distrust.

Jake had a lot more questions than answers at this point, and first thing in the morning he intended to ask those questions and demand some answers.

"Just as I thought, nothing but trouble," he muttered.

"What's nothing but trouble?" Abigail's voice came out of nowhere and made him jump. "Maybe I can help."

"Maybe you can." Jake turned to her. She stood a few feet behind him, silhouetted by the moonlight. The glow made her look like an angel. For a moment he couldn't find his words.

She hugged her arms around herself. "I couldn't sleep."

"I'm sure this is different than anything you've ever experienced. It has to be unnerving."

Abbie laughed. "That's an understatement." She looked over her shoulder toward the fire. "Actually, it's more the men's snoring that's disturbing me. Each time I drift off I have a nightmare about being back on the train, which startles me right back awake. I didn't sleep much on the train, afraid I'd sleep through my next stop."

Jake found himself smiling at her words. "I hardly think you'd sleep through the squealing of brakes and loss of speed."

"You'd think as much. But during my medical training we'd be woken up at all hours. There weren't many nights where we'd sleep straight through. We became accustomed to sleeping when and where we could, and when we did we slept hard. Now that I've finished my training, I still experience the same problem."

The breeze tossed Abbie's hair, and the scent of lye drifted to him. He'd never thought lye a pleasant aroma—until now.

"Can I ask you a question?" Jake folded his arms and pinned her with his gaze. He hoped she wouldn't bolt. "Make that several questions."

She turned candid eyes on him. "Of course. What would you like to know?"

He searched for the right words. He didn't want to offend her or scare her off. "Can you tell me how you alone survived a brutal Indian attack when more experienced men didn't have a chance?" He closed his eyes and chastised himself. That wasn't quite the gentle approach he'd planned.

Silence greeted his question. He opened his eyes and looked at her, half expecting her to have disappeared into the darkness. Instead she stood nearby with soundless tears coursing down her face. Tears that he'd put there as surely as if he'd captured water droplets from the lake and dropped them onto her cheeks. But genuine pain lay behind the tears.

"I'm sorry. I didn't mean to make you cry."

She shook her head, still hugging her arms around her chest. "It's not your fault. It's me. You see, I did a terrible thing."

Jake's heart sank. Just as he'd suspected. And if she'd set up an attack on the outlaws, what fate did Jake and his men have at her hands? This was a side Caleb hadn't had time to warn him about. Or more than likely, a side Caleb hadn't even known about. The band of Indians still roamed the hills nearby. They wouldn't have had time to go far. "I see. Please continue." He could hear the coldness in his own voice.

Apparently she did, too, because her eyes hardened as she continued. "Coming out on the train, we were held up by train robbers. They singled me out to go with them as a hostage—or something—and my new friend, Hattie, sank down onto her knees and prayed for my deliverance. Almost immediately help arrived in the form of Bat Masterson." She glanced at him. "Of course, at the time I didn't know who he was. I just appreciated that he was kind and he intervened and got me safely back on that train." Her voice lowered. "He was very kind and handsome, much like you."

Jake had to lean forward to hear her words. She thought him kind and handsome? Another piece of ice thawed inside his heart. But she'd just admitted it was her fault that Bert and his men were brutally murdered. Perhaps he should keep his mind on the matter at hand and not allow himself to be swayed by her charismatic charm. He realized they were only inches apart. He quickly stepped away, wishing instead that he could step closer and pull her into his arms. He cleared his throat. "Please continue."

Her voice shook. "Last night we were making plans for this morning, and Bert reminded me that today would be our wedding day. One of the men, Bill, had been injured. This morning after I woke up, I checked his injuries and realized that moment might be my only chance to get away. I quietly packed my valise and grabbed Hamm. I prayed that God would intervene and save me from my fate as Bert's wife. I had my horse, ready to lead him out of the area, but suddenly a horrible yell pierced the air. I wasn't sure what was happening." The tears turned to sobs, but she continued. "I hid behind a boulder and dropped to my knees. I remembered what Hattie had done for me, and I followed her lead. I bowed down to the ground. I prayed. I prayed God would help me."

"You said you killed Bert and his men."

"I did. I killed them as surely as if I'd done it with my own hands."

"How do you figure?"

Her voice became a whisper. "I prayed them dead."

Now, as she stated the comment in a flat tone, he recalled her earlier comment at the scene of the massacre. She'd uttered the same words then.

"You prayed them dead?"

"Yes."

He softened toward her. "Doc, you can't pray a person dead."

"But I did. The result was almost instantaneous. I prayed, and they died. As simple as that. And I alone survived."

"You were behind a boulder?"

"Yes."

"And the Indians never saw you?"

"They did."

Jake hesitated. They'd seen her and didn't kill or capture her? Perplexed, he pushed her. "Are you sure?"

"Positive. We had words."

Stupefied, he stared at her. "You had words. With a ferocious Indian."

"Yes."

Surely she was in shock. She had been at the time and now she was from the memory.

"What words did you exchange?"

"Oh, we didn't exchange words. I was the only one who spoke."

"Perhaps you should try to explain what happened word for word."

Abbie took a deep breath, and her mouth formed the words several times in silence before she actually voiced them. Again they came out in a whisper. She shivered as she relayed them. "The dust of the area seems to annoy my senses. With all the dust stirred up at the savages' arrival, I sneezed. They'd already done their damage, and I was hoping they'd go away."

Jake winced at the images in his mind. Her terror. The screams of the men. The scent of blood that would have floated around her. And her nose tickling with a sneeze that surely would mean her immediate death.

"But they didn't, and you sneezed."

"Right." She paced a few feet away and turned her back on him. "Silence greeted my sneeze. Suddenly my fear turned to blind fury. I've never been so angry in my entire life. I'm a strong, independent woman. I looked forward to this trip to see my brother. Then the train was held up, Bert stole me away from the station, he told me I'd been promised as his wife, and I spent the longest days of my life with a band of outlaws and watched as they shot at each other, each time wondering if a stray bullet would find its way to me. I lost all my confidence. And in the end, I prayed up an Indian attack."

Jake tried to keep up with her thoughts and explanations. "What did you do after you sneezed?"

"I froze. I couldn't breathe. I heard soft footsteps on the ground, coming my way. I knew it was all over and I was about to face the same fate of the brutal killings I'd heard. It made me angry. I grabbed Hamm and jumped to my feet." Her arms gathered around an invisible Hamm as she spoke. She hissed her words through clenched teeth, as if reliving the experience too clearly in her mind. "I jumped to my feet and screamed all my rage at the Indian who approached. He fell backward and did a complete flip before returning to his feet, staring at *me* as if I were an apparition. I rushed forward and poked him in the chest with my finger. I told him about my trip out here and about everything that had gone wrong. I told him if he was going to kill me, to do it and be done. He continued to stare, along with his men. We stood that way for what seemed forever until suddenly Hamm poked his face out from the blanket."

"You'd wrapped Hamm as you would an infant?"

"I suppose so. I never really thought about it. But yes, that's how I carried him."

"What happened when Hamm poked his head out from the blanket?"

Abbie considered his words. "Hamm squealed, and a look of pure panic passed over the warrior's face. He screamed something to the others, and they retreated. I sank to my knees behind the boulder and remember falling into a deep sleep. Next thing I knew, you and your men were there."

Jake felt a huge peace descend upon him. She hadn't set up the attack, nor had she had anything to do with it. Indeed, it was quite the opposite. He still didn't understand why the attack had taken place, but perhaps it was simply a random situation that would never be fully explained. He did know one thing. With Abbie's wild blond hair and her total lack of fear as she clutched a "baby" to her chest during the warriors' arrival and then a pig's snout and squeal emerging from the wraps, the Indians must have thought her a spirit for sure. As superstitious as they were, she must have terrified them. The image had his mouth twitching with a desire to smile.

He took one look at the genuine devastation on Abbie's face and fought off the urge.

"Doc. Listen to me." He stepped close and took her by the arms. "Look at me."

As the moonlight shone down, she raised her eyes to him and pain reflected from their depths. The breeze stirred again, this time from the west, carrying the scent of the lake their way. It teased the silky strands of hair that lay beside her cheek. The dust swirled at their feet, and Abbie sneezed.

Her half laugh turned into a sob. Jake pulled her against him.

"You didn't pray them dead. You sent up a prayer for intervention, and coincidentally, the intervention came on the heels of your prayer. Their fate was already sealed. I do believe you were divinely protected. Are you a believer?"

"Not really. Though after all I've been through, I'd like to learn more."

"I can help you out with that." He pushed the hair from her face with a tender finger, more tender then he'd ever thought he could be. "But I want you to understand and know that you didn't cause their deaths. Do you understand? The circumstances are unusual, but their fate was sealed without your help." He moved away from her and paced beside the water's edge. "Did any of the men get away?"

"Only Boggs."

The hairs raised on the back of Jake's neck. "Someone did survive?"

"I think he left during the night, long before the attack."

"So he could have been involved. He could have planned the attack. Why else would he leave that particular night?"

"It wasn't like that."

"How so?"

"I actually encouraged him to go. I knew with my pending marriage as a distraction, Boggs could get safely to his family and take them away. Bert had used them as a threat to keep Boggs at his side all this time."

Jake nodded. After what Bert had done to Caleb, he could see him doing the same to others.

"But what kind of man would leave without you? He doesn't sound like much of a man to me."

"Jake, he was a perfect gentleman. He begged me to go with him, but Bill, one of the other men, had been shot during one of their bouts of drunken shooting and I needed to care for him. Otherwise he would have died."

"He died anyway."

"Yes, but I didn't know he would at the time."

Her response solidified his trust that she was telling the truth. Otherwise, what was to keep her from escaping during the night with the other man?

They heard the snap of a branch nearby, and both looked in the direction of the sound. Jake held out a hand to stay Abbie while he checked it out. He couldn't see anything in the moonlight, but the lighting had dimmed and he couldn't guarantee what—or who—had made the sound. "Doc, I want you to return to the campfire and try to get some sleep. We'll have a long day tomorrow, and I want you well rested."

The crackle of brush sounded again, a bit farther away. Whoever—or whatever—had been there had left. Jake couldn't tamp down the feeling that someone had listened to their conversation. He escorted Abbie back to her bedroll and stood nearby as she settled in. The others lay about, snoring as she'd said. Only Hank was unaccounted for. He'd been on watch duty and appeared promptly from the other direction. He'd had time to circle back around, but Jake couldn't be sure. Hank entered the cleared area, and firelight reflected off his face. He sent Jake a look of challenge, and Jake motioned him to rest. Jake would remain on watch for the rest of the night. He'd do everything in his power to prevent Abbie from experiencing any more fear on this journey. If someone lurked in the shadows, Jake would roust them out and deal with them without her knowing.

Chapter 9

Jake stepped quietly through the brush surrounding their site. The wind blew over the lake's surface, bringing along a chill breeze. Though the moon was bright, he didn't see any signs of an intruder. Small night animals scurried through the brush, but other than that no other sound broke the silence.

He circled around to the far side of camp and stood just outside the clearing. Everything appeared to be as he'd left it. Their gear, neatly piled near the horses, stood ready for morning's first light. One of the horses snorted and shuffled around on the hard-packed dirt. The fire burned low, emitting just enough heat to keep the area warm. On the far side, Abbie slept, her angelic features framed by her mass of hair. Her face wore an expression of peace, something he hadn't seen during her waking hours. Red coughed and shifted to his back, but Scrappy and Grub didn't budge.

Jake sat down and relaxed against a large boulder, just out of sight of the fire, and laid his rifle across his lap. He leaned his head back so he could rest but didn't let down his guard. He stayed in that position until the sky began to brighten in the east. The mountains were silhouetted as he stood to rouse the others.

Grub stretched and emitted an incoherent grumble as he slowly started over to prepare their morning meal. Scrappy rubbed at his eyes, tried to focus on Jake's face, stiffly worked his way to an upright position, and headed over to look after the horses. Red jumped to his feet, always ready to move on, and began to sort through the things that needed repacked onto the horses.

"Hey, Doc. Time to wake up. I want to make an early start." Jake held back his smile as she groaned quietly and pushed to a sitting position. Her hair, though cleaner, looked almost as rough as it had the morning before when they'd found her. She smoothed it with her hands and surprisingly, for the most part, it pressed into place. She squinted her eyes and blinked at him. From her actions, it was clear she wasn't an early riser by nature. "We need to keep moving so we can get to the safety of the ranch."

"It's still dark. You aren't kidding about an early start." She stretched, glancing around at the others. Jake did the same.

Hank still lazed on his back, his hat pulled over his face, as the others worked to move out. Jake toed him with his boot. "Hank. Up and at 'em. We need to get moving."

Before Hank could respond, Scrappy let out a yelp of pain. One of the horses reared. Abbie was on her feet and at Scrappy's side before Jake realized anything had happened. He hurried forward as Abbie led Scrappy to a rock to sit down. Red spoke quietly to the stallion, calming him.

"You have to relax, Scrappy. I just need to take a look."

Jake bit back a grin as Scrappy batted at Abbie's hands. "Scrappy, take it like a man. Doc needs to look at your leg. Last night you were tripping over each other to get her attention."

Scrappy shook his head and ignored him. "I like you and all, Doc, but you ain't gonna be touchin' me on my leg or anywhere else."

"Don't be silly, Scrap." As she talked, she continued to roll up his pant leg, appearing oblivious to his oppositional hands.

"What does a petticoat doctor know about doctorin' men?" Scrappy succeeded in rolling the coarse fabric of his pants down a notch. "Just because Grub fell under your charm doesn't mean I'm gonna. I ain't gonna be your guinea pig."

"Goodness gracious, Scrappy. I've doctored plenty of men during my training. I trained with all women doctors, but we had plenty of male patients. And I'm not going to do surgery out here. I just need to see what stung you. Red, could you please bring me my bag?"

"I bet it was a scorpion. Did you see it, Scrap? Those things can be deadly. First you have trouble breathing and you can swell all up. I hear it's an excruciating way to die."

"Red!"

Jake and Abbie's voices melded in unison as they both chastised Red for his untimely comment. Scrappy's face froze in a mask of fear. His blue eyes watered more than normal, and Jake had the uneasy feeling that the grown man was about to cry.

"I think my chest feels tight. Am I swelling? My pant leg feels tight." He sucked in panicked breaths of air.

"You're making yourself breathe too hard, Scrappy. Try to breathe slow and deep. You're going to be fine." Abbie glared over her shoulder at Red. "I really need my bag." She turned to her patient. "It's not a scorpion bite, okay, Scrap? You're going to be fine. Unless—" She glanced up at Jake and bit her lip, worry creasing her pretty features.

"Unless?" Scrappy's voice raised an octave. "Unless what?"

"Are you sensitive to bees?"

"Not that I know of. But I've never been stung before, either."

"Isn't it a bit early for a bee to be about?" Jake pulled his hat off and ran his fingers through his hair. Couldn't any aspect of this journey be easy? They should be pulling out, and instead they were all gathered around Scrappy, with no food on the fire, and the horses still unpacked.

"Apparently this one doesn't know that and is an early riser." She looked across the camp. "Unlike Hank over there."

Jake looked over at his newest hand and stalked across the ground. He should let him go on the spot. But for now, the more hands they had the better. There was safety in numbers. And until they escorted Abbie safely onto the ranch, he wanted all the numbers they had.

"Hank, I told you already to get up and prepare to pull out. We need to get out of the area." He paused. "You saw what the Indians did to Bert and his gang. Do you really want the rest of us to end up that way?"

The man went pale at the thought, and he hurried to stand.

"Scrappy was stung by a bee. Doc's taking care of him. I need you to prepare the horses while Grub gets our food ready. Can you do that for me?"

Hank nodded and headed in the direction of the horses, but he kept his gaze on Abbie the entire time. Red returned to his assigned area and sorted through their gear. Jake hurried back to Scrappy's side. "How's the patient, Doc?"

"Doin' just fine, boss."

Jake laughed at her attempt at a drawl. "I'm not your boss."

"More or less you are." She grinned up at him. "Until we reach the ranch, I'm at your mercy and need to do my part. I don't mind getting my hands dirty."

"Well, you seem to be doing fine earning your keep just by using your doctoring skills. We're mighty blessed to have you along with us."

"I'm glad to hear that." Without looking up at him, she settled on her knees and dug through her bag. She pulled out a scalpel.

Scrappy slapped at her hand. "What are ya doin' with that thing? Doctor or not, you ain't cuttin' nothin'."

Red and Grub hurried over and crowded in close to watch.

"Will you relax?" Abbie's voice dropped to a soothing tone. "I only plan to use it to scrape the stinger from your leg. If we pull it out with tweezers, more venom will seep in. The more venom in your body, the sicker the sting can make you. And if you aren't sure about sensitivities to a sting, we need to be very careful. If you have a reaction to the sting, we could be in trouble. You need to tell me if you have any difficulty breathing or feel anything out of the ordinary."

"I feel pain."

Abbie laughed. "That's to be expected."

"You ain't cuttin' nothin'?"

"No." She glanced at the other men. "Don't you both have better things to do?"

Amused at her authoritative side and his men's rush to oblige her, Jake continued to watch from nearby.

Abbie scraped the stinger out, applied salve to the irritated area, and dusted her hands on her skirt as she stood. "There you go. That should do it."

"It's hurtin' somethin' awful. Are you sure you got it all? And are you sure it was a bee sting?"

Abbie placed a comforting hand on his shoulder. "I'm afraid it will hurt for the better part of the day. And yes, I'm sure it's a bee sting. Bees die after they sting, and your little fella is right over here." She pointed to a spot near Scrappy's foot.

He raised a boot and stomped on the insect.

"Oh." Abbie's hand flew to her mouth. "I guess he deserved that after the pain he inflicted on you, though he was already dead to start with." She looked over at Jake, laughter dancing in her eyes.

So the good doctor had a sense of humor.

"Well, now that the crisis has been dealt with, what do you all say we hit the trail? Grub, pull us something together that we can eat as we go. We've lost too much time."

Grub pulled out some cold biscuits and passed them around. Red and Hank had the gear stowed and their mounts ready to go.

They rode steadily through the morning and early afternoon, and several times Jake felt the same sensation that they were being watched. Though he stopped to look around, he never saw a sign of anyone trailing them.

Jake reined in Steadfast and motioned for the others to join him. "Let's head down toward Nephi, and then we'll cut from there over toward Mount Pleasant."

Hank leaned forward in the saddle. "So we're looking at a few more days on the trail?"

"More or less. We've made good time today. We'll set up camp just ahead, this time near the base of the mountains."

He pushed them until sunset. He wanted to double back around and see if he could flush out their pursuer.

"You seem worried."

Obviously Abbie's skills as a physician didn't stop at treating ailments, but she also had a knack for assessing a person's mental state with apt precision.

"You did well today, keeping up and all."

"Don't change the subject."

"I didn't." He grinned and crossed his arms as he leaned back against a large tree trunk. "I merely started one of my own. And wouldn't you say I have reason to worry? I need to get you back to the ranch. We need to get your trunk and our wagon and secure your passage through the mountains. There could possibly be a band of Indians following us, anxious to do the same thing to us as they did to Bert and his gang."

Her face crinkled into a frown. "You think someone's chasing us."

How she could hone in on that one item from his comments, he didn't know. But she was a mite too close to the truth, and he didn't want to worry her.

"I've kept watch all day and haven't seen any physical sign to prove that we're being followed."

"That was a good attempt at a nonanswer. But still, you think someone's following us."

She was tenacious. Her raised eyebrows dared him to deny what she felt she knew. The top of her head didn't even reach his chin; yet she stood straight, waiting for him to respond.

"I'd like to double back and check to be sure."

Now her expression became troubled. "Do you think that's wise? What if the Indians have tracked us? You saw what they did to a whole group of men. Do you think they'll hesitate when it comes to one lone man?"

"I'll be careful. You don't have to worry."

"Why doesn't that make me feel any better?" She huffed out a breath and narrowed her moss-colored eyes. "I've had plenty of doctoring experience on the trail without your adding to it."

"Then I'll take one of the men with me. Would that make you feel better?"

"I suppose. But of course, that leaves only three of us here."

"You're right. Doc, I need to go alone. The more of us that go, the more noise we'll make, which in turn will jeopardize my security. There's no reason for all of us to go. Grub needs to start dinner, Scrappy needs to rest his leg, and Red needs to reorganize our gear. Hank can care for the horses."

"I can help with some of that. Just tell me what to do."

"You, Doc, need to check Grub's hand and look at Scrappy's leg, then you need to relax. Tomorrow will be another hard day of riding, and after that we'll cut through the mountains. I want you rested for that leg of the journey. It won't be easy."

She measured him with a look and turned away. "Grub? Could you use an extra hand with dinner?"

"Yes, ma'am. My hand is stinging a bit, and it's hard to work this way."

"I'll be over in a moment to see it. We'll need to change the dressing anyway."

If she noticed Jake's scowl when she turned back around, she didn't give any indication. A tiny dimple formed at the corner of her mouth as she smiled. "It looks like everything's set on our end. You'd best be on your way."

Jake needed to be on his way—away from her. Somehow the helpless, prissy woman from the train station had turned into an opinionated, independent taskmaster. In a way he wished he could stick around to watch her whip the motley crew into shape. But for now, he needed to go round up their tracker.

At the last moment he decided to go on foot so he could melt into the trees. He felt sure their pursuer advanced alone. Thoughts of the interesting woman he escorted kept interrupting his concentration. He was pleasantly surprised to see how well she'd adapted to every change that came her way. Any other woman would have turned heel and headed back to Pennsylvania after the train robbery. Instead Abbie continued to push on, no matter what trials the journey brought her way. He was mighty impressed.

The crackle of a stick up ahead brought his thoughts back to focus. He slipped farther into the woods and waited as the unsteady gait of a large man— or possibly a bear, considering all the noise being made—approached. He rested his hand on his gun where it rested in its holster on his hip and prepared to draw. He saw a flash of color through the trees. Now he had his physical sign.

"Don't take another step." Jake stepped from the shadows and held out his gun.

The man froze and about tipped off his feet. Sweat beaded on his forehead, and his eyes were glazed with fever. Though he led a horse, he traveled on foot. He rested against the horse as he stared warily at Jake.

"Why are you trailing us?" Jake took a step closer.

"I'm trailing Miss Hayes, not you." He stopped and took several deep, pain-filled breaths. "After the Indian attack—when you showed up—I needed to know she was in good hands."

"She's in good hands." Jake narrowed his eyes and moved forward again. "How do you know Miss Hayes?"

"I met her the day she arrived at the station."

"And just happened to run into her again at the attack?"

The man shook his head. "No. I rode with Bert."

"How'd you survive the attack? No one else did, save Abbie. Miss Hayes." Jake was close enough now to see the dried blood on the man's shirt. From the volume of it, he'd bled heavily at some point.

"I left the night before."

"Boggs?"

"Yes." He heaved several breaths and glanced up at Jake. He wobbled on his feet. "How'd. . .you. . .know?"

"Miss Hayes mentioned you."

The man tipped forward, and Jake grabbed him. "Do you think you can get back up on your mount?"

"Don't know. Hurts too bad."

Jake sighed. He came out here to flush out their pursuer and instead ended up mollycoddling him.

It took every bit of strength Jake had, but he finally got Boggs up on the horse and was able to lead him back to their camp. His crew had everything set up. Abbie stirred something in the pot over the fire and glanced up at his approach.

Upon seeing Boggs, she darted over to grab her bag and met them on the near side of the fire. "Set him down here." She laid out several blankets and motioned to them.

Red and Scrappy worked as a team with Jake to lower the man to the bedroll.

"Mr. Boggs!" Abbie's gasp of surprise told Jake what he needed to know. Boggs must have befriended her, which didn't surprise him based on his ranch hands' reaction to the woman. "What on earth happened to you? I thought you'd have collected your family by now and be well out of danger's way."

"I couldn't leave you. I tried to go, but I couldn't leave you at Bert's mercy. I know. . .how he is." He gasped in obvious pain. "As I returned to our site, I ran into a warrior. He stabbed me and left me for dead. He was intent on attacking the encampment, so he didn't take time to make sure. I managed to get to camp, but I passed out again. I saw you leave with these men and have followed you since, wanting to make sure you were okay."

Jake watched the interaction with interest. Abbie could take the crustiest of men and calm them.

She shushed Boggs. "There'll be enough time for talk later. Right now I want to tend to your wound."

"Too late." Boggs waved her away.

"Let me be the one to decide that." She motioned for Red and Scrappy to roll him on his side, and she gently cut the back of his shirt. Her face crinkled with concern. "Grub, I'm going to need some hot boiled water."

"I'll collect some water." Scrappy grabbed a small bucket and hurried off to a stream they'd located in the woods. He reappeared a few minutes later, water in hand. Grub took it and put it over the fire. In the meantime Abbie laid out the items she'd need. When she got the water, she dipped a clean cloth into it and cleaned the open wound. Boggs grabbed onto the blanket and moaned.

"The angle is good." She spoke to Boggs as she worked. "You did lose a lot of blood, but I think once I sew you up you'll be fine. It's going to be tender. The outer area is a bit red, but I'll give you something to prevent infection."

She stitched him up and saturated the area with salve before wrapping it in fresh bandages. "He won't be able to travel for a couple of days."

Jake's jaw worked. "We can't afford to sit here."

"Then I'll stay put with him, and we'll join you in a few days."

"No."

"No?"

"I'm here to escort you to the ranch, not to leave you in the forest with a stranger while rogue Indians roam the area."

"Then leave one of your men with me. We'll be fine."

"You didn't seem to think I'd be fine earlier when I went to see who was following us."

"Then you do admit you knew someone was following us."

"I admitted it already! Stop talking in circles. You're not staying behind and that's that. We'll have to figure out a different solution." He ran his hands through his hair. The woman exasperated him. They couldn't afford to sit tight. It wasn't safe.

Chapter 10

Jake allowed Boggs two days to recuperate before they hit the trail again. Abbie suggested a longer wait, but even Boggs insisted he was well enough to move on and that it wouldn't be safe to wait any longer. They left at dawn and planned to stop in Nephi for supplies before the final leg of the trip to the ranch. In midafternoon they approached the outskirts of town, and the horses picked up speed.

"I think they must know they'll get a good meal at the livery at the rate they're moving forward." Abbie laughed. "And I have to admit, a solid meal at a regular table sounds mighty good to me, too."

Her enthusiasm dulled, though, as she realized the ramifications of her journey and how much easier it would have been on all of them had it started here.

Jake pulled up beside her. His brown eyes, full of concern, studied her. "Hey, Doc, why did you get so quiet all of a sudden?"

She felt her mouth contort into a wry smile. "I just realized this is where my original train destination was to end. If my trip had gone as originally planned, so many things wouldn't have happened the way they did."

"It was hardly your fault. How were you to know that Bert would plan such a ruse and lie to you as he did?"

Abbie nibbled on her lip. "Still. I walked right into his plan. You'd think I'd have thought things through better. I blindly trusted a stranger and look where it got me. I'm an educated woman. I'm supposed to use my knowledge and think things through in a way that reflects that education."

"But Bert manipulated the situation, correct? How were you to know? You can't continue to berate yourself for things that are out of your control."

"You're right." She sighed. "And it's not like I can change any of it now. I can only use the experience to avoid such situations in the future."

They rode along in silence, the town looming bigger and bigger on the horizon. This is where Jake had planned to pick her up. And where her trunk hopefully awaited her.

"Will we have a way to transport my trunk—if it indeed made it down here—to the ranch?"

"I left a wagon at the livery. We can bring your trunk and any other supplies that we'll need with us from here."

"Good."

Jake pulled ahead, and Abbie studied him from her place behind him. He sat tall in the saddle, and his quiet strength inspired confidence within her that he'd keep her safe. Apparently his ranch hands felt the same way, based on the constant respect they showed him. Hank, who they explained had only recently joined the group, was the only one reticent with his approval, but Abbie figured that could be explained by his need to grow to trust his new boss.

She returned her attention to Jake. He wore his dark hair pulled back with a brown leather strap, where it lay against his tan neck. His white shirt, rolled up at the sleeves, contrasted nicely against the deep brown of his skin. His feet rested casually in the stirrups, and she wished she had his ease in the saddle. Though she'd become more skilled, she continually tensed her body to stay in place, which caused more aches and pains than she wanted to think about each night when they finally dismounted from their day's trek. The two-day break, though tedious, had been a welcome relief from the horse's back. She tried to mimic Jake's casual stance and nearly fell from the saddle.

"I'm not sure I can catch you if you fall off, Doc." Boggs's quiet laugh sounded from over her left shoulder. "I'd hate to tear open the wound you so nicely sewed up for me."

"I'll keep that in mind and try not to challenge your healing." She grinned over her shoulder. The man had become her self-declared protector.

The warm spring sun felt good as it shone upon her back. The blue sky stretched endlessly before them, and she marveled at the mountains in the distance. Jake had told her that they'd pass through them on their way to Mount Pleasant. While Boggs recuperated, she'd explored their immediate vicinity with Jake or one of the hands always nearby. The trees, streams, and open area spoke quietly to her heart. She didn't know what the future held, and she'd need to discuss her options with Jake at the soonest opportunity, but for now she held onto the dream that somehow she could still stay out here and help treat the local families as a physician. Jake spoke often of his relationship with the Lord, and she tucked the tidbits away for further contemplation.

She again felt a pang of guilt over her happiness. She hadn't properly dealt with her grief over Caleb's death and didn't want to succumb to it in front of these kind men. Though they were caring, they wouldn't know what to do, so she forced the grief away. She'd been trained to hide her emotions when dealing with her patients. Some of their situations were heartbreaking, and she'd learned to put a shell around her emotions as a way to deal with the deaths of small children or men and women who met their end too soon.

Hank rode up beside her and pinned her with his glare. She returned his gaze with raised eyebrows, and he shook his head and rode on.

Boggs leaned forward in the saddle and rested an arm on his thigh. "What did you do to that one to make him so full of animosity?"

Abbie shrugged. "I have no idea. At first he seemed semi-friendly, then he changed and hasn't said anything kind to me since. But for the life of me, I can't think of a thing I did to deserve his anger."

"Some men don't need a reason." Boggs shrugged. "Just stay away from him, okay? Something about him sets my nerves on edge."

"I completely intend to stay away from him, don't you worry."

They arrived at Nephi and left their horses at the livery. Jake checked on his wagon and asked that they have it ready for them upon their return. He and Abbie walked to the train depot and asked about her trunk. She was thrilled to find it waiting for her.

Abbie smiled up at Jake, unlocked the trunk, and ran her fingers lovingly over her medical books. Everything seemed to be accounted for.

Jake returned her smile.

"You'll send it over to the livery?" Abbie verified with the stationmaster.

"Will do, ma'am. We'll make arrangements to get it over there right away."

Jake led her down the bustling walkway and toward the restaurant. They ate alone, and she felt comfortable in his presence. Jake had a knack for making her feel relaxed.

"I'll escort you to the store and head over for the horses and wagon while you shop." Jake held the door open as they exited the eating establishment. They walked leisurely along the boardwalk. Several carriages bounced along the dusty road beside them. He placed her hand on his arm and led her across the street to the mercantile. "Take your time. I'll round up any of the hands I find on my way over, and we'll meet you back here."

"I thought you needed supplies, too."

"I placed my order for supplies when we passed through before. I'll pick them up when I return for you."

Abbie stood inside the door for a few moments and let her eyes adjust to the dim interior. She smiled as she surveyed the well-stocked shelves. A small table covered with checkers sat near a small stove. Several chairs surrounded it. The rest of the store was packed with supplies of every kind.

"May I help you, ma'am?" A robust woman stood before her, a warm smile on her face.

"I'm sure you can, but it will take me a few minutes to figure out all I need." Abbie laughed. She felt as if she'd been away from civilization for months instead of a couple of weeks and wanted to savor the experience of walking through the narrow aisles.

The woman appraised her in return. "You've been traveling?"

"Several long days by train and a week by horse." Abbie wrinkled her nose. "It's that obvious?"

"You don't exactly look like you just stepped out of the hotel. Your dress is a bit disheveled. I'd be lying if I said otherwise."

"My trunk continued on without me, and I've just now caught up with it. I could use a few new lightweight dresses for the rest of my journey. Do you have any ready-made dresses for sale?"

"We sure do!" She gestured for Abbie to follow her. "Right over here. We have several that should fit you." She stepped back and studied Abbie's outfit. "Perhaps you'd like something that isn't quite so austere?"

Abbie glanced down at her full, dark skirt and jacket. Her scuffed boots peeked out from below her hem. The outfit worked well in the city, but out here it did feel rather oppressive. She nodded.

The storekeeper chose several dresses, and Abbie fingered the soft material. "This would feel heavenly after the stifling heat we've endured on the ride down."

"While you were traveling by coach?"

"No, by horse."

The woman's eyebrows raised in surprise. "You rode horseback in those fancy clothes? You must have sweltered at times." She dangled the dresses in front of Abbie. "These will be much better suited for riding, and you'll love the airiness of the fabric."

"I hope so. That sounds delightful."

"Come over to this storage room, and you can try them on."

Abbie stepped into the small room as the door to the shop opened. She closed the door behind her, but could still hear the shuffle of the new shoppers' feet. As she unbuttoned her jacket, she heard Grub's voice and Scrappy's response. She smiled. By the time she was finished, they'd probably be done, too, and they could all leave to meet Jake together.

"I'm telling you, the petticoat doctor ain't what she appears to be."

Hank's words froze Abbie in place. She tried to get her fingers to move, but they wouldn't cooperate. What was he thinking saying such a thing? She realized she'd inhaled a breath and held it, and now she forced herself to release the air from her lungs.

"What're you talkin' about, Hank? You ain't liked Doc since she joined us, but we ain't seen no reason to back up your claims."

Dear, precious Scrappy. She wanted to give him a hug.

"I heard rumor that she planned that Indian attack on Bert and his men."

Red's voice carried through the thin wooden walls as a chair scraped on the floor. "That can't be true, and I won't have you bad talking Doc. She's not here to defend herself. It ain't right. You're just jealous because her intentions seem to be toward Jake instead of you."

Abbie felt her face flame. She didn't have intentions, did she? She enjoyed Jake's company, but only because he was kind. It wasn't any different with Boggs. She appreciated their protective instincts after years of looking out for herself. Though she did have to admit she felt drawn to Jake in a way she didn't feel with Boggs. But the realization that Red and possibly the others had sensed it made her blush with embarrassment.

And here she stood holding the most beautiful pale green dress in her hands. She couldn't deny that when she first saw it she wondered what Jake's reaction would be when he saw her in it. Time was running out, and she slipped out of her skirt and blouse and slipped the light cotton garment over her head. It fit perfectly. After the heavy wool of her other garments, she felt light and carefree in this new one.

"I could care less if Jake gets all her attention, if you know what I mean." Hank's guttural laugh knocked the air out of her. She closed her eyes and again held her breath, waiting for Red's response. "But rumor had it back in Salt Lake City that our good doctor told Bert he'd be sorry, and now he and all his companions are dead. And there she waltzes out from behind a rock without so much as a scratch."

"I've seen no sign of Doc being anything but kind and caring. Bert and his men kidnapped her. They met their demise at their own hand. It had nothing to do with Miss Hayes."

Abbie wanted to hug Grub, too. And she wished Boggs had entered the store with the others instead of waiting with the horses. He'd have set Hank straight in a moment.

Hank's voice intruded on the thought. "Fine. Think what you want. But I don't trust her, and I'd advise you all to rethink where you place your trust, too."

"I think we have." Red's voice, surprisingly strong for a man who Jake said ran from any altercation, finished the discussion.

She heard Hank stomp to his feet and slam out the door.

"Doc ain't like that," Scrappy said, sounding sad.

"No, she ain't," Grub agreed. "Don't you worry about it, Scrap."

"She's taken right good care of us," Red finished. "Hank's had something bothering him from the moment he joined us. Jake isn't happy and plans to release him as soon as we get back to the ranch."

The men's voices quieted. Abbie jumped as a knock sounded on the storeroom door. "I have a towel and some wash water for you, dear."

Abbie heard the hands get to their feet and mutter farewells to the storekeeper. The outer door opened and closed and only after silence settled over the area did Abbie open her door.

"Oh, honey, you look beautiful in this dress. It softens your rough edges."

"Rough edges, huh? I'm Abbie Hayes, by the way. If you're going to be so blunt, I guess we'd best know each other by name."

"Madeline Costner. My husband and I own the store. And I didn't mean any offense by my statement."

"None taken." Abbie surveyed herself in the blurry mirror in the room. The storekeeper was right. With her hair pulled back so severely and the oppressive, heavy dress, she had looked hard and unapproachable. This dress softened her and made her look and feel more feminine. She turned with a smile. "I like it."

"What about the others?"

"I'll take all three. And I'll need new bonnets to match, too." As she thought back, she couldn't remember a time she hadn't worn black, brown, or tan. The pastel blue, green, and pink dresses brought her back to her childhood when she'd tagged along with Caleb and he'd tugged her matching ribbons from her braids. If the garments brought back even a touch of those carefree days, they were well worth the purchase. "Do you mind if I wear this dress now?"

"Not at all. Hand me your other outfit, and I'll wrap it for you." She raised an eyebrow as Abbie handed it over. She held it out by her fingertips. "On second thought, I'll wrap it separately from the others. It's a mite dusty."

Abbie laughed and closed the door, returning her gaze to the mirror. One by one, she pulled out her hairpins. She ran her fingers through her unruly curls and then twisted the strands back up into a softer style, allowing a few tendrils to drape casually around her face. The change in her appearance was drastic. She smiled. The men would likely walk right past her and wouldn't even know it. She snatched up the towel and scrubbed the travel dust from her face. The action made her cheeks glow with color. Her eyes appeared brighter and reflected the green of her dress.

Her first thought was to wonder what Jake would think. The thought reminded her of Hank's accusations, and her heart sank. Jake might not think anything at all. Or he might believe Hank's lies and think Abbie did indeed have something to do with Bert's death. And if she searched her heart, she knew he was right. She inadvertently did.

Chapter 11

Jake returned to pick up Abbie and walked right past her before looking again and stepping back to stare. "Doc?"

She nodded, a blush filling her cheeks. Her eyes darted to look off into the distance beyond his shoulder. She refused to meet his gaze.

"Wow. You look. . ." He stopped short of telling her she looked beautiful. From the expression on her face, she wasn't in a mood to be fussed over. But the difference from the stodgy woman at the train station and this one that stood before him was remarkable. "Different."

"Oh. Thank you." She glanced back at him and something akin to disappointment filled her eyes.

He'd gambled with his words and lost. He'd said the wrong thing.

She quickly tried to cover her reaction and forced a smile to her face. "I'm ready when you are. Let me just get the things I bought."

"I'll get them." Jake hurried over to the counter where a brown paper-wrapped package waited. "The wagon is just out front. At least from now on you'll travel in style."

Abbie nodded, gathered her skirts in one hand, and headed out the door.

He followed, ruing his doltish response. "Doc. . ."

She turned around to look at him, her features a mask of innocence. "Yes?"

He pulled his hat from his head and stood on the boardwalk, wondering why he hadn't just let the uncomfortable moment pass. She stared at him and nibbled on her lower lip. He should have just bustled her out to the wagon and been done with it. But she did look pretty, and it suddenly seemed important to him that she knew.

Two men passed by, jostling him as he stared awkwardly at the beautiful woman. They tipped their hats at Abbie, bidding her a good day, and she responded to them with a pleasant grin. He silently fumed. Suddenly he wanted all her attention on him. He wanted her to respond to him—and only him—with her flirtations.

"Jake?"

"What?" He didn't realize he'd been glaring at the two men as they walked down the walkway until she interrupted his musings. He sent them one last glare for good measure and returned his gaze to her. "You look beautiful." He snarled the words.

Her laugh circled the air around him. "Thank you. I think."

"You think?" He'd just uttered the hardest words he'd ever had to say in his life, and she "thought" she thanked him?

"I'm not used to having compliments snarled at me." She fussed with the delicate lace at her wrist.

She had tiny wrists. How had he missed that before? Somehow in her matronly garb she'd appeared much more sturdy and self-sufficient. Now he found himself wanting to do everything for her.

"I didn't mean to snarl. When those nefarious men so blatantly flirted with you, my compliment got all mixed up."

"Jake! They didn't flirt!" Her face turned several shades of red. "They were simply being friendly." She pinned him with her green eyes. "Honestly. The things you say. I never can get my bearings when you're around."

He grinned. She might put on her scientific front, but underneath she apparently felt just as muddled around him as he felt around her. He'd take that as a good sign.

Whoa, buddy! He stopped that line of thought in its track. There needn't be any muddling or befuddling or anything else when it came to Abbie. She was Caleb's sister. He had an obligation to get her to her brother. He didn't need any romantic interests to distract him from his mission. The last thing he needed to do was moon around because of some female.

He wiped off the grin and cleared his throat. "We'd best be on our way."

Confusion clouded her eyes, and with her expression perplexed, she nodded and headed for the wagon. Before she could even reach for the handhold, he'd swept her up and onto the seat. He registered as he let go that his hands fully circled her waist.

"Oomph." She gasped and glared at him for a moment before leaning forward to fluff her skirts. She sent him another glare and settled back onto the hard wooden surface, arms folded defiantly across her chest. "I'd appreciate it if you'd warn me next time before you manhandle me in such a way."

"Manhandle?" he stalked to the other side and climbed up beside her. "I merely lifted you to your seat as any gentleman would, including either of those two men you batted your eyes at a moment ago. Would you chastise them for doing their duty as a male?"

Abbie's eyes narrowed, and she huffed out a breath. "I didn't bat my eyes at them. They tipped their hats and greeted me, and I in turn responded. If they'd dared to touch my waist as you just did, I'd have pounded them with my reticule for taking such a liberty with me."

He smirked. "Yet you didn't pound me. Interesting." He could tell his words irritated her further. He sent her an innocent smile. He'd taken a liking to riling her up.

"Of course I didn't pound you. I—I. . ." She stopped to gather her thoughts. "You're my escort to the ranch. I can't afford to alienate you."

"Right."

She shifted on her seat and turned toward him. Her raised left eyebrow quirked and quivered. "What's that supposed to mean. '*Right*'?"

"I think you might have liked the feel of my hands on your waist. *That's* why you didn't 'pound' me." He raised his eyebrow back, but held his steady—no nervous twitches there—which gave him the upper hand. "You know I made a commitment to your brother. I'm not going to abandon you on the streets, no matter how snide or biting your comments can be. And surely you know that. Therefore I have to assume that you appreciated my gallant attempt to assist you onto the bench."

"I know nothing of the sort." She faced forward and pulled her skirt closer to her legs. "But what I do know is that the men are waiting for us up ahead and from the looks on their faces, they're curious as to what has us sitting here wasting time talking."

Irritated, Jake looked over and saw the men sitting on their horses just as she said at the edge of town. Scrappy waved. Jake waved back. He gathered the reins and urged the horses forward.

Abbie glanced at the wagon bed. "Oh!"

He slowed.

"You have my trunk!"

"I do."

"Thank you."

Her charming grin dispelled his irritable feelings, but he wasn't about to let her know that. He forced out a grumpy, "You're welcome."

They joined the men. Boggs had waited with Hamm and now placed him in the wagon beside the trunk. He winked at Abbie, but Jake noticed none of the others would meet Abbie's eyes. He sent her a questioning glance and noticed that she stared at Hank with pain-filled eyes. What had Jake missed?

"Hey, um, Doc?" Scrappy's voice pulled her attention from Hank. "Can I speak to you for a moment?" He glanced at Jake. "Uh. In private?"

What on earth could Scrappy have to say that Jake, his boss, couldn't hear? It was downright disrespectful.

"Scrap. Anything you need to say to Doc can be said in front of me." They needed to remember who was in charge of this trip.

Scrappy sent Jake a sideways glance and peered anxiously up at Abbie. He lowered his voice. "Doc?"

Abbie looked around and pointed to a stand of trees up the road. "We'll meet you over there."

His face relaxed, and without a further look at Jake, his *boss*, he hurried back to his mount.

"I need my men to respect me, Doc, or nothing will be done correctly."

"We mean no disrespect, Jake, but a patient's confidence needs to be respected. If he needs me to speak to him in private, as his physician, I need to honor that. So do you."

Jake mumbled under his breath, but directed the wagon toward the trees. "Make it quick, please. We've wasted enough time in town. We need to find a place to set up camp before nightfall."

He watched as she dropped gracefully to the ground. She picked up her black bag and carried it off to meet with Scrappy. After some furtive hand movements on his part, she opened the bag and pulled out a small container. She dispensed an amount to him, and he disappeared behind the trees. Abbie slowly meandered back Jake's way, and he wanted to bellow at her to hurry. But with Scrappy behind the trees, they couldn't exactly rush off. He knew his frustration was due to the fact that Abbie had ingratiated her way into the hearts of all his men, while seeming to hold him at arm's length.

Scrappy reappeared and hurried to his mount. He led it their way and asked if he needed to assist Abbie onto the wagon. She sent him a charming smile and thanked him for the courtesy, but Jake hurried to her side and helped her into place. Jake choked back his comment and just stared at her with questioning eyes before hurrying back to his place beside her.

Abbie narrowed her eyes at him. "What?"

"What what?" Jake slapped the reins on the horses, and they moved forward.

"You look like you just swallowed a sour lemon."

"No I don't."

"How can you say you don't when you have no mirror? I'm looking at you and can see it plain as day. You, on the other hand, can't possibly see your sour face or countenance. It's ridiculous to assert that you can."

"It's my face. I can certainly assert anything about it that I want."

She snickered, the sound completely incongruent with her prissy outfit.

"Now you're laughing at me?"

"I can't help it. You sound like one of my disgruntled pediatric patients back home."

How many times could one woman insult him in a few moments' time? "Anything else?"

"No." She sat demurely upon the bench, her hands folded in her lap. "By the way, it's a chafing problem."

"A chafing problem?" He couldn't keep up with her rambling thoughts.

"Yes. Sometimes a small rash, if left untreated, can grow to cause a person a great deal of pain and irritation. That, in turn, can make a man cantankerous."

Jake was horrified by her newest topic. From time to time a man might get a small rash from being in the saddle too long, but it certainly wasn't any of her business either way. "I don't have a chafing problem. My problem is that you seem to be undermining my authority with my men."

She stared at him.

He tried to stare back, but couldn't meet her eyes with the present topic under discussion.

"My comment referred to Scrappy's medical issue. The saddle has caused a rash on the back of his thighs."

"Huh? Oh. Of course."

"He said I could tell you, since you're *the leader* and all."

"Good. Good. I appreciate that." Jake shifted in his seat.

She pointedly glanced down and back up with a guileless smile. "Are you sure you don't have an issue we need to discuss, too? I have plenty of salve."

"This topic is highly improper."

"Not really. Not for me." She sighed. "I'm sorry. My whole adult life has been centered on the hospital, my training, and my patients. I'm not used to social situations." Her eyes clouded. "I didn't mean to offend or to say anything improper."

Again he shifted. Her medical observations made him uncomfortable. Her personal observations made him more uncomfortable. Everything the woman did suddenly made him uncomfortable. And instead of just stating the fact, she'd made him nervous and now thought he had a chafing rash. Next time a pretty woman turned his head, he'd keep his thoughts to himself. And he'd stick with the innocuous word "different" instead of the all-telling word "beautiful."

"Hank!" Jake ignored her and spurred the horses on.

Abbie placed her hand upon his arm, a look of alarm passing across her features. "What do you need with Hank?"

"I'm going to switch out with him for a while and take the lead. I need to see what's up ahead."

"No, please! Anyone but Hank."

He didn't miss her panicked tone and urged the horses to slow. "What did Hank do to you?"

"Nothing."

"Doc. If something inappropriate or offensive was said or done to you by one of my hands, I need to know. And if it helps, he's already on his way out of my employment. He'll be let go as soon as this trip is over."

She stared straight ahead, and he studied her, waiting for her response. Her brow furrowed in concentration. "I overheard him at the general store."

"Overheard him say what?"

Her face contorted, though she gave a valiant attempt to keep her tears at bay. "He said I'm responsible for Bert and his gang's death. He tried to convince the other hands to turn their trust from me."

"Scrappy showed you otherwise."

"I'm not sure what you mean."

"Did the hands know you were there, in the store? Did they know you'd overheard?"

She shook her head. "No, I was in the storeroom with the door closed."

"You think it's coincidental that Scrappy just now had a chafed area bothering him? He's not been in the saddle all afternoon. If he had a problem earlier, wouldn't he have told you about it at that time?"

He watched as Abbie turned her attention toward Scrappy, who clowned around in the saddle as always. "He sure doesn't look to be in pain."

"That was his way of showing his confidence in you."

Her face transformed with her smile. "But. . .chafing? He couldn't come up with something other than that?"

"Apparently not. But regardless, his trust is fully in you, and I can assure you Red and Grub feel the same way."

She looked up at him through lowered lashes. "And you?"

"My trust is with you, too." He chuckled. "If I ever have an issue with chafing, you'll be the first to know."

"I'm honored."

Her teasing grin told him otherwise, but he let the issue rest. "And about his other comment? We've already discussed that and put the topic to rest, haven't we?"

"To an extent."

He sighed. "To what extent?"

"I still prayed for them to leave me alone, and they died. How can you explain that?"

"Sin."

"Sin?"

"You run hard enough from God, and eventually sin will catch up with you. Bert and his gang were long overdue their day of reckoning."

"So you're saying it was coincidental?"

"Pretty much." He held the reins loosely in his left hand and watched her worry her skirt with hers. "God likes us to speak to Him through prayer, to petition Him, but He's not a magic genie ready to do our bidding."

"So when we pray, He won't always answer?"

"Oh, He'll answer. Just not always in the way we want."

"Bert's death wasn't what I wanted. I just wanted to get away from him."

"I know." He reached over and pushed a tendril of hair under her new bonnet. "And God knows."

"But if He doesn't answer our prayers specifically, why are we to petition Him? It's confusing."

Jake dug deep for words that would help her understand. He sent up a quick prayer for guidance.

"As a small child, did you ever petition your ma or pa for something?"

"Of course."

"Did they give in every time you asked?"

"No, of course they didn't."

"Why not?"

He watched as she contemplated his question. "Well, I'd always want more than my share of peppermint sticks when we'd go into town, and they'd say no because it wouldn't be in my best interest."

"Exactly. But you were allowed to ask."

"I suppose I was."

"That's how it is with God. We can pray and ask and petition, but He sees the bigger plan and knows when to say yes, when to say no, and when to say not now."

"But I asked Him to rid me of the gang, and He did say yes. So that goes back to my request causing their deaths."

"Not necessarily." Jake rubbed his forehead in frustration and gave the matter some more thought. "Did you pray and ask, 'Smite them down in my very path, Lord'?"

She gasped. "Of course not!"

"Then you didn't cause their death. You didn't ask God to take their lives. You only asked Him to get you out of that situation. The attack could have been coincidental, and it could have been God answering your prayer, but correct me if I'm wrong, you didn't personally ask God to kill them."

Peace flowed across Abbie's features. "No, I didn't ask Him to kill them."

"And also correct me if I'm wrong, but Scrappy seems fine with your doctoring skills, even to the point of possibly concocting a false ailment—an ailment most men would rather die from than ask a petticoat doctor for assistance with. No tough cowboy likes to admit his thighs are chafed from sitting in the saddle."

She laughed. "You're correct."

"The men all stick together. If Scrappy trusts you, they all trust you."

"All except Hank."

"Hank doesn't enter into it. He hasn't fit in since day one, and I wish I'd seen it before we left."

She nodded her acceptance. It was never easy to watch a person die. Surely as a doctor she'd seen her share of death. And in her case, as a physician, it had to be even harder to watch helplessly as everyone around you died a terrible death and you couldn't do a thing to save them. Even with that, he thought she'd truly let go of her responsibility in the other men's deaths. But even as he acknowledged the fact, a dark foreboding settled into his chest.

Chapter 12

After their Hank discussion, Jake stayed in control of the wagon and kept Abbie close to his side. She enjoyed his company, but his mood seemed to become more sober with every mile that passed. She counted her blessings that Hank kept his distance. She'd become accustomed to sleeping under the stars, and now that they had the wagon, she made a bed in the back and slept even better at night. And with her trunk in her possession, she had access to all of her personal items. Though she tucked her new dresses aside for her future home, she didn't have to wear the stuffy outfit she'd arrived in.

Abbie hadn't yet faced her emotions regarding her kidnapping at Bert's hand, the massacre, or anything else. She continued to keep her feelings carefully tucked away until she could examine them in private. The time would come—a time when the men didn't lurk everywhere nearby—when she could deal with all that the trip had brought her. She wanted to talk to Jake about Caleb, but the minute she did, she knew she'd fall apart. And she refused to fall apart in front of her new friends.

In the meantime, she determined to focus on the good in her life and to enjoy each new experience the journey brought her. In that way, everything would be perfect, if Jake would only open up to her again. The sun peeked over the horizon with the clear promise of a new day. Abbie closed her eyes and deeply inhaled the fresh air. The crisp blue sky went as far as her eyes could see, filled with fluffy white clouds.

"You seem to be in a good mood this morning."

She opened her eyes to see Jake surveying her with a grin.

"As opposed to. . . ?" She raised her eyebrows. "I try to keep my mood pleasant all the time."

He nodded. "I've noticed. And I appreciate it. The men seem to reflect your mood, and they've been much more relaxed in your company."

"All except for you." She hoped her bluntness wouldn't cause him to shut down on her again. "You've been more distant as the days have gone by. Ever since we left Nephi and I commented on Hank. I didn't mean any offense."

Jake squinted his eyes and tilted his head her way. "Why would I be offended by your comment? I asked you to share about what happened with him."

"I don't know. He works for you, and I felt that perhaps I spoke out of turn.

Why else would you grow so silent?"

"I can promise my moods have nothing to do with you."

"That's not what I meant." Her hand flew to her mouth. Did he find her too outspoken? The last thing she wanted was for him to think she felt responsible for his every mood. "I didn't mean to imply. . ."

He waved her away. "It's not you. I've had this feeling. I'm trying to stay focused."

A chill ran up her arm. "What kind of feeling?"

"Nothing I can back up. It's more of a foreboding, and I don't usually pay much thought to that type of thing. I've spent time in prayer and have tried to ignore it, and the oppression hasn't gone away. It's probably nothing, but just in case it is discernment and God's giving me an advance warning, I want to be prepared."

Abbie studied his profile. "You've felt this way for days? Why haven't you shared with me before now?"

"I didn't want to upset you. Especially if I'm wrong. You've been through enough."

"And what if you're right? Don't you think I deserve to know what we're up against?"

"That's just it; we don't know what we're up against. It's only a feeling."

"A feeling you don't often have."

He swallowed. "Yes."

"So we have to assume there's something to it." She stared into the thick trees that ringed the mountain beside them. Anyone could hide there and watch as they passed, and they'd be none the wiser. "I'm tougher than I look."

He nodded, and his mouth quirked into a grin. "I've noticed."

"Two of us can watch more carefully than one."

"That's true."

"Do the other men know?"

"Yes."

"So I'm the only one who wasn't told, which allowed me to babble on when you could have focused better without my constant chatter."

"I wouldn't say you 'babble on,' and I happen to enjoy your chatter."

He didn't look her way. Instead he looked pointedly in the other direction, but her heart did a little jig at his words. "You do?"

"Yep."

A rustle to their left had Jake's full attention. He didn't slow their pace, but Abbie could sense a subtle change as his wariness increased. "What is it?"

He didn't answer. He whistled a strange sound as if spurring on the horses. But he'd never used that whistle—at least that Abbie had ever heard. The horses picked up speed. She reached up and held her bonnet on her head with one hand while bracing against the bench with the other. She looked ahead and noticed Scrappy and Grub sat higher in their saddles. A casual glance backward showed Hank and Red also on alert. Boggs rode alongside them to her left. Abbie shifted in her seat and watched the trees but couldn't see a thing out of place.

She didn't dare speak. Her heart pounded with fear. Unknown fear that weakened her knees with all the unanswered questions. She'd lived through one attack. She knew what the aftermath looked like. She forced her thoughts—and the shaking—to stop. She'd just told Jake to let her in on his concerns, and she wouldn't fall apart and prove that he'd been right to keep her naively blasé to what was going on.

She studied his handsome profile. Though he remained silent, his face betrayed his concern. His lips pressed down into a firm, straight line. "If I tell you to move, I don't want you to question me. Get into the bed of the wagon as quickly as you can and take up the rifle that's behind this seat."

"Okay."

"You remember how to shoot?"

"Yes." He'd insisted she practice with each of his weapons. After the events of the past week, she didn't hesitate to agree. Though she'd been a good marksman as a child, she'd not handled a gun in years. Jake's instruction quickly brought back her technique.

"Good. If we come into gunfire, you have to shoot back."

"Oh." Shooting at trees was one thing. She hadn't thought about shooting at living targets.

He risked a glance at her. "What?"

"I hadn't thought that part through."

"What part?"

"Shooting at someone."

"You didn't think our target practice was so you could shoot a tree in case of attack?"

"I didn't really think about it all that much. I just enjoyed being near. . ." Flustered, she let her voice drift off. She'd almost admitted she let him train her because she enjoyed being near him. "I enjoyed the lessons."

"The lessons were intended as preparation in case of an attack."

"I'm a physician. I took an oath to save lives, not take them."

"I understand that. But there comes a time, possibly today, when you have a choice. You can take a life or lose your own."

"That sounds selfish. Why would my life be worth more than the person who might shoot at me?"

"Because you're a good person, and you're needed. If someone evil is intent on killing you, you need to defend yourself."

She hugged her arms around her waist. "I'm not sure I can."

"Then what if someone plans to hurt Scrappy? Or Red? Or Grub? Boggs— or even Hank?"

Or you?

The thought passed through her mind, and she knew in an instant she'd do whatever it took to protect any of the men—even Hank, but especially Jake— from any evil adversary that set his sights on her new friends.

"I'll do what I have to do."

"Thatta girl." He tightened his hold on the reins. "I'm going to slow for a moment. Get over the seat as fast as you can, but be careful. We can't afford to stop and scrape you off the ground."

She narrowed her eyes and glared. Though his expression didn't change, a hint of humor resided there.

"Go!" Jake slowed slightly and grabbed Abbie's arm, keeping her steady as she moved.

Holding tightly to the back of the seat, Abbie swung her leg over the back and ducked down to do as Jake had instructed. Her heart beat a staccato rhythm against her chest as she leaned against the rough planks and lifted the rifle into her arms. She suddenly hated the cold weapon. Only a little bit hesitant, she prayed she'd not need to use it. Hamm squealed with excitement that she'd joined him and snuggled against her legs. She welcomed his warm body against hers. Scrappy had taken a liking to the piglet and had insisted on caring for him until they retrieved the wagon. She'd missed her little pet.

She held her nerves at bay by talking to the runt. "Looks like Scrappy did a good job of keeping you alive and out of Grub's cooking pot."

Hamm squealed, and she quickly covered his snout, not wanting the men to get distracted by his grunts and squeaks.

Jake spurred the horses on, and Abbie dared a peek over the sidewall. She saw movement in the trees, but only a brief glimpse. She settled with her back against the bench and rested the rifle on her skirt.

She watched as Red lifted his weapon and took aim toward the trees and shot off a warning round. Abbie jumped and closed her eyes. Several yells rang out from the trees, and Abbie dared a quick look forward as more gunfire joined in with Red's. Both Scrappy and Grub shot toward the trees. Silence filled the air as the wagon bounced along the hard path.

"Stay low for a few more minutes."

"I'm not in any hurry."

She heard Jake's quiet chuckle. "Good."

Red pulled alongside the wagon on the left while Hank did the same on the right.

"I think we scared them off. That'll gain us some time."

"Thanks, Red." Jake didn't change his pace. "You okay back there, Doc?"

"I'm dandy; thanks for asking." Her backside wouldn't agree, but hopefully she'd be back in her seat beside Jake before long—if her legs would still cooperate after all the bouncing around.

Hank looked away, but she thought she saw the first hint of a genuine grin on his face as he turned. He didn't look half bad when he smiled.

After another thirty minutes with no further sightings, Jake pulled the horses to a stop. Boggs, Grub, and Scrappy circled around to join them as Jake spoke.

"I think we're clear for now, but I don't want to take any chances. It's obvious where we're headed."

"Could you tell who it was?" Scrappy kept a white-knuckled grip on his reins.

"I didn't get a clear view, but I'm guessing it was the same Indians who attacked Bert and his gang."

"Why would they be after us?"

Jake shook his head. "I wish I knew. With the majority of tribes on the reservations down south, I'd have to guess this band contains some of the disgruntled few who are holding out."

Abbie stood on shaky legs and got her footing. She stepped over the side of the wagon and placed her foot on the sideboard before allowing Jake to assist her back onto the seat beside him. "But why would they attack us? Why Bert and his men?"

"I guess because they're angry and we're all easy targets. Other than that, I don't know. Why did Bert and his men do the things they did? As the Bible says, we live in a fallen world."

"You look upset, Doc." Grub shouldered his way past Hank and surveyed her with worried eyes.

"Things like this don't exactly happen in Pennsylvania."

"Yeah." Jake also looked her way. "I guess they don't."

"So what's next?" Red still looked nervous, though he'd rested his rifle on his lap.

"We continue on and put some distance between us." Jake's expression didn't show his anxiety, but Abbie's trained eyes didn't miss the nervous jiggle as he held the reins. "But I don't want to move into an ambush."

"Could we take an alternate route?" Abbie searched the road ahead but couldn't tell anything about the terrain up ahead or the passes through the mountains.

"Not any that would be convenient. They'd all take us days out of our way."

The jiggle moved to his leg. "There's a pass we all used to use, but it's fallen apart and no one can get through anymore."

Abbie thought back to one of the articles she read coming out on the train. "I think I may have an idea."

Chapter 13

Jake, Grub, Red, Scrappy, Boggs, and Hank stared at her expectantly. She hesitated. What if the plan didn't work? She'd spoken without thinking, a tendency that often got her into trouble back East.

She felt a flush creep up her face. "I read an article on the train coming out. There was a group of settlers a few years back that came upon a seemingly impenetrable cliff. They ended up blasting their way through."

"Blasting their way?" Scrappy scratched his head. "You mean they blew it up?"

"They were at the top of the cliff. It was steep. They had to blast it down to different levels so they could lower their wagons down the side."

"Doc?"

"Yes, Hank?"

"I don't know if you noticed, but we don't exactly have any cliffs around here. We're actually at the bottom of the hills."

Abbie pinned Hank with her gaze. For a few moments there, she'd thought he was softening toward her. "I'm well aware of the fact that we don't have cliffs, Hank, but thanks for clarifying." She didn't know what she'd done to rub the man wrong, but she'd had enough of his snide remarks. As if speaking to a child, she enunciated her next words for Hank's benefit. "My point is, maybe we can find a pass, an older one that isn't often used, and as this gang chases us through, we could blow the opening behind us."

"Doc, that's a good idea." Abbie saw both admiration and amusement in Jake's eyes. "I think I know of a perfect spot not too far away."

Grub stared into the hills. "I think I know the place you're thinking of. Will the wagon make the trail?"

"It'll be tight, but I believe it will. I don't think we have another choice."

"Sure we do." Hank glared at Abbie. "We could always stay on the well-traveled path and hope whoever is behind us changes direction."

"And if they don't?" Jake's eyes targeted Hank. "What then? We sit and let them attack us like they did Bert and his gang? I'm sure you're aware we picked up a case of dynamite in Nephi to use at the ranch. One wayward shot and we'll be blown sky-high. I don't intend to sit around and let that happen."

Hank winced. "There's no guarantee they're still after us."

"You saw the aftermath—from *afar*. We laid the men to rest. We saw each and every wound."

Abbie watched with interest. Apparently his patience with Hank had run out about the same time as Abbie's.

"I saw all that I needed to see," Hank retorted.

"Boss, I don't want to see that again. I vote we go with Doc's idea." Scrappy pushed his scraggly hair from his face and nodded at Abbie.

"I second the idea." Grub glared at Hank.

Red didn't speak, but stepped closer to Abbie's side and squinted his eyes at Hank with an unspoken challenge. Boggs joined him.

"Looks like you're outvoted, Hank." Jake leaned down to pluck a long piece of grass and put it between his teeth as he surveyed the trail ahead of them. "We'll continue as we're going. The pass isn't far ahead. We won't reach it tonight, but can camp just below. First thing in the morning, we'll make our way up the mountain and put our plan into action."

This was the only part of the plan Abbie didn't like. "What if we're attacked as we sleep?"

"We'll keep watch. The location I have in mind has good visibility in all directions. There's no way the Indians got ahead of us, so we'll only have the lower area to watch. If we can't see them on this overcast night, they shouldn't be able to see us. There's a clearing they'll have to cross to get to us. We'll camp just on the other side of it."

Abbie felt the air whoosh out of her mouth. "That sounds fine." She couldn't stand a repeat of the other attack. Especially when she hadn't cared for the other men at all, and even with Hank's sour disposition, she cared about each of these men.

Jake raised the reins in preparation to move out.

Scrappy pulled his battered hat from his head and worried it with his hand. He sent Abbie an apologetic look before returning his gaze to Jake. "Um, boss? One thing."

"Sure, Scrap. What is it?" Jake stilled his hands.

Again Scrappy looked over at Abbie.

"Go ahead." Her forehead creased as she wondered what he didn't want to say in front of her.

"The canyon we're entering. Isn't it where the massacre happened?"

"That was a long time ago."

Jake's eyes also slid over to Abbie. He didn't elaborate.

She placed a hand on his forearm. "What happened? I need to know."

"I was only a boy. A small group of unarmed immigrants cut through the canyon, Salt Creek Canyon, and they were attacked by Indians. Only one man escaped and made it to Ephraim alive."

She swallowed. "Oh."

"They used a tomahawk on the lady of the group."

Why Scrappy felt led to share that little tidbit of information, Abbie didn't know. But she'd have been fine without it. His words brought back more memories of the attack on Bert's gang. Her breathing hitched, and Jake turned his eagle eyes her way. She quickly concealed her emotions.

"Then I'd best be extra cautious."

Jake nodded approvingly at her and urged the horses on, not allowing time for any of the others to comment. About an hour into the journey, they began to slowly make their way up the steep side of a mountain. Small groupings of trees hid their progress. Even Abbie's untrained eyes could tell the trail had seen better days.

"It's not used much, is it?"

"No, not any more. There's a quicker way to Mount Pleasant now."

She sat in silence and worried her lip.

"What is it?"

"I'm just wondering. . ." She looked over at him. "Maybe you should have listened to Hank and taken that more traveled route. Surely we would have seen others. And there's safety in numbers."

"The other path isn't exactly well-populated."

"The story you told. . .did they ever capture the Indians responsible?"

"I don't recall." His dark eyes stared into the trees beside them.

"Then maybe. . ."

"If you're thinking what I think you're thinking, you're wrong. Those Indians are long gone. This attack might have been modeled after the original. But whoever these men are, I think they're a renegade group."

"How can you be so sure?"

"It doesn't happen that way anymore. And my instincts tell me otherwise."

"Your instincts are never wrong?"

"Never." He glanced at her with a wry grin. Her heart sped up at his nearness. The setting sun glistened off his black hair, and she could see her reflection as his brown eyes looked into hers. He was extremely handsome. "At least, not yet."

She quirked an eyebrow in response, and he laughed. His levity broke her tongue-tied mood.

"Let's hope that instinct doesn't let us down now, hmm?"

❧

They reached their destination at dusk. A small stand of trees sheltered them, and with practiced ease, they set up the most basic of camps. After a dinner of cold biscuits and dried beef, everyone but Abbie settled onto the ground. She slept in the wagon, and Jake sat protectively upon the seat, his rifle posed on his lap.

"I won't sleep a wink with you so close." Her voice, while quiet, sounded loud to her own ears.

His soft laugh drifted her way. "Are you that intrigued by me then?"

She huffed. "I'm not intrigued at all. I'm simply not used to sleeping with a rifle pointed over my head."

A moonbeam drifted through the trees and shone down on him as he stared at her. "Not even a little bit intrigued?"

He sounded disappointed.

"Maybe a little." She smiled in the dark, glad he couldn't see her expression as well as she could see his.

A grin tipped up the corners of his mouth. "Good."

She waited, but no other comment was forthcoming. Though she had no intention of sleeping, the security of his presence relaxed her enough to do just that.

❧

The next morning they woke at dawn. Red and Jake went ahead to survey their trail. Abbie gathered their supplies while the men loaded the bedrolls onto their mounts.

"Wouldn't it be easier to put your things in the back of the wagon? Then you wouldn't have to secure them each time we break camp."

Boggs smiled. "A cowboy needs to be ready at all times. If we had our supplies in the wagon and something happened to separate us, we'd be up a creek."

"Oh, I hadn't thought of that." Another lesson learned for the city girl.

They were ready by the time their scouts came back.

Jake secured Steadfast to the front of the wagon and climbed up beside Abbie. They took the lead and the others fell in behind.

"How'd you sleep, Doc?"

"Just fine." She kept her gaze forward, embarrassed by their late-night conversation.

She could feel his stare.

"Did anyone ever tell you that you snore?"

She gasped and turned to face him. "I do not!"

Though his eyes were tired, a teasing smile lit up his face. "You most certainly do."

He looked very much like the dangerously handsome man she remembered from the train station. Though he tossed out playful banter, she saw that his wary eyes never ceased to search the area around them.

"You're trying to distract me with your teasing."

97

"What teasing? I'm merely stating a fact."

"I don't snore."

He raised an eyebrow her way. "You can hear yourself sleep?"

"I'd know."

"How?"

"My roommates would have told me."

"Would they now?" The eyebrow went higher.

He grinned, and she held back a sigh of contentment. How wonderful it would be to have such a good-natured man by her side for life. The thought caught her off guard. Never before had she given thought to a future with a husband. Her choice in becoming a doctor limited her prospects. Most men she'd met didn't like the idea much of a wife with more book knowledge then they had. Though she knew her education would most likely prohibit her chances of marriage, she hadn't realized until now just how severely her life would be affected. She'd never before met a man like Jake.

After she finished medical school, she'd suddenly realized how restricted her options were. Though she could continue with her work at the hospital, without her training schedule she'd suddenly felt adrift and very lonely. The offer from Caleb came just in time to give her direction. But what would she do now? She didn't belong on the ranch without her brother.

"Hey, Doc, why the sudden scowl?" Jake's words went from teasing to gentle.

She hadn't realized her thoughts were so clearly written on her face. Horrified, she felt the tears she'd held back form behind her eyes. She whipped her head around to face the empty landscape. The dry ground in this part of their journey matched the dryness in her heart.

"Doc?" Jake didn't slow their pace, but his soothing manner cajoled her to look his way. "You're crying! I didn't mean. . ."

She waved his words away. "It's nothing you did."

How could she explain? No way would she admit to him that she'd looked at him and saw a future that wouldn't be hers.

"As soon as I see to my brother's affairs, I'll head back to Pennsylvania. All this will have been for nothing."

"See to your brother's. . ." He stared at her, perplexed. "He didn't bring you all the way out here just to watch you leave again."

"Watch me leave?" Now she felt confused. "But Bert said he was. . ."

"Dead? No way." The smile returned. "Your brother is alive and well and anxiously awaiting your arrival."

A wave of emotion passed through Abbie. Laughter won out. "He's alive?" She stared at her companion in wonder. "All this time. . .I thought. . ." Again she laughed.

"I'm sorry, Doc. I had no idea."

"You never spoke of him."

"Neither did you."

"I couldn't. I knew I'd break down if I tried." She stared hard at him. "You mean it? He's all right?"

"He will be by the time we return. He did have a run-in with Bert. He had a hard time of it, but he pulled through. He's doing better, but wasn't up to the trip to meet you. I just assumed you knew."

"No. But I'm so glad to hear you say it now."

"Better late than never."

"Yes." She couldn't stop smiling. "I have a home."

Jake scowled. "Of course you do. Even if something had happened to Caleb, I'd have made sure you had a place to live."

"I wouldn't have expected you to."

"Caleb would have."

She wondered if Caleb was the only reason. Would he have done it of his own accord? She shook away the silly question. Without Caleb, he wouldn't have known about her.

After a few moments of silence, Jake spoke again. "All this time, since the station, you thought you had no home?"

"Yes."

"Yet you never brought it up."

"What good would it have done?"

"I could have put your mind at ease."

"I didn't know that at the time."

His forehead creased as he watched her.

"What?"

"You're not used to leaning on others, are you?"

She shrugged. "I've not had much experience with that."

"Why didn't you come to Caleb immediately? After you lost your parents?"

"I tried." Wistfully, she wondered how her life might have been different if she had. "I didn't know where he was. He left when I was fourteen." She contemplated the thought. "I was busy with my training, and it took me a long time to track him down. But I wouldn't trade the way things turned out. I enjoy doctoring."

"I can tell." He surveyed their surroundings and relaxed slightly in the seat. He propped a worn boot in front of him on the wagon's frame and rested his right wrist on his leg. "May I ask you something?"

Intrigued, she smiled. What could he possibly want to know? How her training had come about? How she'd fared in her classes? "Sure. Ask anything."

"Why didn't you ever marry? If you had, you'd surely have several children by now."

Anything but *that*!

"My question offended you."

She fanned her warm face. "No. But it certainly caught me off guard. I thought you'd meant to ask me about my work."

He laughed. "So family never entered into your thoughts?"

She shrugged. "Perhaps at some point, but then. . ." She let her voice drift off. What could she say? That no one ever cared enough to ask? More accurately, she chased off each suitor before they had a chance to ask. The right man hadn't come along. Only after accepting that his daughter faced a future as an old maid had her father reluctantly agreed to let her pursue her studies.

"Then. . .what?"

"It just never happened."

"Good."

Again she whipped her head in his direction. "Good?" Her heart picked up in tempo. Did he feel a connection with her, as she did him?

"You would have missed this whole adventure."

"Oh." Her voice faltered. So he didn't feel it. She cleared her throat and continued. "Of course. To miss the adventure. . .that would never do."

She forced a smile.

His countenance changed, and his lips parted. Lips that commanded her attention. He seemed to be on the verge of saying something important when Hank's sarcastic call broke into their conversation.

"Hey, boss. Maybe you ought to ride over here and take a gander at this view."

Hank and Red had moved ahead during their discussion and now waited at the top of a rise.

"We'll talk more later." Jake spurred the horses on, and they pulled up alongside the men. Boggs, Scrappy, and Grub joined them.

Abbie bit back a groan as she surveyed the scene. Barren cliffs blocked their path, and the small opening they needed to pass through was filled with huge boulders. If their pursuers were indeed on their tail, they'd be trapped.

Hank swung off his horse and dropped to his feet. "This is what we get for listening to your precious Doc."

"That's enough, Hank." Jake jumped down to join him. "We've all had enough of your complaints and whining, and I won't stand here and listen while you verbally attack Doc."

"He has a point." In this situation, Abbie had to agree with the caustic man. Guilt threatened to drown her. She couldn't bear to be responsible for the massacre of the men she'd grown to love. She cared about each and every one of them—even Hank with all his abrasive ways.

"We said we'd likely have to blast our way through before closing it back off.

What did you expect to see?" He paced a few steps nearer Hank. "But your attack on Doc won't help anything. I've had enough of that."

"And I've had enough of you mooning over the doctor while making poor decisions that affect the rest of us."

Before anyone could stop him, Jake reared his arm back and punched the man. Hank stumbled backward and landed on his backside. Red and Grub jumped forward to stop him as he bolted to his feet. He struggled, but they held tight.

"You'll be sorry you did that."

"Really?" Jake fisted his hands at his side and moved close to the man. "The way I hear it, you accused Abbie of saying those same words just before the attack on Bert and his gang."

"I don't know what you're talking about."

"Yeah. I think you do. I heard that's what you told the other hands back at the general store in Nephi."

Hank glared at the other hands. They each shrugged.

"It wasn't them, Hank. It was me." Abbie hopped down from the wagon and joined the men. "I was there." She forced the quiver of anger from her voice. "Every man at that camp died. I had nothing to do with their deaths."

Hank winced.

Boggs walked up beside her. "Abbie didn't do a thing to hurt any of them men in the gang. She even saved one man's life. I won't hear talk about her like this again."

Abbie redirected their attention to the matter at hand. "So we blast our way through the opening. The settlers I mentioned needed to work their way down the cliffs. We just need to go through."

The men followed her lead and moved forward as one.

"I think it will work, Doc." Jake climbed a few boulders, testing them for stability. They didn't budge. He climbed higher and peered over the top. "They're stacked on top of each other, but aren't very wide." He worked his way back down and jumped to the ground beside them. With hands on hips, he backed away and looked at the mound from several angles. He sent Abbie a grin. "It'll work."

The men moved into action. Boggs moved the horses a safe distance away as Jake led the wagon and Abbie over to Boggs' side. Scrappy pulled some burlap bags from a crate in the wagon's bed and cautiously carried them to the pile of rocks. Hank refused to help and surveyed the action from afar, his feathers still ruffled.

As they surveyed their handiwork, Abbie noticed the approach of someone from down below.

Chapter 14

The tuft of dust grew larger as their pursuers came closer. Abbie's heart pounded. From this vantage point, she could identify them as Bert's killers.

"Hurry! They're coming!" She yelled the words, but the men didn't pay her any attention. They were too focused on setting the charges in place. Jake's hair brushed against his collar, and he tucked it haphazardly behind his ear. He held a wick in his lips for a moment, his face a study of concentration, while he carefully worked with a stick of dynamite. He pulled the wick free and pressed it into the paper-wrapped stick. He set it aside and repeated the process.

Abbie glanced over her shoulder and saw that their pursuers were moving steadily closer. They weren't going to have time to blast the rocks out of the way and get through the opening before facing the impending attack.

Boggs prepared the animals and held them securely at his side. When the blast came, it would be up to him to keep them from bolting. Scrappy and Grub assisted Jake with the dynamite, placing it securely as directed. Red had cautiously climbed over the wall of rocks and disappeared from sight, presumably planting a few sticks on the far side. If all went well, the blast would completely clear their path. Abbie didn't want to think about what would happen if their path remained impassable.

Hank worked at the farthest edge, securing the explosive into a crack between the cliff wall and rocks. He'd have the hardest time getting back and through the opening safely. Abbie had been told to remain with the wagon, but she grabbed hold of her skirts and ran forward to snatch a stick of dynamite from the pile Jake had set behind him. She chose the one with the longest fuse.

She knew enough about the explosive to be cautious. She held it gently in the palm of her hand and reached for a match. Jake and the others were busy unwinding long lengths of wick so one fuse could be lit to blow the entire area.

Abbie might have been invisible for all the notice they gave her. With shaking hands, she struck the match. It lit and went out just as quickly. She hurried back over to get a few more. She laid them carefully beside her on the wagon's tailgate. Again she carefully struck one and this time shielded it from the slight breeze. The flame caught and grew tall. Stepping away from the wagon, she held it under the fuse, whispering a prayer for their safety and for success.

Sparks flew from the wick, and it disappeared far more quickly then she'd expected. She stepped backward, swung her arm back, and hauled her arm forward with all her might. Covering her eyes, she peeked through her fingers to watch as it hurled end over end and arced down the mountainside. Midair, just before it reached the other men, it blew. She watched as their horses reared, spewing the riders in all directions before hoofing it back down the trail. The men scrambled to their feet and took off in pursuit.

Only then did Abigail think to look over at the men she rode with. They all stood with mouths agape, their skin void of all color, staring at her in horror. Jake got his bearings first and stalked up to her.

"Wh–wh–," he sputtered, the word not fully releasing from his angry lips. "*What* do you think you're doing?"

She pointed downhill and saw his eyes register the scene below.

"That's them?" His brown eyes pierced hers. "Why didn't you say something?"

"I did! I yelled. I walked right behind you, and you were so focused on what you were doing that you didn't hear."

Jake didn't respond. He finished his assessment, hurried over to pick up the fuse, and continued to unroll it. "Let's go! We don't have much time before they catch their mounts and regroup."

Red had climbed to the top of the pile at the sound of the explosion, but now dropped back out of sight. Scrappy headed over to help Boggs with the animals while Grub took Abigail by the arm and led her back to the wagon. "Get down below the bed. After the percussion dies out and you're sure no rubble will come your way, head for the seat and be ready to go."

He handed Hamm to her, and she wrapped him securely so he wouldn't escape. He lay shivering in her arms from the first explosion as it was. She slid under the wagon as Grub had instructed and crooned quietly to the pig.

"Grub?"

He ducked his head and peered at her. "What?"

"What if the horses startle?"

He grinned. "They didn't a minute ago when you tried to blow apart the mountain."

She rolled her eyes. "I didn't try to blow the mountain. I only meant to detain them and buy you some time."

"Which you did."

"But the horses? This explosion will be much closer."

"I think they'll be fine. Watch carefully and roll fast if they startle." He saluted her and hurried off to join Jake. They discussed the plan and resumed their positions.

Abbie held her breath as Jake lit the fuse. He ran her way and dove down beside her. As the explosion rocked the hillside above them, he held her close and placed his upper body protectively over hers. She sneezed as the air filled with dust and smoke. He pulled her face against his shirt, which, since he'd rolled in the dust to get under the wagon, didn't help much.

But she relished the stability and closeness of his warm chest. She felt safer at that moment than she had in a long, long time. She clutched his shirt and took comfort in the rhythmic beat of his heart.

Unfortunately, the moment passed much too quickly.

"Let's go!" Jake rolled back out, secured Abbie in his firm grip, and dragged her along with him. She scrambled to her feet, and he assisted her—and Hamm—onto the wagon. Scrappy, Boggs, and Grub already moved through the newly opened pass. Red appeared safely on the other side, laying the last few sticks of dynamite in the hopes that they could reclose the opening before the other men arrived.

"Hurry, they're coming!" Abbie watched behind them as their pursuers resumed their trek up the hilly mountain. Their fast pace didn't bode well. She'd bought her group some time, but she'd raised their enemies' ire in the process.

Hank rounded the edge of the remaining boulders, assisting Red with the extra sticks. "Hank, c'mon!" Jake jumped onto the wagon and urged the horses through.

Abbie couldn't help herself. She scooted over to his side and clutched a piece of his sleeve in her hand. Jake didn't seem to mind. She felt his muscles bunch as he adjusted the reins and guided their mounts forward. After they were a safe distance from the explosives, he slowed and handed the reins down to Grub.

Hank's voice followed them. "Light the fuse. I'll be right behind you. I want to make sure everything is set."

Concerned, Abbie touched Jake's arm. "You can't light it until he's through."

"We can't afford to wait. He'll be fine." Jake slipped to the ground, leaving Grub to assist her.

"Jake, it's *dynamite*," she called. "You can't be sure. We can't take the chance."

"He'll be fine, Doc. We talked over the plan, and he'll be right behind us. Red scouted the area and told Hank exactly where to go as soon as he passes through. The repercussion shouldn't affect him at all."

Abbie had learned a lot during the past few weeks. And the main thing she learned was that she wanted Jake's—and Hattie's—strong confidence in their future. If this plan didn't work, one way or the other Abbie and the men would likely meet their Maker. She intended to meet Him as one of His chosen children.

God, the other times I've talked to You, the results haven't been exactly what I wanted. She hesitated, not wanting to hurt His feelings. *I mean, I appreciate all the help You've given me, but I didn't mean for Bert and his gang to be killed. I'm just learning the ropes of how prayer works, and, as I'm sure You know, how You work. I understand now that I didn't "pray" the others dead, but if possible, I'd like a nicer ending from now on.*

"Move it, move it, they're gaining on us!" Scrappy's panicked voiced interrupted her prayer.

She glanced up, willing Hank to rush through. He didn't appear.

I want to make things right with You. I need to make things right with You. Jake's been explaining how a relationship with You works, and I want that. I want to know You're guiding my choices and watching over me in all situations. And especially in this one.

"Abbie, get under the wagon, *now!*" Jake knelt beside the fuse and watched the opening for Hank.

Abbie bent down so she and Hamm could return to their safe haven.

I give You control of my life. I believe, Lord. I've watched Jake's quiet faith, and I want to experience that for myself. I hear Caleb has become one of Your followers, too. I want to see my brother again soon, but if I can't, I want to be sure I'll see him in heaven. Please watch over him for me in the meantime if something goes wrong in the next few moments.

"Hank, where are you?" Jake sat posed with one knee on the ground and with the wick and a match in hand. He'd be ready to run as soon as he lit the match. The fuse would sizzle its way to the explosives, and if all went well, they'd be safely on the far side of the cliffs from their enemies.

Hank's voice carried from between the cliffs. "I'm coming. Jake, light the fuse!"

Lord, get Hank safely through this. Please make him hurry. I want him to have a chance with You. I haven't been very nice to him. I don't want that on my conscience. If You'll give him another chance, so will I.

Though she still felt anxious about their present situation, she also felt a cloud of peace descend. No matter what, she'd be all right. At worst, she'd be in her Creator's presence. And at best, she'd have a chance to meet her brother and see what the future brought with Jake. Her hand nervously thrummed against the hard-packed dirt.

Even under the circumstances, Abbie felt her face crease into a smile. She'd done it. She'd turned her life over and was now a follower of Christ. No matter what happened, she'd be okay.

Jake lit the fuse. Abbie held her breath. Hank moved into sight, but stumbled as something from behind rocked his body, knocking him off his feet. A flow of blood ran down the front of his arm as he fell. It was obvious that Hank wouldn't make it through the pass before the explosion. Abbie scrambled out from under the wagon. Time slowed. She screamed as she rushed forward. This had been her idea. She wouldn't be responsible for another man's death and live to tell about it. It was one thing for her to meet her Maker on this day, but quite another for Hank to meet his. She wasn't sure he was ready. And she wasn't ready to see him die before she'd had a chance to share her newfound joy in her Savior. Hank had to live.

Abbie tripped and fell. Jake pulled out his pistol and shot at the wick. He missed. Hank pulled himself frantically along the ground. Jake shot again. This time the wick stopped glowing. Abbie gathered her skirts and headed his way. Jake tackled her and held her down.

"Stay back. It could still blow. I'll get him."

Abbie pushed to her knees and watched Jake move cautiously forward. Another gunshot rang out from the other side of the opening. A bullet whistled over her head.

"Doc, stay down!" Jake hit the ground. He continued to inch forward on his stomach, nearing the injured man. Boggs now stood beside her and covered the men with his rifle, shooting over Jake's head through the opening in the cliffs. She heard a scream of pain from the far side.

Jake had reached Hank's side. Just as Abbie breathed a sigh of relief, she heard a rumble from overhead. The percussion of gunshots along with the earlier blast created an avalanche that effectively blocked the pass but now tumbled down onto Hank's helpless form. Jake was trapped beside him.

Chapter 15

Jake!" Abigail tried to rush forward, but Boggs held her back.

Scrappy and Grub hurried over to Jake while Red dropped down on his knees beside Hank.

"Jake." A sob tore at her throat. She had to help him. She tried to shake out of Boggs' grip.

Hank lay motionless nearby, held captive by the pile of rock.

"I need to get to them."

"Now, Doc, you need to settle down. We'll stay over here where it's safe. It won't do us any good for you to get injured. Grub and Scrappy will bring them to you."

He had a point. They hurried to the wagon, and she jumped up onto the wagon's bed where she'd stashed her black bag. Boggs tugged her trunk out of the way and lowered it to the ground. Hamm squealed at all the noise.

"I'm off to help Red." Boggs hurried away.

When she had her supplies ready, she glanced up to check on the men's progress. Jake, supported by Scrappy, walked her way. He was alive and well. She closed her eyes with relief and thanked God for his safety. Grub joined Red and Boggs, and all three worked to dig Hank out. She saw Hank's foot move. He, too, had survived. She prayed his injuries were as minor as Jake's appeared to be. She couldn't do anything with Hank until they freed him, so she turned her attention to Jake.

"You scared me." She skewered the man with a glare.

He grinned. "I sort of scared myself there for a few minutes."

"Well get on up here and let me look you over."

"I'm fine, Doc. I need to go help with Hank."

She narrowed her eyes at Scrappy. "Don't let him move an inch until I've given my approval."

"Yes'm." His eyes widened, and he shifted nervously back and forth on his feet. "Um, boss. . ."

Jake sighed. "It's fine, Scrap. You head on over and help the others while Doc fusses over me."

Scrappy didn't wait to be told twice.

"I'm not fussing."

Jake hopped up to sit on the tailgate of the wagon. "What do you call it then?"

"An examination."

Dirt smudged across his forehead, and his face had several small scrapes and bruises. His shirt was torn, but otherwise he looked intact.

"How do you feel?"

"Like I came out on the bad side of a wall of rocks."

She poured astringent on a clean cloth and began to clean his wounds.

"Ouch!" He tried to pull away, and she gently tugged him back.

"Do you hurt anywhere?"

He snorted. "I hurt everywhere."

She tossed the cloth aside and placed her hands on her hips. "You're not going to make this easy. Do you want me to do a full examination?"

His gaze became wary. "What's that supposed to mean?"

"A full examination." She enunciated each word carefully. "I'll check every part of your body. Twice if need be."

"Whoa." He jumped to his feet and waved a hand in the air. The effect would have been more successful if he hadn't wobbled and grabbed the wagon for balance. "I'm fine, Doc. Nothing's broken. I have no gaping wounds for you to sew up. Sorry to disappoint."

"I hardly *want* you to be hurt." She grasped his chin and looked into his eyes and felt a jolt travel up her arm. She tried to ignore it. He was her patient after all. "Look into my eyes."

"My pleasure." His mouth formed into a foolish grin as he squinted his dark eyes and peered into hers. "How do I look?"

Breathtakingly handsome. But she wasn't about to tell him that. His pupils looked fine. She covered his eyes with her hand and was glad he couldn't see the tremble he brought on.

He leaned close, his face only inches from hers.

Her breath hitched. "Will you let me concentrate?"

"I thought I was."

Though he seemed okay, his unusually flirtatious actions made her think he'd suffered a small concussion in the fall.

She quickly moved her hand and watched his pupils tighten to small pinpoints in response to the light. He squinted, still way too close. As she studied his eyes, his pupils dilated, and she saw hunger replace the humor.

"I think a kiss would make me feel better."

His eyes began to close.

Abbie panicked. She'd never kissed a patient and wouldn't start now, but all reason seemed to escape her. She *wanted* to kiss him.

"You're concussed."

He paused and stared at her. "I'm what?"

"You hit your head and have a concussion."

"That's what your exam tells you?" He reached up and twisted a strand of her hair around his finger.

"It's what your actions tell me." She busied her hands with reorganizing her instruments. If she didn't look at him, maybe he wouldn't have such a hold on her.

"Hey, Doc."

"Yes, Mr. Maverick?"

His deep laugh told her the formal title didn't throw him off.

"I'm not 'concussed.'"

His words stayed her hands. She didn't dare look at him. She waited until she heard him walk away before she turned around. The ranch hands had almost cleared the debris from Hank's inert form, and Jake hurried to help them without a backward glance.

Jake had flirted with her, she was sure, and she didn't know what to make of it. She'd had official suitors back East, but they were painfully formal and nothing ever came of their attentions. With Jake things were different. He made her heart beat faster, her breath hitch, and her knees feel weak, almost as if she had an affliction. She smiled a secret smile. If she had to suffer an affliction, this is the one she'd choose to have.

"Doc, we're coming your way!"

She shook off the silly notions and focused on her newest patient. The men carried the unconscious man over and positioned him in the wagon. She settled beside him and began her exam. "I'm afraid he's suffered a few broken ribs. I'll need some strips of cloth to secure them. He also has some pretty nasty gashes. He'll need stitches. Grub? Could you boil some water for me?"

Grub hurried away to do as she asked.

The other men hovered nearby.

She gently cut away Hank's shirt.

Jake squatted opposite her on the wagon bed. "What can I do to help?"

He sounded suspiciously normal all of a sudden. She raised an eyebrow at him. He shrugged.

"Find something for them to do. I don't need an audience, and I doubt Hank will appreciate waking to see them all gathered around staring at him."

"Scrappy, see what you can do to help Grub. Red, keep an eye on the passage. It closed back up and looks unstable, so stay off the rocks. But just to be on the safe side, make sure we don't have any surprise visitors. And, Boggs. . ."

"I'll take care of the animals."

"Thanks."

The men scattered, and Jake resumed his place at Hank's far side. "Now tell me what I can do to help you."

The thought of him so close sent her nerves into a dither, but she knew she needed his assistance. She set him to work cleaning the surface wounds while she cleaned the deeper wounds and stitched them up.

"Hank." She checked his eyes and saw no response.

Jake leaned an elbow on his knee, his face full of concern. "What do you think?"

"His pulse is weak, but steady. His worst injury seems to be the ribs, but I don't think they punctured a lung. His breathing is strong." She frowned. "But I have no idea why he hasn't regained consciousness."

"Could he have suffered a head injury?"

"Definitely." Diagnosing in these conditions, where so many things were unknown, was her least favorite part of her job. "But I see no signs of a blow to his head. You suffered a bigger bump than him."

"What else could cause the unconsciousness?"

"He could have internal injuries. I have no way to care for him out here if that's the case. I can't very well do surgery."

Jake pulled his hat from his head, his expression troubled. "Wouldn't there be signs?"

"Yes. In most cases. And I don't see any at this point. I'll keep watch, but so far there's no bruising on his abdomen or back and nothing on his chest to show anything like that. That's encouraging. But only time will tell. I have him as stable as possible for now."

"Then continue to stabilize him as well as you can, and we'll head out immediately. We can reach the ranch in two more days, one if the conditions remain steady."

By conditions she assumed he meant they didn't run into Bert's killers.

The men packed up, and Boggs helped Jake lift her trunk back in beside Hank's still form.

"I'll ride back here with him." Abbie settled her skirts around her. Hamm pressed close against her side.

❧

Jake spurred the horses on, wishing they had a smoother path. The jolting wouldn't make Hank's trip any better. As they traveled, he had a lot of time to think. More time than he wanted. He wished Abbie were sitting beside him instead of back with Hank, but he knew the other man needed her more.

He hadn't missed the fact that Abbie's soft hands gently skimmed over Hank's body during her examination. The unconscious man didn't know what he was missing. She hadn't examined Jake that thoroughly. He felt a tinge of jealousy and grimaced. In all fairness, she'd threatened to do just that, and he'd waved her away. Maybe he should have taken her up on it.

And what kind of man felt jealousy over such a thing? Abbie was only doing her job. Maybe he had a touch of a concussion after all. Why else would he be dwelling on the good doctor and her bedside manner?

He needed to focus on something else. Their homecoming. He always loved coming home to the ranch, and this trip was no exception. More than ever he craved the stability and consistency of their ranch. Home. His home. Caleb's home. And now Abbie's home. He pictured her in the ranch house, cooking meals and cleaning, and the domestic image put marriage on his mind. He shook it off.

Would she cook and clean? After all, she was a medical doctor. He frowned. His thoughts had returned to the beautiful doctor sitting in the wagon behind him.

"Jake! Slow down."

Jake reined in the horses and motioned for the others to stop. He jumped down and hurried to her side. "What is it?"

"Hank. I think he's coming around."

She caressed the man's cheek, and Jake fought off his urge to scowl. The man had been nothing but trouble the entire trip, and now he lay on Abbie's lap while she caressed his cheek. Life could be so unfair.

Jake rested his arms on the wagon's side and waited. The other men paced around behind him.

A low moan escaped Hank, and Abbie's face lit up with a smile.

"Hank." Again she caressed his cheek. "Can you open your eyes?"

His eyes fluttered open and closed.

"That's it," she crooned.

She'd never crooned over Jake's injuries. With him she acted more like a ruthless taskmaster. He allowed himself to scowl this time. The action made him feel better. "Hank! Doc said to open your eyes."

Jake hadn't meant for his command to come out quite so loud or harsh, but at least Hank opened his eyes.

"There you go." He gently pulled Abbie's hand from Hank's face. "You can stop touching him now."

She smirked. "Jake, are you feeling all right?"

"I'm feeling fine. But the man doesn't need you mollycoddling him after all he's been through."

"I'm not mollycoddling him. I'm using a caring bedside manner."

Jake didn't even want to think of her at Hank's bedside. Ever. Especially looking like she did right now. Her hair blew freely in the wind, the long blond strands pulled loose from the day's events. Her delicate hands lay primly in her lap, and her features crinkled into a look of amusement at his expense.

"No doctor I know would caress a man's cheek to wake him up," he growled.

"Well, I suppose not since all the doctors you know are likely male."

"That's just my point. You aren't male, so you don't need to be doing—," he fluttered his hand, "that."

"I'd do the same for any of my patients, Jake, including you."

The thought had his face warming.

"If you all don't mind my interrupting, could someone please explain what's going on?"

Hank's words interrupted their verbal sparring.

"Of course!" Abbie turned her full attention on her patient, promptly dismissing Jake.

Jake renewed his vow to fire the man the moment he was healed. He half listened as Abbie filled in Hank on the avalanche and his injuries. As she talked, she examined the man.

Hank muttered something Jake couldn't quite make out.

Abbie's chatter quieted. "What did you just say?"

Hank tried to sit, but she stilled him with her hand. A hand Jake suddenly wanted to claim as his own—in marriage.

"Bert. He's my brother."

Jake's thoughts suddenly diverted from Abbie to Hank. He clenched his teeth and gathered his thoughts before he spoke. "Bert, the man who kidnapped Doc, is your brother." He didn't question; he stated the fact.

"Yes."

"You were in cahoots with him all along."

"Yes."

"Is that why you hired on?"

He nodded, grimacing in pain.

"And the reason you were 'sick' and slowed us down?"

"Yes."

Jake wanted to punch him. "If you hadn't slowed us down, Abbie never would have been kidnapped. And Bert. . ." He stopped, realizing what his next words would have meant to Hank.

"Go ahead, boss, say it. Bert wouldn't have been killed."

So Hank had been living his own personal hell. Jake had been there plenty of times himself. He sighed. "It wasn't your fault."

"Yeah. Thanks. That doesn't bring my brother back, though, does it?"

So now Jake knew where Hank's bitterness came from. Self-hate was a harsh emotion.

"I blamed you, Doc. I figured if you hadn't—I don't know—existed, I guess, things wouldn't have turned out as they did."

"Why are you telling us this now?"

"I almost died back there." He shifted and gasped in pain. "I thought I saw God. Then I felt unbearable pain. It was so bad, I thought God had sent me away. To. . .the other place. Then I realized He'd just left me here on earth." He looked up at Abbie. "Then I felt your hand on my cheek and heard your soft voice and thought maybe I'd gone to heaven after all."

Jake loomed over the man, his stance meant to intimidate.

Hank laughed harshly as he looked at Jake. "Yeah. And then I saw you and knew I surely wasn't in heaven."

"Very funny."

Abbie snickered.

"I figure if God spared me from what I deserved, a brutal death like my brother experienced—though the way my ribs feel, I'm not sure I was spared anything in this case—God must have other plans for me."

"I bet He does, Hank," Abbie soothed.

So when had she become such a theologian? Jake echoed her words sarcastically in his mind before feeling chastised. Hadn't he wanted Abbie to grow closer to God?

As if reading his mind, she looked over at him, and her soft lips curved into a serene smile. "I made my peace with God, Jake. I prayed about my salvation and turned my life over to Him."

"You did?"

"I did."

Jake couldn't stop grinning. "I'm glad to hear that."

"I thought you might be." She glanced back at Hank. "I prayed for you, too."

"That so?" Hank narrowed his eyes. "I think it's probably a good thing. I'd like to hear more later."

"We can sort this all out when we get to the ranch." They'd lost enough time for now. They wouldn't make it in by nightfall, but if they got back on the trail, they'd reach the ranch by midmorning. "Doc, is he stable enough to travel?"

"Hank? What do you think?"

"I want to get home. That is, if I still have a place there."

"Of course you have a place. Right, Jake?"

Abbie looked at him, her green eyes captivating, and he couldn't refuse her. He was in trouble. He already dreaded telling Caleb all that had happened while Abbie was under his care. What would Caleb think when Jake admitted that in the process of botching up the entire trip, he'd fallen in love with Caleb's baby sister?

Chapter 16

"The ranch lies just beyond that ridge up ahead."

Abbie's heart beat in anticipation. "I can't wait to see it. To see Caleb."

"Scrap?" Jake called. "Ride ahead and tell Caleb of our arrival."

Scrappy, looking relieved to be free of the stressful journey, spurred his horse and hurried out of sight.

The midmorning sun rose high as they traveled the last few miles. Hank had pulled through and lay snoring in the wagon's bed. He hadn't talked much since the previous afternoon when he'd cleared his conscience, but the few times he did speak, his manner was kind and relaxed.

Jake slowed the horses and looked at her. "About the ranch, Doc. I've not been totally up front about—"

"Well, it's about time." Caleb's rich voice interrupted whatever Jake was about to say. His teasing words met them as they cleared a rise that overlooked the ranch. "I send you off on a six-day trip, and two weeks later you mosey back—that's just great!"

"Caleb!" Abbie slid down from the wagon before it had completely stopped and threw herself into her big brother's embrace. "I thought you were dead."

"Dead?" He looked over her head toward Jake. "What made you think I was dead?"

Scrappy hovered in the background.

"Bert Sanchez told me as much. Let me look at you." She held him at arm's length and stared. His features were stronger. He'd filled out. His blond hair had darkened, but the long, sun-bleached strands gave him a rugged look that hadn't been there when he'd left the city. "Where's the prissy city boy who walked out of my life all those years ago?"

A grin transformed his face as he wrapped his arm around her neck and bumped his forehead up against hers. He stared into her eyes. "Now, little sister, let's get one thing straight. I ain't never been a city boy, and I never will be. That's the whole reason I came out here when I did. The city was smothering me. But here? A man can breathe with all this open space."

"I'm beginning to see what you mean." Abbie exchanged a look with Jake. "Now that I have the train robbery, the kidnapping, the massacre, and the explosion behind me, I'm starting to see the better side of living out here. The city. . .it was boring in comparison. Noisy, dirty, crowded, and did I mention. . .boring?"

Caleb stared hard at her for a moment then threw his head back with a wild laugh. "That's my Abigail. You might be a fancy doctor these days, but I'm glad to see you haven't lost your imagination and spunk." He looked at Jake who still rested on the seat of the wagon. He watched their exchange with an air of amusement. "Growing up she was a tomboy to beat all tomboys. She gave our parents fits. She gave most of the neighborhood bullies fits."

"Caleb, some things are better left in the past."

"Well, at least now you're making restitution by patching people up instead of sending them to the doctor in a coma."

Abbie sucked in her breath. "That only happened once."

Jake choked on his laugh. Abbie glared. Caleb smirked.

"But was it ever an event when it did happen."

"Tell me about it." Jake leaned forward, much too eager to hear the story at her expense.

"I don't think this walk in the past is necessary. We need to get Hank settled in." Abbie folded her arms across her chest and tapped her foot with exasperation.

"I'm fine. I want to hear the story." Hank, now fully awake, lounged against the wagon's sidewall.

Caleb used a walking stick to move closer to the other two men, completely dismissing Abbie's request.

"It was the year I left." Now he turned her way. "What were you, eleven? Twelve?"

"Almost fifteen."

"Fourteen then." He returned his attention to his rapt audience. Now Red, Grub, and Boggs had joined the cluster.

She glared at them. "I treated every one of you and will treat you again in the future. You really want to think about your actions."

Abbie's threat went unheeded, and a couple of the men actually shushed her.

"Though a tomboy at heart, she'd clean up right pretty when our folks forced her to attend town events." He winked her way. She flushed and rolled her eyes. "The suitors would come out of the woodwork."

"Suitors? They were mere boys."

"I think fending them off is what sent our pa to an early grave."

"It was not! He died of a weak heart, and you know it."

"What *weakened* his heart, hmm?"

"Nothing I did."

"Anyway. . .she'd ride up all haughty and pretty and the men—boys—would absolutely flock. Most of them would scatter by a well-directed look from my father or myself." He laughed. "But there was one in particular who continued to give Abbie a hard time. He'd stay at a respectful distance if one of us were around, but one day I had to run back inside the church after a town meeting to find my hat—"

Abbie interrupted. "Ha. You snuck around behind the church to steal one more kiss from Penelope Myers."

"While I was gone, Petey Piker snuck up to the wagon and tried to do some stealin' himself."

"He was a despicable boy."

"I'll agree with you there. If you hadn't put him into a coma, I surely would have."

"So Doc really let him have it, huh?" Scrappy sat so far forward on his saddle he looked like he'd topple over the front at any moment.

"Scrappy, if you break your neck at my expense, I won't doctor you up."

He scooted back a few inches, and Abbie released her breath. She still held her arms protectively crossed at her chest, though, as if that would protect her from her brother's story. How charming that he'd jumped right back into his annoying brotherly ways. She fumed and huffed, willing him to hurry up.

Jake stared at her, much too pleased with the present events.

"Oh she let him have it all right. As rumor has it, he climbed up beside her and tried to steal that infamous first kiss all the males were vying for."

"And she was only fourteen?" Jake sounded impressed and sent her a look that said just that.

"Fourteen but looking like she was sixteen."

"Wow, Doc, I guess you've always been pretty." Scrappy's awe was palpable. "So what'd you do, punch him?"

"Nah, she's too much of a lady. You wouldn't punch anyone, would ya, Doc?" Grub held his horse by the reins and munched a piece of jerky.

Abbie opened her mouth to answer, but Red interrupted. "I bet she whipped out a pistol and shot 'im right then."

"I did no such thing!"

Jake seemed way too amused by all the comments. She'd ask him the reason later.

"Nah." Caleb had their full attention and dragged the moment out. "She did carry a pistol half the time, though our parents would have died on the spot had they known. She wore it strapped around her thigh. She could outshoot the best of us *city boys*. And she had been known to punch a few boys back in her younger days."

"I think I'll head on down to the ranch by foot. It didn't seem to wind Caleb too much. He seems to have plenty of gumption for talking after his long stroll."

They were so attuned to Caleb's words that no one even noticed she'd spoken.

"C'mon, Caleb. Tell us. What'd she do next?" Boggs spoke to Caleb as if he'd known him all his life.

"Well, he climbed up on the wagon bed, taking her by surprise. When he leaned in for the kiss. . ."

Abigail remembered that horrible moment and shivered with disgust.

"She screeched for the horses to pull out."

"Wow, did she throw him off?" Red sent her a look of raw appreciation.

"Not at that moment. He clung for dear life, having been caught off guard. He would have been fine if she hadn't suddenly jerked back the reins." This time his expression held a touch of pride as he stared at her, his baby sister. "Poor Petey didn't expect it and went flying headfirst over the front."

"And then she ran him down?" Scrappy almost drooled with anticipation.

"Not according to Abbie. Right, sis?" He looked back at the men. "According to the story she told, the horses spooked and ran him down of their own accord."

"So you really ran over a helpless man. Doc, I'm stunned."

Jake didn't look stunned. The teasing glint remained in his eyes. He also looked intrigued and. . .charmed? Regardless, she had no intention of letting them all continue to tell stories at her expense.

She turned and stalked off toward the buildings of the ranch. She heard the group disperse. The men each tipped their hat as they passed. The wagon rolled by at a fast pace, and she looked up in disappointment. Caleb held the reins.

"Doc."

Jake's quiet voice called to her from behind. Slowly, she turned.

He stood in the same spot where Caleb had been while regaling them with stories.

"C'mere."

They met under the cooling shade of a juniper tree.

"You let Caleb take the wagon."

"Yep."

"Now we really have to walk."

"Looked like you were doing just that anyway."

"So why'd you stay behind? Surely you're eager to get home? If you'd stayed on the wagon, you'd have been there by now."

"I thought about asking you to hop back on, but in your present mood, I was afraid you'd turn me down in front of my men." He chuckled. "And I didn't want to take a chance you'd reject me and try to run me down."

He moved closer. His brown eyes crinkled at the corners where laugh lines betrayed his attempt to be serious. His dark hair blew freely in the breeze, and she wanted to tame it. The strands reflected the wild heart of the man who wore them, a heart she longed to capture.

Her breathing hitched. "Why would I want to run you down?"

They were mere inches away now.

"Because," he whispered. "You knew I'd do this. . . ."

He leaned forward and dusted his lips across hers. She closed her eyes and smiled. He kissed her again. This time his lips lingered, and the kiss intensified. Her entire body went weak, and she was grateful that his strong arms surrounded her, keeping her firmly on her feet.

"I've wanted to do that for a long time." He leaned his forehead against hers, the effect completely different from Caleb's brotherly move. Jake's mouth remained an inch away from hers. She could feel his breath mix with hers.

"I wouldn't have run you down."

He leaned back so he could see her eyes, keeping her tucked securely in the circle of his arms. "What was that? I'm afraid I didn't hear you."

She could tell by his twinkling eyes that he had.

"I said I wouldn't have run you down." She couldn't look him in the eye. "I saved that kiss, from all those years ago, just for you."

This time his eyes registered surprise. "All those suitors and all this time. . . and you saved your kiss for me?"

"I did. I didn't care for any of those suitors. I care about you."

"Oh." For the first time he seemed to be without words.

"Petey almost ruined it for you."

"I should hunt him down and punch him."

"Nah." She laughed. "He met his match in his wife. There's nothing you could do to make him any more miserable."

"Then justice has been served. Twice. After you put him in a coma—"

"My *horses* put him in a coma."

"I'd have thought he'd pick a mild-mannered woman to marry and live out his years."

"That was always Petey's problem. He never did learn from his mistakes."

His mirth abated, and he studied her, his eyes warm. She shivered at his intensity. "I know we've not known each other long. . . ."

"I feel like we've known each other a lifetime."

"We've been through a lot the past two weeks."

"And I'd love to go through a lot more, as long as you're by my side."

"I need to speak to your brother. Though we're partners in the ranch—"

She interrupted. "Partners?"

"Yeah, partners. I tried to tell you that just before we ran into Caleb."

"I thought you were the foreman." She grinned.

"Does it matter?"

"Nope."

"So you don't mind if I talk things over with my partner?"

"What things?"

She knew from his expression he aimed to give her a hard time. "Things like which, if any, of the cattle took ill while I was gone. Did our supplies come through? How is the newest litter of kittens in the barn? That type of thing."

"Oh, that's all?" She punched him softly in the arm and turned to walk from beneath the branches of the tree.

He grabbed her by the arm. "Other than one other little detail." He pulled her back into the circle of his arms.

"And what would that be?" She held her breath.

"How would he feel about my getting hitched with his pretty little sister?"

"Oh."

"Just 'oh'?"

"What if he says no?"

"He's not going to say no."

"How can you be so sure?"

"I can be very convincing."

"I can imagine."

He knelt down on one knee, and a tear coursed down Abbie's cheek. He reached up to wipe it away. "Aw, Doc, don't cry."

"I can't help it. These are happy tears."

"Think you can hold back the happy tears until I've actually proposed the question?"

"I'll try." Now her tears coursed freely down her face.

A rumble of laughter sounded from his chest. "I'm in trouble."

"The best trouble of your life." She dropped to her knees to stare into his eyes.

"You've got that right." He cleared his throat, his own eyes misting suspiciously. He searched her eyes. "Doc?"

"Yes?"

"Will you do me the honor of becoming my wife?"

"I will."

They kissed to seal the agreement under the juniper tree.

≈

Caleb hadn't seemed too surprised at Jake's marriage request. His only requirement was that they have the ceremony soon so he could be released from the burden of watching out for his wayward younger sister. Jake and Abbie were all too willing to appease him.

A few short weeks later, they stood beneath the very tree where he'd proposed and now said their vows. When they were done, he pulled her into a deep kiss and spun her around to face their witnesses. He held her close against his chest. Along with the preacher, his motley band of misfits comprised their entire wedding party—and guest list—but Abbie didn't care. Between them, her brother, and Jake, she had everyone dear to her in attendance. They gave their well wishes and slowly drifted off, leaving her alone with her groom.

"So, wife. What do you think?"

She remained where she was, leaning back against his chest. "What do I think about what?"

"All of it. The journey. The ranch. Me."

"I wouldn't trade the journey for anything. It led me to you."

He rested his chin on her head. "Hmm. Good point."

"The ranch—" She surveyed the buildings and pastures below them. She saw the men going about their chores. They were her family now. She no longer felt so alone. "Is simply breathtaking. I can't believe I get to live and work here forever."

"And me?"

She turned in his arms. "There are no words with enough depth and meaning to describe my feelings and love for you. If there are, I certainly haven't learned them."

"Really?" He glanced down at her. "With all the book learning you've put in?"

Grinning, she nodded. "Really. Hard to believe, but true." Happy that he embraced her status as physician instead of resenting her schooling, she laid her head against his chest and listened to the beating of his heart.

"Well, I suppose you could try to *show* me in actions what your words can't seem to say."

"I'll keep working on the words." She met his kiss with her own. "And as for the actions, that's exactly what I plan to do, every day, in every way I can, for the rest of our life together. I love you, Jake Maverick."

"And I love you, Abbie Maverick. And by the way. . ."

"Yes?"

"Those words you just stated said everything I need to hear. You don't have to study any further."

"I guess sometimes the simplest words say all that we need to hear."

"Yep." He took her hand, and they headed down the hill, ready to start their new journey.

Carousel Dreams

Dedication

To Doug and Lyn W., my inspiration for the characters in this book.
We love you!

Chapter 1

Great Salt Lake, Utah Territory, 1895

Grandmother. . .these books can't possibly be correct. If they are. . ." The melodic feminine voice drifted off momentarily then resumed, stronger. "Did Papa keep another set of books somewhere? Maybe that would explain things."

The raised voices carried through the open window. Bascom's steps slowed on the walkway as he neared his destination—the large front porch of the resort. He'd just arrived in town and couldn't wait to see the owner's face when he presented the plan for his newest, hand-carved carousel. Of course, true to his reputation, he'd saved the most special pieces to carve once he arrived at the site. He never added his signature touches until he knew the personality of the owner.

"No, Ellie, he only kept one set of records."

This voice, decidedly older, contained more control, didn't sound as panicky. Bascom had to lean forward to hear. It wasn't that he wanted to eavesdrop, but he didn't feel comfortable intruding on someone during a personal discussion, either. He glanced around, weighing his options. There weren't any other buildings nearby, and his entire caravan of wagons that had followed him now waited to be unloaded. Bascom only needed to ask where to direct the drivers. He motioned for the nearest wagon master to wait a moment.

"Gram, what was Papa thinking? This can't be right. According to these numbers, Papa spent most of his fortune just before he died. How can that be?"

"Child, you can't question your grandfather's motives when he isn't here. It's not proper." The older voice didn't contain any of the worry the younger one portrayed. "Your grandfather had his reasons for everything he did."

"And his reason for this, do you know what it was?" Now the speaker spoke with venom. "It says here he purchased something. The paper is smudged, and I can't make out what it is."

A sigh carried through the air. "He purchased a carousel, Ellie. He wanted to surprise you."

Bascom heard the sound of papers shuffling.

"A carousel? For this outlandish amount? Why would Papa do this?"

Despair crept into her words.

Bascom felt a pang of sympathy. He also felt a tug of panic. His works were usually embraced with enthusiasm. Never before had he approached a buyer who held such resentment. Yet his men waited to complete the delivery so they could be on their way to well-deserved breaks while he made the finishing touches and put the large structure together.

His apprentice, Sheldon Lavery, hopped down from the wagon and approached him. As usual, the man looked remarkably well-groomed with every dark hair in place, even after the long trip. "What seems to be the problem, boss?"

Bascom nodded toward the open window as the women resumed their discussion and put a finger to his lips to silence Sheldon.

"I suppose he thought the purchase would help us out."

"What would help me out would be to have that money in hand to help run this place." Footfalls sounded as the speaker paced. "I mean, really. His entire life's savings? How are we going to keep the resort afloat?"

Now guilt joined Bascom's sympathy and panic.

He heard Sheldon's snicker beside him. "This is grand. We arrive with their carousel only to find out they don't want it."

Bascom silenced him with a glare. He didn't see any humor in the situation at all. His one-of-a-kind masterpiece had become his client's worst nightmare.

"Competition's fierce of late, Ellie. You of all people know that. Your grandfather knew we had to have an edge to keep the resort filled with guests. Amusements such as the carousel are the newest way to ensure such a thing."

Bascom could see silhouettes of the women through the window, though he couldn't clearly see their features. While the younger woman paced, the older one sat in her chair, some sort of needlework in her hands.

Sheldon leaned closer. "Are we just going to stand here and listen in on their conversation? Or are we going to alert them to our presence? Because. . .I don't think they're going to improve their image of us if they look out to see us cowering behind this rose trellis listening."

"What do you recommend I do, Mr. Lavery? The woman obviously had no clue this was in the works. She's financially strapped due to our gain. I'm trying to figure out a plan."

"Could we resell it to another client?"

Bascom shook his head. "It's doubtful. This one was pretty specific, and all our clients have their own minds when it comes to what they want to see designed for them. The odds are against someone else wanting a carousel of this nature."

"Then we seem to have no choice. The contract is sound. It's too late for them to back out."

If only it were so simple. Bascom didn't hurt for money, and these people obviously did, but he couldn't afford to write off or walk away from a project of this magnitude.

For the first time the older woman lowered her piecework. She tipped her head to stare over the top of her spectacles at her granddaughter. "The Lord always provides, dear. You know that better than anyone."

"Of course He does, but I believe He also expects us to use common sense when planning how to use what He's provided."

"Ellie Lyn, you know how your grandfather felt about you. You've always been his pride and joy. We've both sat back and watched the spark flow right out of your eyes. First when you lost your parents and later when you lost your sweet husband. The carousel purchase wasn't about the money.... It was your grandfather's way of making a smile reappear on your face. He felt concern for you, and this is what he wanted to do with *his* money." She paused as if to emphasize the point. "What's done is done, and I suggest you move forward with that fact and focus on the next thing. The contract has been signed, long ago, and the carousel is on its way. Like it or not, there's no changing that."

"Well, perhaps I can implore the builder to take it away and sell it somewhere else. Or I can refuse delivery..."

The grandmother's patience must have been spent, judging by the volume of her sigh. "And what good will refusing delivery bring? The money's already spent. It's gone. If you refuse delivery, you'll have nothing to show for your grandfather's well-intended decision."

"I guess you're right." The younger woman paced again from one side of the window to the other and momentarily disappeared from sight. "But I have to wonder what kind of dirty, rotten scoundrel takes advantage of an old man on his deathbed. Surely the builder knew of Papa's condition. Maybe we could hire an attorney, prove that the builder deceived or tricked Papa into this transaction."

Sheldon snickered again, and Bascom made his decision on the spot. It was one thing to regret a purchase of such magnitude, especially in this case without having any knowledge of the expense, but it was another thing altogether to stand there and insult his company and his name. He stalked up the stairs and knocked firmly on the door.

The voices instantly quieted. After a moment the door was yanked open, framing the most beautiful dark-haired, green-eyed beauty Bascom had ever seen.

۶۹

Ellie stared in confusion at the bedraggled man on her front porch. Had she forgotten about a guest's arrival? Surely they didn't have anyone planned that she'd overlooked. Their rooms were full. But things had been rather chaotic lately with her papa's death and trying to get the resort shuffled around. "Can I help you?"

"Miss Ellie Lyn Weathers?" He looked perturbed, but for the life of her, she couldn't imagine why. She'd never seen the man before in her life. His unkempt brown hair brushed the shoulder of his jacket and looked in need of a good combing—or better yet, a nice visit to the barber. Confused blue eyes stared at her with consternation.

"I'm sorry. Do I know you?"

"I guess not. I'm Bascom Anthony, the dirty, rotten scoundrel that you think took advantage of your grandfather on his deathbed."

"Oh dear."

Her grandmother's soft laugh echoed from behind. " 'Oh dear' is right. Ellie Lyn, I've warned you that your quick tongue was going to catch you in a spot."

"Thanks, Gram, that really helps." Ellie now felt as exasperated with her grandmother as she did with the stranger standing on their threshold.

The man continued to stare, and Ellie didn't know what to do. Fortunately, her grandmother picked that moment to join her at the door and motioned the man inside. He removed his dusty hat and hung it on the rack that stood near the door. He walked with a slight limp as he moved into the foyer.

"I apologize for my appearance. We've just arrived in town, and I came straight over."

"We?" Ellie leaned past and peered over the man's shoulder. She gasped when she saw all the men and wagons. Each wagon contained several large wood crates.

"Yes, we. I have a caravan of men that have helped me transport the attraction, and they're waiting for direction on where to unload. I'm sorry if we've caught you at a bad time, but they really need to be able to get on to their other destinations. They'll move on while my assistant and I do the finishing touches."

"But how big can this carousel possibly be?" Ellie's wayward curls had tumbled over her shoulder, and she brushed them back with frustration. "I thought it would be brought in and that would be that."

Bascom laughed. "It isn't that easy. I still have to put it all together. There are still a few pieces to carve and design. I'll be here awhile."

"And where will you stay?"

"According to my contract, I'm to stay here. Your grandfather was most specific. He wanted me to have full access to my work while putting the carousel in place."

Ellie's grandmother stepped forward. "I'm so sorry. We haven't even properly introduced ourselves. Let's start over. I'm Mary Case, and this is my granddaughter, Ellie Lyn."

"Pleased to meet you both."

126

Ellie muttered under her breath. "I'm sure."

"Excuse me?" The man appeared baffled. Surely he wasn't that daft.

"You can't possibly be pleased to meet us under these circumstances. If you overheard my comment about the wool being pulled over my grandfather's eyes—"

The man had the audacity to interrupt. "I believe the phrase you used was, 'dirty, rotten scoundrel.'"

"Right. I believe it was something like that. Though from outside I'm sure you couldn't hear clearly."

"Your words were loud and clear, ma'am."

"And for my words, I apologize." Ellie couldn't look him in the eye. "I'm sorry you overheard that conversation."

Bascom's mouth quirked up to one side, the action more grimace than smile. "So, you're sorry I overheard, but not as sorry for your words?"

"Well, you have to understand how it looks from my view point. . ." Her voice trailed off as she caught her grandmother's scowl.

Grandmother pushed Ellie aside, none too gently, and ushered the man into the parlor. "Have a seat here and let me get you a cool drink. I'll send someone out to serve your men cool drinks as well while they wait."

She left Ellie alone with the stranger. He stared expectantly at her. She felt she owed him an explanation. "You see, my assistant, Wanda, and I had this dream. We thought we could compete with the bigger resorts if we offered a novelty, such as a carousel. We researched and decided the expense too great to justify for a resort of our stature. My grandfather must have overheard our plans and decided to take control of matters on his own." She wrung her hands together. "We lost him recently, and the last thing I anticipated was that he took everything he had and put it all into your creation. To say the least, the whole idea has caught me by surprise."

Bascom studied her. "Perhaps your grandfather felt it a final gift to show his love for you. He had faith you could use the attraction to the resort's best interest." He glanced toward the kitchen as Grandmother brought in his drink. "He confided in me and said as much. He didn't tell me he wouldn't be around to see his plan put into action. I am sorry for your loss."

Ellie felt shame over her words and attitude. "I do want to apologize. I really am sorry." She took a deep breath. "And we'll figure out a way to make things work so we can carry out my grandfather's final wish."

"I have the perfect solution." Gram didn't seem at all remorseful about her obvious eavesdropping. "Since the upstairs rooms are full, Ellie, you can move into Priscilla's room. She has a large bed, and you know she'll love the arrangement. Wanda can move into your room, and Bascom can use Wanda's room off the kitchen until his stay is up. With its private entrance to the porch, he'll have freedom to come and go without disrupting the household."

The plan could work. The family quarters were at the back of the house on the main level. Having a man around would be awkward to say the least, but it wouldn't really present a hardship. As her grandmother had said, he'd have privacy and so would they.

The kitchen door burst open, and Ellie's five-year-old daughter, Priscilla, flew into the room. "Mama, look! I made a snake!" A piece of dough dangled from her fingers, having been rolled into a snake's form during her table play while under Wanda's supervision.

Ellie feigned a shiver of disgust, which earned a giggle from the little girl.

"It's not real—it's pretend. Like the Land of Whimsy." Prissy froze and stared as she finally noticed her mother and grandmother weren't alone.

"Prissy, this is our newest guest, Mr. Anthony. He'll be staying with us for a while. He has a special project that will help the resort bring in more business." Or at least she hoped as much. Winter was always tough on Great Salt Lake, and this year had been no exception. Bigger hotels were moving in, and new attractions—such as the newly famous Saltair Resort—made the competition fierce.

Bascom smiled at Priscilla, a genuine gesture, complete with dimples that transformed his face.

"I'm glad to meet you, Priscilla." He glanced at Ellie. "Please tell me about the Land of Whimsy. It sounds most intriguing."

A warm flush moved up Ellie's face. "It's nothing really."

"It isn't nothing, Mama!" Prissy gasped with indignation. She turned to their guest, her eyes sparkling with enthusiasm and her voice lowered to a whisper of awe. "The Land of Whimsy is our special place. Mama tells me Whimsy tales every night before I go to bed. Whimsy is a place full of sea creatures and princesses and all sorts of exciting adventures."

"Is that so?" To his credit, Bascom really did seem intrigued, as if the information had been set aside for further thought. Though why he would care about Ellie's make-believe world was beyond her.

Chapter 2

Ellie placed a pan of cookies onto a rack and slammed the oven door closed with too much force, an action that earned her a questioning glance from Wanda.

"I don't understand why you're so upset." Wanda dusted her flour-coated hands against her apron and began to knead the large ball of dough before her. Her robust form pressed against the countertop as she worked the lump into smaller circles that would soon become their dinner rolls. "This is our chance. We've dreamed of this opportunity for a long time, and thanks to your grandfather—rest his soul—we now get to see our carousel dreams come to life."

"It's. . .I don't know. The whole thing feels wrong." Ellie strode over to look out the open kitchen door. A gentle breeze blew in and cooled her overheated face. Her eyes were immediately drawn to the action near their largest outbuilding behind the resort. The men, *Bascom's* men, had lined up their wagons and worked as one to move each crate along a human chain before the wooden boxes disappeared into the carousel's new home. One wagon would be unloaded and the driver would move out of line and another would take its place. She shook her head. "Look out there! All those men are rushing around in such a hullabaloo of activity for such a silly notion. My grandfather should not have taken my fantasy to the point of fruition."

She folded her arms across her chest, leaned against the doorway, and watched. She started when she felt Wanda's gentle hand wrap around her arm.

"You're feeling guilty."

The comment took her by surprise. "Guilty? Why do you say that? I didn't order the contraption."

"No, but you wished for it, and you feel that your dream put the event into motion."

"And didn't it? Papa would never have thought up such an outlandish idea on his own. He carefully planned and plotted out every detail of his life." Her voice rose in agitation, regardless of her attempts to quell it. "And then he threw everything away to appease me. He wasted his life savings. We have nothing to show for his hard work, all his planning. . ."

"You just said yourself that your grandfather was a careful man. Do you really think he'd risk it all if he didn't have good reason? Maybe he knew you were onto something great and without a push you'd never take the necessary risk to reach that goal."

Ellie nibbled her lower lip and considered Wanda's words. Though only a few years older, Wanda always had wise advice. "Maybe."

"And the reality is—the attraction is here. Delivered by a very handsome man, I might add." She nudged Ellie and received a reluctant grin. "You have to admit Bascom is a nice bonus to the deal."

"I'll admit no such thing." At that moment Bascom glanced her way and waved. She quickly moved away from the door.

Wanda's quiet laugh followed her. "Then why did you just run away from his wave? The man is only being friendly."

Flustered, Ellie pulled open the oven to peer in at the under-cooked pastries. "I thought I smelled something burning."

"Perhaps it was your ears. They're burning red all the way to your hairline. And all because a man you don't find attractive sent you a good-natured wave." She tsked and moved back to her rolls.

"Can I help you with those?" Other than removing the last of the cookies from the oven, Ellie's own chores were done. Though they had extra men to feed, they'd prepared a hearty beef-and-vegetable soup earlier in the day, so dinner would be easy. Wanda's crusty rolls and Ellie's snickerdoodle cookies would round the meal out nicely. The majority of their guests had taken advantage of the noisy evening to escape to nearby Saltair Resort for dinner.

"I only have to place them on the pan. You sit and relax while you have a chance. I'll join you in a moment."

Ellie did as advised and with a few minutes to spare watched her friend work. Even this late in the day Wanda as always looked as neat and fresh as she had upon rising early that morning. Every hairpin remained in place, holding Wanda's soft brown hair in check while Ellie's own dark curls fell out of her pins in tumultuous chaos. Though she repaired it several times a day, the outcome always remained the same.

The comparison made her feel like a wild filly next to Wanda, the pristine mare. If Bascom had any intent through his wave, it was probably to capture her shapely friend's attention. She sighed.

Wanda chose that moment to set a cup of tea before her. She sank into the opposite chair with a smile. "Talk to me. Why all the anxiety?"

Ellie's eyes returned to the activity outside their window. "I've worked hard these past two years since losing Wilson to his illness. Priscilla and I have made our own way, and we've succeeded." She realized she was scowling and forced herself to relax. "Bascom takes up a much-needed room here at the hotel."

"Your room wouldn't have been rented out, Ellie. Our shuffling around didn't change anything. And the carousel is new and unique and bringing in crowds at other hotels. I think this is a much needed move. Your grandfather didn't enter into his decision easily. He never did." A soft smile shaped her mouth. "And I think God handpicked Bascom to build it for us. I've seen the paperwork. He gave us a great price. You know that having a B. A. Carousel can only help with our future finances. People are buzzing over his work, and he's careful to only create one masterpiece per area. We're blessed to have been accepted as clients. When word gets out that we have an original, people will come to see it—people who wouldn't have come here otherwise. I can't wait to see the theme he's chosen."

"Theme?" Ellie wrinkled her forehead again. "I thought carousels were pretty standard. A few benches, moving horses of various color, and sometimes swans that rock back and forth."

Wanda's eyes lit with anticipation. "Bascom's carousels always have a theme, built around the personality of the person who orders them."

"But whatever would Papa's theme be?" Ellie couldn't imagine how her grandfather's life would be immortalized. "He worked hard. He rested in his rocker on the front porch in the evenings while smoking his pipe and visiting with the guests. I'm not sure that will make for a very exciting attraction."

"This is where the fun begins!" Wanda sent Ellie a pointed grin as she walked to the oven and removed the final tray of cookies. The scent of warm cinnamon and sugar drifted through the room. Wanda placed the pan on a cooling rack with the others before she replaced it in the oven with the two pans of rolls. "Bascom always gets to know the owner before finishing the final design. Since your grandfather is gone, you'll be the center of Bascom's plan."

Ellie felt a momentary panic. She didn't like being the center of anything, let alone the focal point of a stranger's plan. She felt like a specimen under the lens of a man who studied a scientific process.

"I'm more predictable than my grandfather. How will he ever come up with a theme about me? This carousel will be his first flop." Ellie did her best to stay out of the limelight. She buried her face in her hands. This latest information was disheartening.

Wanda's laugh surprised her. "Oh, honey, why do you always underestimate yourself? If anything, he'll have to juggle ideas and choose which is best to encompass your personality into one small project such as this. You'll be his greatest endeavor, just you wait and see."

Ellie noticed the activity outside had slowed. "It looks like the men are down to the last wagon. They'll soon be ready to eat. I'd best go wake Prissy and Gram from their naps."

She shivered with dismay as she mulled over Wanda's words and felt a chill move across her skin. Her friend had always been lavish with her praise. But the last thing Ellie wanted was to be part of Bascom's plan.

❧

"For someone who owns a resort, the woman sure doesn't seem to be the friendly sort," Sheldon observed.

Bascom started from where he leaned against a crate, taking a momentary breather from the backbreaking labor of unloading. Sheldon stood nearby and apparently had seen the wave and lack of response.

"She's had hard times of late. She lost her husband and now recently she's lost her grandfather. He's the one I did business with." He raised an arm from the crate and pushed his hair from his forehead. A visit to a barber would be high on his list of things to accomplish during the next few days. "I think she's probably friendly enough. We just arrived with an unexpected surprise. I'm not sure I'd feel any differently if someone invested my fortune all in one purchase. It would certainly be a shock."

"I see."

Bascom didn't like the tonality of Sheldon's response. It was almost as if he read into the statement something that wasn't there. He pushed off from the box and gingerly put weight on his bum ankle. "Let's finish up with this wagon. I'm ready to get off my feet and settle in for the night." His ankle had been healing nicely and hadn't been a problem, but this past week he'd set himself back. Especially today with all the unloading, he'd pushed his recuperation to the limit. If possible, he'd find a way for a long hot soak to soothe the throbbing appendage.

"Sounds good. From the aroma wafting out the door from the kitchen, I'm ready to call it quits and sit down to a nice meal."

A lot of the men had waved off the offer of food, anxious to return home or to move on. But a handful remained, and they were all famished after the long trip. Prissy ran outside and directed them to the pump where they could freshen up.

"Mama said to come in through the side door and to make yourselves comfortable in the dining room. Dinner will be served. . ." A frown twisted her features as she thought for a moment. "Promply."

"Thank you, Priscilla." Bascom hid his smile at the young girl's earnestness. "But could you please tell your mother we'd best eat outside?"

Priscilla frowned. "Why?"

"We've worked hard all day. I'm not sure it would be a good idea for all of us to traipse into your mother's pretty dining room."

"Oh, 'cause you're dirty?" Understanding dawned on her young features. She was a perfect miniature of her mother—complete with a long tangle of black curls—until you got to her eyes. Where her mother's were a deep emerald green,

Priscilla's were a soft light brown.

"Yes, that's exactly why."

"Mama won't care. We feed lots of dirty people here because of the salty lake and sand. Mama says that's just part of life on the Great Salt Lake." She leaned close. "A lot of them even stink 'cause of the algae. You smell lots better than some of our guests do."

Several of the men chuckled at her bluntness.

Bascom glanced at Sheldon, who shrugged.

"Well then, I think we'll take your advice and eat in the dining room. . .if you're sure."

"I'm sure," she called over her shoulder. Mission accomplished, she skipped back toward the main building.

Several of the men deferred on eating in the formal dining atmosphere and asked to be served their meal outdoors. Sheldon and Bascom joined the handful of guests that were left on the premises. Though the large room was elegant with ornate wall coverings and polished hardwood floors, the atmosphere was cozy and relaxed.

Ellie kept glancing at Sheldon, and a frown hovered in her eyes. When the last guest left the room, Bascom asked her about it.

"I've just realized your assistant will be staying with us, too. I haven't a room for him."

So that was it. "If it's all right with you, Sheldon will stay in the storage room off the building where we'll be working. It's just the right size for one person. He's already moved his things in there."

The tension drained from her shoulders. "That'll be fine. But what about the other men?"

"They'll all move on tonight. They're ready for a night in town. Only Sheldon and I will remain."

"Then that's settled. I feel much better." She still looked uncomfortable. "Thank you for understanding. Your arrival caught me by surprise."

"I noticed." He hoped his smile would soften the words. "But I do understand. You didn't exactly expect us, and with a full guest list, we put you in a rough spot."

Wanda began to clear the dishes while Ellie, Priscilla, and Mary led the way to the parlor. Sheldon made his excuses as they passed through the central hall, and loaded down with a lantern and other supplies he'd need for his new quarters, bid everyone a good evening. Bascom figured now was as good a time as any to finish up details with his hosts and settled down onto a soft rose-colored wing chair. It felt heavenly to take the weight off his ankle.

Ellie watched for a moment as he tried to find a comfortable place for his foot, then she hopped up to move a padded footstool in front of him. He lifted his foot and rested it carefully on top.

"Gram, Wanda, Priscilla, and I have our own private parlor at the back of the house. The area we're in now is the original house, but my grandfather added on the large extension at the side for guests when the area started booming as a tourist location a few years back. The guests are welcome to use this parlor and the front porch anytime they like, so please make yourself at home. Most guests are tired after a day of activity and retire to their quarters after the late meal."

Bascom nodded. "I aim to do the same myself soon. I'm ready for a good night's sleep."

Priscilla climbed onto Ellie's lap and snuggled into her arms. Her eyes were heavy. "Mama, is it Whimsy time? I'm tired."

Ellie lowered a kiss to the girl's soft curls before glancing his way. "It is. Let me finish up with Mr. Anthony first and make sure he has everything he needs."

"Please call me Bascom." Bascom disliked formal titles. Back East the lines of propriety were well defined, but he hoped those boundaries were dimmer this far out West.

"Bascom it is. Well. . .now that we have everything settled, do you require anything else before we retire for the night?" She hesitated and glanced down at his ankle. "Forgive me for intruding, but your ankle—it seems to be bothering you. You've worked hard today. Would you like to soak it?"

Wanda entered the room and overheard. "Of course he would! I'll set a pot of water to heat on the stove right now." She bustled back out, and they could hear pans clanging about in the kitchen.

Ellie turned to him with a smile. "That's taken care of then. When Wanda sets her mind to something, there's no talking her out of it."

"So I see. I didn't even have a chance to try." Bascom had the feeling she spoke from experience.

"Is there anything else we can do for you?"

"I'd love directions to a good barber. Will I find one in town?"

Mary's blue eyes brightened. "I'll do better than that. I'll cut it right here. Let me get my things."

"Oh no, I couldn't ask that of you. One more day won't hurt any." His voice tapered off as the elderly woman stood, and ignoring his words, hurried from the room.

Ellie smirked. "You'd best stop arguing right now. First thing you need to learn now that you're staying is that once Gram sets her mind to something, she doesn't back down easily—same as Wanda." She exchanged an amused glance with her daughter, and then looked back up at him, her eyes suddenly nostalgic. "Gram loves to cut hair. She misses fussing over Papa. It would be nice if you let her cater to you."

"Mama, my Whimsy tale?"

"All right." She mouthed a silent apology to Bascom for the interruption. "Once upon a time, in the Land of Whimsy, Princess Priscilla woke up in a strange place. Nothing looked familiar. . ."

Mary returned and directed Bascom to a straight chair and went to work. Wanda set a large wash pan beneath his foot and filled it with steaming water. Bascom took advantage of the quiet and tuned in to Ellie's soft words as she spoke to her daughter of a private, magical world. As she painted word pictures of adventurous pirates, beguiling mermaids, and various sea creatures—some he'd heard of and some he figured were created from her imagination—he began to develop his plan for the carousel's theme into a fully detailed image.

Chapter 3

Bascom woke at dawn and tested his weight on his ankle. He'd learned through experience that if he didn't exercise it, he'd be stiff later. The soak had done its job; the ache was mostly gone, and the appendage felt much better now after a rest. He gingerly dressed and stepped onto the front porch.

Mist hung over the lake in the early morning air, and he decided to walk closer to the water and explore. No one else was up and about at this hour. The quiet refreshed him, and he felt a peace that had been absent for a long time. The hustle and bustle of Coney Island seemed far away from this quaint place.

Even this early, Coney wouldn't have had a quiet or isolated place for Bascom to catch a thought. And there wasn't a moment that someone else hadn't been in sight, whether sleeping off too much imbibing from the night before or getting started early on the day's work.

He began to walk along the shoreline, his gait gaining steadiness as he went. He'd heard tell that the area was known as "the Coney Island of the West," but in his experience he didn't see any resemblance at all. The lake spread out before him, water as far as the eye could see. If he didn't know better, he'd assume by the vastness that it was open water like the ocean. But where the ocean roared toward the sand with mighty waves, the water here seemed gentler, lapping against the shore's edge.

A soft breeze drifted across the water. Mountains in the distance stood tall against the blue sky. The sun shone down, warming his shoulders and back. For the first time since losing his wife and son, he felt alive again. The warmth eased the iciness that had filled his heart for so long.

He thought about his newest carousel, the first since the accident, and wondered if his returning to work caused the burden to lift. But the burden had prevented him from working, his focus refusing to move past all the grief and all that had happened, until now.

Whatever the reason, Bascom rejoiced and savored the warmth that filled his soul. He whispered a prayer of thanks to God, with whom he'd recently started a relationship, for bringing him to this place of healing. Though his heart still ached over his losses, he knew he was on the path to recovery. The prompting he'd felt to take a new contract, this one specifically, was a good thing.

"Mr. Anthony. Mr. Anthony!"

Bascom stopped in his tracks as he heard the young voice calling from behind him. He turned to see a pink-enveloped Priscilla hopping along with a clumsy skip. The sight brought a smile to his lips.

She wasn't much older than his son had been, and both had the same enthusiasm about life. The pang of loss was with him, but Priscilla's arrival distracted him from dwelling on it.

She stood before him and grinned. Her plaited hair draped behind her back. Though her dress appeared to be new, her worn brown boots told a different story as she dug her wiggly heel into the soft sand at the water's edge. "I'm not s'posed to be down here without an adult. But you're an adult, right?"

He squatted to meet her gaze. "I am. Did you tell your mother or anyone else that you're out here? They might be worried if they can't find you."

"I told them I'd be out on the porch. . .then I saw you."

"So if they come outside, they're going to worry. They won't know you're with me."

She giggled. "Silly. They will if they look around like I did!"

"All the same, I'd feel better if we return and receive permission for you to be at the water's edge with me."

"Yes, sir." She sighed. "But they might make us stay to eat if we do that."

Bascom's stomach rumbled at the thought of a good, hot breakfast. "I can't think why that would be a bad thing. My stomach says it's a great idea."

Priscilla, apparently not having a shy bone in her body, reached up and clutched his hand. "Then let's go find your stomach some food." She stopped and looked up at him. "But can we walk to the water again later?"

"Only with your mother's permission."

"Yes, sir."

They rounded a slight bend, which brought the resort back into view. Ellie, arms crossed against her chest, strode toward them. She stopped as she saw her daughter clinging to Bascom's hand.

"Mama! How'd you know where to find us?" Prissy let go and skip-hopped to her mother's side where she threw her arms around the woman.

"I followed your footprints in the sand."

"I was with an adult."

"I see that. But you need to tell me next time."

"Mr. Anthony told me that. He was bringing me back."

Ellie addressed him for the first time. "I appreciate that. I'm sorry if she's been a bother. I hope she didn't intrude on your quiet time."

Bascom waved her words away. "She wasn't a bother at all. She's welcome to join me at any time"—he glanced down at the smiling little girl—"*if* she first receives approval from you."

Mother and daughter exchanged a look, and Ellie nodded. "I suppose that will be fine."

"Thank you!" Priscilla buried her face in her mother's long skirt for a quick hug before returning to grasp Bascom's hand.

"Breakfast is almost ready. Can the walk be postponed until after?"

Bascom knew he needed to start work on the carousel after the morning meal, but when Priscilla's face fell with disappointment, he couldn't help himself from saying, "We can take a quick stroll after we eat. It's good for digestion. But I'll need to get to work soon after."

"Oh, she can wait until another time. Please don't let my daughter keep you from your work."

Bascom couldn't tell if her words were a reprimand, directing him to follow his contract and finish his work as soon as possible, or if she only spoke to give him a way out of walking the lakeshore with her daughter. Though he knew her rooms at the resort were at a premium and he took up one of them, he also knew the room he occupied wouldn't be rented out even if he left early, so he threw caution to the wind. Returning the smile to Priscilla's face took far more precedence than finishing the carousel a few moments earlier.

"We'll walk. I need to balance my time, and part of my work is getting to know you both so I can properly capture your essence in my project."

Ellie's eyes darted to his in mortification and then just as quickly looked at the lake.

He chuckled. "I didn't mean to embarrass you. But I do need to get to know you better if I'm to make the carousel work for your resort. You need to have a draw."

"I can't imagine what that draw will be. We're a simple sort."

Bascom had to disagree. There was nothing simple about the stunning woman that walked beside him. He wondered what had brought her to the point of believing such a thing. She walked with an air of confidence, yet she seemed to shut herself off from the world around her. He felt sure she hadn't seen the beauty in the view before her for quite some time. Instead, her eyes focused on the building they moved toward while her thoughts remained far away.

"You just be yourself, and I'll create the draw."

Priscilla yanked his hand, bouncing up and down. "I love to draw. Can I draw the picture with you?"

Bascom chuckled. "Sure you can. The picture wouldn't be complete without you."

Ellie laughed softly. "There are different meanings to the word *draw*, Prissy. In this case, the word refers to a way to bring in more guests to the resort. We want to use the carousel to draw—or bring in—more business."

They watched as Priscilla sucked in her bottom lip with concentration. "Oh. And sometimes, Mama, you *draw* me bathwater from the pump."

"Exactly! So you can see there are different meanings to that word."

"Well, I'd rather you draw me a picture of a bath than make me take one." Her eyes took on a mischievous glint. "Or, Mr. Anthony could take me swimming in the lake, and I wouldn't have to bathe at all."

"I thought you said people came out of the lake all smelly from the algae," Bascom teased with a tweak to her braid.

Ellie's gasp caught his attention. "Prissy, you didn't!"

"Yes I did. They do stink sometimes, Mama."

Bascom wrinkled his nose. "And that's what you want to smell like after you bathe? I'm not so sure that's a very good idea."

"I guess not." She looked disappointed for a brief moment, then her eyes brightened. "I know! You can take me for a swim and then Mama can *draw* me a bath for after!"

Both adults laughed.

"Your daughter doesn't lack in negotiating skills. She'll be a fine businesswoman someday."

"I guess she will at that. Though I'm not sure her precociousness is a good thing at this age."

"Nonsense. You need to cultivate the trait in her from the start. How else will she learn to follow her heart—and do an about-face—if she's held back now?"

Ellie's sigh much resembled her daughter's. "I suppose you're right. But it is a hard balance to find."

"I think you're on the right track, and from what I've seen, you're raising a fine daughter here."

"Thank you."

Bascom turned his attention back to the little girl tugging on his hand. "And I'll have you know that in this case, though our attraction will create a *draw* for tourists, we also need to draw the ideas onto paper so I have a plan to work with. I'd still welcome your help with that."

"What kind of ideas?"

"Secret ones." Bascom put a finger to his lips and smiled. "Your mother can't see the final product until it's ready. If you assist me, you'll have to keep quiet on what we're creating."

Ellie looked worried. He understood. She didn't know him well. "And only the proprietor has to wait for the final unveiling. Miss Wanda and Mrs. Case are free to come and go as they please, as long as they promise not to tell any details."

Now she sent him a look of annoyance. "So this entire thing is about me, but I'm the one who can't see it until the unveiling?"

He nodded. Priscilla giggled.

"And what if I don't like the finished product?"

Bascom put a hand to his heart in feigned horror. "I've not yet found one client who isn't satisfied with the final result. You'll dearly love the carousel I build. In fact, I dare say you'll be shoving the small children out of your way just so you can have the first choice of character to ride."

"Mama!" Priscilla's chagrined voice interrupted. "You wouldn't."

Ellie glanced down at her daughter. "You never know. According to your Mr. Anthony, I just might."

He liked this playful side of his employer.

Priscilla stared out over the water for a moment, contemplative, her brow furrowing with concentration before she whipped around to speak to them.

"Then I'll draw a special carving just for me to ride. I'll ask Mr. Anthony to make it too small for you to sit on."

Their laughter carried across the water, and Ellie pulled her daughter close for a hug.

"Is that what all that staring at the water was about?" Bascom teased. "I thought for a moment you'd become distracted from our conversation and were looking for a mermaid."

"No, silly."

"Oh, that's right, because mermaids are pretend?"

"No. It's because nothing like that can live in the Great Salt Lake. It's too salty and only tiny brine shrimp can swim in it."

"Ah. So I'd best put away my thoughts of breaking out my fishing pole and catching us all a good dinner."

Priscilla sent him a sideward grin. "You didn't *bring* a fishing pole, Mr. Anthony. I watched you unpack your wagons, remember?"

He ruffled her hair as they stepped onto the porch. "And how do you know I don't have one packed away in one of those many crates?"

Again her face creased in thought. "Oh."

She hopped up the several steps and thumped onto the hard planks that led to the front door. "Well, we can *draw* you one, and you could carve it."

"That's a fact." He grinned over her head at Ellie. "But what would be the point if now I know I'd never catch a fish?"

"Well, it would give you something to do while you sit and watch me swim." She smiled impishly and hurried through the front door. Ellie's laugh filtered back as she followed.

The general corruption and cutthroat competition between carousel designers back East on Coney Island seemed far away. For a short time the pleasant walk with Ellie and Priscilla had pushed the violence of his former life to the back of his mind. Whether the beautiful climate or the two females created a balm for his soul, he didn't know. But if time spent in their company would continue to make him feel alive again, he'd carve a fishing pole for each of them, just to give him an excuse to share their company. He'd always worked hard, and this job would be no exception, but he'd also have time to relax—and he intended to use his rest time to get to know his hosts better. Maybe in turn he could make Ellie's life a bit easier by helping out a bit.

He had a feeling he was going to like it here, and after two years of grief, healing might just come packaged in the duo that had entered the resort before him. He could only hope the tormentor who'd made his life a living nightmare had finally given up his quest for vengeance now that Bascom had moved out West.

Chapter 4

Ellie shifted the pan full of green beans that rested on her lap and tried to focus on her daughter's words as she snapped the vegetables for dinner. She usually loved their early morning time together, but today she felt restless. Bascom had given Prissy a small wooden carousel horse to play with the evening before, and Prissy now sat at her feet on the worn planks of the porch, keeping up a continuous dialogue about the pony's adventures. With half her focus on listening to the little girl's rambling chatter, Ellie found herself watching for any sign of movement near the outbuilding and had to keep redirecting her thoughts away from the curiously interesting man.

She smiled as she acknowledged the fact that she was the curious one. She couldn't deny the fact that Bascom piqued her thoughts about where he'd come from, why such a kind man was alone in the world, and how he'd ended up with the limp. Had he been born with it? She didn't think so. His cautious steps made the injury appear to be a fresh one, still tender to movements or overwork.

Though he did work hard, even with the injured ankle, she quickly corrected herself. The man had definitely kept busy during the first week of his stay, so busy in fact that she'd hardly seen him, and according to both Prissy and Wanda, he'd made a lot of progress on his work. But at what expense to his health? Did he neglect and overwork his ankle in order to be out of her way since she'd made clear the hardship his arrival would cause the resort? In the end, they'd all shuffled over a bit, and he'd done nothing but liven up the place with his good humor during the few times she'd seen him. He did seem to be a very nice man.

"Mama, you're smiling. Do you like my story?" Prissy peered up at Ellie, her eyes squinted against the brilliant sunlight that filtered under the covered porch.

"I always love your stories. You know I do." Ellie answered, again having to refocus her thoughts away from the man and back onto her daughter.

Priscilla stared a moment longer. "You were smiling over at the big building. *Not* because of my story."

"Oh."

"I know what you were thinking about. . ." The amusement in Prissy's impish smile matched the amusement in her twinkling brown eyes.

"You do?" Ellie put a hand to her heart and patted it, flustered. If her young

142

daughter could read her thoughts, how much more obvious must they be to any adult that might be watching?

"*You're* thinking about how to sneak in and take a peek at your new carousel." Prissy's giggle filled the air.

Thoroughly disconcerted over her wayward musings, Ellie sighed with relief. Maybe her silly notions weren't as transparent as she'd thought. "Oh, and is that what you'd be doing if things were flipped around and *you* were the one waiting for the surprise?"

"Yes, ma'am, it's exactly what I'd be doing."

Ruffling her daughter's hair, Ellie snapped the last bean and set the bowl aside. "Well actually, I was thinking about the new carousel *and* wondering how Mr. Anthony hurt his foot. It seems to be a new injury, and I'm wondering if he might need some doctoring or if he should even be up and about, walking on it as he does. *That's* where my mind had wandered off to. Though I was still listening to your story, and you can quiz me on that fact if you feel you must."

"No, I know you always listen." Prissy grew quiet as she followed her mother's stare at the building. "Do you think he hurts? He's nice. I don't want him to hurt 'cause of the carving."

"I'm not sure, but I think I'll ask him about it today at lunch."

"He injured it in a fire."

Both females jumped at the intrusion of Sheldon's voice as he walked around the corner of the house. His silent steps hadn't warned of his arrival, and Ellie couldn't help but wonder if he'd been eavesdropping.

He grinned. "Sorry if I startled you. I thought I'd take advantage of the early hour and do some exploring."

"Oh, I thought perhaps you were both already hard at work on the attraction." Ellie stopped, realizing her words sounded judgmental, as if the men should have been up and working away. "I mean, I hadn't seen either one of you, so I figured you'd made an early start." There she went again, her words insinuating they should have been doing just that.

Sheldon leaned lazily against the support post and waved her words away. His dusty boots attested to a stroll along the lake, but that didn't mean he hadn't been listening to what they'd discussed a few minutes before. She didn't like the thought.

"We have started early most days, but Bascom's ankle must be acting up because he wasn't out there this morning. I decided rather than mess something up by guessing what he'd want me to do, it would be better to wait and see what we'd be doing when he made an appearance."

"You mentioned a fire?" Ellie didn't mean to pry, but her concern for her guest overrode her better judgment.

143

"Yep." Sheldon, unasked, took the stairs two at a time and pulled a chair close to Ellie's. She fought the urge to move hers a few inches in the other direction. His presence unnerved her. Partly due to the fact that they'd discussed Bascom behind his back, but also partly because he'd moved too close to her. She felt crowded in his presence.

Bascom always kept a polite and proper distance between them the few times they'd been together, during their walk and at meals. She preferred his standards to Sheldon's.

Though she felt smothered by his nearness, he obviously felt nothing of the kind because with his knee almost touching Ellie's he still leaned forward to close the space between them as he spoke.

"Coney Island has become very competitive between businesses, sort of like what you're experiencing here, but much worse. The area is thriving, and the resorts compete to keep the upper hand so that their place will be most popular the next year. The attractions are getting bigger and better, and the builders of the attractions are just as competitive as the people hiring them."

"Bascom doesn't seem the competitive sort." Ellie felt she needed to defend the man for some inane reason. Probably, again, due to the fact he wasn't around to defend himself as they gossiped.

"He's not. That was part of the problem. Crime has escalated right along with the influx of tourists."

"The vacationers are criminal?"

"No, not the vacationers. But the people that vie for their business aren't above finding ways other than attractions to force some of the business operators out."

Ellie gasped. "That's terrible."

"It is. Organized crime has moved in and now they work different operators and charge for their protection. At times, that 'protection' includes setting fires or using other methods to put an overly competitive neighbor out of business."

"And is that what happened to Bascom?" Ellie couldn't believe people would sink to such lows, but then again, she knew her desperation to keep her own resort afloat. That nature, she felt sure, drove some people to drastic and scandalous measures.

Sheldon reached over and tugged at her skirt in a most inappropriate manner. Her emotions must have reached her expression because he smiled and held up the end of an errant green bean for her to see. "Didn't want it to stain your pretty dress."

Ellie nodded, wanting him to continue and then be on his way.

"A little over two years ago, Bascom and I had just finished a carousel for a place on the beach, our most beautiful creation yet. Much like your competitor to the east. . ." He gestured in the direction of which he spoke.

"Saltair."

"Thank you. Much like Saltair, they had a dance pavilion, cottages for the guests, and a huge boardwalk that went out over the Atlantic Ocean. The carousel was the focal point, and people were scheduled to arrive the next week to see what Bascom had created. In the meantime, a corrupt man named John McKane controlled the area, and he often would ask for money in exchange for protection."

"And he did this to Bascom?" Ellie was horrified at the thought. She knew there were evil people in the world and that bad things happened to people who didn't deserve it. Her loss of her husband proved that. But she would never understand what drove people to purposely hurt others or how they could live with themselves if they did.

"Not directly. No one knows for sure who was behind the accident. But we have our suspicions." He glanced at Priscilla, who had moved to the far rail and now balanced her horse upon it while talking quietly to herself, and lowered his voice. "Bascom's family had arrived the day before, his wife and young son, and were free to enjoy the facilities during the week prior to opening. After a swim with the family, Bascom left them to enjoy the carousel while he went to nap. Like I said, we'd worked hard, and he took advantage of the break between projects to catch up. A fire started in the building that housed the carousel, a fast-moving and ferocious fire. Bascom's wife and son were trapped inside. By the time Bascom was summoned, it was too late. Bascom, out of control from grief, tried to get to them, but the few people that had arrived by that time held him back. He fought them, broke free, and entered the structure just as the roof collapsed, which trapped his ankle under the outer beam. The bystanders were able to pull him out."

"How awful!" Tears collected in Ellie's eyes and slipped down her cheeks. She didn't even try to hold them back. No one should ever have to endure such horror. Though she'd lost her husband, he'd been taken from her by natural causes. A severe illness had claimed his life. She lowered her voice to match his. "To watch your spouse and child burn to death in front of your eyes—I can't even comprehend."

Sheldon looked at her then looked off toward the outbuilding. "It's only fair to tell you—there was another version of the story that floated around for a time. I'm sure the authorities have dispelled their concerns on that one, though, or he'd be in custody by now, just like John McKane. . ."

"The city boss?"

"Right. He was arrested around this same time period for his criminal activities."

Ellie felt a shiver of apprehension pass through her. She didn't want to hear. Bascom, at this time, was her employee. She felt the right to know if his injury would prevent him from successfully doing the job he'd been hired to do. But based on Sheldon's last words, they were now bordering on pure gossip, and she didn't like it. "Perhaps it's best we leave it alone if the authorities have cleared him."

"I feel you need to know. Hear me out for my peace of mind, and then do with the information as you please."

She nodded but felt like a traitor.

"The other story has it that Bascom himself set the fire and that he was injured during his escape."

"Are you insinuating Bascom had something to do with McKane? That he committed arson—and murdered his own wife and son—in order to prevent other businesses from succeeding?"

"I wasn't around at the time. We'd finished our job and didn't have another lined up yet. Though we had a lot of requests, Bascom hadn't chosen one."

"You're his friend and assistant. I've not known the man for long, but I have a hard time believing the man I've met would ever be capable of committing something as cold-blooded as the act you've just told me about."

"I have to agree. Like I said, I wasn't around at the time. I've only heard rumors, and I'm sure that's just what they are. But I felt I owed you both explanations for what happened. You deserve to feel safe here, and I'd hate to see bad things start happening to you."

The shiver returned, but Ellie couldn't tell what caused it. The fact that Bascom might have done exactly what the rumor insinuated? Or that his assistant's final words sounded almost like a threat?

She watched as he hopped up from the chair and dropped to his knee at Prissy's side. He glanced at Ellie with a covert smile. Then he asked Prissy what she'd named her magnificent creature, and the little girl giggled at his magnified antics when he requested a turn to play.

Bascom exited the kitchen door at that moment, carrying a plate piled high with breakfast foods. A look of concern crossed his features when he saw Sheldon at the far end of the porch. He quickly reined it in and sent Ellie a smile.

"May I?" He motioned to the chair beside her.

"Of course." Ellie watched as Bascom balanced the plate in one hand while moving the chair back to a proper distance away from her with the other. His light brown hair looked tousled, as if he'd forgotten to brush it upon awakening. More likely, according to its shine, he'd brushed it, and it preferred to flop about his head at will as usual.

She realized he stared back at her with an amused expression as he took his first few bites of food. His blue eyes twinkled over his private thoughts, and again she had a hard time believing that this man, who'd made her feel so at ease in his company, could ever hurt anyone.

He ate in silence for a few minutes, and she dug through her pan of beans to be sure she'd properly prepared them for cooking amidst all the distractions.

"Ellie." Bascom's soft voice caused her to glance up. A look of concern had replaced the amusement as he glanced from her to Sheldon and back again.

"Please be careful who you trust. Not all people are as they seem."

The shiver returned. She couldn't be sure whether his words referred to Sheldon—because his eyes again moved in that direction after the statement—or if he knew of their little chat and the words also referred to him.

Regardless, she'd take his words to heart and trust no one. That was the safest thing to do.

Chapter 5

P
lease be careful who you trust. Not all people are as they seem."
Bascom's words echoed over and over in Ellie's mind. She considered their meaning as she did the laundry, her least-liked chore. She put a hand to the small of her back as she straightened from leaning over the washtub, forcing her aching muscles to cooperate. Though she'd risen early to begin her work, the washhouse heat caused beads of perspiration to roll down her face and back. Her dress wilted against her, and she couldn't wait to finish. Maybe she'd reward herself and Prissy with a swim later in the afternoon. The water would feel refreshing, even if they would have to rinse off afterward so the salt wouldn't cake on their skin.

She glanced out the small window where the morning sun had just begun to light up the sky. The day promised to be a beautiful one, with a brilliant blue sky and very few clouds. She felt alone in the world at this hour, with everyone else snuggling under their covers for the last hour or so of sleep. Though some guests trickled down early, most slept later than they usually would, savoring each moment of their visit.

A droplet of sweat ran down her forehead, and she used her sleeve to wipe it away. She shook away her musings and again bent over the washtub, anxious to get as much work finished as possible before Priscilla woke up and ran out to "help." Her thoughts again wandered to the two men staying on the premises. Surely her grandfather had investigated them thoroughly. He wasn't a man to make a rash decision, and she felt sure he'd have researched carefully before committing such a task—and such an amount of money!—to just anyone.

But none of it made sense, beginning with why her grandfather would even do such a thing with their inheritance. And even more alarming, why, if Bascom had meant she shouldn't trust Sheldon, would Bascom have the man working as his assistant? Surely she'd misconstrued his meaning. Sheldon seemed nice enough. Perhaps Bascom only meant that with so many strangers coming and going at the resort, she'd be well-advised to use caution as to who she spent time with since he'd seen her so easily visit with both Sheldon and himself. She also entrusted Priscilla to the men's company, but always under the supervision of Wanda or her grandmother.

She felt secure with such measures but would be sure to keep her daughter

148

under one of the females' constant care. Times were changing, more guests were using their facility as word spread and as the community grew, and even though they had wonderful neighbors and townsfolk, bad people with ill intent usually interspersed with the good ones as towns expanded and strangers moved in. She'd do well to keep better track of her daughter, and in light of that, she welcomed Bascom's thoughtful words and advice.

Ellie decided she would read no more into his intent than that, a mere warning to be cautious with her trust. Growing up at the resort had built hospitality into her nature. Though it stretched her to warmly welcome strangers into her home, she'd become acclimated to doing just that, even if her personal level of comfort strained in the process. But in doing so, she'd also become overly trusting and tended to forget to keep in mind that not everyone who passed their way would be deserving of that trust. And even though Bascom had extended the warning, she'd do well to steer clear of him as much as possible as well.

After snagging up another armload of sheets, Ellie placed them in the water she'd carried from the pump. They'd rigged up an old stove years before to boil the water, and she'd already filled it with a measure of Ivory soap flakes. The handle on the washtub creaked in protest as she began to rotate it, the action forcing the paddles inside the barrel to mix the bedclothes around. As one arm began to ache, she switched to the other.

"If you'll step aside, I think I've found a way to make your chore a bit easier." Bascom spoke from the doorway directly behind her.

Ellie jumped as his voice intruded on her thoughts. Hadn't she just made the decision to steer clear of the man?

She straightened but was sure he didn't miss her stiffness upon reaching an upright posture. The wash water sloshed with the abrupt break in rhythm, then silence filled the room.

"Pardon?" Ellie, flustered by his appearance, pushed her hair away from her face. Quiet and private, the man had a way of staying in the background, doing his work, and letting others do theirs. His invasion into her work space felt personal.

Bascom motioned to a contraption he held in his hand. "There are easier ways to do some of the things that are done around a place like this. I watched you on laundry day last week and, though I know my time is to be spent on the carousel, it didn't take much effort at all for me to put this together." He hesitated. "I used my spare time in the evenings and my experience with the carousel to form a similar steam engine setup to help with your laundry chores."

"Really?" Intrigued in spite of herself, Ellie grinned at the thought. No one had ever done such a thing for her. "How does it work?"

"If you'll step aside, I'll rig it up and show you." He moved closer into the room, and Ellie rounded the washtub and backed toward the door. She stood in the doorway and relished both the break and the cool air that filtered past her.

She watched as he hooked the contraption to the handle of the washtub. "I'll use the same system you use to heat the boiling water to run this smaller version of the engine that will power your carousel." He continued to work as he spoke.

Priscilla arrived and greeted Ellie with a hug before slipping under her arm to peer inside at Bascom. "Whatcha doin', Mr. Anthony?"

Bascom paused and sat back on his heels, shifting a bit to accommodate his injured ankle. "I'm putting together a steam engine to ease your mama's load on wash day." He sent her a crooked grin that highlighted a deep dimple in his left cheek.

"Oh, can I help?"

"Sure. C'mon over here and hold this tube for me." He helped Priscilla grip the rubber tube before glancing over his shoulder toward Ellie. "Don't worry, we're not hooking up the steam yet."

Ellie appreciated the way he took time to acknowledge her daughter instead of continuing his work while offering his explanation—or worse, ignoring her questions completely. She also liked that he directed his reassurance to Ellie without making Priscilla feel unneeded.

Bascom spoke quietly throughout the process and patiently answered Prissy's many questions. With a warm chuckle he glanced at Ellie. "I think she'll be able to build her own as soon as we're finished here. It looks like I'm going to have competition in my business if I don't watch out."

Priscilla's delighted giggle filled the air. "I'm too little to do business."

"Is that so? You could have fooled me."

Prissy glanced at Ellie and rolled her eyes. Ellie responded in turn. They shared a conspiratorial smile.

"Great job!" Bascom stood and wiped his hands on his trousers. "Let's see how it works."

Ellie moved forward to watch. Bascom explained as he went. "The water will heat up, and the steam will put pressure on this piston and exert force. I've rigged it up like the process used to make the carousel horses move up and down. That same force will, in turn"—he grinned at Ellie and she felt her heart skip a beat—"turn the gears that make the washtub do the job all on its own."

As he spoke, the process did just that, and Priscilla jumped up and down with excitement. Ellie just barely restrained herself from doing the same.

"Pure brilliance, that's what it is!" Ellie stepped closer, enthralled. "But how decadent to allow a machine to do my work for me."

This time Bascom let loose a laugh that startled them all. "I hardly think you'll be a lady of leisure with just this indulgence. You'll still need to gather the laundry, create the steam, load the linens into the tub, and hang them to dry. The upside is you'll be able to do most of that while the washtub does the most strenuous task for you. You'll be less tired. Now c'mon, give it a try."

She didn't even try to contain her smile as she moved forward and sailed through the process. He moved to do the same setup with the wringer, and before she knew it she had a full load ready to be aired in the slight breeze. The most remarkable part was that she could do just that while the next load churned away without her.

કૈ

"Thanks for letting me invite Mr. Anthony along on our swim trip, Mama!" Prissy skipped ahead, and her voice carried back to where Ellie and her carousel builder friend followed at a more sedate pace.

Ellie glanced at Bascom. He raised an eyebrow in amusement, and she quickly looked away. "It's the least we could do after he freed up my time so we could enjoy the afternoon."

"That's the only reason you asked?" His tonality revealed he was just as startled as she by his choice of words.

She kept her eyes forward, telling herself it wouldn't do to trip on a stone and sprawl flat on her face. But she knew her real reason for not meeting his eyes was the emotional reaction she felt every time their gazes met. While her intentions to keep him at a distance were sincere, her heart and daughter and every circumstance about them seemed determined to throw them into each other's path at every turn.

"What other reason would I have?" Her question, asked innocently, caused him to scowl.

"I'd like to think you might enjoy my company, too."

"Well, there's that, I suppose." She glanced at him just long enough to quirk her mouth into a teasing grin. She couldn't deny that he intrigued her or that she'd enjoy his company while Prissy splashed about in the water. "But I do want to thank you for lightening my load. I never dreamed such a thing possible. Your steam-powered washtub is simply amazing."

"I can't take the credit for inventing the steam engine, you know." He waved as Prissy hopped along backward, gesturing for their attention. "I can only take credit for having the right parts to make it work for this situation."

"Well, even so, it's wonderful, and I do appreciate it."

"Just make sure to keep it oiled as I showed you. Don't add too much at a time or it might splatter over the wash."

"I'll remember. Just a few drops to keep it lubricated."

Prissy dropped to the ground and began to pull off her boots. Ellie hurried

151

to join her, knowing patience wasn't her daughter's strongest virtue and if they dallied she might jump in boots and all. Bascom joined them, pulled a blanket from the basket he'd brought along, and expertly flapped it into the air so it settled flat on the small beach that abutted the shore.

Ellie kept one eye on her daughter while helping Bascom unload their picnic lunch. Surprised, she marveled over how at ease she felt in the man's presence. While in business mode, she managed to appear halfway intelligent, but in social situations, her tongue became mired in knots and she usually tripped over her words.

"You're not joining us?" Bascom nodded toward Prissy where she bobbed and dipped in the lake.

"Not today. I originally intended to, but. . ."

"My presence interfered?" A shadow of concern passed through his eyes.

"No, actually, the salt irritates my skin, and I'd have to bathe again. . ." She stopped midsentence, mortified that she'd blathered about such a personal situation, so comfortable was she in his presence.

"To remove the salt, I understand." Bascom finished her sentence casually without making her feel any more ill at ease.

"Exactly." She busied her hands setting out more of their lunch. "And since you made my morning so much easier, I don't feel the need to cool off as much as relax and enjoy my newfound leisure."

"Then I'll let you get to it while I go swim with that bobbing cork of a girl. Don't you worry about her being out there alone?"

He looked confused.

"It's the salt. You'll see once you immerse yourself. The buoyant quality of the water won't let you submerge, even if you try. You'll pop right back up to the surface. The lake is also known for its medicinal benefits. It will benefit your ankle, and you'll feel better for it."

"Sounds nice. And fun. I believe I'll try it right now. You just relax." He nodded toward her book and headed out to join Prissy where the little girl's gleeful shout welcomed him.

❧

Later, Bascom reclined and watched mother and daughter interact from between his partially open eyelids. He enjoyed their camaraderie and playful personalities. He knew from his own experience that life as a widower wasn't easy, but having Prissy certainly seemed to soften the edges of grief for Ellie. He knew the child's presence also brought additional challenges, and he was glad he could lighten Ellie's load in this small way and allow her more time to spend with her little girl. For the first time in more than a year, he allowed himself to fall into a deep sleep.

He awakened to Ellie's soft hand on his shoulder. "The sun's moved. We need to head back."

Priscilla slept beside him, curled up against his side. He didn't want to move. The scent of her sweaty, salty little-girl skin washed over him, and Ellie's eyes softened as a small smile curved her lips. He liked being in their presence and wanted the moment to last forever.

"She looks so content. I hate to wake her," Ellie said as she moved to do just that.

Bascom stopped her with a hand to her arm. "Then don't. I'll carry her if you'll gather up the blanket."

"I can't let you do that with your sore ankle."

"You can and will. She can't possibly weigh much more than that basket did when full. My ankle is much better, and it feels good as new after my soak."

"I think that's a stretch, but if you're sure. . ." Ellie studied him a moment. "You'll let me know immediately if it begins to bother you?"

Bascom nodded. He knew he wouldn't admit any such thing. Though his ankle did feel good enough, he doubted it would be an issue. Prissy snuggled against his chest, and his heart hitched. A throbbing ankle would be well worth this special moment in time. He'd lost his chance to enjoy such pleasures with his own son and wife. Back then, time had seemed to stand still and he had everything to look forward to in his future. He worked hard and spent too much time away from his loved ones, knowing they always had tomorrow. But he'd been wrong. Their tomorrows had run out, and all he had left were empty dreams he would never live to see. God had removed him from his grief, and for now this moment felt near enough to what he'd dreamed about before he lost the two most precious people in his life. If he'd learned anything, it was to savor the special moments as they came.

Chapter 6

B ascom carefully worked to carve out the shape of a mermaid. He blew to clear off the dust and wood chips that had settled in the various nooks and crannies. A miniature replica of the carousel piece rested upon a table at his side, the finished painted object a map for this creation. He'd already decided that upon finishing the merry-go-round, he'd put the sample pieces into a miniature carousel for Priscilla to play with. She could remove them for individual play or attach them together and, with the help of a small motor he'd fabricated, watch as the tiny figures mimicked the movements of the amusement that would reside in the building outside her window.

Pleased with the thought, he stood and tucked the tiny mermaid out of sight. Prissy arrived at the most inopportune moments, and he had to work hard to keep her from seeing the miniscule replicas. He'd already given her a few of the standard horses, a move that had kept her attention from the other models that lay around at times. So far she'd proven herself to be trustworthy with their plans, an accomplishment most five-year-olds would find impossible to achieve.

The outer door opened, and Bascom glanced over to see Sheldon walk in from a break.

"Hey, boss, what do you want me to work on next?"

Sheldon's question grated against Bascom's nerves. He'd asked his assistant numerous times to refrain from addressing him in such a manner. They'd worked together for years, and the title had become unnecessary in Bascom's opinion. But they were now to a point where Bascom ignored the annoying word.

"You've finished the seahorses?"

"Yes. The paint should be dry, and if so they're ready to put into place."

Bascom rose from his stool and stiffly walked to where the two pieces rested. They were magnificent. "These are your best work yet, Sheldon, and you've done a lot of good pieces."

The praise came easily. Sheldon had proven himself to be a worthy carver, and Bascom felt sure it wouldn't be long until the apprentice moved on and began to carve a name out on his own. He grinned at his unintentional pun.

"Thank you."

Bascom looked around. "We're down to only a few pieces. I'll let you take your pick." He moved to the table with their sketches.

Sheldon perused them and plucked up a drawing of a simple horse. "I think I'll take this one for now."

"Then I'll let you get to it."

He watched as Sheldon stepped over to walk amongst the finished pieces they'd transported from their warehouse back East. Most of the basic horses were carved and ready to paint, but they'd waited to paint them until deciding on the theme. After matching the number on the drawing with the proper horse, he moved the piece over to the painting area.

Bascom returned his focus to his own piece. Since this part came naturally to him, without needing much thought, he talked to God as he carved. It wasn't long ago that he'd cut God out of his life. But after the darkness of losing his wife and son had subsided some, a pastor friend had spent several weeks pulling Bascom from his grief and bringing him teachings which restored his hope and drive to move on.

Though it hadn't been easy, the memories and pain dimmed, and good memories and peace filled the void his losses left behind. The pastor taught him a lot, and Bascom read the Bible continuously during those final weeks of their time together. By the time his friend needed to move on, Bascom had given his life to the Lord and vowed to live for Him, a promise he'd kept and intended to keep forever.

He knew the hard times were far from over. Memories would sneak up out of nowhere and send Bascom spiraling into a grief that set him back for days. When that happened, Bascom spent more time in the Word so that he would continue to grow and not lose sight of the God that loved him. It had worked up until now, and with this new stage, stepping out of the haven of familiarity where he'd grown up and married and loved and lost, he knew more adventures were in store.

The sky darkened outside their window, and Bascom realized he'd worked nonstop for several hours. He set aside his tools, dusted the mermaid, and nodded with satisfaction at the workmanship. She was developing just as he'd hoped. He froze as he realized the character's face mimicked Ellie's own. Mortified, he wondered what she'd think about being immortalized into the shape of a mermaid for everyone to see and for guests from all around to ride. She was such a quiet woman; she most likely wouldn't take too kindly to his recreating her into an amusement piece. Oh well. He couldn't change it now. Perhaps he could paint the features different than hers, but his will resisted that thought. He wanted his masterpiece to resemble the object of his inspiration. He'd find a way to highlight the mermaid without insulting or offending his employer.

Sheldon had already left the building while Bascom contemplated his deep thoughts. Dinner would be ready soon, and Bascom had taken to visiting with

Ellie on the front porch during the short period prior to the evening meal. He had just enough time to freshen up in his room before meeting her.

&

Ellie leaned closer to her work and caught up a small bit of fabric with the needle before pulling the thread away, closing the gap in the small tear. The pile of mending in the basket beside her had dwindled during the afternoon, and she realized how much Bascom and Sheldon's help at the resort freed her up to get other things accomplished. She and Wanda had stared at this basket for months, and neither one had the time to make a dent in the pile of linens that rested inside. But now she had only one more and would actually reach the bottom of the pile! Wanda, in the meantime, had more time to do what she loved best—to dabble in the kitchen formulating new creations to bring the guests back to their table over and over.

Sheldon supplied the woodshed with cut logs while Bascom found other heavy work to assist with. The barn sparkled. The horses' coats glistened. Delivery wagons from town were unloaded within minutes of their arrival and the goods placed strategically where they were needed. Neither man would accept Ellie's or Wanda's directions to stop and focus on the carousel. According to both men, they could only do so much in a day before needing to do manual labor in order to free their creativity so they could be productive again the next day.

Ellie had her doubts about whether the words were the complete truth, but regardless she appreciated their hard work and assistance. She also secretly enjoyed her evening discussions with Bascom on topics ranging from current politics to what folks were wearing and doing back East. Bascom seemed open to discussing anything she wanted to talk about, and with the constant influx of guests from all over, there wasn't ever a shortage to her list.

She knotted the thread and snipped it loose from the finished piece. Just yesterday they'd talked about his training in carousel carving and design, and only after she'd broached the subject of his wife and son had he shut down. She promised herself she'd be more careful of topics in the future, as she still felt the pain of losing her husband and grandfather, and she didn't want to cause Bascom similar grief.

"Mama, look at my spinning!"

Ellie glanced at her daughter, allowing her eyes to adjust from her detail work, and enjoyed the little girl's glee as she spun in circles on her swing. The contraption was another of Bascom's ideas. He'd hung two pieces of rope high in the branches of a tree and had formed a plank into a seat for Prissy to sit upon. She loved for someone to push her whenever possible, but otherwise contented herself with lying on her belly and flying into the air with a push of her feet or sitting upon the seat and twisting the rope before leaning backward as the swing spun around in circles.

"That's wonderful spinning, Prissy. I'm afraid one of these days you're going to spin yourself free of that tree and spin off into the sky."

Her daughter's giggle bubbled over to her. "That's not poss'ble, Mama."

"Whew, I'm glad to know that. You had me worried." Ellie sent her a teasing smile and reached for the final piece of mending. At this rate, she'd have the burdensome chore finished before Bascom's arrival. What a nice feeling that would be! She looked forward to evenings of watching Priscilla play or visiting with her guests without feeling like the mending loomed over her.

She heard footfalls on the path and smiled with anticipation. Bascom usually approached through the house, but today he must have changed his plans.

"Good evening," a deep voice called out. The voice didn't belong to Bascom. She glanced up in confusion and paused with her needle midair.

"Oh, good evening to you." She quickly stood and smoothed her skirt. Priscilla had stopped swinging and now sat watching the newcomer with curiosity. "I'm sorry. We weren't expecting any new arrivals. But we do have a room available if you're in need of one."

The man waved her words away. "No need to bother yourself. I've just come to introduce myself. I've hired on over at your neighbor's establishment and wanted to offer my services to you, too."

A tingle of suspicion ran along Ellie's back. She didn't know why, but the man unnerved her. Perhaps it was his sudden arrival, much like Sheldon's at times—so silent that she didn't know he'd come until he spoke. It was almost as if he'd wanted to look things over before making his presence known.

"Your services? I'm afraid I don't understand."

"Allow me to explain." Without an invite, he climbed the steps of the porch and settled into the chair next to hers.

Ellie fought the urge to wave him away and turn down his offer before he even voiced it. She already knew she didn't want the burly man working anywhere around her resort, her daughter, or the other ladies that lived with them. She settled back into her chair but hoped Bascom would make his appearance sooner rather than later.

❧

Bascom took the back stairs two at a time and entered the back hall in a rush. Mrs. Case had just exited the doorway that led to the ladies' private quarters, and she squealed as he nearly ran her down.

He caught her by her arms and gently steadied her. "I'm so sorry."

She stared over her glasses at him with knowing eyes and smiled. "Well, somebody certainly seems to be in a hurry."

"Yes'm. I am. I'm usually out front talking with Ellie by now, and I don't want to keep her waiting."

"Ah, it's a good man that abides by a customary routine. I'm sure she'll be delighted at your diligence and is waiting in anticipation, but you might slow down or you'll scare her with your intensity."

"Yes'm." He echoed his previous statement, wishing the woman would move on and allow him to be on his way. He adored Ellie's elderly grandmother, but now wasn't the time to chat. With her anyway. He knew if he didn't hurry, Sheldon would take his place on the porch, if he hadn't already.

"Go on now. And try not to run anyone else down in your hurry to get out front."

He could have sworn he heard her snort with a laugh as she walked away. Bascom felt an unusual flush flow up his neck. His actions were too transparent. But he couldn't deny the pull Ellie had on his heart, nor his attraction to his pretty host. If everyone else saw it, so be it. As long as Sheldon didn't feel the same way about her. And to prevent that, he needed to beat him to the chair. *The* chair. The one that should belong exclusively to him because it rested nearest hers.

He entered his quarters through the kitchen and splashed water over his face before toweling it dry. He grabbed a comb, pulled it through his hair, and splashed his hair with a dash of water when it wouldn't cooperate and lie right. The uncooperative strands cost him another few precious moments. He felt compelled to hurry and wondered if God prodded him in an effort to save Ellie from Sheldon's company. After changing into a clean shirt, he left the room at a safer pace, but still moved forward as he buttoned the white fabric into place. He stepped into the parlor and muttered under his breath as he heard a male voice droning away from the direction of the porch.

Maybe it was just a guest passing time with Ellie until supper. Who could blame him? With her sweet charm and feminine ways, she had a habit of making every guest feel special. But maybe the voice belonged to Sheldon. If so, Bascom would have to resort to alternative means to keep the man working late from now on so that he, Bascom, would be able to claim the coveted chair on the porch first. The jealous thought startled him. He didn't know where it came from, but decided to leave it for further exploration at a later time.

The closer he moved to the door, though, the more his hair stood up on the back of his neck. The voice didn't belong to Sheldon, and from his body's natural reaction, he didn't think it belonged to a pleasant guest, either. Bascom stopped just short of the door, listening to the man on the other side.

"So, if you'll pay me a small fee, I'll make sure no harm comes to you, your guests, or your fine establishment."

Ellie's soft gasp filled the air. "You're telling me someone is purposely damaging the area's resorts? What would be the purpose?"

"Ma'am, just because people like you and I are decent folk doesn't mean there aren't bad folk lurking about, too."

Bascom could hear Priscilla singing slightly off tune near her swing. He prayed she couldn't hear the man's words. Unbidden, images from his life on Coney Island came barging back into his memory; memories of a man in a similar fashion trying to get them to pay for his protection, memories of the madman competitor who made their lives miserable, memories of his wife and son dying in the fire. A fire that had been set as a trap for Bascom, and a fire that his loved ones had walked into instead. The killer had never been caught or punished—a fact that was a constant thorn in Bascom's side and one he tried over and over to set at the foot of the cross.

More often than not, though, he'd hurry back over and pick up the burden once more, figuring it was his to carry for his lack of foresight or action. He determined the same fate would not come to Ellie, Priscilla, Wanda, or Mary. He returned to his room, pulled a small gun from his satchel, and secured it into the back waistband of his trousers, his dinner jacket hiding it from sight.

Upon returning to the door, he heard the man speak again. "You really need to reconsider. My price is fair for the service I provide. You don't want to live in fear on your own premises."

Bascom slammed the door open, and he felt a jolt of satisfaction when the man startled before turning in his seat to face him.

"The lady said she doesn't want your services." Bascom stated the comment in a firm voice, accentuating the last word for emphasis. "She's hired her own help and doesn't have need for outsiders."

Ellie raised her eyebrows at him in confused amusement, but the action didn't hide the concern and fear that had been on her face upon his arrival.

The man stood to his feet and moved closer to Bascom. "Oh really. And you're the one that's going to protect her?" His scorn, evident in the way he talked and looked Bascom over, turned Bascom's stomach. A man like him shouldn't be within a mile of Ellie or her resort. Bascom didn't have time to analyze his own defensive attitude. Ellie and her family had become his friends and no matter what, she deserved his loyalty and protection.

"Yes, I am. And based on that, I'll have to ask you to leave the premises."

The man stepped closer still. "Who's gonna make me?"

Bascom reached behind him, pulled his gun free, and shoved it against the burly man's chest. "I am."

Ellie stood and backed away from the two men.

The man paled and stepped backward, his hands raised in surrender. "No need to go over the edge, mister. I'll take my leave. But mark my words. By refusing my offer of protection, you've opened yourself up to all kinds of danger."

Bascom kept the gun leveled at the man's chest. "That sounds like a threat."

"Take it as you want." The sinister man stomped down the stairs and stalked away up the path toward their nearest neighbor's place. "Bad things are happening to folks up and down the shores of the lake."

Most definitely, Bascom would treat it as a threat. First thing the following morning he'd be in town, discussing it with the sheriff.

"Where on earth did you get that awful weapon?"

Ellie's distraught question broke into his thoughts.

"I always carry a weapon when I travel. It wouldn't be safe to travel any other way."

"Well, of course, but even with your full caravan of men? Surely their presence alone would ward off any thieves?"

Bascom sighed. "I wish you were right, but you aren't. That man there should be proof that you can't trust anyone, anywhere."

"But what if Prissy would have found it? She could have been hurt. We have guests to consider, also." Though she lowered her voice to a whisper, her pitch rose with anger.

"Ellie, calm down." Bascom took her by the arm and led her to her chair. She shook, whether from anger at him or from fear concerning the man who had just left, he didn't know. "I keep it in my satchel on a high shelf that Prissy can't reach. I always keep my door locked when I'm not in there. Priscilla is safe. Remember, I'm a father. . . I *was* a father. I know about safety and children."

"All the same, I'd feel better if you kept it off the premises. Could you at least keep it out at the pavilion?"

Amusement curled his lip. "Pavilion?"

Though she fought a smile, it peeked through. "Yes, pavilion. We can't very well keep calling the carousel's roost 'that outbuilding,' now can we?"

"I suppose we can't." Bascom opened the gun's chamber and spilled the bullets into his hand. "And I'll keep this out there if you prefer, but I strongly caution you to reconsider. If that man is any indication, we're in for some rough times ahead. It would be best if the gun resided within easy reach if that's the case. Men like that strike in the dark of night, not during the day when I'd have easy access to the weapon in the *pavilion*."

Ellie rolled her eyes at his use of the word. "Very well. Keep the gun in the house, but please use every precaution to keep it away from Prissy."

Bascom nodded and glanced at the little girl. Having missed the altercation, she innocently dug in the dirt with a stick while hanging from the swing by her stomach. Her sweet song reached his ears. As he watched, she glanced up at him and grinned. He waved, and she waved back. He'd do anything in his power to keep the little girl—and her loved ones—safe.

Chapter 7

Another week passed with no return visit from the offensive neighbor. Each day without vandalism or a threat brought Ellie a measure of peace. Though she'd not had problems in the past, the strange man's threatening behavior and words concerned her. The previous night Bascom had again waved off her fears. He assured her he and Sheldon would be on the lookout for anything out of the ordinary and that the women shouldn't concern themselves with things that couldn't be changed.

"Bascom, I've thought about it a lot since our last discussion and I still can't come to terms with why the man would be so forceful about his protection." No matter how hard Ellie tried, she couldn't let the topic drop.

With a sigh, Bascom scooted his chair back from the dinner table. "I didn't want to bring this up, but I guess it can't be avoided. When we worked on Coney Island, there were a lot of 'wars' between competing resorts and restaurants. The town became corrupt, and men of ill repute took over. They had a lot of pull with the governing men and began to bribe owners of various establishments with requests of payment in return for their protection." He hesitated and looked at Ellie, as if waiting for her to encourage or discourage him from going on with his explanation.

Ellie nodded and motioned for him to continue.

"Unfortunately, the men demanding the fees for protection were actually the ones the owners needed to fear most. Most likely, that man is one of them. He's capitalizing on the way things were back East. If an owner refused to pay, the men would damage the business in one way or another."

"Such as?" Ellie knew her face reflected her feelings of disgust at the thought. Instead of neighbors helping neighbors, as she was accustomed to here on the lake, those very bonds would be stretched to the limit in such a scenario. She found it very sad to think about.

"Such as fires were set. Buildings burned down. Rumors were spread about good, decent people to drive away their legitimate guests. Anything and everything that could be used to ruin the reputation would be put into play."

"That's horrible. Despicable! Why?" Ellie felt sick to her stomach.

"Nothing more than greed. When a person desires what he cannot have and he doesn't have a solid foundation of training to carry him through the tough

161

times, he'll do terrible things that previously wouldn't have been considered."

"And this solid foundation. . .what does that entail? Admittance to the right schools? An education? A proper upbringing in the right family? What sets a person on that course?"

"A lack of faith, improper upbringing with no moral training—there are lots of reasons a person will turn to that lifestyle, but riches and education aren't at the top of the list. I'm sure they'd contribute. If a person is poor enough or resentful of others that might have better educational training, I'm sure he can find a reason to justify his poor behavior. But by solid foundation, I'm referring to spiritual training, faith in Jesus, and good morals."

"I see." Ellie contemplated the way she brought up Priscilla. The little girl acted like an angel, very rarely throwing a fit over anything, but did she miss out by not having the spiritual training Bascom referred to? Would her daughter's lack of spiritual training cause her to become like the vandals he referred to back East? Ellie's grandparents had always read the Bible as part of their daily routine, but Ellie's parents hadn't done the same. Though Ellie was familiar with her grandparents' faith, and she felt their beliefs were a nice guideline as a model of how to live one's life, Ellie hadn't been brought up that way before coming to live with her extended family as a young adult. At first she'd made an effort to understand and do as they did, but the daily practice of their routine had never completely taken with her; in time she'd let herself drift away. "Do you think I'm doing Priscilla a disservice by not reading the Bible to her on a regular basis?"

Bascom's expression gentled, and he laid his hand upon hers. "I think it's always a good habit to start for everyone, no matter what the reader's age."

He meant her, she could tell. She wondered if he thought her a bad person. Here she'd spent hours and hours weaving stories of whimsy to her daughter, but she'd sorely neglected her daughter's spiritual training.

"The habit of reading is important, but building a relationship with Jesus, as the Bible instructs, is what matters most."

Before Ellie could voice another thought, shouts sounded from outside. Bascom flew to his feet and headed out the door, and Ellie followed close at his heels. Mary and Prissy stood near the door to the private family quarters, while Wanda hurried into the hall from the kitchen.

"What's all the commotion I hear?" Wanda asked, her hands still coated in flour from supper preparations.

"I'm not sure," Ellie replied, motioning to the door that had slammed shut behind Bascom. "We heard shouting."

They moved forward to the door and peered out. Nothing seemed amiss. Ellie motioned for her grandmother to stay behind with Priscilla, and she and Wanda stepped onto the porch. From there they could see billowing puffs of smoke rising from the far corner of the pavilion.

"The pavilion's on fire!" Ellie yelled, catching up her long gray skirt in her hands as she ran for the pump. She grabbed a bucket and began to fill it while Wanda scurried around, gathering up more.

The air crackled and Ellie could hear the fire popping as it ate at the dry wood of the older building. She thought of all Bascom's hard work sitting inside, the wood pieces representing her grandfather's fortune, and pumped for all she was worth.

Scorched, wood-scented air filled Ellie's nose, and she sent up a hollow prayer for help. The words felt empty and seemed to fall on empty ears, too. She had no idea if God heard the prayers of those who hadn't talked to Him for such a long time. But surely one had to start somewhere and He understood that.

They pumped hard and filled each bucket as Bascom and Sheldon ran back and forth to douse the flames. The fire had been caught early enough that they were able to put it out before it caused substantial damage.

Bascom rounded the corner a final time, his face smeared with soot and sweat, and motioned for them to stop filling buckets. "I think we caught it in time. I'll watch it this afternoon and tonight to make sure it doesn't restart, but I think we got it all out."

Gram and Priscilla joined them as they surveyed the aftermath.

Prissy seemed fascinated with the whole process, which concerned Ellie and made her more determined to see to the child's spiritual training. They'd continue their Land of Whimsy tales, but they'd study the Bible each evening first. Ellie didn't have a clue where or how to start, but she knew her grandmother would be happy to guide them.

❧

Ellie watched from her chair on the back porch as Bascom scrubbed the soot from his face by the pump. His clothes were ruined, but she'd insisted he change so Wanda could try to salvage them by soaking the scorched odor from the fabric. He walked over to her, and she noticed his face glowed a bright red. She hurried to her feet. "You're burned."

"No. I'm only flushed from the heat. I'll be fine as soon as I rest a bit." He settled into the chair beside hers. "I need to keep an eye on the pavilion, but I'll be able to see any smoke that starts up from here."

"I'll be right back." Ellie slipped into the kitchen and poured lemonade into a mug. The beverage was cool since Wanda had just made it up fresh from the pump's cool water. She stepped back outside and handed it to him. "Drink this. I'll only be a minute."

Ellie slipped inside again, this time to get the soothing liniment they used for burns. She returned, and Bascom eyed the ointment warily. "You're not slathering that on my face."

"Oh yes I am, and you're going to let me." If there was one thing Ellie could handle, it was a cantankerous man who didn't want to admit he needed nursing. Between her grandfather and her husband, she'd dealt with her share of stubborn males.

Bascom glared but didn't say anything more. She dipped her finger into the tin and rubbed her hands together to equally disburse the cream. "Look up at me."

"I'm gonna stink so bad no one will want me at the table tonight." Though he growled the words, he did as he was told.

"Quit complaining. There isn't a scent to this at all. If anything, your face will shine a bit, but after everyone hears about what a hero you are, no one will give your face another thought."

"No one needs to know about the fire or about my putting it out with Sheldon, ya hear?" Bascom, agitated, jumped to his feet. "I don't want to hear another word about it."

Ellie stood and watched in shock as he jumped from the porch, stalked to the pavilion, and disappeared around the far corner.

"Well, he certainly has a bee in his bonnet."

Sheldon's voice startled Ellie again. How was it he always seemed to creep up on her when she least expected it? Perhaps because she always so heavily focused on Bascom when he was around—or a lot of times even when he wasn't—that her thoughts weren't directed toward what went on in proximity to her. She told herself to concentrate more on the activity around her, especially now that they'd been vandalized. Or had they? Maybe the fire had started out of pure coincidence or chance.

"Sheldon, what—or who—do you think started that fire?"

"Coulda been most anything, I suppose." He climbed the steps and leaned against the rail, keeping his distance this time.

"Do you think it's possible it started on its own? Just a random spark or something? Did either of you leave a lantern burning out there when you left for lunch?"

Sheldon looked at her with amused eyes. "In broad daylight? We don't often leave a lantern burning throughout the day. There's plenty of natural lighting in the pavilion for us to work without wasting fuel and effort."

"Oh. You have a good point." Ellie frowned and stared at the building.

She didn't have the answers, and neither did the men. Staring wouldn't bring anything further to mind. She turned her attention back to Sheldon, who was remarkably untouched by the event. His clothes were none the worse for wear, and he didn't look the least bit flushed or burned. But in his defense, he'd mostly been the one to run back and forth for buckets, so he hadn't been as close to the heat or scorch of the fire.

She hated to ask her next question, but it needed to be voiced. "Do you think the act could have been the vandals the man from last week mentioned?"

Sheldon nibbled on a piece of grass he'd snagged somewhere on his walk. "I suppose anything is possible. Except. . ."

"What?" She stared hard at him. "Don't hold back any information from me. If you know something, I need to be told."

He glanced at the pavilion, consternation on his face. "I know, but this is hard."

She watched as he contemplated her request without answering. She reiterated her request. "I really need to know everything that's going on or that might be going on. Even if you don't think it's significant, I need to know."

Several emotions passed across his face as he carefully chose his words. "It's not that it isn't significant, but I owe a loyalty to Bascom. He's trained me well, and he's been good to me. I don't like to gossip about him."

"Bascom? What does he have to do with this? He worked hard to save the building and everything in it." Ellie's confusion pulled her mouth into a frown. She corrected it, not wanting Sheldon to know where her emotions lay.

"He might have nothing to do with the fire, and he might have everything to do with it."

Ellie's patience wore thin. "Out with it, Sheldon. What are you trying to say? Indirectly, you work for me, too. You owe me a certain loyalty as long as you're here. I have a small daughter. If you have any concern about a safety issue, I need to know it now."

Sheldon raised his eyes and peered into hers with a coolness that caused a shiver to run up her back. Though his hat sat low on his forehead, his eyes looked like black orbs in the added shade of the porch. "I'm concerned because a similar fire broke out at the pavilion back East, just before the bigger fire that killed Bascom's wife and child."

"So someone could be harassing him. Maybe someone set him up and is doing it again?"

"Maybe." Sheldon tossed the weed to the ground. "But why? The authorities scrutinized him while we were back East. They found no enemies, other than those jealous of his success. There were quite a few of them, but they were all cleared. Though competitive, they were all upstanding businessmen."

"What about the others, the organized crime I've heard about? Surely they could have followed Bascom here. You arrived with a caravan! You weren't exactly subtle. And how well did you know all the men who helped drive the pieces out here anyway?" Ellie knew she desperately grasped for straws, but she had to. She couldn't wrap her mind around the thought of the gentle man that had befriended her and the others around them as a malicious criminal—or murderer.

Especially a murderer of his own family.

"There were those in organized crime, but their goal was to chase the competition out. What would they have to gain by following us way out here? The area isn't that developed."

"Well, the area is apparently developed enough if I have a man coming to my doorstep with an offer of protection that bordered on extortion. He also threatened me. Bascom wasn't that man."

Sheldon nodded as he thought about her words. "True."

"Is this a coincidence?" She pinned him with her glare. "Surely not."

"I don't have the answers you're looking for, Ellie. I wish I did. What I can do is keep my eyes open and try to see that nothing else happens." He pushed away from the rail and prepared to leave. "If you'd like, I can discreetly order a copy of the newspaper that told of the other fire and Bascom's interrogation. Maybe something in there will help you decide whether or not to trust the man you hired."

Ellie hated herself for it, but she nodded her agreement. She doubted the paper would arrive in time to do them any good, but it was worth a try. The man before her spoke of Bascom as a good boss, yet in a way Sheldon seemed very eager to have her distrust his employer. She wanted to trust Bascom, but now she didn't know if she could. Did Sheldon have her best interests in mind? Or did he have ulterior motives for wanting her to dislike Bascom? Perhaps it was something as simple as rivalry for her interest. There weren't many available females out this way, and both men seemed lonely and in want of her attention.

Chapter 8

Bascom half listened to Priscilla's chatter as he studied Ellie's mannerisms. Every movement of her body screamed discomfort, but she'd assured him through a strained smile that everything was fine. Still, she'd definitely been distant the past few days.

"Mr. Anthony, are you listening to me?" Prissy danced beside them as they walked. "I'm telling you something very important, and you're staring and staring at my mama."

Bascom felt his face flame as Ellie turned to scrutinize him with a stare.

"It isn't polite to stare, you know. My grammy tells me that all the time. I mostly only stare at people at the dinner table, but only if they're funny looking." Priscilla tilted her head and stared at her mother. "Do you think my mama is funny looking?"

"Prissy!" Ellie admonished. "That isn't something you ask a person."

The child's face crinkled into a look of genuine confusion, and Bascom had to bite back his smile. "I don't find your mother funny looking at all. As a matter of fact, I find her to be quite beautiful, just like you."

"You do?" Now a sly smile replaced her frown. "You could marry us. We need a husband around here."

Ellie gasped audibly. "Priscilla Anne Weathers! You stop that kind of talk this instant. You know better."

"But it's true! The other husband that lived here died when I was too little to remember him, and now I don't have a daddy. Bascom's a nice man."

"Young lady, if you don't hush right now, we'll turn around this moment and return to the house, where you'll spend your afternoon in your room."

"You mean *our* room. Miss Wanda took your room. Mary Ellen Marchison told me that if you married Mr. Anthony, you could sleep back in your room with him and I could have my room back." Apparently mistaking her mother's speechless mortification for hurt feelings, she hurried on. "I like sharing a room with you. You're very warm to snuggle with. But now Mary Ellen and I can't play in there because all your things crowd my things. And Mr. Anthony would probably like to snuggle with you, too, so you wouldn't be lonely."

Bascom grinned. He didn't realize a person's face could turn so many shades of mottled purple and red at one time. Ellie refused to acknowledge Bascom's amused perusal.

Her voice grated out from between her clenched teeth. "Young lady, turn around and march your little body back to the house at once."

Still completely unaware of her mother's chagrin, Priscilla stared at her a moment. "If we return home, we won't get a chance to look for the North Shore Monster."

Indecision battled across Ellie's features. "Then that's a decision you'll have to make. By continuing your stream of completely unacceptable questions to Mr. Anthony, you'll make the choice to finish our walk right now."

Bascom decided to rescue them both. He could see their similarities didn't end with their looks. Stubbornness seemed to run a close second, and at this point both ladies had dug their heels into the ground and the line was drawn. He understood Ellie's need to corral her young daughter and discipline her for disrespect, but if that were to happen, their walk would end prematurely, and Bascom wasn't ready for it to be over. He needed to find out what caused the original distress in Ellie's countenance.

"What's the North Shore Monster?" He feigned fear, looking all around them.

Prissy giggled, and the moment of tension passed. "It won't hurt you. It lives in the water."

Bascom glanced at the lake. "It lives in the water where I swim?"

"Yes."

"Then perhaps I'll continue to walk when I feel a need to stretch my muscles. Our swim excursions will have to end."

The young girl looked horrified.

"Perhaps you should tell me about him. Maybe I'll change my mind."

"Like my mama just did when I talked about the. . ."

"Prissy!" Ellie warned with a hiss.

"Sorry. Well, he's called the North Shore Monster and—"

"Wait a minute."

Prissy scowled at Bascom's interruption. "What?"

"This is the south shore."

She glanced up at her mother and registered Ellie's nod before she returned her gaze to him. "Right."

"Shouldn't we be looking for the South Shore Monster, then?"

Rolling her eyes, Prissy let out a breath of exasperation. "No. There isn't a South Shore Monster. It's only the North Shore Monster."

"Hmm." Bascom offered Prissy his elbow, which she delightedly clasped with her small hand, which allowed Ellie to tread alongside and gather her frazzled nerves. "Tell me more."

"He's large, with the body of a croc'dile and a head like a horse. Some men saw him when he chased them, and they had to run away and hide until morning!"

"Indeed?" Bascom surveyed the water once more before easing her in the direction away from shore. "Did this happen today?"

Priscilla laughed the deep belly laugh he loved to hear and in return pushed him back toward shore. "No. It happened weeks and weeks ago." She released her hold on his arm and ran ahead.

Ellie quietly snickered.

Bascom glanced at her with raised eyebrows.

"It was sighted mid-1877," she whispered, amusement written all over her face. "So more like years and years ago. Eighteen to be exact."

"I see." He knew his own eyes mirrored the humor sparkling in hers. Relieved that she regrouped so quickly, he also noticed she'd lost the earlier distance she'd put between them. "Has this monster been sighted since?"

She shook her head no. "Rumor has it the creature they saw is nothing more than a buffalo."

"Mr. Bascom Anthony!" Prissy bellowed. "C'mere!"

She crooked her finger his way. He walked over to her and bent close. "Some one else saw it, but they said it looked like a dolphin out by that island." She pointed. He saw a landmass opposite them across the lake.

"So, much closer in our direction." He acknowledged her comment with raised eyebrows.

Ellie caught up to them. "Yes, but that sighting was over thirty years ago. So if that's the case, the North Shore Monster, if they were one and the same, moved north from here, not the other way around."

"Oh, Mama," Priscilla pouted. "If he moved north from here...can't he move back to the south? Doesn't the north water touch the south water, too?"

"I suppose it's all one and the same." Ellie lifted her petite shoulder and shrugged in defeat.

"She has a good mind." Bascom watched the little girl run ahead again.

"That she does." She matched her steps to his as they followed along after the lively child. "She must get that from our original husband."

He glanced over, worried that she'd go into her dour mood again, but only saw laughter in her expression.

"I'm sorry if she embarrassed you or put you in an awkward position. I honestly don't know where she gets such ideas. Sometimes she wears me out with her constant questions and fast-thinking responses."

They walked in silence for a few minutes.

"And I suppose she might even be right. If we had a husband around as she says, a lot of things would be easier. We wouldn't be such an easy target for the arsonist or the man that wants me to pay him off for protection. We'd have our own."

Her voice drifted off, and he didn't know what to say.

She hugged her arms around her midsection, an action both defensive and lonely. He wished he could give her the security she needed. Perhaps this was why she'd been so distant and quiet earlier.

He chuckled. "I'm not sure if you're proposing to me or just speaking your thoughts aloud."

She whipped her head his way, her hands flying up to cup her cheeks, this time blushing to her ears. "Oh goodness, no! Maybe Priscilla does get a touch of her precociousness from me. I didn't mean anything. . . I. . ."

He waved her words away. "I'm only kidding. I wanted to see a smile reappear on your face. You've looked much too serious for most of this walk. If my company upsets you so or causes you concern, I can walk the other direction next time."

Her eyes widened before she looked away, a sure sign of guilt. Surely she didn't mistrust him! He had no idea why she'd feel that way. He considered her reaction. More than likely he'd only hit close to the truth with his words. She did have concerns, but as his hostess, she didn't feel she could burden him with them. The man's visit to coerce money for protection must have shaken her up more than she let on. Then, with the fire on top of his visit, she had reason to worry.

Bascom couldn't do a lot, but he could definitely patrol the resort's grounds during the night. Wanda had mentioned in passing that the early season had been slow to start, and he was sure Ellie didn't have the budget to hire security. Perhaps he and Sheldon could take turns standing watch. He dismissed that idea as soon as he had it. For some reason, he felt the need that he alone should watch out for and defend the four females and their guests. He'd begin his patrols that very night.

᪣

Ellie finished the evening's Bible reading and Whimsy tale and lifted the sleepy Priscilla into her arms. Her grandmother had nodded off over her knitting sometime during the Bible story. She'd tuck her daughter in and then return to assist the elderly woman to her bed.

Prissy didn't budge as Ellie lifted the comforter over her sleeping form. The moonlight shone in through the open window, and a cool breeze blew into the room. Ellie considered closing the window, but if she did, the room would become too hot. She shook off her apprehensions and hurried out the bedroom door.

"Gram," she said after returning to the parlor. She gently shook the older woman's arm. "It's time for bed. Let me help you to your room."

Her grandmother abruptly roused from her slumber. "Nonsense, Ellie Lyn. I won't have you tucking me in like a little child. I'm perfectly capable of getting myself to my chamber."

"Yes, ma'am." Ellie bit back her grin and helped her grandmother to her feet. She carefully put the knitting needles and yarn into the basket beside the rocker as her grandmother shuffled away.

Ellie cringed as the older woman reached for the wall, using it to aid her balance and offer support. Support that Ellie was more than happy to give. Stubbornness apparently ran through more than two generations in the family.

"Everyone tucked away for the night?" Wanda entered the parlor from the kitchen. "I finished the dishes from dinner and prepared for tomorrow's morning meal. We should have a few more guests than usual. Things are picking up again."

"They are. I've noticed. Besides our regulars, the supply wagon has dropped off letters of request from new customers, too." Ellie wrapped her arms around herself and stood at the window, peering out into the dark. The moon grew bigger every night but didn't cast much light on the land between the house and lake. The wind picked up, and a gust blew in and knocked over several pictures that had rested on the small round table in front of the window.

Wanda and Ellie both reached for and stabilized them before they could fall to the floor.

"I'd best close this window before the furniture starts to move!" Ellie joked. The winds that blew over the water could be extreme at times, especially during storms.

"You do that. I'm going to settle here and try to catch up on my reading. That is"—she peeked over the top of her glasses—"unless you have something more for me to do?"

"No, there's nothing at all. You rest here. I'm going to go onto the porch and sit outside the door until the wind chills me or blows me back inside."

"I don't blame you. It's a beautiful night right now. Enjoy it while you can. Storm'll be here before you know it."

Ellie wandered outside, knowing she was safe with Wanda's presence on the other side of the wall. She sat in her favorite chair and looked out over the water. The sky had darkened where the storm clouds gathered. It would be a cozy night. Her thoughts, as usual, drifted to Bascom, and she wondered if he'd turned in early.

As soon as she had the thought, she saw a dark figure slip around the far side of the house. All the guests had retired for the night and were safely ensconced in their rooms. She didn't want to wake any of them, but the intruder had headed in the direction of the pavilion. If she took time to alert Bascom, she'd lose sight of the person. If she didn't follow him now, it might be too late. She knew it wasn't the smartest thing to do, but it would only take a scream to wake everyone at the resort. Without a further thought for her safety, she slipped from the porch and followed the dim figure around the building.

She walked as quietly as possible and stepped into the darkness at the side of the house. A strong hand grabbed her arm and pulled her close against the intruder's chest. As she started to scream, a hand clamped across her mouth. The inappropriate thought that her captor smelled nice crossed her mind. And she had to admit, if she was going to meet her demise, she'd rather it be the most pleasant experience it could be. She'd rather her dying breaths not be filled with a strange man's bad body odor or sweat.

"Ellie Lyn, what are you doing out here at night like this? What if someone else had grabbed you instead of me?"

"Bascom?" His use of her grandmother's personal endearment for her didn't slip past her notice. "I could ask you the same thing. Why are you skulking about my resort in the dead of night? You didn't even come up to the porch to chat with me."

She realized he still held her close in his embrace. His rapid heartbeat sounded against her ear, and she wanted to hold tight and absorb his security and strength. She didn't feel as if she were in any kind of danger.

"I wasn't skulking. I was patrolling."

"Then why not stand out where you can be seen? Wouldn't that make more sense? Once trespassers knew you were here, they'd surely leave."

"Not if they're the ones I dealt with back home."

His words caused a shiver of dread to pass through her, and she pulled away slightly, trying to see his face in the murky light from the cloud-encased moon. "You think they followed you? But why?"

"I don't know for sure. But the fire the other day felt like a warning." He gently set her away from him. "A warning I intend to heed."

She felt adrift now that she was out of his arms. She hadn't been held by another man since Wilson died, and she'd forgotten how wonderfully reassuring a man's strong embrace could feel. But it was improper for them to be out here, unchaperoned in the dark while in each other's arms.

He led her onto the porch and sat her in a chair. The sound of Wanda just inside the door, where she conversed with Sheldon, carried out to them. Bascom settled close beside her, his warm breath caressing her cheek.

"Ellie, where do you stand spiritually?"

Not the words Ellie had expected to hear from him. What she'd hoped he'd say, she didn't know, but words of endearment that followed her line of thought a few moments earlier would have been nice, or probably more practically, words of explanation on why he'd been patrolling her area without talking to her about it.

"I'm concerned about you. I'd leave, but I'm not sure whatever's been put into action would stop with that. I want you to be safe. I don't want to bring you trouble, but if history—my history—is going to repeat itself, I want to know you've made things right with God."

"Bascom, you're scaring me. Maybe we should involve the sheriff."

"And tell him what, that we think all this stuff we can't prove? I've been through this before. I lost my wife and son in a fire, and it tore me up inside. Sometimes I don't want my ankle to heal because as long as it gives me pain, I remember. I wish I could go back and take the pain for them. But I can't. Instead I found Someone who can take my pain away, and only after I turned my life over to Christ did I finally get the courage to move on. I want you to find that same strength and peace."

Ellie stared at him. He had tears in his eyes, and his voice broke as he talked about the details surrounding the loss of his wife and son. She didn't see how someone who cared so much could ever hurt someone he loved. She could sense that Bascom's faith was real. And she knew she wanted to find the same peace and strength for herself. Bascom was right. It was time to set things right with God.

"I need you to help me."

"It's simple, not like some of the traveling preachers make it sound. The Bible is very clear that all we have to do is realize and accept the fact we can't make it through this life and into heaven unless we allow Jesus to have full control of our lives. Ellie, without faith in the fact Jesus is the only way to God, we'll just not make it. I know some folks believe we can work our way there, but the only way is to accept God's gift—His Son!"

Ellie smiled. "I believe and accept. Will you pray with me? I'm not sure what to say."

Relief filled Bascom's eyes as he returned her smile and shifted closer. "I will. Let's pray together right now."

Chapter 9

"What is it now?" Ellie didn't want to know, but she had to ask. Bascom and Sheldon stood near the water pump, hats in hands, deep in conversation. During the several days that had passed since Bascom started his nightly patrols, the vandalism had stepped up, and it seemed various events now occurred or were noticed on a regular basis.

Bascom looked at her with somber eyes. "Which incident do you want to hear about first?"

Ellie raised a hand and held it against her rapidly beating heart. "There's more than one today? Why doesn't someone catch the person responsible? I mean. . .I know you've both worked hard to cover the grounds at night. But how is this person getting past you?"

"We have been working hard, but whoever is doing this continues to outwit us." Sheldon's exasperation carried through in his words. "It seems wherever we patrol, the vandals hit us from another angle."

"I know it's not your fault," Ellie hurried to soothe. "The night patrols are over and beyond your carousel duties. I hope you know how much I appreciate you both. I'm just wondering. . ."

"Go ahead," Bascom prompted. "You're wondering. . .what?"

"Maybe it's time I go ahead and hire a security team. No one's going to stay here if we're continually under attack."

"Can you afford it?"

"I'm not sure that's the proper question. Can I afford not to? Word gets around, and while I know we've heard rumblings of similar activities happening at other resorts around the lake, the majority seem to be—or at least feel like—they are happening to us here. I can't afford to lose any of the customers that are expected to arrive for the season. I need to assure them their stay will be pleasant and they will feel safe." She sent Bascom an imploring look as tears of frustration pushed against the corners of her eyes. "And right now, even I don't feel safe."

"None of the attacks have been against a person." Bascom, apparently determined to make her feel better, had hit her main concern on the head.

"Yet. But what if they soon are? I don't feel safe outside at night. How can I expect to let my guests walk the shores of the lake by moonlight? If they were to stumble upon the vandal committing a crime, who knows how either party might react? I sure can't tell them in advance to take caution and not to approach a villain. That would send people running right out the door."

Bascom nodded but didn't say anything. Instead he stared off into the distance for a long moment. "I think you're jumping the gun, but I understand what you're saying."

Ellie uncharacteristically found herself taking in his appearance more than his words. He always looked tidy in the morning, and even when ruffled later in the day with wood shavings clinging to his clothes, he took care to present himself neatly. Today he wore a blue woven shirt that buttoned down the front. His light wool pants would surely snag on the wood chips as he carved. His clothes always carried the fresh aroma of outdoors along with the nose-tingling scent of newly cut wood. His hair shone gold in the early morning light, and when the sun caught his eyes, the brilliant blue sparkled with an inner light. Even now, when stressed, he also wore a sense of security and peace.

She thought about their late-night chat earlier in the week and his encouragement that she put her focus on living her life as a follower of Jesus. The conversation had kept her awake late during the following nights, but while she knew he spoke from experience, she didn't see how putting her faith in something she couldn't see would help her while dealing with a destructive force she couldn't see. Right now her focus needed to be on finding the person or persons responsible for the attacks on her resort, not on musings of things unseen in the spiritual realm.

"Ellie?" Bascom's question broke through her thoughts.

Just like her focus should be on Bascom's words right now and listening to his idea on how to better protect their establishment. "I'm sorry; I got lost in my thoughts for a moment."

"I'm saying I don't think we need to rush into a decision like hiring a team. Let's take a bit more time and see what happens. Maybe the attacks will slow as the season begins in earnest. If it's a competitor, surely the busyness of life will stop further meddling with us."

Us. He said the word as if he had a vested interest in her place. While on the one hand, she appreciated having a strong man around to give her support in running the resort; on the other hand, she resented having him move into her territory when she'd been doing fine on her own before his arrival.

And though she'd been feeling more at peace about Bascom's presence and her ability to trust him, she again felt the fleeting undercurrent of distrust at his words. Did he discourage her from hiring more protection because he honestly felt up to the task on his own? Or did he discourage her because he didn't want extra interference while trying to carry out the task of ruining her?

But what reason would he have to ruin her? He'd been a stranger before her grandfather hired him to build their carousel. *The carousel. . .* He'd said it was his best yet. Could it be that he became so attached to his creations that even though working for hire, he couldn't bear to leave his work behind in the hands of others?

"How many carousels have you built and sold?" Her question burst forth without thought of the consequences or of how odd she would sound asking such an inane thing in the midst of a crisis.

Bascom let out a small laugh while looking perplexed. "Carousels? Well, I suppose around a dozen or so. Why do you ask?"

"Just wondering." She felt silly. If there were that many then he surely didn't grow abnormally attached to his work. Unless. . .another disturbing thought occurred to her. "Have there been other—incidents—with any of the other attractions? If so, how many?"

A cloud passed over his eyes. Whether from her question or her distrust she didn't know. And at this point, she didn't care. She just wanted answers.

"Well, other than the one that took the lives of my family"—he hesitated and peered into her eyes—"none."

"I see."

"Do you?" His eyes narrowed and a look of hurt passed through them. "Why would you ask?"

"I'm just trying to understand what's going on. The attacks started after your arrival. . ." Her words tapered off as she realized how awful and accusing she sounded. "I'm sorry. I didn't mean. . . I just. . ."

He waved her away, and her heart dropped. She hadn't meant to hurt him. He'd done nothing but help her, and she'd insulted him.

"Bascom, please. Listen. I'm just wondering, could someone be following you, perhaps someone trying to pursue a vendetta? We've talked about this. Do you think your past is connected with the present vandalism?"

"I've thought long and hard, and there isn't anyone that I know of. But there was the fire that killed my family. That wasn't an accident, so yes, I guess someone could possibly be following me." He stared at her a long moment, disappointment evident in his censuring gaze. He then looked past the resort and toward the water. "I think it's best if I pack up and leave. Sheldon's capable of putting the finishing touches on the carousel."

"No, Bascom. I don't want you to leave. If this is a vendetta against you or a tactic of the competition, your departure isn't going to make it all better. If anything, it will make things worse. I won't have. . ."

She flushed as she realized what she'd almost blurted out. *I won't have your steadfast support and strength beside me.*

"You won't have what?" He sounded tense, ready to move on. Or could he possibly be worried that she'd figured out his plan?

A low growl of frustration escaped her. "I won't have your support, and I've really grown to rely on your presence. I mean, I know you have to leave soon, and we'll be on our own at that time, but—I want you to finish what you started. I want you to be here when the carousel is completed."

"As you wish."

His agreement to stay could have been a bit more heartfelt instead of voiced with frustration, but he had a reason to be upset. She'd attacked his character, insulted him, and disappointed him all in a few choice sentences. She'd read some verses in the Bible somewhere during the last few days about guarding the words that came from your mouth because of their power to hurt. This must be what that teaching referred to. She'd just have to work extra hard to make things up to him and to right her wrong.

"I'm sorry if I offended you. It wasn't my intent. I know we're all testy right now, and you, especially, must be very tired." That didn't come out right, either. Now it sounded as if she blamed him for their stilted conversation, based on his lack of sleep.

This time his eyes twinkled as he took in her dismay. "Apology accepted. Would you like to see the damage now? Or would you prefer we just deal with it?" He motioned between himself and Sheldon, who had become silent during their exchange.

"I'd like to know, please." She stepped closer, surveying the pump to the well. The handle lay on the ground, the connector smashed beyond use. "Oh. We can't fix this, can we? It won't fit back on, and even if it did, there's no way to secure it." Without the pump handle, they couldn't access their water. Ellie felt overwhelmed with despair. Why were these things happening to her? She fought the tears that again threatened to overfill her eyes.

"Aw, c'mon, Mrs. Weathers," Sheldon reached over and awkwardly patted her upper arm. "We'll get this thing going again. It won't be a problem for us at all."

Bascom nodded. "We have everything we need in the pavilion. This will be a breeze. The other thing we need to show you is a bit more problematic."

He led her to the side of the pavilion, the main side her guests would see, and she saw the huge splatter of white paint that ran down the wall to the ground. "Someone had to use a full bucket to do this. Why?" Her voice was a frustrated squeak as she studied the mess. Since it had already dried, washing it off wasn't an option.

"We tried to clean it, but the hardest scrubbing didn't do a thing. It's there for good." Bascom watched her reaction.

She pulled herself together. She wouldn't fall apart in front of these men. "Well then, that does leave us in a predicament, doesn't it?" She lifted her long blue skirt by grabbing two handfuls of material and strode closer to study the wall. After a moment of thought, she again lifted the heavy layers of material and paced back the other way, stopping some fifteen feet away from the offensive wall. "I have a solution."

"What's that?" Bascom voiced the question, though both men looked at her with amusement.

"We'll paint the entire wall white." Her enthusiasm grew as she spoke. "This is actually a blessing in disguise. Look at the building with fresh eyes. It's worn and the wood is tired. A fresh coat of white paint is just the ticket to brighten the place up and make it appear more festive."

Sheldon whistled through his teeth as Bascom laughed. He walked over and grasped Ellie by the waist, swinging her in a circle. "Why, I do believe that's just what this old building needs. You're right."

He set her down, and for a moment she thought he planned to kiss her. Regardless of Sheldon or anyone else that might be watching, she hoped he'd do just that. Instead, he caressed her cheek with his work-worn hand and walked over to peruse the structure. "We'll need to get to it right away. Are you thinking a full coat of paint? Or would you prefer we try to whitewash over the area and do the entire building that way? I think we might be able to scrape away enough paint that the whitewash would cover it well."

"I don't want you two to go to any trouble at all. I'll buy paint in town, and I'll take care of painting it."

"Nonsense. This isn't an easy job."

"You think I'm not up to it?" Her question held a challenge, but she kept her tone teasing.

"I absolutely think you're up to it, but you have a lot to do to prepare for the season. Sheldon and I can do this between rounds of paint on the carousel characters inside. . ."

Ellie glanced at him as his voice tapered off. "What is it?"

"I just realized something. Wait here a minute, will you?"

She nodded and looked at Sheldon, who shrugged.

Bascom disappeared into the building. When he reappeared, he blanched. "Whoever did this used paint meant for the horses and creatures of the carousel."

Ellie could feel the color leach out of her skin. "Did they destroy your work?"

"No, but I'm surprised they didn't. I think I'll take to sleeping out here from now on just to be sure they don't reconsider and try that in the future. Something like that would be devastating."

"Yes, I suppose it would be."

Sheldon motioned toward the pavilion. "I can move from my room out into the pavilion, Bascom. There's no need for you to uproot your living quarters for this. Or I can sleep with my door open. I'd hear anything that went on out here. And whoever is doing this would surely need to light a lamp, so I'd see them before they saw me." He paused. "As a matter of fact, I'd guess my presence is what prevented them from damaging our work in the first place. They must have come in for the paint, heard me rustling around, and instead turned their attention to the outside wall."

"Perhaps. But all the same, I'd feel better, I think, sleeping out here for now."

"What about the ladies?"

"What about them?" Bascom looked at his partner.

Ellie watched the interchange with interest.

"Who will watch over them if we're both out here? What if another fire is set, but this time in the house?"

"I hadn't thought of that." Bascom rubbed his chin with his thumb while he considered his options. "I suppose you're right. It would be best for me to remain where I am. But you'll need to be extra diligent out here." He sighed. "I wish we could do more."

"For now I think this is all we'll need," Ellie hurried to soothe. "I do appreciate what both of you are doing. If necessary, Wanda and I could take turns with the watches, too."

"Absolutely not."

Ellie startled when both men answered at once. One thing for certain, the men didn't want the ladies interfering with their plans.

She went to bed that night as conflicted as she'd awakened. Distrust and suspicion for both of the carousel designers battled for her desire to believe in them. Alternating between the emotions wore her out. Both men seemed to be in the vicinity of vandalism each time, but only after the fact. Why did they miss the culprit? Was the person that good? Or were they working together for a more sinister reason? Maybe they were partners in crime and thrived on the power to make innocent people cringe with fear. The thought didn't go along with the character of the men she'd come to know.

Since she'd been reading the Bible every night and trying to trust God with her daily life, she decided to trust God with her confusion. She addressed her fears through prayer and asked God to direct her on whom to trust. Peace descended upon her, and she fell into a deep sleep.

Chapter 10

B ascom, could you please stop the wagon for a moment while I speak with my neighbor, Miss Adams?" Ellie placed her hand briefly on her escort's arm, and he urged the horses to the side of the dirt road.

Her elderly neighbor worked in a flower garden alongside the white fence that defined the front of her property. While the small two-story house sat within sight of the resort, they didn't often have a chance to talk.

"Why, Ellie Weathers, it's so good to see you! What brings you out this way?"

"It's good to see you, too." Ellie hid a smile at the woman's playful hat. Her round straw sun hat sported a huge bluebird upon the brim while long black ribbons held it firmly in place under her chin. Considering the fact that the sun lay low on the horizon, there wasn't any need for such a contraption, but people from far and near knew about Miss Adams and her love of hats. "I like your bonnet. It's very pretty."

Miss Adams flushed with pleasure and pushed it back a bit from her face. "Why thank you, dear. It's a gift from a couple that stays here often." A cloud passed across her features.

"What is it?" Ellie hurried to step down from the wagon, concerned that by the sudden change in expression the woman might be ill.

"I'm sure it's nothing. . .but the other day when they were here, they said they saw someone creeping around in the dark. I'm sure there's a reasonable explanation."

Ellie sent a quick glance to Bascom but stopped herself short of telling the neighbor that they, too, had suspicious events of late. Nothing new had happened since the paint incident earlier in the week. There was no need to worry her when Ellie felt sure the events at their place were personal and directed at some-one on the property. If a guest of Miss Adams had seen someone, surely it was because the guilty party had trespassed across her property to get to Ellie's place. She skillfully redirected the conversation. "Miss Adams, I'd like you to meet my escort for the evening, Bascom Anthony. And of course you remember Wanda." She motioned to Wanda on the far side of the seat. "And up ahead, waiting on the horse, is another guest at the resort, Sheldon. We're heading over to Saltair for the evening."

Ellie had an ulterior motive for leaving with both men. In a way she hoped something would happen at the resort while they were gone—nothing that would harm her grandmother or daughter, of course—but anything that would clear her suspicions of Bascom. Just to be on the safe side, she'd informed the retired sheriff that happened to be staying with them for the week of her concerns. She promised him a free night's lodging if he'd watch out for anything suspicious. He assured her he would sit up late with her grandmother and keep on eye on things. Only that knowledge had given her peace on leaving for such a long evening.

His wife had pulled Ellie aside and thanked her for both giving her husband a chance to relive his "glory days" and for allowing her a quiet evening to read and catch up on correspondence. They were a quaint couple, and Ellie hoped they'd come around more in the future. They'd even discussed them staying on permanently, due to the recent events, for free room and board in exchange for the sheriff's security, a notion which gave Ellie tremendous peace. Ellie left her grandmother and Priscilla in the parlor with the couple, and the small girl sat enthralled with the sheriff's stories from his past. Priscilla surely wouldn't miss her Whimsy tale on this special night.

Miss Adams's voice brought Ellie out of her musings.

"You young people have a good time. Hurry on now; don't let me slow your plans." She dusted her hands against her faded blue skirt, leaving a streak of dirt, and bent down to her work.

Bascom helped Ellie back onto the seat before climbing up to sit beside her. They had a tight squeeze on the single bench, but the air around them felt balmy and a nice breeze kept them cool, so no one seemed to mind the arrangement. And if truth be told, Ellie liked sitting so close to Bascom and absorbing his strength when her arm brushed against his.

Bascom and Sheldon had invited all the ladies to accompany them to dinner at the infamous resort, but her grandmother had begged off, insisting she stay back to feed their guests. Prissy, enthralled with her new sheriff friend, surprised Ellie by asking to stay, too. The excursion didn't happen often, and Ellie found herself looking forward to the trip with anticipation. She enjoyed the place, but only for a brief visit. The larger resort had activity all around, and that came with a lot of noise. Though she found Saltair to be very beautiful, she preferred their quiet, much smaller, much cozier place.

Ellie had an awful time getting ready, first trying to decide on suitable attire and then styling her hair. She finally chastised herself for worrying so over her appearance and quickly twisted her hair into a stylish knot at the nape of her neck.

The entire time she dressed, her thoughts had drifted to Bascom. What would he think of her hair? Would he think her elegant or pompous? Would he like the long pink skirt and the way she paired it with the tailored cream blouse she'd chosen to wear? Would it be too dressy or too casual? And why on earth did she care what Bascom thought anyway? She'd pushed the bothersome thoughts aside and hurried out to the parlor. Now they rode in silence, all lost in separate thoughts. Was it a coincidence that Miss Adams's guest saw someone lurking around? Had the person meant harm, but instead took off after seeing the guest in the window?

"Bascom, you heard her. . . . What do you think?"

"About the trespasser?" Bascom asked. "I think it's disturbing in light of what we've experienced, but with no harm done, I don't think she's in any danger."

They rode a bit farther. Saltair appeared on the far horizon.

He cleared his throat. "Her place is tiny. Does she rent rooms? She mentioned a guest."

"She has a small boardinghouse, yes. But she's never had a bit of trouble to my knowledge. She's the sweetest lady you'll ever meet. . .next to my grandmother." She grinned. "It's interesting, though. You put the two of them together, and you've never heard such loud, boisterous females."

He laughed and hurried the horses onward. He nodded toward Saltair. "Tell me about this place."

The resort loomed ahead, big and beautiful.

"Most people come from Salt Lake City by train. As you know, the owners planned it to be 'The Coney Island of the West.'"

At this comment, Bascom's face tightened, and he pressed his lips together in a frown.

"Did I say something wrong?"

"No. It's just that the reference to Coney Island doesn't bring back the most pleasant of memories for me. Remember, that's where the original attacks and fire broke out. It just feels rather ironic. Maybe it's a little too much like Coney in my experience."

"Hmm. I hadn't thought of that. Do you want to change the plans? We can turn around and go home if you'd like."

Ellie felt Wanda take in a deep breath in anticipation of his answer. When he shook his head no, her friend released her breath in a quiet whoosh.

"Anyway, they brought in a famous designer, Richard Kletting. His plan called for large posts to be driven into the bottom of the lake as the foundation. The lake has about a foot of sand on top of sodium sulfate. Engineers decided they could force steam down steel pipes to loosen the sodium sulfate compound. They put the posts into place, and after a few hours it hardened again and made the posts virtually immoveable. We've had some huge storms out this way with high winds, and no matter what damage the rest of the place sustains, the resort itself has remained solid."

She glanced from the resort toward Bascom. He stared at her in surprise.

She felt a blush flood through her features. "My grandfather had a certain fascination with the place. He read every article in the newspaper and often talked about the grandiosity of the resort. I'm guessing that fascination had something to do with his 'surprise' of the carousel."

Wanda laughed. "To say he was fascinated is an understatement. I think even Prissy could pronounce *sodium sulfate* as one of her first phrases."

"It is pretty amazing, you have to admit. There aren't many structures such as this around here."

By now they'd neared the monstrosity, and Bascom whistled through his teeth. "I can see why he was impressed. How long did it take to build?"

"Less than a year."

The structure stood several stories high with several towers topped with domes surrounding the various sides. Ornate trelliswork finished out the trim.

They found a place to leave the wagon, and Sheldon tied his horse nearby. They joined the throngs of people entering the arched doorway. Wanda and Sheldon quickly disappeared into the crowd, and Bascom firmly gripped Ellie's arm to prevent her from doing the same.

He leaned close. "Do you want to try and find them? Or would you prefer to head outside onto the boardwalk?"

Ellie motioned for him to continue on through the large building and out the far door. He led her up to the second level, where they stood near the rail overlooking the water. Sunset wasn't far off.

"I'm glad you chose a spot away from the train terminal." Ellie didn't think her nerves could handle the constant noise of the trains that came and went at steady intervals. She could see people dancing inside the large hall behind them.

"It's not quite the atmosphere I envisioned." Bascom's voice, full of remorse, came from nearby. He leaned in so he could be heard. "I thought we'd have a nice, quiet dinner where you could forget about your worries for a night. Instead, it's noisy and not the least bit relaxing."

"Oh, I don't know. I enjoy the excitement. Though I admit I prefer the quiet of our resort for the most part."

Another couple joined them at the rail, overlooking the swimmers in the lake below.

"Ellie?"

Ellie looked over to see another neighbor beside them. "Good evening, Delores. Hank." She introduced Bascom. "It seems to be the night for resort owners here at Saltair."

The couple exchanged a troubled look.

"We didn't leave our resort for the evening without giving it a lot of thought," Hank supplied. "I'm still not sure it was the best idea to come here."

A chill ran down Ellie's back. She had a feeling she knew what her neighbor would say next.

"We've had some. . .occurrences at our place and were hesitant to leave for an evening. Have you noticed anything peculiar over your way?" Hank's blue eyes connected with hers as he waited for a reply.

"We've had a fire and a few pranks pulled around our place. I'm sure it's an unruly neighbor boy or two out for a good time." She didn't know why she added that last part, since the thought had never entered her mind before now. Perhaps denial or wishful thinking had caused the spontaneous words.

"I'm not so sure," Hank continued. "I've talked with the others, and we've all been having some hindrances to our businesses."

Ellie asked the date when his vandalism began and had to mask her concern when she realized the date lined up with Bascom's arrival.

"Well, we'll leave you and your beau to your evening." Delores waved, and the couple continued walking down the wooden planks.

Bascom stared out over the water. Though the sun had begun its descent, neither one spoke of the splendor. Ellie watched the colors filter through wispy clouds. Blue, pink, orange, and finally deep purple as darkness began to fall.

"I can imagine what you're thinking." Bascom's voice, even with the din around them, sounded strained. "This has all followed us here. Whatever is going on seems to be caused by our arrival."

Ellie placed a hand on his arm, trying to gain a bit of warmth as her body shivered in apprehension. For the first time, though, the apprehension dimmed in Bascom's presence. Ellie sent up a silent prayer for discernment and then determined to enjoy their evening.

"Not necessarily. It could all be an awful coincidence. Let's not worry about this for now and enjoy the moment instead."

Bascom agreed and led her to a quieter table overlooking the water. Most swimmers had come ashore, but there were still enough people out there to make their dinner entertaining.

"The water seems shallow here." Bascom bit into a roll.

Ellie nodded. "It is. There's rumor of the water receding enough to put the resort in jeopardy. If it does, the swimmers will be far from the water's edge with a field of mud between them and the water. And the stench and flying bugs won't make visiting here pleasant."

Bascom made a face. "I hope for their sake that doesn't happen. It's a beautiful place."

"It is. And I agree. I'm fortunate that a dry season won't affect us in the same way. Our location is on deeper water."

The sun had set completely and small lanterns lit the tables. The moon shone down on the water, illuminating a path across its surface. Ellie looked in the direction of their place. She couldn't see it from this distance, but suddenly the desire to be on her own quiet porch with only Bascom for company overran the desire to stay in the beautiful but noisy place.

Bascom seemed to read her thoughts. "Shall we find our travel companions and head back home?"

Ellie nodded and allowed him to assist her to her feet. The dinner and company had been wonderful, but the noise and chaos were grinding on her nerves. She spotted her friend across the dining area, and Wanda also stood to her feet. She motioned toward the front of the building, and Ellie nodded. She followed her dapper companion and wished again that the situation were different. Bascom possessed all the attributes she'd want in a father for Priscilla. And in a husband for herself. She brushed away the fanciful musings. Apparently her lack of a Whimsy tale for the evening had her imagination racing in directions where it didn't need to tread. Along with Bascom's arrival came too many questions that remained without answer. And only time would tell if the questions would be answered in a way that she found pleasing.

Chapter 11

Y ou seemed very relaxed in Bascom's company last night." Wanda handed the last breakfast plate over to Ellie, and Ellie began to wipe it dry.

"Did you have a good time?"

"I did. . .and I didn't. Wanda, I'm so confused!" Ellie tossed the dish towel on the counter and settled into a kitchen chair.

Wanda hurried to pour them each a cup of coffee before joining her. "What did I miss? The rides there and home were both pleasant. Bascom seemed to be a model gentleman and escort. . ." Her eyebrows furrowed. "Or was he? Did something happen after we were separated?"

"Oh no, nothing like that." Ellie hurried to wave her concerns away. "Bascom only acted in the most proper of ways. I enjoyed his company."

"Then what? I don't understand."

"I don't either—that's just the problem! I really have grown to enjoy his company. I love our evenings on the front porch when we discuss so many topics. He's very educated."

Wanda placed her hand upon Ellie's. "As are you. I'm sure he's found great pleasure in realizing a woman can carry on such intriguing conversations about so many topics. Your grandfather did you a favor by drawing you in to so many deep talks."

"Indeed, he did at that." Ellie smiled, the memory of their many discussions a fond one. "And I do believe this is part of what draws me to Bascom, now that you mention it. He reminds me a lot of my grandfather."

"He's very handsome."

"Yes. Very." Ellie ran her finger back and forth across the side of her mug. "I love the way his hair flips down across his forehead, partially hiding his eyes. It makes him appear shy. Yet his eyes, they watch every move and miss nothing. His intelligence is mirrored in them. And then there's his one dimple when he does that crooked smile. It makes him appear very gentle and sweet."

"Just to name a few things." Wanda smirked.

Ellie realized she'd been sitting there for several moments, staring off into space with a ridiculous grin on her face. "Wherever is my head today? I need to check on the new reservations, make sure the books are up-to-date, clean the rooms of departing guests. See? He has me all in a dither—yet I can't even trust him. How can I make good choices if my emotions are all tangled up when it comes to Bascom? All my grandfather's training, his trust; I can't betray him now. Nor can I properly raise my daughter if I let a man I barely know throw me into such turmoil."

"I'm afraid I don't understand." Wanda looked genuinely perplexed. "You think he's handsome. He's kind and considerate. He's intelligent. You've known him about six weeks now and have had nothing but exemplary behavior from him. And that makes you a poor judge of character?"

"No, but all the events since his arrival point to his involvement in some way. I can't let my heart rule my common sense. You heard what Miss Adams said about a person in her yard. . . ."

"Who could have been anyone, not necessarily someone up to no good."

"And then we ran into Delores and Hank. They stated they've had some 'hindrances' along with other neighbors."

"He didn't mention what those 'hindrances' were? That could mean anything."

"Well, they were bad enough occurrences that he said it took a lot of thought to get them away for the evening."

"Hmm." Wanda stood and walked to the window.

Ellie leaned back in her chair and crossed her arms, waiting for Wanda to share her thoughts. She'd always trusted her friend and knew she had good insight into such things.

"He's a good man, Ellie. I just know it. He's kind and truly loves the Lord. I don't think you can show that type of devotion without meaning it with the heart. I've heard bits and pieces of the talks you two have shared while out on the porch, and I've had my own conversations with him on the subject. He's very strong in his faith, and it's important to him that those in his path also hear the truth. What reason would he have for deception with such a thing?"

"Oh, I don't know." Ellie joined Wanda at the window and looked out. Dark storm clouds again lingered on the far horizon to the west. The wind had picked up and now blew an old rag across the open expanse between the house and pavilion, plastering it against the porch. "Maybe, if he's a trickster, he just enjoys toying with a trusting female."

"I don't think his personality shows any indication of that at all. . .and I don't think you believe it deep down, either." Wanda turned to face Ellie, and Ellie wrapped her arms around her middle in a defensive gesture. "What I do think is that you've been alone for a long time. I think you feel something for this man and something—guilt? fear?—is gnawing at you and building a protective covering around your heart. Look at you, hugging yourself as if you can protect your heart even now from being broken."

Ellie deflated, relaxing her arms and releasing her tight hold. What silly notions her friend had. As if her embrace could protect her heart from being broken. "You know me too well."

"I know you as all good friends should know each other. Ellie, don't let your fear cause you to miss out on a special man. I know you've begun a relationship with Jesus over the past few weeks. Let Him guide you and pay attention to what's going on around you, but don't push Bascom away and ruin this chance."

"Speaking of, how did *your* evening go with Sheldon?" Ellie decided if she couldn't win the conversation, she could at least divert it. After all, as Wanda had said, she'd learned from the best—her papa.

"My evening didn't go nearly as well as yours. Sheldon is a gentleman, but I had the feeling he only spirited me away in order to allow you and Bascom your privacy."

Ellie felt the blush rise up in her face. "You mean you think they planned it?"

"No, I don't think *they* planned anything. I think this was entirely Sheldon's idea. He forced me right into the heart of the crowd, and we were carried along straight out the back door. I saw you divert to the side and motioned for Sheldon to follow, but he only smiled and continued to press me in the other direction. We had a good time, but his heart wasn't in the evening or events. He was a pleasant companion, and he even took me dancing."

"Wanda!"

"I know, but I was curious. We only stayed a few moments. I should know better at my age, but I wanted to experience the feeling of being held in a man's arms while being whisked about on the dance floor."

"At your age. . .you're only a few years older than me!" Ellie teased. "And as for the dancing, how did it feel?"

Wanda sighed. "In all honesty, it felt flat without being held in the arms of a man that I love. I watched the other couples. Their eyes never left each other's face. You could see the love. I think without that, something lacks in the experience."

Ellie felt like an awful friend. In all the years that they'd been together she'd never once noticed how lonely Wanda was or that she longed for her own romance to sweep her off her feet. "Well, I'll be the first one to pray that you find that man for yourself."

"I appreciate that. And you know I'm content here with you and Priscilla and your grandmother. I can't imagine a better place to live and spend my years."

"Priscilla." Ellie's emotions plummeted again. "I have to consider her in all this. She's becoming too fond of Bascom, and I can't chance her getting hurt. Maybe I should busy her with other tasks and keep her out of his work area for now."

"Nonsense. She adores him. Just as you miss your husband and grandfather, she misses having a man involved in her life. Bascom seems to enjoy her company. We just discussed all this a moment ago. Why take that relationship away from them?"

"Because something isn't right, and I can't figure out what it is. I can't take a risk that my daughter will suffer for my poor decisions." She grasped her skirt, pulled it up from the floor, and stalked across the kitchen. "Why did the damage to our area start just after his arrival?"

"Do you really think Bascom and Sheldon are the only new arrivals in the area? We all run resorts or hotels or boardinghouses. Newcomers are arriving and leaving on a daily basis. The area has grown quite a bit, and with growth comes crime. Surely you remember all the articles from the newspapers your grandfather loved to discuss with you."

Ellie froze in her tracks. "You're right! I haven't thought of any of those articles in some time. Each week he'd read of new crimes that had happened in town. It's only natural that the criminals would find their way out to us eventually."

"Right. There's bad in the world, no matter where you live."

"I suppose we'd do well to secure the place a bit better. And perhaps we even need to consider buying a weapon of our own." She shuddered at the thought. "Though it's highly unlikely I could ever hurt another person, even if he presented a danger to me."

"What if an intruder presented a danger to someone you love?"

Ellie scowled. "I'd use it in a moment."

"Then I agree this is something we should check into."

Ellie threw her arms around Wanda. "Thank you, Wanda, for helping me sort through my jumbled thoughts. I'm going to check on Prissy."

"You're welcome. Anytime." Wanda turned and busied herself with her bread dough. During the course of their conversation, it had risen past the top of the towel-covered bowl.

Ellie hurried out to the central hall.

A loud roll of thunder sounded from the other side of the window. Ellie smiled, knowing that within moments Prissy would catapult herself around the doorframe from their private quarters and into her mother's reassuring arms. When the little girl didn't appear by the time Ellie had reached their shared room, a small pang of worry filled her chest. She pushed open the door. Though Priscilla's dolls sat at the small table her great-grandfather had fashioned a couple years earlier, the silver tea set sat upon it untouched. Each mug held water, so her daughter's tea party had started after breakfast as the little girl had planned, but where was she now?

The laundry room. Prissy found a certain fascination with the steam-powered washing machine and went out to watch it at every chance. Ellie's heart plummeted with relief at the realization. She headed out the door, only to have it wrenched from her hands by the strong wind. The scent of oncoming rain hung heavy in the air, and the clothes on the line whipped furiously in all directions. Ellie wanted to reassure her daughter, but she needed to get the linens down before they were drenched.

Since her daughter hadn't appeared, Ellie could only imagine that the noise in the laundry was so great that the child hadn't heard the thunder. Another loud boom sounded, and Ellie jumped. She spurred herself into action and began to pull down the laundry into her arms. Wanda joined her, her voice lost in the blowing wind.

Ellie's arms were full, so she motioned with her head in the direction of the laundry room. Wanda nodded and continued to pull down bedsheets. Ellie entered the small room and glanced around as she placed her laundry in a woven basket. Her heart skipped a beat when she noticed Prissy's favorite rag doll lying on the ground. She couldn't remember if Prissy had left it there earlier or not. Ellie scooped up the doll and called Priscilla's name.

"Sweetheart, it's Mama. It's all right to come out now. The storm's not yet here, and if we hurry we can get to the house before the rain arrives."

No answer.

Ellie returned to the open door in time to see Wanda hurry into the house. She pulled the laundry door closed behind her and followed suit. Surely Prissy had returned to their quarters, seeking out her mother. But again only a silent empty room greeted her.

A quick peek into their parlor had showed her grandmother's sleeping form without the companionship of her great-granddaughter.

A sob caught in her throat as she entered the kitchen. The reassuring aroma of baking bread swirled around her, totally incongruent with her sentiments at the moment. Never had Prissy strayed from the house alone.

"Wanda!" Ellie tried to tamp down her terror, but the emotion carried through her panicked voice. "I can't find Prissy anywhere!"

"Ellie? Priscilla's fine. She's in the pavilion with the men. She asked to go earlier in the morning, and Sheldon was here topping off his coffee. He offered to take her. I didn't think you'd mind since she's been out there so many times before. And after we had such a pleasant time last night with the men, I didn't think there'd be any harm with the arrangement."

Ellie lashed out in anger. "Well, you obviously didn't think at all. I've said she could be out there with you or with Gram. I've never said you could leave her alone. I trusted you to..." Tears choked off her words. They'd just had a conversation about Bascom and her concerns. Not once had her friend mentioned Priscilla at that very moment was in the sole custody of those men. They could finish this conversation at another time. For now she just wanted to go and retrieve her daughter. "She's probably terrified."

She hurried through the door, leaving her devastated friend behind. "Prissy!"

The wind whipped against her as soon as she left the protection of the back of the house. A wall of rain immediately soaked through her clothes. The lake provided a smooth surface for the winds to blast over, and now she had to lean forward to avoid being blown back as she forced her way to her daughter. She prayed the men had the sense to keep the little girl under their care with the storm raging outside. She prayed even harder that the men would indeed be *in* the pavilion with her daughter. What if they'd taken off with her? Maybe Bascom missed his own child so much that he'd decided to take Prissy as his own. "Prissy!"

The pavilion door burst open and slammed back against the wall. Even over the high wind Ellie could hear her daughter's lighthearted and slightly off-tune voice singing along with Sheldon. Ellie didn't notice she'd frozen in her steps with relief until Bascom grasped her arm and pulled her inside. The interior felt cozy after the raging storm outside. But that was nothing compared to the storm of fear raging inside Ellie's heart.

"How dare you take my daughter without my permission? How dare you!" Ellie pummeled her fists against Bascom's chest with anger. Bascom stood there and allowed her to vent her frustrations. He finally pulled her into his embrace, and she cried, "I was so scared. I couldn't find her anywhere."

Sheldon appeared at her side. "I'm so sorry, Ellie. I had no idea. I figured Wanda would tell you I had Prissy out here."

"Well, she didn't." She knew her attitude toward her guests and best friend was inexcusable. But she'd never felt so terrified in her life. She tore herself away from Bascom's solid arms and swiped at her tears. Everything in her life felt like it was falling apart. Everything felt in an upheaval. She reached for her daughter, pulling her tight against her chest. "Oh, baby, let's get back to the house."

"At least wait until the storm abates. It isn't safe to be out there right now." Bascom's worried eyes surveyed her.

"I'm soaking wet and need to get into dry clothes. I'm not leaving my daughter for another moment. And look, I've already drenched her, too."

"Then at least allow me to accompany you back to the house." He snatched an overcoat from a hook on the wall. He gently pried Prissy from Ellie's tight embrace and pulled Ellie up against his side. He draped the coat across her and Priscilla and led them back into the storm and to the house door.

The winds diminished once they were on the back porch and directly out of the brunt of things. Bascom stared at her for a long, silent moment. He passed Prissy back over to her. "I'd never hurt you or your daughter, Ellie. I'm disheartened that you'd even think such a thing. Her safety is both mine and Sheldon's utmost concern when she's out in the pavilion with us."

Ellie opened her mouth to speak, but no words came out against the disappointment in his eyes. He hurried back out into the storm, disregarding the fact that he, too, was now completely soaked. She pulled Priscilla close against her chest and sank back against the wall. She'd have a lot of apologizing to do, but for now she'd get them both into fresh clothes. Only later, after they'd changed, did she realize she'd entered the forbidden pavilion and hadn't even bothered to take note of the carousel's progress.

Chapter 12

Bascom ducked his head against the wind and hurried out into the driving rain. The large drops pelted against his eyes, blinding him as he moved toward the pavilion's door. Once he arrived, he fought to pull it open. The relentless wind fought back. He slipped through the small opening, and the door slammed back into place, barely missing his hand as he snatched it out of the way. He leaned against the door, exhausted, the rough wood hard against his back as he stared across the room. The sizeable attraction loomed in the dusky interior, and for the first time, Bascom felt doubt over a project.

Always before he'd known he'd captured the essence of what the prospective owner envisioned. But in those cases, the person who'd hired him had been either the potential owner and known exactly what he wanted or an overindulgent parent wanting a small carousel horse for a child's gift.

Ellie had resented his presence from the start, and now with the vandalism and unrest that followed soon after his arrival, her resentment moved into distrust. And even with all that aside, even without the interference of the attacks on her place, he just wasn't sure she'd like the creation he'd developed. She saw the purchase as an extravagance they hadn't been able to afford. Bascom had no clue as to her financial status and he, too, questioned whether her elderly grandfather had made a poor choice in purchasing the carousel. But there was no turning back now. No one else would want a merry-go-round with this theme— it was exclusive to Ellie.

He sighed. He'd just have to make it unique enough to become the draw her grandfather had hoped for. Maybe if she could think of it like that, as a way to honor his final request, it would help with her frustration.

Wandering forward, Bascom looked at the beautiful merry-go-round that filled the room. He caressed the shiny wood of the completed horses. The specialty wood carvings were coming together and would soon be set into place beside the traditional ones.

Bascom slipped out of his dripping overcoat and moved to his favorite design, the mermaid. He ran a hand down the side and felt rough edges. The rote work of smoothing and shaping rough edges into soft curves welcomed him. Working with wood always relaxed him, so he picked up a chisel and started chipping away.

If only he could smooth Ellie's rough edges as easily. A small smile tipped his mouth at the thought. He knew he wouldn't change her even if he could. Her rough edges were also tempered with softness, judging from the warm way she responded to her daughter and to the consideration she gave her grandmother and Wanda.

She easily switched from concern to gracious host. He'd observed that transition several times during their evenings on the porch when he arrived unexpectedly. She'd be lost in thought, staring out over the lake, her forehead furrowed with concentration, but as soon as she registered his arrival, a smile would slip into place and she'd welcome him with cheery warmth.

A quiet chuckle sounded behind Bascom. "You work that mermaid any harder and she'll collapse into sawdust the moment a child sits upon her." Sheldon left the doorway of his private quarters and approached the work area.

Bascom surveyed the piece. "I guess I did get a bit overzealous for a moment there."

"What were you thinking about? The way you were digging into the surface, it looked like you had a personal vendetta against the poor girl."

More like a vendetta against whoever keeps putting a frown on Ellie's face. Bascom didn't share the sentiment with his friend.

"It's Ellie, isn't it?"

Sheldon straddled a high-back chair and slapped his work gloves against his palm. The noise grated on Bascom's already shredded nerves.

"It's everything." Bascom put down his tool and paced across the hard-packed dirt floor. "It's like Coney Island all over again. I don't understand. It's like a personal vendetta, but I have no known enemies."

"The men responsible are all behind bars, correct?" Sheldon stopped the annoying slap-slap-slapping and held the gloves still, contemplative. "Do you suppose there's a chance that one of them is free or that perhaps one of the captured men had help from someone on the outside who's still on the loose?"

"I have no idea about any of it. I only know that my family paid the price for an attack planned against me, and I won't stand by and watch the same happen to another family."

"What are you saying? Do you want to leave?" Sheldon's eyes narrowed. "I suppose I can handle the finish work. You've taught me well. But I'm not sure that will stop whatever's going on."

Bascom, deflated, sank onto a chair and sat opposite his apprentice. "That's my concern, too. If I left and something happened to any of them, I'd feel even worse. Perhaps by staying I can figure out what's going on and prevent another tragedy."

"Then we need to figure this out together." Now Sheldon paced the length of the pavilion. "Can you think of anyone you might have outbid for a project? Did you ever have a run-in with a competitor that blamed you for getting a contract he wanted?"

"No, nothing. I'm contacted by my clients; I don't go seeking them out. If ever there was a situation like that, I know nothing about it." Bascom thought hard but couldn't come up with a thing he'd ever done to warrant the violence and anger of which he'd been a victim. "I can't even think of a situation where that would be possible. Carousel designers are a small breed. There aren't many of us available. So there's more demand than supply in this case. You know that. Why would anyone care about a contract when there are plenty more for the taking?"

"That's a good point."

Silence pressed in, but nothing new came to Bascom.

"Perhaps. . ." Sheldon hesitated, measured Bascom with a glance, then continued. "Perhaps it's personal."

"What do you mean by that?" Bascom had no idea to what his friend referred. "What kind of personal situation would ever drive a person to commit murder?"

"I can think of quite a few instances. The newspapers are full of stories. Maybe someone courted your wife before you and the fire was his way of lashing out?"

"Not that I know of. Susan only had eyes for me." Bascom shrugged. "And if there ever was anyone else, she never spoke of him."

"Never? Surely she had other suitors. Your wife was a very beautiful woman." Sheldon walked over and stared at the rain running down the window in tiny streams. "Maybe it was someone she toyed and flirted with, someone who thought he meant more to her than he really did?"

"Susan? Not a chance," Bascom snapped. "She didn't have a mean bone in her body, and she had a good sense about her. She'd never lead a man on for the thrill. You knew her better than to ask that."

"Then someone who *thought* she felt that way? Maybe someone mistook her sweetness for interest? She might have been the intended target all along." Sheldon spun around at this new inspiration. "All this time you thought you were the target. You've tortured yourself with the thoughts of what you could have done differently, how you could have saved them, correct?"

"But what else could it be? You agree that Susan didn't have a mean bone in her body. Surely the cruel act against them was intended for me alone."

"In a roundabout way, yes. In this person's eyes, you 'stole' Susan away from him. By his hurting her, you'd be hurt, too. Especially if during the process of an inquisition, a seed of doubt about your reputation could be instilled in everyone around you. And when you think about it, that's exactly what happened."

Bascom thought about his words. Sheldon could be right. If so, Bascom wasn't directly responsible for his family's death as he'd thought. He'd only been a victim of the same crazed person's scheme. But a missing piece didn't make sense. "What about the men put away for the crime?"

Sheldon raised a shoulder. "I don't know, but I guess they were still guilty for the lesser charges. So even if they were honest when they denied the attack against your family, they still deserve to be right where they are."

"That's true. They still stood guilty of setting the other fires at the other establishments and the coercion."

The rain had slowed, and Bascom stood and walked to the window. He saw movement near the porch and even through the blurry window knew Priscilla hopped back and forth across the porch in play. He'd grown to love the child in his short stay and determined again to see things through so that when he moved on, it would be with a clear conscience and the knowledge that all was well with the ladies. "And what of the attacks against the other resorts?"

"The killer could be pacing himself so he doesn't end his quest too quickly... or maybe he's just trying to throw off suspicion by not doing all the acts in one place." He walked to the outer door. "The rain's slowed enough that I'm going out for some fresh air. Let me know if you need anything."

Bascom nodded, already slipping away into his thoughts. Sheldon had given him a lot to think about. Things he should have realized long ago. His grief had been so deep that he'd never even considered any other reason for the violence—other than the crime being directly related to his work. All signs had pointed toward arson with the intent to destroy the newest project because of the owners' refusal to pay for protection. Instead of Bascom telling his wife and son to stay home, he'd led them right into the trap.

But what if Sheldon was right? What if a jilted lover—or worse and more likely—someone who thought he had the potential to gain Susan's love took advantage of the already heated situation at Coney and used that as a cover to get even with them all? A shiver of terror rolled down his back. If so, then the person had followed them here—not a hard thing to do with all the wagons and hoopla that surrounded their arrival—and now Bascom's friendship with Ellie had put her and her loved ones right into the path of a lunatic.

He had to figure out a plan. If he went to the authorities, they'd think him insane. He needed more evidence before they'd take him seriously. Or worse, they'd point the finger of blame toward him once again. Since he'd never invited his family to a work site before, they'd scrutinized the case heavily. The fact that no other sites had ever been located at such a wonderful family destination didn't seem to matter to them. With the other suspects behind bars, Bascom alone would be their prime target.

A sardonic laugh slipped over his lips. A target explained exactly what he was. No matter what, whoever had chased them down made him just that. His guilt over another person's pain, his worry of what would happen if he couldn't stop the attacks, his ending up in jail because the authorities blamed him. . .all added up to a situation of vengeance where Bascom couldn't see a way to clear his name. Maybe the original intent was to hurt Susan, but whoever the killer was, he apparently wasn't done with inflicting pain on the people Bascom loved.

Since the authorities weren't a viable alternative, Bascom would have to find his own way to figure out the mess. He considered all his options. Telling Ellie wasn't the best idea since she already distrusted him and blamed him for various things from financial woes to taking advantage of her grandfather while the old man lay in a feeble state. While Bascom had had no way to know of such a thing, Ellie obviously hadn't come to that realization yet. He could do nothing and keep watch, but that went against Bascom's nature. He needed to be a step ahead of the tormentor. Susan and Billy didn't have a chance. They had no warning. This time Bascom did, and not to act on it seemed ridiculous.

His strongest plan would be to spend more time in Ellie's company, hoping any further assaults would force the killer out into the open and into a confrontation. If so, then Bascom, along with Sheldon and any male guests that were around, could hopefully subdue the criminal before further damage was done. He'd finally know his enemy. That's when they could bring in the law. At the very least, Bascom would feel better knowing Ellie rested safely under his care. He would protect her to the best of his ability. He smiled, knowing the rain had been a blessing in disguise. Given the killer's favorite method of attack seemed to be through fire, the wetness of the drenched structures would prolong another round.

Since Ellie had left in a huff and wouldn't necessarily be open to Bascom's company, the opportunities to spend more time together would be harder to come by. But still Bascom determined this angle to be the best remedy for that situation. If Susan were here, she would be the first to attest to the fact that when Bascom turned on the charm, he was hard to resist. She'd said many times over that Bascom had done just that with her, and she'd had no eyes for anyone else from that moment on.

Of course if Susan were there, none of the bad stuff would have happened and he wouldn't be in this mess. If the same reaction rang true with Ellie, Bascom could keep her nearby at all times, under his watchful eye. Daytime hours wouldn't be a problem. There were too many people around, and no attacks that he knew of had been initiated during those hours. Bascom could finish the carousel and ready it for their grand opening. He had some ideas to share with Ellie, and now that he thought of it, that would be the perfect opening into spending more time in her company. She'd consider his words in the name of bettering her resort and its reputation. Now he only had to put his plan into effect.

Chapter 13

Y ou still don't trust me."

Ellie froze in place at Bascom's direct words, her hand still resting in the water where she trailed it over the side of their small wooden boat. "That's not tr..."

But she couldn't deny what they both knew to be fact. His words *were* true. She'd avoided all contact with him during the past few days and sat in the boat with him now only because Wanda hadn't given her a chance to refuse Bascom's invitation after lunch.

"I can see it in your eyes, not that you'll look at me very often."

She now raised her eyes to his, sure he could see her regret. His mouth curved into a sardonic half smile, but his blue eyes held no trace of humor. She winced at the hurt that filled them.

"I'll leave if that will make you feel better. Sheldon can finish up the few loose ends and put the final touches on the carousel."

He'd stopped rowing and now rested the oar across his legs. The water dripped off the end of the thin piece of wood, the sound of the droplets as they hit the surface of the lake the only sound to break the silence. From where they sat far from the shore of the lake, they seemed to be the only life around. No one would interrupt the conversation in time to rescue Ellie from responding. If only she'd insisted on bringing Prissy along....

But Ellie knew the talk was a long time coming and overdue. She'd missed Bascom's teasing banter and friendly wave across the open area between the house and pavilion. She'd grown accustomed to their evening chats, and now, ever since she'd lambasted him about Prissy's disappearance days earlier, Bascom hadn't even tried to come around. At first she told herself his lack of presence spoke louder than words about his guilt and that she'd been right in her tirade, but time and Wanda had convinced her of what her heart already knew. Bascom kept his distance out of respect for Ellie and her feelings, not because of any guilt or wrongdoing on his part. Only her stubbornness and lack of a plan on how to fix things kept her from making things right.

"I don't want you to leave." She'd made a mess of things, and she was the one that owed him an apology. And she needed to do so quickly because the thought of Bascom leaving left a queasy feeling in her stomach. "I know you meant no harm to Prissy. . .or to me. She's missed you." Ellie looked away, the intensity in his eyes doing strange things to her stomach. She glanced back and saw that his smile came more naturally. Hope now filled his eyes. "I've, uh, I've. . .missed you. . .too."

For the first time in days his eyes lit up and his mouth quirked into the heart-tugging grin she'd missed. The grin she'd wiped from his face. He leaned toward her and grasped her wrist, tugging her forward toward the seat closest to him. She'd purposefully chosen the farthest seat from his place at the stern. Her heart pounded in her chest as she hesitantly moved forward, clutching the folds of her skirt while balancing carefully in the most central part of the vessel. She stepped over the bench with one leg and swung the other over quickly as the boat rocked, causing her to plop quickly onto her seat.

The silence spread around them, but this time it was a comfortable silence, and she no longer wished for Prissy's presence.

Bascom leaned close, his knees brushing against hers. "I've missed you, too. I've missed our chats. I've missed watching you wave while almost walking into the doorway in distraction over my presence."

Ellie gasped, tugging her hand from his. "Not true!"

Bascom's rich, bubbly laugh filled the air. "It is, too. Last Saturday morning you walked straight into the door in your hurry to get inside and avoid me."

She pushed against his egotistical shoulder. "I tripped into the door when my boot heel stuck in the crack of the floor and held me in place when the rest of me thought I'd continue forward. It had nothing to do with your wave, other than the fact that I didn't pay attention to my steps."

"So you admit my presence causes you a distraction."

"I admit nothing of the sort." She cupped her hands against her flaming cheeks and rested her elbows on her knees to avoid his intense stare, a move which caused her to lean forward and increased Bascom's nearness.

"I'll admit it." Bascom also leaned forward, his forehead almost touching hers. "I'll admit you've caused me distraction from the moment I first laid eyes upon you. You've brought the first sign of joy back into my life since I lost my wife and son. You and Prissy fill a void left inside me. I want to explore that further."

"Bascom!" Ellie didn't know what to make of such bluntness. No man, not even Wilson, had spoken so freely in her presence of his feelings and emotions. She imagined her eyes now reflected her horror and panic at being in such a quandary. She covered them with her hands so he couldn't read the emotions within.

"Ellie." He gently pulled her hands away and forced her to look up at him. "If I've learned one thing, it's that relationships can be fleeting. There's no guarantee of the time one might have with another." He shifted in his seat and repositioned the oar. He worried his lower lip with his teeth and watched her thoughtfully before resuming his speech. "There might not be a second chance if you let something special slip through your fingers. I don't want to live with regrets. Not any more than I already have, anyway. I care for you, Ellie—a lot— and I care for Priscilla. I feel that you sense the same emotions; you're just afraid to acknowledge them."

He was right, but she didn't know how to let go and trust with all the suppositions careening around in her thoughts. She'd grown through her prayer time and her reading of the Word, but what if in this situation she still went by her own emotions and not God's? She didn't trust her spiritual maturity yet. What if she put herself and Prissy into a dangerous situation because of this confusing and tumultuous feeling of love? The realization of the intensity of her feelings toward Bascom surprised her. If she didn't care deeply about him, why would she miss him so much or care what he thought?

"Love?"

She didn't realize she'd whispered the word aloud until Bascom repeated it and a look of confusion passed over his face. She froze in place and felt his hands tighten around hers.

"Love?" he repeated. "Maybe. I've not dug that deep. But Ellie, the carousel is almost complete, and when it is I'll have no choice but to move on."

"No choice? Why? Must you hurry off? Can't you stay on awhile longer?"

"Not if I don't know where we stand. Not if we can't get past this distrust that has you doubting my every move and intent."

"I don't want to distrust you. But nothing happened here before you came. And you've said yourself that it's eerily reminiscent of your time on Coney. Even Sheldon. . ." Her words tapered off. There wasn't a need to bring the other man into the conversation.

A muscle worked in Bascom's jaw. "What about Sheldon?"

"It's nothing." She relaxed her hands in his and watched as his right thumb traced the length of her left one.

He squeezed. "It's something or you wouldn't have brought it up."

A sigh escaped. "I shouldn't say anything. But he's voiced his concern a few times, too, about the similarity of the events matching up to what happened to your wife."

Hurt passed through his eyes again. "And you still believe I had something to do with that?" He shook his head in disgust, and this time he pulled away, taking up the oar and pulling it firmly through the water to spin the boat toward home.

Did she? She didn't answer immediately, wanting to be sure her words were genuine. She said a quick prayer and felt peace descend. "You know what? I don't. Bascom, I trust you in every way. I think I've known it in my heart all along, but sometimes my worries carry more clout than they should."

She reached out and touched his arm, her contact staying his motions. He searched her eyes, and she smiled in return.

"You're sure?"

"I'm sure."

Bascom closed his eyes and let out a sigh of relief. "Thank you."

They sat staring for moments before both leaned forward in unison. Bascom cupped her chin in his hand and tilted it up to meet his kiss. Emotions exploded through Ellie, and a sob caught her throat. He kissed her several more times before they pulled apart, and he gently pushed her hair back from her face.

"Why are you crying? That wasn't my intent."

"Mine, either. But I've been alone so long. I doubt my every move and question my every thought. You bring out emotions in me that are overpowering, but in such a safe way that I feel I can finally let go, that I have someone on my side. But..."

She stopped.

"But?" He jiggled her hands, encouraging her to go on.

"But...you might leave soon, and I don't know how I'll deal with that."

"Or I might stay. How will you deal with that?" he teased.

She wiped at a tear. "Really?"

"Really. If you'll have me."

"We have that workshop out past the pavilion. Maybe you could set up shop there and stay around awhile? You could still work on other clients' orders."

A smile lit Bascom's face from one side to the other. "You're sure?"

She nodded. "I'd like that."

"On one condition."

"A condition?" She quirked an eyebrow at him. "And what might that be?"

"I've had some ideas about the resort. I'd like to share them with you. Do you trust me? Completely?"

"I do."

"Okay then. Every night I've heard you tell Prissy your Whimsy tales. They're good. Very good. I think you should write them into booklets and share them with your guests and others who might be interested."

"Oh goodness, no. I couldn't."

"Why not?"

"Well, because...they're personal. They're just entertaining little snippets for Priscilla. No one else is going to enjoy them like she does."

"And again I ask, why not?"

"Because. . .they're. . .whimsical. Not many people have time for fluff like that."

"Other children don't deserve a touch of whimsy in their lives?"

"Of course they do, but their parents will provide that, suited to their own child's nature."

Bascom smirked at her. "And you think all parents can just pull stories out of their heads on a whim like you do?"

"Yes. And much better suited to their own child's nature, too. Prissy loves tales of the sea and adventure, but not all children would like that. Some might prefer stories about the animals of the woods or creatures from the desert around their own homes."

"You have no concept of your ability, do you?"

Ellie shook her head to clear it. "Concept of my ability? I'm afraid I don't understand."

"You have no idea the talent it takes to create a story such as yours. You have a gift. You should share it with children and families that don't naturally have the ability to create a make-believe world of their child's dreams."

"Your parents didn't tell you stories at bedtime? Mine did. And my grandparents told stories before that. It's just something we've always done."

Bascom caressed her fingers again, muddling her ability to think. "Maybe so, but you have a knack for it that most other people don't."

"And. . ." He again jiggled her wrist, and she returned her attention from his fascinating hands back to his face.

"And?"

"And I've seen Prissy's drawings as you spin your story. They're quite good."

"They're stick figures and outlines of her imaginings. A child's sketches, nothing more."

"But I'm telling you, they'd sell and sell well. If she draws the most simple of pictures and you write down your tales, we could sell them and bring in more money for the resort."

She smiled at him. "You're serious."

"Very much so. At Coney there were people who made good money just drawing a caricature of the tourists. The rendition suited the person's features, but in a silly, overdone way. Priscilla's drawings are much better than that."

"Hmm. I'll give it some thought. With you and Sheldon around, Wanda and I have been able to turn our attention to other pursuits. Before, we worked nonstop." She glanced up at him and saw his eyes were gentle and completely focused on her words. "I know you didn't come here planning to get so involved in the day-to-day running of the resort, but I hope you know how much we appreciate your help."

"I've enjoyed it, too. I'm glad we could make your life easier, as much as we've also complicated things and brought worry and fear along, too."

Ellie now realized what her heart and head tried to tell her all along—the man sitting before her had nothing to do with the vandalism at the resort or his wife and child's death. She regretted letting the notion fill her mind for even a moment. "I'm so sorry. I know whatever is going on around here is either coincidental or completely out of your hands. I trust you, Bascom. Completely. Please forgive me for ever doubting you."

"You have every right to suspect me."

"No, I don't. You deserve the benefit of doubt just like everyone else. And Bascom. . .I have an idea, too! If you want to help out, why don't you create miniatures of your carousels and let us sell those, too." Ellie almost tipped the boat with her enthusiasm. "We can set up that front corner of the pavilion— the entry—as a small shop of sorts. Maybe we could even open a refreshment stand and offer food items to bring in guests from other resorts."

Bascom steadied the boat and contemplated her words. "Are there enough people in the area?"

"I think so. We all encourage our guests to sample the amenities at each other's places. With Saltair closing down due to the receding water, there's need of another diversion out this way. It might be temporary until they get back on their feet, but for now, we could give it a try."

"You might have something here." Bascom quickly rescued the oar that Ellie's fervor had knocked overboard. "I could do some small carvings. We'll have to discuss it some more. But for now," he motioned to the storm clouds that hung on the far horizon, "we'd best get back to solid ground and batten down the hatches before that next storm hits. Saltair might not have anything to worry about if the rain keeps up."

"Another storm? Goodness. But they're fleeting, so the rain doesn't add up very fast."

The brightness of mood brought on by their clearing the air dimmed as the storm clouds filled the sky. Ellie shivered and knew the sudden urge she had to return to shore had nothing to do with the man sitting across from her.

Chapter 14

Bascom rowed hard, using both oars to push his way through the rapidly building waves. He'd been so caught up in Ellie and their conversation that he'd missed the approach of the oncoming storm. He'd never forgive himself if he allowed something to happen to Ellie while she remained under his care.

A gust of wind caught up Ellie's hat. Even as she reached for it, the wind pulled it from her head and sent it spinning across the water. It landed a good four yards away and rode flat upon the waves. He faltered, glancing at Ellie for her reaction.

"Let it go. We need to get back to the dock." She had to yell to be heard over the rising wind. Though her words said to move on, her eyes said otherwise, anguish pulling at their depths.

"It's important to you."

She nodded. "It was my last gift from my husband before he passed away. But if he were here, he'd rather us make it safely to shore than worry over a trifle object and risk our lives. Please, continue on to shore."

The last word carried through on a sob in her effort to remain brave and do the right thing. Bascom made a quick decision and turned the boat slightly in the direction of the floating straw contraption. The wind helped them reach it in moments, and he snagged one of the long ties with an oar and pulled it close to the boat. After leaning down to retrieve it, he smiled into Ellie's grateful eyes, but the worry that lay behind the expression urged him to hurry on.

Thunder rumbled overhead and lightning flashed in the distance. The lake wasn't a safe place to be in a storm. Rain began to pelt against them, and Bascom had to squint to see through the deluge that soon surrounded them. Ellie rocked the boat as she cautiously moved to the bench next to him, her presence reassuring.

"Give me an oar. We'll go faster if we both row."

Bascom shook his head and continued to make progress, albeit inches at a time it seemed. He might be tiring, but he wasn't about to let Ellie exert herself because of his poor planning.

"Bascom, give me an oar. Who do you think does my rowing for me when you aren't around? We'll make better time, and we don't have a moment to lose.

205

Now let go of any ridiculous male notions and allow me to help."

She refused to budge, so he lifted the oar up and let her slide underneath before he settled it against her lap. She instantly clutched it and began to push with all her might. He had to admit they immediately made better time as they focused on their own sides.

"We make a good team," he called to her with a grin as they neared the dock. Though she sat inches away, she had to lean close as the wind tried to blow his words away.

"Like two oxen strapped to the same plow, that's us," she laughed back, relief evident as she handed him the oar and crept cautiously forward to the bow.

He used an oar to push closer to shore, and Ellie wrestled the rope and grabbed on to the dock. With practiced skill, she wrapped the braided material around the post and cautiously jumped onto solid ground. He waited to make sure she was stable and then quickly followed suit. He tied his end to the other post, and they hurried up the walkway to shore. Wild waves crashed against the beach, and the wood dock groaned at the onslaught.

"I see Priscilla waiting on the porch—let's head that way." Ellie called over her shoulder, but Bascom would have followed her anywhere, even without the invite.

"Mama, Mama, hurry!" Prissy's worried voice carried to them. "Don't let the thunders get you. C'mon! Run, Mr. Anthony!"

"Prissy, stay put." They'd reached the stairs, and Prissy lunged for her mother, tears coursing down her face. After a moment's hesitation, Ellie pulled the little girl into her embrace. "We're going to have to stop these wet hugs, don't you think?" Priscilla didn't move. Bascom felt exhausted and knew Ellie had to be even more tired. They were both emotionally drained from their talk and physically drained by their adventurous return from the water. "Let me get her."

Though she initially resisted, Prissy finally let him pull her into his arms, and he carried her into the bright warmth of the parlor.

"Oh goodness, let me get you some blankets. Prissy, I told you to wait inside." Wanda looked flustered as she hurried into the room. "I only left her a moment to check the hot cocoa. I thought you'd return soon and knew that a warm drink would be welcome."

"It sounds mighty nice, Wanda, but maybe we'd better get into some dry clothes first."

"Of course. Let me take Prissy and you two can do just that."

"She's soaked through, too." Ellie laughed. "She met us on the porch, but I'm afraid our hug of greeting messed up your plans to keep her dry. "I'll just take her with me, and we'll be back out here shortly."

She reached for her daughter.

Bascom waved her away. "I'll carry her to your door."

Wanda hurried back to the kitchen while the three of them continued on through the back hall.

Prissy laid her head upon Bascom's shoulder and felt like a cuddly rag doll in his arms. He didn't want to release the warm and snuggly girl to her mother. But her dress was damp, and Bascom knew she risked becoming ill with the cold. He could hold her later.

"We'll meet you in the parlor." Ellie reached for Priscilla, her eyes softening as she took in the sight of him holding her daughter with such concern. "Unless Prissy falls asleep. I think her vigil on the porch drained her. As relaxed as she appears to be, once she gets into warm clothes, she might drop off for a nap."

"Not tired, Mama," Priscilla's drowsy voice stated.

They exchanged grins over her head at her denial.

"Warm clothes will feel good," Bascom agreed. He wished he could join the ladies and all three could catch a nap together—as a family. The thought startled him, but he knew their day in the boat had solidified his feelings for Ellie and Priscilla. He wanted to be around to care for both of them, to be their shelter in the storm. He mulled over the protective thought and hurried off to don dry clothes.

❧

Ellie laid her lethargic daughter on their bed and peeled her own drenched clothes off before helping Prissy out of hers. If she tried to change the little girl while as soaked as she was, her daughter would be dripping wet again in no time. Since the back of Prissy's dress had remained dry, she simply pulled a warm quilt over her daughter to keep her warm in the meantime.

She made quick work at changing into a simple pink dress then helped her daughter into a warm nightgown. Since the day promised to remain dreary and with the late afternoon hour, Ellie doubted Prissy would wake before nightfall. And if she did, it wouldn't be a problem for her to take a light dinner in the kitchen in her gown.

Ellie wished she could do the same. Though most of the time she loved running the small resort, there were other times she longed for a private home where she could settle in away from the public and while away her day as she pleased. If nothing else, a small getaway far from all neighbors would be a welcome respite.

She shook off the silly notions and turned her attention to her hair. After the hat had blown off, the wind had taken advantage and whipped the long strands into a fine mess. She pulled the tangled locks from the braid and brushed her hair into shape before winding it up at the nape of her neck. The hair would dry better this way, but again she longed to be able to leave it down and not worry. It wouldn't be appropriate to be so casual in front of her guests, though, and there were Bascom and Sheldon to consider, too.

She felt a warmth flow across her cheeks when her thoughts turned to Bascom. She loved the man. She'd realized it that afternoon as they'd talked in the boat. She sank down onto her dressing table chair and laid her forehead against the cool table. She knew it was time for a heartfelt prayer.

"Oh heavenly Father, would it be possible for Bascom and me to move into the permanent relationship of marriage? I'd love to have a steadfast man like him in my life again." She paused in her musings and wondered at the prayer. Did she really want to move into marriage again? Had she known the man long enough? Not long ago she questioned his very sanity, and now she questioned hers. "I know You led him here, and I know You must have a plan beyond the attraction he's building for our resort, Lord. I feel that You used my grandfather's last request to further that plan. I know You've given me a peace about Bascom's intentions, and that he intends to bring only good to myself and Prissy. He's so gentle with her, and I know he'd never hurt either of us. If You could see fit, I'd love to see an end to the destruction and vandalism and let the guilty party be caught. And then I'd feel free to go ahead and pursue a future with Bascom."

Ellie ended her prayer and raised her head and peeked at her reflection in the mirror. Her eyes sparkled with a newfound joy. Joy in finding her way to God and finding her way back to love. She hopped to her feet and with a last peek at her daughter hurried out the door and into the waiting company of the man she hoped held their future.

She entered the room to find Wanda, Sheldon, and Bascom all there ahead of her. "Sorry I took so long."

"Where's Prissy?" Sheldon looked past Ellie with concern. "I'd hoped to challenge her at a game of checkers."

"She's dead to the world, and I doubt she'll wake before morning. She still needs a nap every few days and hasn't had one for a while. She's played hard today, and I'm sure it's finally catching up with her. I've tucked her in and will check on her in a bit. If she wakes, we'll feed her a little something and send her back on her way."

"She's not been herself all day. I think she's coming down with something." Wanda's forehead creased with concern.

Ellie felt a frown crease her forehead, too, as she thought back to her daughter's countenance. "I didn't notice that she felt warm, but you're right. Now that I think of it, she's quite tired, even more than usual after a long and eventful day."

"And she felt warm in my arms." Bascom stood and offered Ellie his chair. "I thought it was due to our being damp, though, and her coming from inside. Maybe we should go check on her?"

"I think she'll be fine for now, since I just left her."

Sheldon carefully placed his empty mug of cocoa on a doily on the nearby oak table. "Call me if you need me. I want to go out and finish my last piece for the carousel. The unveiling will be tomorrow, correct?"

Bascom grinned Ellie's way, and her stomach tumbled in response. "It is. I can't wait to show it off and see your reaction." Though his words answered Sheldon's question, his eyes were for her only.

Sheldon laughed and excused himself. "I can see that you two would like to be alone. Don't worry, I'll see myself out."

"Nonsense, I'll walk you." Wanda sounded just as anxious to get out of the room and away from the two of them. "Ellie, most of the guests have taken an early dinner and retired to their rooms for the evening. You relax."

Ellie watched as Sheldon held the door to the kitchen open for her friend. A moment later, she heard the far kitchen door open and close from the hallway, and then the door swung partly open as the outer door let Sheldon into the brunt of the storm.

"He should have waited for things to let up. Now he'll be as drenched as we were."

"I don't think he minds. He likes to be alone to tie up his loose ends. I'm sure he figures I'll be busy for a while and he can putter to his heart's content. The carousel is all but finished, but he's a perfectionist and likes to go over every inch to make sure everything's ready for the big day."

Ellie eyed the storm outside the window. "If it continues like this. . .I'm not sure there will be an unveiling tomorrow. We'll be lucky if even the guests try to venture out in this."

A huge crash from the back of the house had Ellie jumping to her feet. "Prissy!"

She hurried through the back hallway and met up with a frazzled Wanda.

"It's just the door—it blew open. Sheldon must not have latched it completely."

The back door swung freely on its hinges, the wind slamming it against the wall as rain poured into the space around them. Bascom hurried to close it, a battle of wills that he finally won. He returned to Ellie's side.

"I'll go check on Priscilla," Ellie said. "I need to make sure the noise didn't wake her and scare her." She hastened into their room. The only light came from the almost constant streaks of lightning that continued to illuminate the world outside their window. But the erratic flashes were enough to show Ellie everything she needed to see.

Prissy's side of the bed lay empty.

Chapter 15

Ellie reentered the hall. "Wanda, could Prissy have snuck into the kitchen without your knowing?" Her voice shaky, she knew the question sounded incoherent even as she asked it. "Maybe the storm scared her and she hid under the table or something?"

"No, I'm sure I would have heard her come in. She's not in the room?"

"No. I left her in bed sound asleep. There isn't any way she'd wake up on her own. Not as tired as she was." She noticed muddy footprints on the wood floor near the door. Her voice rose and panic set in as she pointed them out to the others. "What if someone's taken her?"

"She has to be close by." Wanda's voice dropped to a choked whisper. "We need to check under the bed and behind furniture."

"I checked the entire room. There aren't many hiding places."

"Let's be realistic. If the crash startled her, would she have been able to hide this fast? We got here within moments, and Ellie, you went right in to check on her." Bascom's comments were the first to make sense.

Wanda, clearly flustered, put a shaking hand to her forehead. "Then I'll go upstairs and you all search down here. She wouldn't have gone far."

Bascom sent Ellie a concerned look. "She couldn't have gotten past us. The back door is the only obvious choice. You'd have heard her enter the kitchen, and we'd have seen her enter the parlor. Your grandmother's in her room resting, right? And these wet footprints. . .someone had to have come in from outside."

Ellie's knees gave way, and she almost sank to the floor. She fought the sensation, though, and stayed on her feet. "Then you agree—someone has taken my daughter."

Bascom dropped down to inspect the footprints from a closer angle. He held a lantern above them.

"Tell me what you're thinking, Bascom." Ellie placed her hand on his shoulder, both as a way to feel his solid strength and to capture his attention.

"You don't think she'd go out on her own? Maybe to find us if she didn't completely wake up and thought maybe you were out there since the door stood open?"

"No." Though Ellie tried to sound strong, she failed miserably. "She's a heavy sleeper. She wouldn't have been able to wake that fast and get up. She'd have been sitting up in bed, waiting for me to come."

"What about your grandmother's room?"

"You said yourself she wouldn't have had time to get there after the crash."

She hurried through their personal parlor and looked into her grandmother's room. Prissy wasn't there. She rejoined the others.

"Then where else could she be?" Bascom paced the short hall. "You're absolutely sure she wouldn't have ventured outdoors if she did wake up confused?"

"I don't know. But I doubt it. Storms scare her." The thought of her daughter out there, possibly alone, sent tremors of horror through Ellie's body. The thought of her out there, not alone, brought along worse thoughts. "Bascom, if she did go, she'll never make it out there. You can't see two feet in front of your face, and she'll be lost in moments. The lake is too close and violent. If she falls in. . ." She stared up at him. "And what if someone has her? Those footprints didn't appear on their own."

Her legs no longer held her up, and she sank to the floor. "Oh, Prissy!"

Wanda's voice carried over to them from where she prayed for Prissy's safety.

Bascom took Ellie by the arms. "Ellie, we're going to find her. We need to pull together. We don't have a moment to lose. We've lost enough time as it is. I'm going for Sheldon, and you go round up the guests. Look everywhere you can think of where she might have hidden in the house. Do you understand?"

Ellie forced herself to nod. She had to get a grip. Her daughter needed her.

Bascom hurried into the storm, shutting the door behind him.

Though Bascom seemed inclined to point the finger of suspicion away from foul play, Ellie knew in her heart her daughter hadn't snuck off on her own to hide in fear. She ignored Bascom's directions and, instead, went into Wanda's former room where she pulled Bascom's small gun from a high shelf. She checked to make sure it was loaded and ready and then pulled on an overcoat, determined to join the search outside. Wanda would cover the search inside.

Ellie didn't take time to grab a lantern; the wind would surely blow it right out. Instead, she'd have to count on the lightning for visibility, if such a thing were possible in such blinding rain. She opened the back door, and the wind immediately snatched it from her hold, slamming the heavy wood barrier back into the wall. The strong wind whipped against her as she exited the house, almost knocking her from her feet. She grabbed hold of the banister and got her bearings. She again headed for the outbuilding where they did the laundry. Prissy still liked to play in there and for some strange reason, the room gave her a sense of security.

She pulled her cloak close against her neck with one hand and clutched the gun in the other. She'd never shot anyone before, but if someone had her daughter and meant harm to the little girl, she'd not hesitate to do whatever was needed.

A crash of thunder made her jump, the sound so near she knew the storm now sat directly overhead. She'd almost reached the protection of the washhouse when a strong hand clamped onto her shoulder.

Bascom sighed with relief when Ellie spun around to face him. His relief fled when he noticed the weapon aimed at his heart. He snatched the gun from her shaky grip and ushered her inside the dry room.

"What on earth are you thinking, coming out here armed in this mess? I thought I told you to search the house!"

"There are plenty of people searching in there right now. My abilities are better used out here. We need to find whoever took her and stop him."

"And how do you plan to do that? By shooting some innocent person? How would that help?"

"I didn't shoot you. You snuck up on me from behind and swung me around. I was ready to shoot whoever meant me—or my daughter—harm. If I'd meant to shoot you, you'd be lying on the ground, dead. Now move away and let me continue on. Both of us know Prissy didn't come out here of her own accord, and we both know that someone has taken her. I'll not be wasting my time inside when I can be out here, helping to cover more area." Her hands briefly clutched his jacket front and then slid down his lapel in despair. "Bascom. We're too late. She's probably long gone."

"Don't give up on me, Ellie. I'm going to find your daughter. But I want you to pull yourself together and wait inside the house. Running wild with a gun isn't going to fix matters."

"Standing here arguing won't fix matters, either. You keep the gun, but I'm going to continue my search. I'll go crazy if I have to sit inside, wasting my time while waiting for someone else to find her." She glanced behind him. "You said you were going for Sheldon. . . . Where is he?"

"He wasn't in the pavilion, so I'm searching without him." Bascom softened his voice. "Your time inside won't be a waste if you use it to pray for Priscilla's safety. Trust God, Ellie. I know He'll lead us to her."

"I can pray just fine from where I am."

"Fine. Continue your search, but please use caution." Bascom really wanted to tie her up and carry her back to the house. . .a situation that would surely carry repercussions in their future. But if he couldn't keep her stubborn self safe by force, he could do so with her by his side. It added another dimension to his search, but at least he'd know Ellie was all right. "As a matter of fact, just trail me. I can keep track of you that way."

He didn't miss Ellie's glare or the roll of her eyes, but he was thankful as she fell into step behind him. They exited the small room and reentered the deluge, which immediately engulfed them.

"Stick close to my heels," he yelled. "Grab on to my cloak if you must. But do *not* fall behind."

❧

Ellie heard his command, but the outline of a shadowy figure heading toward the pavilion momentarily distracted her. She knew it could be someone from inside the resort helping with the search, but if so, what was in the bundle the person carried?

She turned to capture Bascom's attention, but he'd already disappeared into the darkness ahead. Without giving further thought to her actions, she turned the opposite way and crept back to the pavilion.

The mud slowed her steps, causing her to slip and slide, but she pushed forward and with the wind at the other end of the building, slipped quietly through the back door and into the room. A flash of lightning lit up the room, and to Ellie's surprise illuminated Sheldon, who knelt in front of Priscilla with his hand clasped over Prissy's tiny mouth.

"Sheldon! You found her!" She started forward and then stopped, confused, as she registered the scene before her.

Bits and pieces of Sheldon's previous conversations flew through Ellie's mind. During the past few weeks, he'd purposely planted doubt about Bascom's past and present actions in order to throw suspicion off himself. All this time she'd suspected the wrong man. And Bascom's trust in his protégé had prevented him from seeing the truth, that the man he trusted the most was the one who least deserved his faith.

Fury roiled through her, and she threw caution to the wind. "Unhand my daughter at once, and move away from her."

She realized her mistake immediately. Sheldon snatched Prissy into his arms and without her weapon, Ellie had no way to bargain for her daughter's safety.

"Mama! Come get me."

Ellie watched as Prissy fought Sheldon's embrace, but the tiny girl's struggling had no effect on his strong grip.

"Sheldon, you're scaring her. Please, let her go and take me instead."

"Why should I do that when at the moment I have you both? You aren't going to leave here without your precious Prissy, now are you?"

Ellie wished for the gun. "No, I'll not leave my daughter. I'm staying with you, Prissy."

Prissy's sobs filled the air, and she again wrestled against his hold. "Let me go! I want my mama."

"No, it looks like I get more than I bargained for tonight. At first it seemed Bascom would keep you safely contained and out of my reach, but luck is on my side. This will be as much fun as the time I took away his wife and son."

Ellie gasped. "What a horrible thing to say." But he was right. If she'd listened to Bascom, Ellie would be safely inside and perhaps Bascom could have saved Prissy from the crazy man before he brought her to harm. As it was, Bascom now stood to lose them both, which would make him crazy with the pain and guilt.

"Your plan wouldn't have worked. Prissy disappeared while Bascom was with me. I wouldn't have suspected him. You've now convinced me, even though I'd already come to this conclusion, that Bascom is innocent of all you've pointed your finger at."

"Really, does any of that matter now? When you two reach your demise, Bascom will be the sole suspect, and I can move on and continue our trade without him. I know all he had to teach me and have no further need of his instruction."

"But why? As you just said, he trained you. He trusted you with his most valuable possession, his knowledge of creating one-of-a-kind carousels."

"Which is why I have no need of him any longer."

"I know he's taught you of other more important things, just as he has taught me. Such as how to have a relationship with Christ. Bascom's the type of man to hand over the reins of the business to you if it meant you'd leave those he cares about alone."

"I have no desire to learn about his God. And he wouldn't share the possession I most desired—his wife."

"His wife?"

"I had her first. We courted, and she knew my greatest desire would be to train with Bascom. She said she had a way to convince him to take me on as his apprentice. I didn't have any way to know that she enticed him to court her and in the process fell in love with him instead."

"But surely, if he'd known, he'd have ended the relationship out of preference to you?"

"No, by the time I found out, the apprenticeship was well on its way. My fiancée made it clear that if I told Bascom anything of our prior relationship, she'd make sure to ruin my future as a carousel designer before it even started."

Ellie felt sick to her stomach. "Bascom had no idea that you'd courted her. Nor did he know of his wife's true nature."

"I suppose he didn't. But that's beside the point. The point is, he ruined my life, and I had to get even. I righted the wrong caused by his wife, and now I'll get even with him by taking over the business he so treasures."

"But if he didn't know you'd courted her first, why would you lash out at him?"

He turned to her with a look that could only be described as pure evil. "Because it makes me feel better."

Ellie froze as Sheldon, thoroughly agitated and working himself into a frenzy, began to pace back and forth in front of the far window. Prissy's terrified cries were muffled by his beefy hand. Ellie wrung her hands, desperate for a way out of the mess. She sent up a prayer for help but knew no one had likely ventured out in the storm, and Bascom had gone on the other way. If she were to free Prissy from this demented man, she'd have to figure out a way to do it herself.

Chapter 16

The storm continued outside, pounding the roof of the pavilion with a vengeance. Gusts of rain lashed against the windows. Prissy's cries became louder as her terror grew over both the storm and the man who held her hostage.

"Sheldon, let her come to me." Ellie struggled to keep her voice steady, though fury and frustration flowed through her. "At least let her feel the safety of my arms."

Rain pounded against the building, and a loud crash against the north wall caused them all to jump. Prissy wailed, lunging for Ellie. Sheldon had to struggle to keep his hold. He jerked her hard against him and hissed into her ear. "Don't move again."

Ellie struggled to hear Sheldon's words over the brunt of the raging tempest. His mood seemed to match the maelstrom outside the window.

Lord, if ever I've needed You, it's now. Please help me find a way to help my daughter and get her safely away from this madman.

Even as she said the words, she felt clarity flow through her. She needed to stay focused. She'd be lucky to have even one opportunity to free her daughter, and if and when it came, she needed to be ready to make her move.

She glanced up, and lightning illuminated a face in the window. Holding back her scream, she hoped whoever was out there had seen enough to go for help.

ૐ

Bascom bit back the curse that threatened to explode from his mouth. Instead, he ranted at God. He'd lost a wife and son. Was history destined to repeat itself by taking Ellie and Priscilla from him, too? He'd lived a good life, had continued forward after his huge losses, and for what? Only to again lose the woman and child he loved?

Had Ellie decided to sneak away of her own accord? Or had the same person that snatched Prissy somehow taken her from under his nose, too?

He'd returned to the washhouse, but Ellie wasn't there. He continued the opposite way he'd come. He knew she hadn't passed him while going the other way. For whatever reason, she'd left his protection and turned a different direction.

The wind howled and his hat blew from his head. Ignoring it, he pressed forward. He heard the faint sound of a woman's voice from up ahead. Hoping against hope that the voice belonged to Ellie, he moved forward at a quicker pace. His foot slid out from under him and raw pain shot through his injured ankle as he dropped to his knees. Gasping, he breathed deeply, trying to quell the biting pain. He struggled back to his feet and continued on, ignoring the stab of agony each step brought.

"Bascom." The voice was closer now, but he realized it belonged to Wanda, not Ellie. Disappointment filled him, but he knew they had a better chance as a team.

"Over here." His voice sounded loud and ravaged. He didn't know whether pain or worry caused the infliction. "Stay near the building. Follow the wall."

He did the same, bracing himself against it for support, and within moments Wanda appeared in front of him. She looked as tormented as he felt. The wind had whipped her hair from its usual neat bun, and now the strands stuck to her face where the wind and rain pelted it. Her eyes were wild as she half ran, half crawled to him.

"I heard you yell." She stopped to catch her breath and grabbed his arm. Whether for support or to hold him in place he didn't know. "I found them. Both Priscilla and Ellie. They're in the pavilion. I saw through the window. It's dark, but the lightning flashed, and Sheldon stood just on the other side of the glass. Bascom, he looks demented and has Prissy clutched in his arms."

Bascom momentarily froze in place. "Sheldon? But why. . . He's the one?" He felt as if a vise clamped around his heart. He thought back to their recent conversation. Sheldon had played him for a fool. His voice came out in a tortured whisper. "I trusted him."

"I don't know why, Bascom. I'm so sorry." Wanda touched his arm. "What should we do?"

Bascom hurried forward, and Wanda blocked his path.

"Wanda, if Sheldon has them, even if he has only Prissy, and he's in the pavilion, he must plan to recreate my wife and son's deaths. He'd have to know he couldn't get away with this. I have to get to them."

Bascom shoved past her and moved toward the pavilion. He felt Wanda's hand as she grasped for his sleeve. He shook her off and continued on, his steps slowed by the throbbing ankle.

"Stop." Her voice commanded him to listen, and for a brief moment he did.

"I can't wait for you. Go for help. I need to get Priscilla away from him."

"You won't do any good if you go off half-cocked. It'll take both of us to stop him. I also saw Ellie standing a few feet away from them. The look on her face..." She shook her head. "I'll never get it out of my head. She's terrified, Bascom."

Bascom let her words sink in. "All the more reason for me to get in there."

"So you can be at his mercy, too? No. I won't allow it. I came for your help. Not so you could brush me aside and plow over me."

"I'm sorry for that. But now isn't the time for formalities. I have to get to them. Sheldon's been the one all along. And I trusted him. Don't you understand? All my grief, he must have savored it. But why? He's been my apprentice, my best friend. Or so I thought. Yet he killed my wife and son. Wanda, I can't let him do the same to Ellie and Priscilla."

"We don't know if he's armed. We aren't. We need a plan."

Bascom fingered the gun that still rested in his pocket, but didn't say anything to Wanda. She might not be armed, but he was. And in light of things, he couldn't wait to use the weapon against the murderous traitor that awaited him inside.

He thought a minute and then nodded. "I'll take a look first, and then we'll talk about strategy."

They crept closer to the windows, and Wanda motioned to the spot where she'd been standing. Bascom ducked and hesitantly moved forward, suddenly thankful for the storm that hid his approach. Lightning burst around him, and he rose up to peek into the dim interior. As Wanda had said, Sheldon still held Prissy, but now, free of terror, she hung limply in his arms. Ellie was nowhere in sight.

❧

Ellie, livid, had watched in horror when Prissy collapsed in Sheldon's arms. She thrust herself forward, only to have Sheldon block her with a solid arm, honed from years of handling heavy wood, and knock her to the floor with a *thud*.

"She's fine. She fainted."

"My daughter doesn't faint. You held your hand too tightly against her mouth. You've suffocated her." Her hate-filled words, sharp with venom, lashed out at the man. "You've killed my daughter!"

She couldn't breathe. The thought of losing her daughter brought Ellie such pain that she couldn't remember how to take in air. She clutched at her stomach and rocked back and forth, struggling to catch her breath. "My baby. . ."

Sheldon laughed. "I love the theatrics, Ellie. If you weren't about to meet your end, you'd do well to take up acting." He continued his hold on Priscilla, but resumed his pacing across the room. "And while we're on that topic, did you also act when spending time with me? Was your devotion real? Or was it also contrived?"

"Any devotion toward you on my part had to be imagined. . .but only by your insane mind." Ellie spat the words his way, but he didn't seem to notice the malice. Prissy made a slight mewling sound, and Ellie almost collapsed on the spot with relief. At least he hadn't lied about her daughter's well-being. "Besides,

I thought you had intentions toward Wanda."

"Wanda? Not a chance. I only spent time with her out of boredom while waiting for my time with you. But as usual, Bascom had to slide in with his debonair ways and snatch you out from under me."

Ellie couldn't believe this conversation. The man was mad and then some. "There was no 'snatching' or anything else. I've been too busy to think about anything other than the resort. And even if I were looking for a relationship, it wouldn't have been with you. You were nice to talk to—or so I thought—but only in the way of a friend. Now I have to wonder if my very soul somehow sensed your evil."

Sheldon's face crinkled into something wicked. "You did care. I saw it in your eyes and the way you smiled at me. I saw you pull back your window curtain at night, searching the dark for my presence."

"I searched the dark for the madman that terrorized the resort. Unfortunately, my naïveté left you out of that equation. If it hadn't, maybe we'd have known sooner and avoided this unpleasant situation."

"Unpleasant indeed. You're going to meet your Maker tonight. Lucky for you that Bascom has spent so much time talking of the Greater Being that would 'save' you. I guess soon you'll find out whether his story is truth or fiction."

Ellie wasn't getting anywhere with her hatred, so she changed tactics. "Sheldon, I believe in God and everything that Bascom has told me. If you'd take a moment, maybe you'd find out the truth, too. It's not too late."

"No, maybe not, but it will be soon if I don't get on with my plan to dupe Bascom. Then I can stand at his side and watch him grieve for another two years." He grabbed her hair and pulled her to her feet. His voice oozed sarcasm. "Move toward my room over there. I think that's the best place to follow through on my intentions. You can thank your God that Prissy won't be conscious or know what's going on."

Just as they reached the carousel, the outer door blew open. It slammed into the wall with such force that Sheldon lost his grip on Prissy. Taking advantage of his distracted state, Ellie threw her body against his and clutched at her daughter. Another body came from the other direction, and Ellie held on to Prissy and protected her as they fell to the floor. Lantern light filled the room, and Ellie glanced up to see Wanda near the back door, dripping wet, while holding the lantern from Sheldon's room high in the air.

❧

Ellie pulled Prissy close and scuttled back toward the wall as Bascom pounded the cowering form of Sheldon. Rain poured into the room until Wanda set the lantern on the carousel's base and hurried over to fight the door closed. The sudden change in loudness roused Prissy.

"It's okay, baby. It's okay. Mama has you now."

Prissy cried softly and clung to Ellie. Wanda hurried over to gather them both in her arms. They sat as a group of three and watched as Bascom towered over Sheldon's prostrate body, lifted a small revolver, and pressed it firmly against Sheldon's head. He cocked the gun.

"Bascom, no!" Ellie hurried to hand Prissy to Wanda and crawled to Bascom's side. "Stop. You don't want to do this."

"Oh, but I do. You'll never know how much I'm savoring the fact that I get to personally put an end to all the pain Sheldon has caused. I get to watch his eyes as I pull the trigger. I want to feel the power of justice done. I want to see him as he goes to his demise."

"It isn't your place, Bascom." She reached over and tilted the top of the gun away from Sheldon's head. Bascom froze in place and glowered at her. "You'll get your justice as you watch the sheriff take him away. And at his trial. If you end things now, it will be over for him. Let the law take control, Bascom, and let Sheldon suffer the consequences legally. Will that not be more justice? To let him sit and rot in a jail cell as he contemplates his fate?"

Still Bascom didn't move.

She dropped her voice to a whisper. "Do you forever want Prissy's mind to carry the image of what she's about to witness at your hands?"

This time her words hit their mark and a look of devastation crossed his features. He remained as he was, with a knee pressed against Sheldon's back, but the hand holding the gun dropped limply to his lap. "What has become of me? What am I thinking?"

"You're thinking a lot of unanswered questions have suddenly been answered, and the answer you were looking for is here along with a lot of pain. It's going to be all right, Bascom."

He reached up and pulled her into his arms, careful to keep the loaded weapon pointed away from her. She leaned into his embrace.

"I'll go for help. You keep him covered." She stood and hurried over to Wanda.

Prissy propelled herself into Ellie's waiting arms.

Wanda waved her toward the door. "You go ahead. I'll stay here with them."

They both froze as they heard another click of the gun.

Chapter 17

I'm sorry I startled you yesterday when I reset the trigger." Bascom scrunched his face into a grimace.

The bright early morning sun shone down upon them as they strolled along the shoreline of the lake, their hands tentatively interlaced. It seemed forever ago that Ellie had felt the security of having her hand held in a man's strong grip. Her thoughts couldn't be farther away from the previous night's events. It took her a moment to catch up with his thoughts, but when she did, she sent him a playful look. "Don't worry about it. The scare kept my mind off the raging storm that I had to carry Prissy through."

He tugged at her, pulling her closer against his side, and she laughed. They walked in silence for a few moments, enjoying the serenity of the lakeside after the furious storm of the previous day. Though the sky showed no trace of the gray clouds, the ground gave testament that they'd suffered mightily from the wind. Debris lined the water's edge, and pieces of wood and cloth bobbed on the water's surface.

Ellie shuddered at what might have been. "Prissy could have wandered into this mess."

"No, Sheldon admitted he snuck back in and took her straight from her bed to the pavilion. He only hesitated to see if the storm would die out, but when he heard you yelling, he hurried on into the brunt of it, which must have been when you saw him."

"And now? What happened after I left the pavilion?"

Bascom chuckled. "You mean after you sent the retired sheriff to aid me? His wife said he was happier than she'd seen him in years when you came through that door, first because you had Priscilla safely in your arms, but then because you sent him to my side. I guess he's been at loose ends of late and relished the occasion to step back into the role of defender of the law."

"So, did he send one of the other men for the sheriff in town?"

"No. He insisted no one go out into the storm and instead sat with Sheldon all night, keeping him under armed guard until I could ride out at daybreak to bring back the law."

"I'm glad someone benefitted from this awful mess. I still don't understand why Sheldon did it all. He explained his reasoning to me, but it doesn't make any sense. Why didn't he have it out with you from the start? If your wife truly loved him, then she moved on, why didn't he just accept that and do the same?"

Bascom sighed. "I'm not sure we'll ever understand the whys and where-to-fors of Sheldon's mind."

Ellie worried her lower lip and contemplated his answer that wasn't really an answer.

"Do you think it's true your wife loved him first?" Immediately she realized the inappropriateness of her question and retracted her comment. "I'm sorry. That was beyond insensitive. This all has to be so painful for you. Don't bother formulating an answer to such a heartless question."

"No. It's a fair question." Bascom looked at her, his pain-filled eyes tugging at her heart. "I've thought about it all night, and I've not come up with an answer. My wife did insist that Sheldon be a part of everything we did. She's the one that begged me to train him under the pretense that it would allow me more time for her. But looking back, she resented carrying my son. I thought she'd adjust after his birth, but instead she seemed to grow more distant and angry. She compared Sheldon's carefree life to our life many times. Maybe she wished she had married him instead. I don't know. But justice has finally been served. Sheldon was caught. And nothing will bring my son back. Trying to figure everything out, well, we'll probably never know answers to all of it."

"I really am sorry, Bascom. I know it has to hurt to think your wife wasn't as faithful as you thought."

Bascom stopped, turned her to face him, and grasped her other hand. "There were lots of things, signs, that if I'd stopped to pay more attention, would have shown me the truth earlier. I'm sure of it now that I look back. Instead I buried myself in work and hoped things would settle down with time."

"But they didn't."

"No. Instead I lost everything. . .but in the process I gained my relationship with God and came through the pain a stronger person. Nothing will ever replace the loss of my son, but I know he's in a better place now and one day I'll be reunited with him."

"And your wife?" Ellie forced herself to breathe. She hated asking him these questions, but they slipped out of their own accord. And deep down she knew she had to hear where he stood on each topic.

"My wife, to my knowledge, never stepped foot in a church or read the Word of God. The few times I tried to get her to go for our son's sake, she laughed in my face. So as I said, I worked. We didn't go to church."

"If it wasn't for you, Bascom, I'd be in the same place. Thank you for caring enough to share the love of the Lord with me."

"You're more than welcome. I'm glad good came from my presence after all the mess I brought along. Maybe it's wrong, but I feel a measure of relief now that the mystery of both places is solved. I'm just sorry we didn't catch on quicker. He threw us off with the vandalism to the other resorts. I wish things had been different, but the facts are what they are. I'll have to work through things, and I know I'll have a lot of things to talk out with God over the next few months, but for the first time in a long time, I feel I can move forward with my life." Complete peace shone through Bascom's eyes for the first time since they met up on the front porch earlier in the day—when he'd grabbed her in a strong, protective hug. After he'd assured himself that she was safe and all was well, the peaceful expression had quickly changed to one of remorse.

Bascom now smiled at her with that familiar crooked grin and pulled her close, his eyes searching hers with a glow of discovery, as if he'd just found a treasure. Her heart picked up its pace as he leaned down and gently brushed his lips across hers.

"Am I a part of that future?" Her voice sounded breathless even to her own ears.

"I sure hope so, Ellie. You and Priscilla both. This is all new to me, but I didn't sleep much last night, and I did give the future some thought. What I'd like would be to stick around and help you here at the resort while basing my creations out of the area." His thumb caressed hers, momentarily distracting her as it sent little trills up her hand and arm. She forced herself to focus.

"You'd still travel and do your carousels, then." She couldn't explain her disappointment, though she knew in part it had to do with the fact that she needed to stay to run the place and couldn't afford to shut down and travel if they were to marry.

A flush warmed her face as she realized how far her own thoughts had strayed, all because of a silly kiss. He hadn't even mentioned marriage. Maybe he had friendship in mind, a protective alliance of sorts. She needed a man around, and he needed a place to live. But deep down she knew it was more than that. A realization hit and a smile formed on her lips. The kiss a few moments earlier had nothing to do with friendship. And it had everything to do with romance. It had enough passion behind it that maybe her thoughts of marriage weren't too far from the mark. The warmth of the flush returned.

Bascom chuckled. "I'm not sure where your thoughts have gone, but I hope the expression on your face bodes well for our relationship. To answer your question, I'd like to stay put and ship the carousels anywhere they need to go. I can interview the purchaser on paper and still custom design each creation. I have some other ideas I'll tell you about later, other ways to make a living with my wood carving. And if I were to take on a carousel project and if I were to travel, if we were married. . . you and Prissy could tag along as a holiday for the short time we'd need to be away. I'm sure we could arrange for someone to watch over things here while we were gone."

Tears filled Ellie's eyes. "Is that a proposal?"

Bascom laughed. "Not the best one I could offer, but yes, it's a very clumsy attempt at one." His words were light, but his eyes were serious as he waited for her answer.

Speechless for once, Ellie only nodded.

He grabbed her up and swung her around in a circle.

Her delighted laugh at his unexpected jubilance rang out. "Oh my. What would people think if they saw us?"

"They'd know they were observing a very special moment." A beautiful smile transformed his features. Bascom closed his eyes and shook his head as if to clear it. "Let me try this again so I can do it properly." His blue eyes softened as he met her gaze. "Ellie, will you marry me? You can take all the time you need, but I know in my heart it's what I want."

"It's what I want, too, and I don't need a lot of time."

"I promise I'll do everything in my power to make you and Prissy happy."

"You've already made us happy, Bascom. I can't imagine a better ending to the past week's events than this."

"How about we forget all that and look at it as our new beginning?"

"That sounds wonderful. So. . .shall we go share the news?"

"I'd be delighted."

Now, with their hands clutched tighter than before, they began their walk back toward the resort.

"I have a question." Ellie glanced sideways at him.

"Just one?" His eyes twinkled in humor at what must surely seem to be her hundredth question of the morning. "Is it the last?"

"Probably not." She looked toward him, squinted into the sun, and sent him a smirk. "How did you know where to find us last night? You arrived just in the nick of time."

"Ah, the question I've been waiting to hear. Wanda saw you and came for me."

"She was the face in the window!"

"Apparently so. And as we crept around the building, trying to figure out a plan, a barrel rammed into the wall, barely missing her leg. We hurried along, but after seeing the distraction the loud bang caused Sheldon, we knew he was jumpy and came up with a plan."

"And the plan was. . . ," Ellie urged him on when he paused, the playful twinkle still in his eyes. "Don't keep me waiting."

"The plan was, she'd throw open the door and cause a diversion to block any noise I might make while sneaking through the back."

"Apparently it worked."

"Indeed it did. And Ellie. . ."

Ellie snuggled against him as his arm wrapped around her shoulders. "Yes?"

"I promise to do everything in my ability to never make you wait. That promise includes any further wait when it comes to the carousel. The unveiling will still be tonight."

Chapter 18

"Mama, Mama, hurry up! Everybody's waiting." Prissy's dramatic voice carried down the hallway and through the open door just before she danced through the opening.

"Everybody?" Ellie teased. Though they'd invited all their guests and a few neighbors to visit the carousel for its unveiling, Ellie would first receive a private showing so she could savor the moment without anyone else present.

"Grammy is serving refreshments on the front porch. I got an extra specially big sugar cookie and a glass of lemonade, too."

Which accounted for her daughter's intensified exuberance at the moment. If the excitement of the event and unveiling wasn't enough to make her daughter bounce off the walls, sweets always made Prissy extra bouncy.

"Can I go get another cookie while I wait?"

"No! I mean, no, I'm almost ready. Let me take one more quick peek in the mirror, and we'll head out."

"Mr. Bascom Anthony is waiting for us out back."

Hop, hop, hop. She tripped on her blue calico skirt and catapulted into Ellie's side. Ellie stayed her with her hands.

"Settle down, honey. And you know you don't have to call him by all his names. Mr. Bascom or Mr. Anthony is just fine for now."

"But I like to call him by all his names. No one else does, so it's special. Until I can call him by his really special name. Daddy. After we get married, I get to call him that, right?"

Ellie quirked the side of her mouth up and smiled in amusement. "Right."

"Are you ready *now*?" Prissy formed her mouth into a pout. " 'Cause we've waited a very long time for you to see your surprise. I don't even get a ride until you see it. We both get to go on the. . .the. . .maiden foyage."

"Maiden voyage?"

"Yep. Maiden foyage." She hopped toward the door. "C'mon, let's *go!*"

"I'm ready, daughter." Ellie settled her hat at a jaunty angle on her head. The hat matched her mood. She reached for Prissy's hand.

"Mr. Bascom Anthony! We're coming!" Prissy bellowed down the hall.

Ellie heard his rich laugh from the back porch. He stepped into sight just outside the door. He made a show of checking his watch before tucking it slowly into his trouser pocket.

"It's about time." He sent her his crooked grin.

Ellie's heart fluttered. Even without the newfound sparkle in his brilliant blue eyes, the man was extremely handsome. The soft breeze tugged at his hair, which again looked ready for a visit with Gram's shears. But she rather liked it this way.

"I'm right on time and you know it," she teased back. "The both of you would do well to learn some patience."

"Patience? We've waited how long now to show you this creation?" Bascom played along.

"Forever!" Prissy joined in.

They began to walk toward the pavilion.

Ellie strolled leisurely between the two of them. "Hardly forever. You haven't known about the carousel forever, Priscilla."

She turned to Bascom. "And you. You might have had the structure in mind a bit longer than Priscilla, but you only finished it yesterday."

Bascom rubbed his chin in contemplation. "Are you sure? It seems it's been much longer." He sent a questioning look to Prissy.

Prissy giggled and nodded. "It has only been a day. But we've been building it for much longer. And we need our maiden foyage."

"Prissy!" Now Bascom clutched at his heart, feigning indignation. "Are you giving away our secrets?" He reached over and tucked Ellie's arm around his other one.

"No, not secrets, only hints."

"So, maiden voyage is a hint, hmm? I thought you were planning a carousel, not a ship." Ellie reached over to tug one of Prissy's dark braids.

"Mama, it's beautiful. Just you wait and see." Prissy's voice became breathless as they neared the building. "Can I run ahead?"

"Sure." Bascom's voice held a hint of mischief. "Wait for us just inside. Tell Wanda we're ready."

Prissy squealed and hurried off.

Ellie looked at him, eyebrows raised.

"What?" He shrugged. "Is it wrong for a man to want a moment alone with his future bride?"

A shiver ran up Ellie's arm as he caressed her hand that hugged his arm. She laid her head against his shoulder, and they walked in companionable silence. As they neared the door, his footsteps slowed. Ellie could hear the sound of an organ from inside the building in front of them.

Ellie looked up at him. "What is it?"

He scowled, looked toward the entrance, and then back at her. "I've never felt this nervous about an unveiling before. I know you'll like it, yet. . ."

"Yet what? How could I not love something you've made with your own artistic hands? I'd love it even if it had nothing to do with me."

"I just want you to be happy."

"I am happy." Ellie could feel the glow reflecting from her face. How could he not see it as well?

He apparently did because relief replaced the scowl, and he grinned her way. "So you're ready?"

"More than. Let me see your creation!"

Prissy stood in the doorway, giggling. She waved inside, and the music grew louder. A wispy piece of fabric hung over the doorway, and Bascom pushed it aside so they could enter the building.

They stopped just inside and waited for Ellie's eyes to adjust to the dim interior. Soft gas lighting lit the room, adding a dreamy quality to the fantasy scene before them. The transformation that had taken place in the room took Ellie's breath away, but her eyes were drawn immediately to the centerpiece, the magnificent carousel in the middle of the room.

THE LAND OF WHIMSY had been hand lettered in elegant script around the side of the carousel's canopy. Wooden seashells and starfish, painted in bright colors to match the sea creatures, framed the words and disappeared out of sight around the curve of the roof. The entire structure seemed to embody the many characters from her stories.

"You've captured Whimsy." Her voice was an awestruck whisper. "It's beautiful."

Bascom and Prissy each took hold of one of Ellie's hands and led her to the platform. She stepped onto the wooden floor of the structure, which wobbled slightly under her weight. Priscilla hopped up beside her, Bascom at her heels. The late afternoon sunlight beamed through the many windows and reflected off the shiny creatures that stood side by side in sets of two around the circumference of the platform. Seahorses, dolphins, huge fish, and even stingrays painted with vivid color and wearing expressions of pure joy danced around before her.

A laugh bubbled out from her. "I absolutely love it!"

She walked around the circle, trailing her hands softly across each carved piece.

"Look, Mama! Jewels. Just like pirate treasure." Prissy pointed out the various jewels that sparkled brilliantly in the sunlight.

Ellie watched as her daughter rubbed her finger over a large sapphire blue gem that had been inset into a dolphin's saddle.

"Are you ready for a ride?" Ellie, so lost in her musings, jumped as Bascom leaned close to her ear.

"It's time for our maiden foyage?" Prissy's voice rose several octaves.

"Aye, 'tis finally time, Princess Priscilla." Bascom swung her up into his arms. "Would you prefer your maiden voyage to be upon the Mighty Schooner?"

Perplexed, Ellie glanced around and watched as Bascom deposited a pouting Priscilla into a small bench shaped like a boat that could seat two or three people.

"This boat doesn't move. You know what I wanted to ride for our maiden foyage."

Bascom winked at Ellie. Wanda's music danced around them.

"I do? Hmm." He glanced around, a frown momentarily pulling his eyebrows closer together. He snapped his fingers. "I've got it."

He walked over and swung Prissy back up into his arms, motioning Ellie to follow. Prissy began to giggle and peeked over his shoulder as if to make sure Ellie had followed his directive.

"Could it be. . .this?" He stopped next to matching mermaids, one slightly smaller than the other. He started to lift Priscilla onto it then stopped.

"C'mon, please?" Prissy reached forward with her leather-encased toe, her blue calico skirt draping around her outstretched leg. "Mama, he wouldn't let me sit on here until you were here to sit on yours."

"Mine?" Ellie stepped closer, noticing for the first time that the larger beautiful creature mirrored her own features. "Oh, Bascom."

"She looks just like you, Mama! And look, mine looks like me."

Sure enough, her daughter's mermaid resembled Prissy in a most remarkable way. Long dark curls were carved in wood and decorated with paint. The younger mermaid's eyes sparkled brown, just like Prissy's.

"I'm not sure I could ever be quite this beautiful, but the coloring, down to the green eyes, and features do mimic mine in a most amazing way." She circled around the mermaid and then did the same with her daughter's. "And, Prissy, you're right. Your mermaid is the spitting image of you! She's beautiful, honey."

Prissy leaned forward and hugged her mermaid. Ellie hadn't realized the scope of Bascom's talent until now. He didn't deserve to be hidden away out here when he could receive accolades from clients all over the world.

He seemed to read her emotions and leaned close. "What brings such a forlorn expression to your face? I thought you'd like them. If you don't. . .I can replace her with something—anything—else. I didn't mean to make you uncomfortable, though you truly are every bit as beautiful—even more so—than this carved figure."

"It's not that." Ellie searched his eyes. "It's just that you have a talent I've never seen before. It doesn't seem right to hide you, or this, away."

"Who's hiding?" Bascom smiled. "I don't need an audience to create. I don't like the hoopla that comes along with the career like some do. I prefer to work and be left alone. I carve to honor the gift that God gave me. But I want the glory of the talent to go to Him, not to me."

"Let's go, let's go, let's go!" Prissy's patience had become frayed.

Bascom waited a moment more, looking into Ellie's eyes for approval. She searched his face for any sign of remorse, but only found love shining out from his eyes. She allowed her mouth to drift into a smile. "If you're sure."

"Positive." He stole a quick kiss and jumped to the center of the attraction where he placed his hand over a small handle. "Prissy, do you remember what I taught you?"

"Yes, sir. I have to hold on tight. The steam has been building for almost two hours. When you pull the lever, the steam will release and we'll begin to spin."

The last word was uttered in pure reverence at the idea. Ellie couldn't help but catch her daughter's exuberance. Bascom jumped back onto the platform and hurried to her side. Before she could move, he gently grasped her waist and lifted her to sit sideways upon her own mermaid. She clung to the bar, not sure what to expect.

"Excellent description, Prissy." He turned to Ellie. "We've primed her for weeks about the process. I can't believe she didn't tell you and that she kept the secret so well. I'm proud of that little girl."

Ellie didn't think any words could make her heart swell any bigger. Hearing the man she loved talk about her daughter's precociousness melted something deep inside.

Bascom returned to the lever. He grinned and sent Ellie a wink. Her stomach fluttered, as much from the wink as from the anticipation. He placed his work-hardened hand upon the shiny piece of metal. Prissy squealed. Slowly, he moved the lever into position and the ride began to spin, slowly at first, but gaining in momentum as the seconds passed. Ellie grasped the pole in front of her for a moment, but relaxed her hold as the ride steadied its pace.

Priscilla laughed with abandon but clutched her own pole with white-knuckled fingers. Bascom jumped aboard and stood between them.

Releasing one hand from the pole, Prissy gripped Bascom's sleeve. "Tell her about the ring."

Ellie glanced at her daughter. The room spun around them, making the gaslights blur behind her daughter's silhouette. "The ring?"

Wanda continued to play a lighthearted tune on the organ, which added a festive flair to the moment.

"The ring." Bascom wrapped one arm around Ellie's waist and pointed with his finger to the edge of the ride's canopy above them. "If you can grasp the ring, you get a free ride."

"Really." Ellie fought back her grin as she studied the small brass circle before it whisked past her head. "And if I miss?"

Bascom's deep chuckle filled the air around her. "Then I suppose you could end up in a heap on the floor."

Ellie now understood why straw had been brought in to surround the structure. She clutched the pole more tightly. "I'd rather that not happen."

She watched as Bascom edged his way around her mermaid. The carved piece of wood rode up and down as the pole moved in a similar fashion. Bascom leaned out and much to Prissy's delight, snatched the ring from its resting place.

"You did it, Mr. Bascom, you did it!" Prissy almost fell off her mermaid in excitement. Ellie clutched her arm and pushed her back into place.

Bascom jumped back to the center flooring and pushed the lever back into its original position.

Prissy cried out in dismay.

"It's okay, Priss. We have a lot of guests waiting for their turn, and you'll be able to ride to your heart's content with them. But for now, I have something special for both of you."

"Yes, sir."

Bascom helped them off their respective mounts, and they stepped from the platform. Prissy ran off to collect Wanda while Ellie's world continued to spin. Bascom kept a firm grip on her arm and led her to a nearby chair. He knelt down beside it and turned his closed fist until it faced fingers up. "I have something for you. I hope you'll accept it."

Slowly he opened his fingers, and Ellie saw a beautiful gold ring lying upon his palm. She glanced over to see the brass ring once again in place on the carousel. How he'd managed to slip it back up there and switch it out with this ring was beyond her.

"This ring will come to mean so much to both of us. It represents the circular shape of the carousel, which first brought us together. It represents my love for you and for Prissy—you've helped me come full circle from my grief to a new hope for the future. And it represents the circle of love that will flow between us and our Lord, constantly growing as we move forward in love for each other and Him."

"Oh, Bascom, that's beautiful. I do accept the ring and all that it represents." She watched as he slipped the golden band onto her right index finger. "I never dreamed my carousel would come with treasure."

"When we marry, I'll take great joy in moving the ring to your other hand."

Wanda and Prissy moved into Ellie's line of vision. Bascom eased himself back to his feet. Ellie waggled her finger at them, and they oohed and aahed for a moment.

Bascom motioned Prissy closer. "Prissy, I have a treasure for you, too."

"Really? Where?"

He walked over to the refreshment counter and reached below to pull out a miniature replica of their carousel, but this one's lettering read differently.

"Carousel Dreams," Ellie read out loud to her daughter.

"My very own carousel?" Prissy clapped her hands together and squealed louder than she had on the ride. She leaned closer. "It even has the Mama and Prissy mermaids."

She turned, and without warning, threw herself into Bascom's embrace. "I love it. And I love you. Thank you!" Tears ran down the little girl's face.

"You're welcome." Bascom, his voice choked up, lifted her high into his arms where she buried her face in his shoulder. "And I love you, too."

Ellie raised her hand to her mouth and watched both through tear-blurred eyes. She caressed her new ring with her thumb as a secret smile moved across her face. Only one more event would supersede the preciousness of the moment, and that special day would soon come.

Epilogue

Mama." Priscilla's voice dropped to a childish whisper of awe. "You're so pretty! You look like the Princess of Whimsy."

Ellie smiled and adjusted her skirts, bending her knees so she could lower to her daughter's level. She balanced on the balls of her feet and whispered back. "No, *you* look like the Princess of Whimsy. Just look at you in that beautiful gown. I'm so proud of you, sweetheart."

Priscilla's gaze grew solemn. "Are we really going to marry Bascom now?"

Ellie could hear Wanda's chuckle from where she stood across the small room. She exchanged a happy smile with her friend. "We really are."

"I like him."

"So do I. He's going to make us very happy."

"We'll make him happy, too, Mama. Remember how sad he was when he came here?"

"I do." Ellie thought back to the day of his arrival. Though deep down her heart instantly recognized her future husband, her mind and rationality had rebelled. She couldn't see past her grandfather's foolish notion to build the carousel, and still reeling from grief over his death, had lashed out at Bascom unfairly. "But now he's happy again. He's getting a new wife and a wonderful daughter."

"That he is," Wanda agreed, coming over to help Ellie up. "And you're going to sweep him off his feet when he sees you. But only if you stop talking and get out there for the ceremony."

"I thought I was the one who was supposed to be swept off my feet," Ellie teased. The sound of voices from outside carried through the wall, and Ellie tried to quell the butterflies that danced inside her stomach. She knew without a doubt that marrying Bascom would bring them all a lot of joy. Things had certainly changed during the past two months.

"And I'm guessing he will. I saw him a bit earlier, and he's heart-stopping handsome in his suit. I saw every woman in the room stop talking and stare after his arrival. You've got a good man there, Ellie, and you'd best hurry out and snatch him up."

"He is a good man. I wish it hadn't taken me so long to realize it."

"I think you both realized it from that first moment in the parlor. Or at least everyone around you did. Your grandmother asked me to begin work on your

233

dress that very night."

Ellie laughed. "Now you're teasing me."

"I'm not!" Wanda faked her indignation, lightening the mood for them both. "She pulled me aside and said, 'My granddaughter has just met her match. If my intuition is correct, you need to start work on a wedding dress for her and fast!'"

Mortified, Ellie laughed. "It was that obvious?"

"To all of us, yes. To the two of you, apparently not. I think Sheldon saw it, too, which is why he started in on his new vendetta so quickly—a plan that failed miserably. But you two, you're both so stubborn it took some time to get past your defenses and see that you'd each met your perfect match."

Ellie took a deep breath and checked her appearance once more in the looking glass. She'd pinned her dark hair up on top of her head, but tendrils had drifted down to frame her square face. Not wanting to take time to set the wayward pieces to right, she ignored them. She smiled at Wanda. "Well then, if you think I'm ready, I'd like to go get hitched."

"You're radiant." Wanda's tear-filled eyes met hers in the reflection. "The dress couldn't fit better, both for you and the occasion."

The full skirt of the white dress brushed the ground. Small white shell-shaped appliqués pulled the sheer top layer's hem up at intervals, holding it in place about a foot above the under layer's hem. The neck scooped down gracefully, finished with tatting also in the shape of shells, and simple long sleeves hugged her arms. The bodice clung tightly and tapered to her waist, where the fabric flared out into the full skirt.

"It does look wonderful," Ellie agreed. "And I have you to thank for that. I had no idea you'd create such an elegant gown. How did you ever come up with the idea?"

"I've only listened to your Whimsy tales for how long? The dress lived in your imagination long before I ever put it to fabric. You might convince yourself that your stories are for Prissy, but I know they really come from your heart. A princess wedding will only be complete if there's a princess. . .or two."

They both looked at Priscilla where she stood on tiptoe, peering out the window toward the festivities. Her daughter, frothed in layers of girlie pastel pink, indeed looked her part. They laughed at her continuous narration of the events unfolding outside their window. "Oh, there's a carriage with the reverend. And his wife is carrying a platter of food. I wonder what they have. I'm hungry—can we eat soon? Will we have Whimsy tale food? What do they eat in Whimsy?"

She didn't seem to notice her mother's and housekeeper's lack of response; she just continued to watch and review.

"I'm ready, Wanda." Ellie hugged her friend and turned to her daughter.

"Come along. Shall we go see exactly what will happen in the land of Whimsy on this day?"

Prissy grabbed her hand and led the way outdoors. The sky was clear with no cloud in sight. Blue stretched before them and disappeared over the rooftop of the pavilion. They strolled slowly in the direction of what had become known as the event of the year. Ellie smiled up at the sign that hung low over the pavilion's door frame. It matched the name on Prissy's new toy.

CAROUSEL DREAMS.

She hoped all those who entered would find a way to reach their own personal dreams. She had every one of hers she could imagine. Good friends, a good life, her daughter, and soon, her husband.

The last few stragglers hurried inside at her appearance. Ellie stopped at the door and waited for Wanda to step ahead. After a few deep breaths to calm her racing pulse, she stepped through the open doorway.

Again, awe and disbelief stopped her just inside, reminiscent of Bascom's first unveiling a few short weeks earlier. He'd formed the entry into a shop of sorts, and small carousels—miniatures of the ones he'd carved on the main attraction itself—lined the shelves. Candies in jars and other small trinkets also lined the counters. The effect was that of a small fair, right inside their pavilion. The carousel embodied the several Whimsy tale characters that Ellie had spoken of—a fish, a dolphin, and a seahorse along with standard horses. The outside edges of the structure, both top and platform, were carved into the shape of waves and rimmed with seashells. The centerpieces, Ellie's favorite part, were the matching mother and daughter mermaids, carved to match her and Prissy's features.

When she'd first seen them, she couldn't stop the smile that filled her face. Bascom, with his unique talent and ability, had captured her imaginary world and corralled it into reality. She knew he must have stayed up late into the night, on many occasions, to get the details honed to match her stories in so little time.

She mourned the talent Sheldon had also brought to the attraction and prayed for him often. She hoped he'd someday lose the bitterness, turn his life over to God, and find joy in living free from the previous burdens.

But today the room had been transformed even more into a fairy-tale setting; sheer fabrics and ribbon and greenery draped from every ceiling fixture available. Expectant faces watched to see the bride's expression. Prissy's warm hand tightened around Ellie's. For once, her daughter was speechless.

And now Ellie, though she'd taken a moment to observe the beauty and breathtaking scene before her, had eyes for only one man. She felt as if she were walking on air as she floated on happiness and stopped before him.

His expression matched her feeling of awe as he drank in the sight of her in the princess dress. "You're so beautiful." His whisper mimicked Priscilla's earlier response to the dress, and tears formed in Ellie's eyes at the display of love reflecting back from his.

"Thank you." She reveled in his presence. He'd dressed the part of a handsome prince. A long black swallowtail coat hugged his slender torso while a deep blue vest that perfectly matched the color of his eyes glistened in shiny fabric from beneath. The top of a pleated white shirt peeked out above the vest, complete with a black silk cravat tied neatly beneath his collar. Slim dark Edgewood pants with tiny blue and white pinstripes completed the ensemble. The style matched Ellie's dress and their Whimsy theme perfectly.

But her handsome prince himself took her breath away. Thick wavy locks of sun-kissed brown hair neatly brushed across his forehead and flipped back over his ears from a side part. His blue eyes twinkled with life, giving the suggestion of an unspoken joke that waited to spill from his lips. And those lips. . .they curved up to the left and highlighted the dimple in his cheek. His whole appearance shone with happiness. The burdens he'd arrived with were left behind, and the new man before her exuded a calm exuberance.

"Where've you been?" His words were low, for her ears only.

Perplexed, Ellie glanced out the window. "In the house."

He laughed. "All my life?"

"Well, no." She laughed back. "But I've been waiting right here."

"I'm glad you waited."

"Me, too." She leaned closer. "And I'm glad you found me."

"Me, too," he echoed. He closed his eyes and leaned his forehead against hers.

Ellie could feel his soft breath against her face and savored the closeness. Bascom opened his eyes, captured her hand in his, and brought it to his lips for a gentle kiss. Their audience oohed and aahed around them.

"You're blushing, Ellie."

He didn't have to tell her that. She'd forgotten about their guests; so absorbed was she in his presence that they'd melted into the background. But at their enthusiastic murmurings, she quickly remembered they weren't alone. The pastor saved her from the moment.

He called them all together and asked them to circle around Ellie and Bascom. Ellie distracted herself from further thoughts of her future husband by looking around to see who had come to help them celebrate this most special of days. All her closest neighbors were there, as well as a lot of friends from town. The celebration carried more meaning for those nearby, who could also celebrate the fact that the vandalism had been thwarted and the villain placed behind bars.

She saw guests from the resort and friends of Bascom's that had come from afar, even on such short notice. They'd arrived during the past few days and had filled her resort and several others around them. She also saw a few reporters.

"Why do the men over there have cameras? They look too official to be guests."

Bascom followed her gaze. "They're friends from back East. They caught the train in when they heard about Sheldon and the wedding."

He caressed her hand and leaned close to speak into her ear. "They'd followed the story back in Coney and tried hard to find a witness or anyone who could help shed some light on what happened. When they couldn't, they felt they'd let me down. Those men followed my entire career and were devastated, almost as much as me, when things fell apart. I felt it only right to let them know things had come to a close in that area of my life and also to know that a new chapter was about to begin."

"They're doing a story on our wedding?"

"The wedding, the attacks, and Carousel Dreams. We'll get a lot of publicity from this. I'll promote your books. . ."

"Which aren't even written on paper yet."

"But it's never too early to start the publicity."

"Always thinking ahead, aren't you?" Ellie realized her husband-to-be had a lot of facets to him that she'd never examined. She knew it would take years to examine them all—and she savored the thought.

"You're going to be a success, Ellie. I'll make sure of it. You'll never worry again about the resort or money or being alone. Not if I can help it."

"Judging by the crowd around your figurines, we won't have to worry anyway."

"I know." Bascom frowned. "They're getting more attention at the moment than our wedding. And you, my princess, deserve to be the center of attention—not the wood carvings. We need to do something about that."

Before she could say another word, he spun her around until her back pressed against his chest and she faced their guests. He wrapped his arms securely around her waist and snuggled his head against hers. She clutched his hands with hers. Never one to like being the center of attention, she clung to his solid strength. "I'd like to thank you all for coming to see this fairy-tale wedding between my beautiful bride and myself. If you all don't mind, we'd like to get the process started so we can begin our life together."

Everyone laughed and the crowd moved closer. Prissy pushed her way through, and Bascom leaned down to peek around and smile at Ellie. "Are you ready?"

"More than." She'd never been so sure of anything in her life.

With Priscilla's hand clutching one of hers and her other securely tucked under Bascom's steady arm, Ellie turned to face the pastor. In her eagerness she had to force her feet to stay flat on the floor. Like Prissy, bobbing up and down beside her, Ellie wanted to bounce the ceremony away.

The words drifted past in a blur, and finally Ellie heard the words she'd been eagerly awaiting. "I now pronounce you man and wife. You may kiss the bride."

Prissy's distraction of the guests was perfectly timed as she squealed with joy and clapped her hands.

Ellie took advantage of the moment, entwined her hands in Bascom's lapels, and gently tugged him forward. She grinned at his expression of surprise. She had a few facets for him to learn about, too. "Kiss me, Bascom Anthony."

Bascom leaned closer. "Yes'm, I believe I will."

The Greatest Find

Dedication

To my husband, Troy, who has offered such wonderful support
for these stories and all the others. I love the adventures we've had,
and I look forward to many more.
I love you!

Chapter 1

Tabitha "Tab" Augustine clasped her hands together against the front of her chest and spun in a circle, taking in the sights and sounds of their newest dig. "Oh, Father, can you believe it? We're finally here in Utah, at one of the most exciting potential dinosaur digs ever. Just imagine! It's supposed to be a huge event, and we're a part of it. All our plans, our dreams—they're about to come to life. We might just win the award and even get the plaque in the Statford Museum with our names on it to record the momentous discovery!"

"*If* there's a discovery." Her father, Peter Augustine, stood next to her, silently taking in the activity before them.

Wagons from town deposited men and supplies at various tents, the horses shuffling nervously at the commotion and chaos. Near the "kitchen" area, men unloaded barrels of water from town—water that would be used for both drinking and bathing. Tab wrinkled her nose. She hated bathing without the benefit of a tub but had learned how to compensate after being dragged all over the world to primitive places by her father. A pail of water, a cloth, and sweet-smelling perfume made all the difference in the world in such a situation.

She turned her thoughts back to their quest. Whoever found the first significant dinosaur bone would be handsomely rewarded, both financially and with recognition. That fact had dinosaur seekers from around the world converging upon the area.

Tabitha paced, stretching her legs after the long wagon ride with their gear. The excavation provided their transportation to the site, with a few horses available on the location for contestants' private use. The dig also provided scheduled wagon trips back and forth to Vernal for anyone needing a trip into town.

Tab continued on, ignoring her father's sour mood. "Just to be here is so amazing. We're a part of this find from the beginning, and if the mavericks"—Tab sent a disdainful glare in the direction of the free-spirited tent-dweller setting up not ten feet away from them—"if the mavericks can keep from decimating the site before we even get started, we have a chance to find the first specimen!"

Her father remained quiet, and she couldn't help but glance at their neighbor again. The blond-haired rogue, hands on hips, stared at them and actually mouthed the word *decimate* in slow motion, as if testing to see how the word—most surely foreign to his day-to-day vocabulary—settled upon his tongue.

Tab stared back with distaste and then turned away, but not before noticing the man tip his hat with a sarcastic flourish in her direction.

"Arrogant egomaniac," she muttered. *Let him look up those words in a dictionary.* She and her father had come across plenty of others like him in their day. His kind tended to be rough around the edges and weren't as educated in the field, a recipe for disaster. She'd never liked their style. Her father, a well-known archaeologist and world-renowned dinosaur excavator, had dragged her all over the world, always looking for the next great find. She'd seen plenty of men like the man across the way. She lowered her voice. "Father, why must they allow men like that into the competitions? You know they're only here for the glory, not for any scientific reason or to further mankind's knowledge."

Her father looked at her for the first time since their arrival only minutes earlier. "You know we want our name on that plaque every bit as much as the mavericks do." He sent Tabitha a smile, but the smile was tight and laced with bitterness and left Tabitha feeling like something was amiss.

Before she had a chance to question her father more deeply, the site coordinator appeared, walking briskly in their direction. Tabitha knew better than to bring up family business in front of others, so she filed away her concern for another time and turned to face the approaching man.

"Dr. Augustine." He lifted a hand in greeting and shook her father's hand. "I'm so pleased to meet you. And you must be Miss Augustine." He also tipped his hat, but with a genuineness that lacked the mocking nature of her neighbor's acknowledgment.

"Yes, sir, and I'm most excited to be here." Tabitha found herself reverting to the training in propriety that dated back to her preparatory school days. At one point, her father had worried over her all-consuming interest in science—an interest not considered ladylike at all—and had sent her to school near her grandmother's house in Boston, determined to make a proper lady out of her.

After Tab debated with several of the instructors about various teachings—and won—they insisted she didn't fit in at the academy and would be better suited completing her education in the field with her father. She hadn't meant to make them look inferior in front of their students, but when they taught incorrect information about places she'd personally visited, she felt it her duty to correct the misinformation.

"I'm Joey Matthews," the coordinator continued. "I'm sure you're familiar with who I am and my position here. I'm in charge of the site and will be happy to help with any concerns or questions."

Since Joey had sent correspondence with continuous updates during the previous few months while setting up details of the dig, she was sure every person here was familiar with his name and position. He'd apparently felt it important to include a staged photograph of himself in the original packet, posing against a huge skeleton of a dinosaur that had recently been found and transported to a prestigious museum back East.

Why did such men always seem to want unending affirmation from those around them? Tabitha's father was a doer. He'd taught her at a young age to go after what she wanted, and she didn't need anyone else's approval to get there.

When neither Augustine answered—her father still miles away in his musings and Tab unintentionally focused on dissecting the pompous man before them—Joey spoke up as if they hadn't missed the opportunity to stroke his needy ego.

"Well, you seem to have chosen your work location well. You have today and tomorrow to set up camp. If you need anything, don't hesitate to look me up. You'll find me somewhere around the dig at any given time."

Her father shook himself out of his deep thoughts and spoke before Joey could step away. "We'll do just that, Mr. Matthews. Thank you. And we're still meeting tomorrow night for a briefing of the rules and requirements, is that correct?"

"Please, call me Joey. We'll be working around each other for quite a while and might as well be comfortable. And yes, we'll meet right over there"—he pointed to an open area over his shoulder that had been kept clear of tents—"tomorrow night, just before sundown. The contest rules will be discussed, we'll have a group dinner, and you'll have a chance to get to know the other men you're competing against."

Tabitha didn't miss her father's scowl at the coordinator's words. "Thank you. We'll make sure to be there. See you then, Mr. Matthews. Joey." She quickly added the last when the man opened his mouth to correct her. Her act of familiarity was rewarded with a smile. She hid a shiver of disgust. Whether he liked it or not, she'd refer to him by his surname from here on out; she didn't want to falsely lead him on. Being the lone woman at most sites, male attention ended up, in all cases, being a hazard to her work. She tried hard to balance courtesy with aloofness, and this dark-haired smooth talker clued her in immediately that she'd do best to steer clear of him. She glanced again at her handsome blond neighbor. He waved. And she'd most definitely do well to steer clear of him, too.

❧

Hunter Pierce looked skyward and silently asked his heavenly Father what he'd done of late to merit having the only woman at the site no more than a horse's measure away from his tent. Women weren't even welcome at these events.

But no one dared stand up to the well-known and much welcomed Dr. Peter Augustine and declare his daughter wasn't every bit as welcome. So wherever he went, she followed. A lot of men considered the very presence of a female a promise of bad luck to come.

Of course, Hunter didn't believe in luck, bad or good. He believed in a Higher Power and was proud to be a follower of Jesus. He chuckled and glanced at his new neighbors as he thought about how well-received that bit of knowledge always was with the scientific types. The topic would surely come up before the dig ended. Though he'd heard of the duo and had read about them and their extensive travels, he'd yet to come face-to-face with them on a dig—that is, until now.

He'd noticed during the past few minutes of his observation that the daughter, Tabitha, came across as both an exuberant young lady and a refined scientific scholar, a surprisingly attractive combination of traits. Now, as he watched, she began to dig wholeheartedly through the two trunks and boxes of gear that had been dropped off by the wagon master's crew. At least she didn't seem the pampered type who sat around complaining while her father did all the work. As a matter of fact, her father still stood and surveyed the work field in silence while his daughter jumped into action.

Hunter felt a small urge to offer his assistance but shook it off. His site was secure. He had worked all day to get things in place and set up. He'd had a goal to arrive early so he could decide on the best place to begin, and he'd followed through. The sun beat down warmly upon his head, and he needed to sit and put his feet up and relax a bit while he could. After tomorrow the days would be long and grueling. He deserved this time of rest. He pulled an empty crate over to the measly shade provided by the side of his tent, settled back into a hardwood chair he'd lugged along, pulled his worn hat over his face, and propped his feet up on the crate in front of him.

He closed his eyes and tried to relax, but Tabitha's grunts and oomphs were hard to ignore. He considered slipping into his tent for a little shut-eye, but with the heat bearing down on him even out in the slight breeze, he knew trying to sleep inside the hot enclosure would not do any good. Besides, the flimsy fabric would do nothing to block the sounds around him. And even though he hadn't slept well during any of the preceding nights before his arrival, he never had been one to stay idle for long. Sleeping during the day felt impossible to him.

He opened an eye, tipped his hat up with one finger, and peeked at his intriguing neighbor. He chuckled aloud as she wiped her lower arm across her forehead, leaving a streak of dirt on her previously pristine skin. Her own broad-brimmed leather hat, much like one a cowboy would wear, clung precariously to the back of her head. Wayward strands of curly blond hair had fallen loose and now framed the petite features of her face, which somehow made her seem more approachable and soft. How women ever coped with their long skirts in this heat had never ceased to amaze him. His mother and sisters worked long hours every day and so did all the other women he'd encountered. His chuckle earned him another dagger of a glare from the woman setting up camp across the hard-packed dirt. He quirked an amused eyebrow in response, much too hot and lazy to move, and crossed his arms over his chest.

A few moments later, Tabitha tugged at an unyielding bundle that suddenly yielded. The entire pile tumbled down on her. Immediately Hunter was on his feet and at her side, pulling the heavy objects away. Her father, as soon as he'd realized what had happened, belatedly joined in. If Hunter had expected warm comments of appreciation, he was way off. He'd have felt safer after freeing a wildcat as ferocious as she was when he held a hand out to help her to her feet.

"I suggest you maintain your distance and keep your dusty hands off me in the future if you don't want to feel the full effect of my wrath," she hissed.

She began to dust her skirts by slapping at them and fluffing them in the air. Hunter smirked as the action reminded him of the piglets back home in St. Louis after a roll in the mud. They'd soak in the rays, and when the mud dried, dust would fly in all directions from their bodies if a brisk wind blew up.

"I don't know what you find amusing. Surely you have better things to do than sit around and stare at me." She resumed her tirade even as she took stock of wounds or injuries. She turned her wrists this way and that and then did the same with her ankles. Her boots peeked out from under the hem of her long, dark blue skirt, but other than a bit of dust, all body parts seemed to have fared well while under the pile of crates. Everything but her temper seemed to be in good order.

Taking into consideration her present mood, he wasn't about to share his mental comparison of her and the piglets back home. He might not be the most scholarly man here, but he knew when to keep his mouth shut, at least most of the time.

"Maybe we should start over and properly introduce ourselves. I'm Hunter Pierce." Hunter offered her his hand, which she pointedly ignored. He dropped it to his side. "And you're Tabitha Augustine, if I recall correctly. I've read about you and your father."

Hunter turned to include the man in his spiel, but Tabitha's father had gone back into his funk, walking over to sit on a previously buried crate, once again watching the flurry of activity around them. The man certainly was a strange one.

Tab briefly glanced up at him. "Interesting how a life of studying science puts you, the scientist, under the same scrutiny your research goes through."

She had stopped her fussing and now stared past Hunter with a faraway look in her clear blue eyes. Her words were laced with pain, as if that scrutiny hadn't been kind. Or maybe she just didn't like writings of her private life being sent around the periodicals of the world. Up close, the woman became all softness, and her beauty literally took his breath away. She focused her full attention on him, her features reverting back to angry lines.

"While you've spent the past thirty minutes doing nothing but gawk at me, I've tried to put our camp in order. Have you nothing better to do than sit over there and laugh at me?" She crossed her arms defensively, but something akin to pain reflected in her eyes.

Hunter felt properly set in his place. If his mother were here, she'd ignore the fact that he was a grown man of twenty-eight and would take a green branch to his backside over his present behavior. "I'm sorry if I've offended you. That was not my intent. But you sent me some well-aimed barbs in the short time since your arrival. And unfortunately, my thoughts have always seemed to reflect openly on my face, much to my consternation, as far back as when I was a young lad in school. I have a way of getting myself into spots that I don't really mean to get into. Like now."

He watched as Tabitha's mouth quirked into a grin. "I've experienced a bit of the same while in school, so I can understand. In light of that, I suggest we call a truce." She held out a delicate hand, covered with small scrapes. "You can call me Tab."

He tugged her toward his site. "Well, c'mon with me, Tab, and let me fix up those scrapes before they get infected." When she started to hesitate, he waved toward the mass of baggage stacked behind them. "Or do you know where your medical supplies are in all that mess?"

She surprised him with a spontaneous, sultry laugh. "I don't know where any specific bag or box is in all that mess, let alone what's in each one. I'll take advantage of your kind offer in light of the truce."

Hunter clasped her delicate wrist and felt a jolt shoot through him. He had the distinct feeling the heavenly Father he'd prayed to earlier now chuckled at him in the same way Hunter had chuckled at Tab. The unnerving thought that nothing in his world would ever be the same slowly drifted across his mind.

Chapter 2

Tab glanced at Hunter as he fixed the scrapes on her hands. His hair had slipped forward over his shoulder, the long strands moving to hide his face as he worked. Upon closer inspection, she realized his hair wasn't blond at all. Instead, sun-bleached streaks of gold sifted through layers of darker brown, a testament to the long hours he must spend out of doors. He wore his off-white shirt with the sleeves rolled up to his elbow. His deeply tanned forearms also attested to a large amount of time spent in the great outdoors.

She startled as she realized his brown-eyed gaze now met hers. A grin surrounded by tiny laugh lines filled out his mouth as he watched her perusal.

"Whatd'ya think?" He settled back on his heels, the gauze held loosely in his hand.

"Excuse me? Oh, about the scrapes? I'm sure they'll be fine."

He laughed, and she liked the sound. "I actually referred to your examination of me. Now I feel like one of your specimens. Do I pass muster?"

A flush spread up Tab's face. "I'm sorry. But you were so intent, and I'm curious about a man such as yourself who seems like a loner yet is so kind to someone who hasn't exactly welcomed him with open arms."

The flush deepened at the mental image of her arms open to welcome him into an embrace. "Oh, I don't mean open arms as in a hug or embrace. I only meant. . .oh, never mind."

His deep laugh filled the air again. "I know what you meant. But we're neighbors, and we need to work in close proximity. I feel it's only right for me to help if there's a need."

"Well, we're also competitors, and surely you have that in the back of your mind. I'm sure not everyone would be as gentlemanly as you've been, especially when it comes to an accident-prone female. A female who isn't even welcome in their presence." She shrugged at her own words, trying to put on a brave front. For some reason, she felt it important that she not look pathetic in front of Hunter.

Hunter stared at her for a moment. "I feel peace over the outcome of the event. Whatever happens, whoever finds the first bone, finds the first bone. It's just the way it will be."

"So you don't care about the win and getting your name on the plaque?" Tab could hear the disbelief in her own voice. She crossed her arms and stared him down. Everyone wanted the recognition. "In all my twenty years, that's all my father has lived for. Surely you didn't sign on and come all the way out here not expecting to win."

"Of course not. I fully intend to do my utmost to claim the prize. But I can only do my best and work in the way I've trained. The rest will fall in place as it will."

Hunter glanced across the road at a couple of rough-looking men setting up camp a few spots down from them. Tab had noticed earlier that the two men couldn't even figure out which way their tent went together. They'd bickered loudly from the moment they'd arrived.

He nodded his head in their direction. "I'm more concerned about the un-trained treasure seekers who are here, that they'll in some way ruin what we've come to do. Though most of the men around the site—excuse me, and you—seem professional and ready to work with careful precision, I'm afraid some of the novices will destroy any find before it's properly recorded."

He abruptly changed gears and turned on his grin again, his eyes crinkling at the corners. "And I have to admit, when I first saw you arrive with your father, I had the thought that even you didn't belong out here and would only be trouble for those around you."

Tab snorted and quickly threw her hand over her mouth in an attempt to cover up the unladylike sound. "And here I've proven you so wrong!"

Hunter's belly laugh caused some of the men, including her father, to glance their way in surprise.

"Yes. And since you've already proven you're destined to be a nuisance to me, why don't you let me give you a hand and we'll get your camp in order."

He gestured for her to lead the way, and though a smart retort of indepen-dence lingered on her tongue, she bit it back and accepted his help. Her father hadn't shaken off his strange mood, and if they were going to have shelter by nightfall, she'd need the assistance Hunter offered.

❧

The next day at lunch, Hunter joined the line of men moving along the food table and accepted his plate from one of the cooks. He'd arrived early, as usual, and had his choice of tables. He chose one that faced his camp, allowing him to watch over his personal area while he ate. Tabitha and her father still hovered over their research.

After a slow morning of going over his notes, Hunter welcomed the chance to meet some of the other competitors. He'd noticed that Tabitha and her father also spent the morning going over notes and textbooks and hadn't had time for more than a brief wave across the expanse of dirt that separated their camps.

Snatches of their conversation had drifted his way as they discussed the climate, weather, work locations, and their setup of camp.

Apparently, they did all their work by the book and used only the most up-to-date scientific procedures to track their progress. They also made meticulous notes of their journey. Though he was intrigued by their devotion, he knew his head would explode if he gave in to such tedious ways.

"Mind if I settle here for a bite of lunch?"

Hunter glanced up at the older man who had staked his claim across from the Augustines to the east. "I'd be happy to have you join me. Have a seat."

The man pulled out the chair opposite Hunter, looking more miner than archaeologist, but Hunter had met all types in this field of work. He studied his lunch companion as he settled in. Worn suspenders held up loose trousers, and his sweat-stained gray shirt had seen better days, but the man wore a kind expression on his face and seemed a kindred spirit.

"Name's Jason Walker." He reached out his hand, appeared to notice the dirt on it, and then shrugged and pulled it back with a sheepish smile. "It's mighty kind of them to provide a cook and the grub so we can focus on our work, don'tcha think?" He tried to tame his wild gray hair with a grimy hand and waited for Hunter's reply.

Hunter, his mouth full, nodded in agreement. He swallowed the surprisingly good food before offering his name.

The man grinned. "Well, Hunter, I can't help but notice that you already seem mighty smitten with our neighboring female."

Hunter choked on the sip of water he'd just taken and glanced around to see if anyone else had heard the comment. After he'd regained his composure, he leveled a look at the older man. "No disrespect intended, Jason, but I'm only trying to be neighborly and lend a hand when needed."

"If I might be so bold—" The man hesitated.

Nothing has stopped you from being outspoken thus far, so why stop now? crossed Hunter's mind. He quickly offered up a prayer for patience and forgiveness for his unkind thoughts and reminded himself that he'd come to lunch hoping to meet some other people.

"Please feel free." As soon as he'd spoken the words, Hunter noticed Tabitha and her father heading his way.

Jason's words carried across the quiet air. "I'd say you've done a mighty fine job of staking your claim on that beauty. She's a looker, that one is—just as pretty as can be. And smart! Why, she could write books with all her knowledge that would rival anything out there, from what I've heard." Jason sent a gap-toothed smile across the table. "Yep, you done did a fine thing in capturing her attention."

Tabitha stopped in her tracks, a look of horrified embarrassment passing across her features. She stared at the two men while her father bumped into her from behind, his dishes sliding dangerously close to his chest. Hunter held his breath in anticipation of a mess, but Dr. Augustine stepped back and righted his tray just in time to prevent anything from spilling. Apparently he was used to his daughter's abrupt stops. Maybe the duo wouldn't realize Jason had referred to Tabitha in his conversation.

"Please, join us." Hunter jumped to his feet and pulled out the chair beside him. Tabitha sent him a look of death and stalked over to place her tray next to his.

"Well, isn't this wonderful!" Jason also stood and offered Tabitha a slight bow. "We've just been talking about you, and here you are. It must be a divine appointment."

So much for her not knowing whom Jason referred to with his flowery talk. Flowery talk at Hunter's expense. And now he couldn't even deny his "claim" on Tabitha without embarrassing the poor woman further.

"A divine appointment? I don't think I understand." Tabitha voiced her confusion after introductions had been made.

"Why, you know, a meeting set up by the Almighty."

Tabitha glanced upward at the sky, following the direction of Jason's up-raised finger. "The, um, Almighty?" Her perplexed eyes sought out Hunter's, the question in them asking about Jason's sanity.

"I think he's referring to God." Hunter turned to his new friend. "Am I right?"

"Well, of course you're right. My Lord and Savior. Who else would I be referring to?"

"It's a bunch of nonsense if you ask me." Dr. Augustine sat and grunted down at his meal.

"You're not a believer?" Hunter asked.

"No. And I take it you are?"

"Yes, sir, absolutely."

"Hmm." His single comment showed his disdain.

Though Jason's comment confirmed he was a kindred spirit just as Hunter had thought, he felt sad that Tabitha, or at least her father, would have a hard time understanding and sharing his belief in God. It would figure that with their training and background, they wouldn't hold the same beliefs as him. And as he'd first suspected, also because of their scientific training, they might have a hard time understanding an intangible concept such as faith. He set the revelation aside for prayer.

❧

Tab enjoyed the rest of her meal with her neighbors. Though at first they'd made her uncomfortable with their personal talk about her and then with their mention of God and religion, the conversation soon moved on to more pleasant topics, such as the weather and the dig. Her father had become surprisingly talkative during the past half hour.

"I'm just saying there's a lot of danger involved in this type of setting. I think each of us needs to be extra careful and diligent and to watch what's going on around us."

The words made Tabitha focus back on the men's conversation. "Dangerous in what way, Father? I've not sensed anything dangerous around us." Her traitorous eyes chose that moment to dart a glance at Hunter. He grinned. She felt her eyes briefly widen. Surely he couldn't read her thoughts and know the very word *danger* made her think of him! And the danger he represented had nothing to do with anything but a danger to her heart. She shook off the silly notion and shifted around slightly in her chair, the movement placing her back to him, which was ridiculous, because now her back was to her dining companions, and how could she hold an intelligent conversation with the three men while facing away from them and into the empty air?

With a frustrated huff, she turned back to the table, grasped the seat of her chair with both hands, and hopped it over a few inches away from the distracting man. Her father sent her a confused look and frowned. She froze where she was and reached up to twiddle with a strand of hair. "Father, the danger? What is it you're referring to?"

He looked away and refused to meet her gaze. "I mean exactly what I've said. Just be aware of your surroundings and be careful."

"Father, why are you so reticent? It isn't like you."

He ignored her question and continued to eat.

Tabitha looked at Hunter, but he seemed as baffled by her father's words as she felt. Something wasn't right, but she had no clue how to force him to open up to her. She felt adrift and alone and suddenly welcomed the companionship and close proximity of the annoying man in the next chair. With her father's withdrawal, she'd have to rely on Hunter if anything did go wrong. The thought was at once both reassuring and alarming. She bent over her plate and hurried to finish. She'd feel a lot better when she returned to the routine comfort of their newest dig.

Chapter 3

The idea of gathering for dinner as a group later that evening made Tabitha most uncomfortable. Never one to be at ease in a large group, she felt even more out of her element when women were so scarce at events such as this one. She glanced around. Forget scarce, make that nonexistent. She alone filled the female category. She knew she stood out like a sore thumb and also knew most men actually resented her presence and would hurry to blame her and "bad luck" for any mishap that occurred while she stayed at the dig.

Her father followed her to the flat side of a rock formation where they'd have a good view of their coordinator when he stood to speak and explain the rules. The setting sun lowered into the horizon on the far side of the butte, allowing them a respite from the heat that had lingered over the barren area throughout the day. Though Tab and her father hadn't thought to bring a crate over to sit on, she refused to perch on the dusty rocks and chose instead to stand with arms crossed defensively over her chest for the contest overview.

She found herself glancing around at the others as they arrived—the area bustled with activity and boisterous talk—and assured herself that she wasn't looking for anyone in particular. She only scouted out the competition. But her traitorous heart picked up speed and skipped a few beats when her eyes met those of Hunter as he approached from the path to her right. Since he'd rescued her from the wall of luggage that had buried her the previous day, and then had helped her get their cantankerous tent stakes deep into the hard-packed dirt, and *then* allowed them to join him for that awkward lunch, it was only natural that she'd greet him with a warm smile of recognition. Wasn't it? The others around her were strangers, and her father continued to be distant. Jason was nowhere to be found, and she needed to feel she had a friend.

Her mouth curved into a smirk over her musings. Her mind hadn't drifted far from thoughts of her intriguing neighbor the entire night before, nor for the majority of her recent waking hours today, even with all that had to be done. She'd been aware of Hunter's every move, a fact that didn't slip past her sharp mind, and those moves pretty much drove her to distraction.

Tab couldn't afford to be sidetracked or unfocused. This project held too much importance to her father and his future. With forty-two years behind him, her father was getting older, and she'd seen a certain despondence come over him of late. She'd determined to help him achieve this one important goal before she had to watch him retire to the scholarly world that awaited the end of his travels. Though she knew he'd be a wonderful professor, she also knew a part of him would die when he had to give up this aspect of his career. She'd do whatever she could to keep him going in the meantime. This last award would go a long way in keeping him young and inspired.

"I see you brought your favorite chair." The quip popped out before she thought to stop it.

"Only in case I met a damsel in distress who didn't bring her own. How fortunate for you and your tired feet that I've arrived with my chair in tow and can offer rest for the weary." Hunter had reached her side and now grinned as he spun the hardwood chair around with a flourish and set it at her side.

He wore his hair pulled back and fastened at his neck with a leather band and had donned another off-white shirt that he'd tucked neatly into dark brown slacks. Tabitha felt grungy and dusty by comparison.

Tab's face warmed with embarrassment for the umpteenth time that day as many sets of eyes turned their way and stared. Never had she blushed so much in any man's presence. "I'm fine, thank you. And I don't need to sit." No way would she sit in a proper chair while all the men around her stood or sat on rocks or on the hard-packed dirt that covered the ground. She preferred to blend in.

Hunter stared her down. "Nonsense. I've watched you work all day—and I didn't miss the refusals to my offers of help. Sharing my chair is the least I can do. Now let me be a gentleman and just for once accept the kindness of a neighbor."

She opened her mouth to argue.

He sighed, placed his hands on her shoulders, and eased her into the seat. "Please sit."

She popped back to her feet, her face flaming more than ever. "I beg your pardon! I'll sit if I want, and I'll stand if I prefer, and tonight I feel like—"

"Tabitha, dear, forget the tirade and do as the gentleman says. He has nothing but your best interests at heart." Tabitha's father had to choose this moment to break his silence of the past couple days. He stood with his pipe in hand and stared down at her with forcefulness completely out of character.

Tabitha didn't see how she could refuse the offer now, with every eye in the place focused their way, without looking petty. She smoothed her skirt over her backside and slid into place on the chair. The relief to her aching feet was immediate, and she momentarily closed her eyes in pleasure. When she opened them, Hunter was watching her.

Always the gentleman, at least in appearance, he tried to hide his smile. "See? That wasn't so bad, was it?"

"It's actually pretty heavenly, I have to admit. But I could have lived without the public spectacle." She scowled up at him before turning her attention on the other men around them. They'd all gone back to their conversations without another thought given to her.

"Then next time be a lady and accept graciously instead of insisting on acting like one of the men."

Tabitha would have shot to her feet to deny his comment, but her father's hand suddenly appeared on her shoulder and held her firmly in place, though he never looked her way. She had to admit Hunter had a point. Her thoughts had strayed to the men around them and her desire to keep on par with them instead of accepting Hunter's offer in good faith.

"I'll keep your advice in mind, though I doubt I'll have opportunity in the future to accept any more of your manly demands." If she thought her face had burned at its hottest level of embarrassment in the previous moments of conversation, she'd been sorely mistaken. That sensation had been a cool breeze compared to the flame of heat that now crossed her features as she realized what she'd just said. The minute the words crossed her lips she wished to call them back, but it was too late. Even her father seemed to be snickering, or else the dust had settled into his lungs in a sudden way that had him grabbing for his handkerchief, which he hurriedly settled over his mouth.

❧

Hunter watched as the coordinator strutted to the makeshift stage.

"Welcome, all, to the Statford Museum's first dinosaur dig. As you all know, this area became known for the dinosaur discoveries that began about thirty years ago." Joey Matthews stood with his heels together, toes pointed outward, and held his jacket by the lapels as he stared out over the audience. "I'm sure you've all received and read the papers I sent outlining the competition, but I feel it's necessary to touch on a few of the more important topics. As you know, Statford Museum is privately owned and located in the state of New York. I'm the on-site coordinator of this event, and all problems and questions need to go through me. We've tried to keep the contest simple and only have a few specific requirements all participants must follow.

"First and foremost, respect the area and the others around you. We'd all like to win the cash prize and the chance for recognition, but let's make sure we only do so by following the rules set before us. You can work alone or in a partnership. Your original papers should be filled out with this information, but if you have a change, please let me know immediately. If you sign on as a partnership, you'll be expected to share the winnings equally. Whatever measures you use, keep the other participants' safety in mind at all times.

"We're looking for the first bone found to signify a dinosaur skeleton. After the find, the bones will be carefully wrapped in tissue paper and dipped in plaster, packed in straw, placed in a sturdy crate, and sent out of here by horse-drawn freight very similar to the wagons that brought most of you out here. Items will then be shipped by railroad to their final destination. We have a doctor available, and we can take trips to Vernal for any of your needs. If you have any questions, I'll be available after this speech."

A thrum of chatter erupted as Joey stepped off the stage. The participants dispersed into small groups and headed back to their tents, a feeling of excitement in the air.

The next morning Hunter had a hard time focusing and settling into a routine with Tabitha's words and charming reactions the night before buzzing through his head. He'd cleared the area for his claim and now worked to set up a rope and stake circumference to enclose the spot he'd chosen. By arriving early, he'd had the pick of the dig site and, through careful analysis, had plotted the best layout.

Though the surrounding outcroppings south of him were also in the dig site, he'd bumped his ropes up against them so no one else could settle in that direction. Tabitha and her father had set up just to the north, and the area to the west was no-man's-land. Thus the rest of the hustle and bustle of activity all happened to the east, allowing them a quiet corner to do their work.

Hunter didn't miss the fact that Tabitha and her father had chosen their dig area just as carefully and with just as much thought. Their tent was placed immediately to the west of their dig site and bumped up against the western cliffs just as he'd bumped his site up against the ones to the south. It made for a cozy and protected setup.

He glanced over and caught Tab watching him. For a woman who had grown up in a man's world, she blushed more than any other female he'd ever met. He found himself wondering about her mother and how she'd come to be her father's sole companion. As she glanced his way once more, he tipped his worn leather hat and laughed aloud as she fumbled the strange utensil in her hand, dropping it to tangle in her long, tan skirt. Her white shirtsleeves were rolled up in the same fashion as his, and he noted that her arms were every bit as tan. He smiled. He liked a woman who didn't cave in to pretentious ways— though the way she and her father traveled, more than likely she didn't even know what convention was.

Tab stood to her feet and hurried his way. His heart jumped in anticipation, a strange occurrence he'd have to dissect and mull over at a later time.

"I'll thank you to please quit staring at me and focus instead on your work." Her hiss was just above a whisper, but the words hit their mark as she'd surely intended. With the sun bearing down, he squinted toward her, trying to figure out if she was serious or teasing.

"I mean it. Every time I look over at you, you're like those paintings where the eyes follow my every move. It's creepy. You have to stop."

Apparently she meant it. He tamped down his amusement as her words made him bristle in anger. Where had their camaraderie of the previous twenty-four hours gone?

He stepped closer. "Then you admit you were staring at me first. Why else would you keep looking over at me? Surely you have enough men at your disposal that you don't have to send simpering glances my way every minute of the day. I have quite enough to keep me busy without you or your glances causing me a distraction."

She gasped and stomped her dainty boot. "Yet you admit I'm causing you a distraction."

They glowered at each other for a few moments before she spoke again.

"And trust me, I'm truly sorry there aren't more women at your disposal so that you're stuck watching my every move during every waking hour."

With her final comment, she turned and huffed back to her father and their dig. And following suit, he huffed and stalked back to his, muttering all the way about women who didn't know their place and strayed into areas that should belong to men alone. He surprised himself as he silently admitted that he didn't at all regret her being the lone woman at his disposal, for he already knew with her around, no other woman would cause him any distraction at all. He enjoyed watching her every move. The thought completely disconcerted him.

As a diversion to his own traitorous thoughts, he grabbed up his dynamite and decided to shake things up a bit. If his progress went any slower, it would stop completely. The process needed a jump start. The way some of the excavators were working, it would be decades before they ever got close to the bones. And the sooner the first bone was found and the wannabes cleared out of the area, the sooner his thoughts could refocus on his work.

❧

Tab carefully settled in with her back to the infuriating male specimen who just had to choose the spot behind them for his dig. Though the annoying thought did cross her mind that he'd been there first and they were the ones who had made the choice to join him, she pushed it aside and continued on her mental tirade. There were so many other men in the area, and any one of them would have been a fine neighbor, if not downright pleasant to share a work area with. But no, she had to be saddled with a wild card maverick with nothing better to do than ogle her and crowd in on her space. She sat back on her heels to ease her aching muscles, resettled her skirt, and glanced around.

For instance, take that nice old man in the spot directly across the road to their east. Jason. He lifted a hand in greeting, and she waved back. He'd be a fine neighbor, but instead had to be all the way across the dusty road from them. That left them too far away to share pleasantries other than the brief wave he'd just sent her when he'd caught her eye and possibly some more discussion over meals. But when she caught Hunter's eye, he smiled that knowing smile of his, yet she had no idea what exactly it was that he seemed to think he knew!

Then there was the quiet young man across the way and to the north of Jason. That man had yet to look her way, content to do his job and leave others to do theirs. And even the coordinator, ladies' man though he seemed to think he was, gave her a wide berth after their initial meeting the day they'd arrived.

Only Hunter seemed to think it was his self-proclaimed duty either to watch out for her or to drive her insane. With the museum provided outdoor kitchen area covering both sides of the road to their north, Hunter alone was the closest "neighbor." Oh well, she'd just have to keep her back to him and allow him to work in peace. Hopefully he'd do the same and things could get on from there.

Before resuming the backbreaking task of meticulously scraping the dirt away miniscule piece by miniscule piece, she reached back to resettle her wayward strands of hair. Her hat always fell backward, so she adjusted it forward to better shade her face. The tiniest bone could signify a find, and even fossils led to other discoveries. She made sure her hair stayed out of her face, which allowed her to have complete focus on the area she processed.

Her father worked with the same methodical precision at the far end of their claim, nearest the kitchen area. They'd slowly process each grain of dirt until they met in the middle and would only then move back to their separate sides to begin the same routine one row over. Both had their own sets of equipment, and seldom did they stop to discuss an angle or process or to consult their plans.

Tab couldn't help herself and glanced at Hunter again, her arms midair in fixing her hair back into the braid that slipped from behind her hat. Now there was a man who didn't seem to even know the word *process*, and she had yet to figure out the rhyme or reason behind his routine.

Even now he stalked back and forth, setting new stakes or something into the ground on the bluff side of his claim. How he ever thought he'd find the intricate makings of a dinosaur while pacing about on his feet was beyond her. She shrugged and knelt into place, her knees lining up with the slight indentations made from her previous work. Her long skirt came in handy while providing a bit of cushion for her sore knees. During the next break, she'd pop over to the tent and retrieve the small knee cushion she'd fashioned for a situation such as this.

Digging through her small crate of tools, she decided to use her smallest pick. Tapping delicately at the crusty earth, she bent close to concentrate on the intricate work before her. She reached for a bigger pick and tapped gently with her hammer to break the unrelenting soil. Several taps later, she'd formed a crack. The area rarely received rain, and though mud would be awful to work in, a bit more forgiving earth would certainly make the tedious job easier. Tipping a chisel in the other direction, she grinned as she levered a large chunk of dirt up, allowing her to peer into a small hole. She placed the chunk into a shallow pan beside her. After finishing with the hole, she'd go through the large piece of dirt before dropping the softened mass back into place and moving on.

She now leaned down on her side, carefully excavating the hole to make it bigger. Disappointment set in. Though she knew they'd be here for weeks, every moment created hope that the next move would find the elusive bone they all strove for. At any minute, even this early in the dig, the cry could come around that the competition was over before it had hardly started, so the stress to make that find constantly kept her on edge.

Tabitha gathered her shaky nerves and leaned closer for a better look. A large magnifying glass helped her see there was indeed. . .nothing to see. With a sigh, she picked up her small pick and leaned in for more digging. Something white nestled at the farthest corner, and she worked to get it loose. The moment took her utmost concentration.

A huge booming explosion rocked the area around them with a repercussion that threw Tabitha forward several inches. Gasping for breath, her heart about to beat out of her chest, she and her father scrambled to their feet while others around them glanced their way before returning to work with shakes of their heads.

"Father, whatever was that? Why are we the only ones who seem alarmed?"

She turned to look at her father, but his attention had settled on Hunter and his claim. She followed his gaze and saw that the man in question stood with his hands on his hips and stared at the wall of sandstone before him.

"Confounded young'uns," her father muttered before walking off in the direction of the outhouse.

Tabitha remembered the "stakes" she thought Hunter had been setting out. Realization overcame her, and before she knew it, she'd stalked his way, stepped over his rope divider, and now stood mere inches away from the crazy man. "Dynamite? You used *dynamite* to clear the rock away from your work area? Are you insane?" She'd heard and read about the maverick methods some men used to clear an area to access deeper locations, but never had she seen it in action until now.

Hunter turned and greeted her with his disarming grin, motioning toward the rock. "What d'ya think? I've watched you itching the ground over there for most of the day to get inches into your work area, and in one blast I just 'dug' six feet into the wall of stone here."

"And you probably 'blew up' six feet worth of relics and artifacts, you big baboon! Any fragment of dinosaur skeleton that was near the surface of the earth has surely just been blown to pieces." Tabitha couldn't even stand in one place, she felt so angry and restless. "Why would you take such a chance and risk ruining history in this way?"

Much to her humiliation, tears formed in her eyes. This was their livelihood, and she truly loved her history. It broke her heart to see the callousness of some of the people in their "field."

"Aw, Tabitha, don't cry. I didn't mean to upset you. Look over here a minute. If I were to pick away at this wall of rock, I'd never get six inches in before the end of the competition. The bones aren't going to be lying on top of the ground waiting for us. We have to dig deep."

"So you throw history to the wind and take the chance of ruining something all for greed?"

He stared at her for a moment in silence. "No. I'm not indiscriminate. If you'll look closer, you'll see which type of rock this is. Have you ever heard of bones being found in such?"

He'd caught her off guard. She stepped toward him and did as he asked. He towered over her, and his nearness interfered with her concentration, but she had to admit he had a point. The blasts had only removed the outer rock that hid the more important area within. Now that she focused more intently, she saw he'd used precision skill to achieve such a feat without endangering the precious rock centimeters away from the blast.

"You're experienced with this."

"Of course. I wouldn't risk anyone's safety. I spent years working with my grandfather in his mining business. I used a very small amount of explosive. I'm sorry the repercussion caught you off guard. I'll warn you next time." He grinned. "*If* there is a next time."

"I appreciate it."

The man seemed to have just as special a touch with the way he handled his explosives as the way he expertly handled explosive women.

Such as her.

Chapter 4

A week had passed with no one claiming a find of any worth. The sun continued its fiery assault on the excavators, causing tempers to flare. More than once Tabitha watched as men gave in to the pressure of stress and heat and allowed themselves to be drawn into a brawl. Several of the confrontations were between the two scraggly men a couple spots down. Each time she noticed Hunter would move into the roadway that ran between the men's site and theirs, and he would either intervene to stop the feud or, if other men beat him to it, he'd stand nearby as if watching over her and her father.

Her father, for the most part, ignored all that went on around them and continued with his work. She still hadn't broken through his self imposed isolation, nor had she figured out what was causing it. So instead, she focused on furthering her detailed work—far away from Hunter's side of the line. She kept her back to him as much as possible to enhance her concentration, but at meals she found herself drawn to him and settled in to eat with the only friend she'd made.

"I take it your father is working through lunch again?" Hunter stood and held her chair as she sat.

They'd taken to eating at the table nearest their claims, while the other contestants filled the surrounding tables and left them on their own. At first, Tabitha felt uncomfortable eating alone with Hunter, but the few times he wasn't there, she'd felt even worse dining by herself. And once, when she'd avoided his table in the hopes that Jason or some of the other men would join him in case she scared them off, she noticed he'd dined alone anyway. After calling her on her action, he'd insisted she not worry about the others and dine with him.

"Yes, he's skipping another meal, and I'm worried about him." She glanced over to where her father continued his work under the hot sun with no break.

"Is it determination to find a bone? Is he always like this?" Compassion shone through Hunter's eyes, and she knew he really cared.

"Not usually. He's never been this determined or stand-offish. His whole temperament is different here. In a way, I wish I could just pack us up and leave, but the competition's too important to both of us, and we'd be sorry later."

Hunter nodded and pushed back his empty tray. "Would it help if I talked to him?"

Tabitha felt the first smile of the day slip across her lips. "If he won't talk or listen to me, I highly doubt he'll give you the time of day."

His look of disappointment made her feel bad.

"It's nothing personal against you, but he's partial to me and hasn't ever been this way before. I highly doubt you, as a stranger, can break through his wall." She sent him a teasing grin. "Dynamite won't even work in this case."

"You're never going to let me live that down, are you?" He captured her hand in his, catching her off guard. "I said I'd not resort to that process again, though you have to admit the technique was well done and pretty amazing."

"Right, and said with such humility." She rolled her eyes. "I still have a bruise on my shoulder from the repercussion knocking me forward. I'm not sure that's a sign of total proficiency and excellence."

Hunter's cockiness vanished immediately. "Why didn't you say something before? I'm so sorry. I didn't have any idea you'd be affected, or I'd have never done it."

Tabitha felt bad that she'd brought it up. "No harm done. Forget it." She pushed her tray away, too, and stood, sending him what she hoped was a cheery smile. "We'd best be getting back."

"Tab."

She froze midstep and turned back to him.

"How can I forget it? I really am sorry. I don't want you brushing this off. You should have told me before that I'd hurt you. That's the last thing I'd ever want to do."

She reached over and tugged at his hand. "I know, and I accept your apology. Now, c'mon. To show that your apology is fully accepted, I'll let you walk me back to my site."

Hunter stared at her a moment, his face a mask of surprise. "I must say, that's a huge step for you! Are you sure you don't mind?" He glanced around covertly. "Someone might see us and realize you are, in fact, a girl."

To her surprise he hadn't released her hand, so she let go of his instead and gave him a mock punch on the arm. "No, I don't mind."

He swung into step with her. "Will your father faint with shock?"

Tabitha laughed at his antics. She'd never met a man as playful and fun as Hunter before. Her colleagues were always like her father, serious and busy. And they all made an effort to ignore her, or worse, pretended she didn't exist. "He'll probably thank you. I think you're his break from me, and since he doesn't seem too big on my company these days, I know I appreciate your companionship and caring."

Embarrassed, she heard the note of sadness that carried over into her words. "I'd better get to work. I have to run over to my tent for a moment before getting busy again."

Hunter searched her eyes for a moment and nodded. "I'll see you at dinner, then. Save me a spot if you get there first."

The last was said in jest, because they both knew Hunter was the early bird, while she and her father seemed to run late at every turn.

Tabitha fluttered her hand at him and stepped over the low-set rope that surrounded their work site. She entered the tent, and the captured humidity sucked her breath away. The area, with only enough space for two cots and each of their trunks of clothing along with a few crates of supplies, was closed off from any breeze and at least ten degrees hotter than the air outside. She hurried to grab the book she needed before heading back outside.

Just as she reached the opening, something hard landed on the end of the tent where she'd stood moments earlier, crushing the back corner to the ground. She screamed and heard footsteps running from outside.

"Tab!"

Hunter's worried voice echoed her father's as both men reached the flap. Tabitha heard them behind her but remained frozen in place, looking at the damage to the interior of the tent. A large tear in the fabric exposed the back corner to the elements. The stake had been ripped from the ground. Her cot lay at her feet, now a splintered mess.

After realizing she was fine, Hunter hurried outside and around the back corner as her pale father led her in his wake. She could hear Hunter's loud words of anger.

They rounded the tent and saw him standing, hands on hips, glaring up at the cliff behind their camp.

"What's going on over here?" Joey Matthews pushed his way through the crowd that had gathered and hurried over to where they stood. "What's causing this interruption to everyone's day?" He glared at Tabitha, as if her very presence drew everyone over.

Hunter spun and glared back at Joey. "What's 'causing this interruption' is a very large boulder that was pushed off the cliff and onto the Augustines' tent while Tabitha was inside."

"Pushed? Now, c'mon, who'd want to do something like that and why? Maybe you ought to keep the accusations down." Joey's face turned red with anger. "I run a clean contest, and I don't like the insinuation that something malicious would happen on my watch."

"Well, then you explain to me how something like this could randomly happen and just as Tabitha happened to enter her tent?"

Joey surveyed the scene. "Well, it's quite possible the boulder just came loose and fell. You did put your tents rather close to a cliff, and surely you must have known something like this could happen."

"If rocks such as this formed the butte, then yes, I'd say you had a plausible theory, but if you'll look closer, this rock isn't anything like the formation behind us. This had to have been brought in and pushed. Someone intentionally planned to hurt Tabitha, or her father, in the process. I demand a full investigation."

Joey swept his hat from his head and pushed his hair away from his eyes before slapping it back in place. "As I said, I run this contest. I can choose who stays and who goes. I'll thank you to remember that. And I'd appreciate your not telling me how to do my job. I'll investigate if and when I feel there's a valid reason." He turned and stalked back toward the crowd.

The men surrounding them didn't budge. Joey faced them. The men began one by one to cross their arms over their chests, fierce looks of protective anger on their features.

"Surely you all don't agree? Especially those who came to me early on and demanded I send Miss Augustine packing?"

Still no one budged.

"Oh, fine. If you all insist I investigate this ridiculous accusation, I'll do so."

Jason stepped forward and stood toe-to-toe with Joey. "Miss Augustine ain't been anything but a hard worker and one of the men—excuse me, ma'am." He nodded Tabitha's way. He returned to his spiel toward Joey. "So you have no reason to speak to her in this way or to ignore Hunter's request."

"Demand is more like it," Joey muttered. "I said I'll look into it. Now clear out and be on your way."

The men stood a few moments longer, staring Joey down, and then turned as one and headed off in the other direction.

❧

Hunter hurried to Tabitha's side. "Are you sure you're okay?"

Tabitha nodded. "I'd just walked away from there. If I'd dallied or waited a moment longer. . ."

A shudder shook her body. Hunter led her to a nearby crate and eased her down on it. He knew how shook up she was, because she didn't argue or give him a fight. He squatted down to face her. "Do you know anyone here from previous digs? Is there someone you've come across before who might have a grudge or a reason to hurt you?"

Tabitha looked at him, her blue eyes reflecting his worry. "No one. I've never met anyone here before. My father and I work mostly abroad. We've not been in the country for a couple of years until now."

Peter Augustine stood with his back to them, staring at the massive boulder. Now he turned and addressed them. "We'll be pulling out first thing in the morning. Tabitha, I want you packed up and ready to go. This isn't worth the danger. You could have been killed."

"No, Father!" Tabitha jumped to her feet and hurried to his side. "You can't mean it. I bet Mr. Matthews is right and this was a fluke. We can't give up so early in the competition."

Her father stared past her and met Hunter's gaze. "You know as well as I do that this wasn't an accident. Tell her, Mr. Pierce."

Hunter hated to go against her, but her father had a point. "He's right, Tab. This was no accident. And since we don't know why someone would do such a thing, there's no reason to take a chance on your well-being. You need to do as he says and go."

The words lanced his heart, and his pain reflected the expression in Tabitha's eyes as she surveyed him as if he were a traitor. With a sad shake of her head, she turned to go, stalking away from him and out of sight around the front corner of her tent.

"Sir." Hunter wasn't sure what to say, but when he saw the look on Dr. Augustine's face, he felt he had to push forward. "If you want to stay, I promise to help watch over Tabitha. Maybe if we're both on guard. Whoever stood on that butte should have been in plain sight. We just didn't know to look. Now we do know, so we can. . ."

Dr. Augustine already shook his head. His color hadn't yet returned, and he looked like a ghost. "Son, I appreciate the offer, but I'm going to have to say no." He opened his mouth to say more but froze, a strange expression filling his features.

"I don't feel so. . ." He began to sway and, with a hand reached out toward Hunter, collapsed.

Hunter caught him and called for Tabitha, who rounded the tent in moments.

"Nooo!" Her cry again had men running from all directions. Hunter heard someone call for the doctor to be summoned as he lowered Dr. Augustine's inert form to the ground. Tabitha hurried back into the tent for a blanket, which they folded under her father's head.

"What happened?" her voice shook, and Hunter prayed she'd not faint. They had enough going on.

"I'm not sure. One minute we were talking, and the next he passed out and fell."

The doctor pushed through the crowd, with Joey on his heels. He sent them a glare that implied they'd done this just to ruin his day.

"I've had enough of you people and your theatrics," Joey growled.

Hunter was on his feet and had the man by the front of his shirt before the words were completely out. "We people didn't ask for any of this. Someone pushed a boulder down on Miss Augustine, and the intent wasn't to scare her.

She could have been killed. The aftereffect caused her father to pass out, whether from a weak heart or shock, I don't know. But *your* operation is causing a safety risk, and I think you'd better focus on finding out who's behind it and why, instead of throwing out inappropriate comments."

He shoved the man away and wished the men behind would have let him fall to the ground. Instead, they reached out to steady Joey, who glared more intensely at Hunter as he righted his clothing. But before Hunter's conscience could prick at him for the unkind thought, Jason stepped forward and intervened.

"Mr. Matthews, I have to agree with Mr. Pierce. This ruckus isn't any of these folks' fault, and I don't think you can find a man here who disagrees." He turned to the others. "Am I right?"

The men voiced their agreement.

"You need to stop meddling with these folks and figure out what's going on. If I'm recalling correctly, they aren't the first people to have a situation occur. We've lost five other teams to accidents that sent them scurrying out of the competition. Someone is determined to chase everyone off, and as the head of operations, you need to be finding out who it is and why."

Hunter hadn't realized others left due to mischief or danger, though he did know a few other groups had pulled out. He assumed they decided they weren't cut out for this type of work. It gave him a new appreciation for Tabitha and her perseverance.

He returned his attention to Dr. Augustine and Tabitha. She stood forlornly at the side of the tent while the doctor did his exam. Hunter could hear Jason shooing the other men out of the way.

"He's going to be okay," Hunter whispered to Tabitha. He wrapped a comforting arm around her and pulled her close. She looked as if she'd join her father on the ground at the slightest breeze. She surprised him by relaxing into his support.

The doctor finished his exam and glanced up at them. "Your father's going to be fine, miss. But I'd like to send him in to Vernal for observation. Has he been eating and drinking enough in this heat?"

Tabitha shook her head. "I've tried to get him to eat consistently, but he's skipped several meals. He hasn't been drinking much, either."

"I'll take him back with me, and we'll have him up and on his feet in no time." He stood and dusted off his pants. "My wife and I live nearby, and she'll take good care of him while I'm here during the day. Don't you worry about a thing."

❧

Tabitha watched him go before turning to address Hunter. "How can I not worry? I have no one to stay with. The doc didn't offer me a chance to go along. Should

I insist on going with them?"

Hunter thought a moment. "They might not have room for you. I think he'd have offered otherwise. As to what you should do, I think you should sit tight and continue on. We'll be extra diligent, and I'll watch out for you."

Though Tabitha was stressed beyond reason over her father's health, she felt a small jolt of excitement at the thought that Hunter wanted to keep her nearby. But then she reminded herself that he probably felt responsible as her closest friend at the dig and did so out of duty.

"Unless, is there somewhere you could go? Someone you could stay with until your father is well again? Perhaps you could go home to your mother or someone else in your family?"

Then again, maybe he only felt obligated and trapped into watching out for her. A chill passed through her.

"My father's all the family I have. My mother died when I was a toddler, and there's no one else." She kept her voice cool and distanced herself from him. "But don't you worry. I'll be fine on my own. I don't need to burden you with my problems."

Realization quickly replaced the confusion on Hunter's features. "You aren't a burden to me. I'd not have offered my assistance if I hadn't wanted to. Haven't we become friends over the past week?" He tipped her chin up and forced her to look at him. "I'm only thinking of your safety."

"I like to think we've become friends. But really, I am perfectly capable of caring for myself. I've done it many times before."

"Well, not this time. Now you have me."

A warm feeling of contentment swept away the chill, and for the first time in a long time, Tabitha felt she had someone else on her side. She sent Hunter a thankful smile and knelt down next to her father.

"I don't know if you can hear me, Papa, but the doctor's going to take good care of you." She'd reverted out of worry to her childhood name for her father. "I'm going to stay here and continue on, but Hunter has assured me he'll watch out for me. So you have no need to be concerned and can just focus on getting well."

She let her voice trail off as she stared into her father's nonresponsive face. A sob caught in her throat as the doctor pulled up in a wagon. She felt Hunter's strong hands on her shoulder, urging her to her feet.

"He's going to be fine, Tabitha. Look, his color's returning and his breathing is steady."

Hunter was right. She stepped back and allowed the doctor, Hunter, and several other men to lift her unconscious father onto the makeshift bed in the doctor's wagon.

"I'll stay with him for the rest of the day and will bring a report on his condition sometime tomorrow." Doc climbed up onto the seat and took the reins. "If anyone else needs my assistance, send for me."

Hunter nodded, and the horses and wagon carrying her father moved out of sight.

By now the sun was low over the buttes, and Tabitha knew there wasn't time to return to work. They'd had a late lunch and, with all the action, had lost the entire afternoon.

"I'm sorry to have kept you from your work. I'm confirming every superstition all the men have about women on a dig site. I'll bet I've been more of a pain than you'd ever imagined I'd be when you first saw me."

"Well, possibly," Hunter teased. "More entertainment than I'd ever imagined, too. Let's head over and snag a table early, and I'll get you a drink while we wait for dinner."

She let him lead her to the tables grouped near the kitchen.

After he'd brought them mugs of water, he settled in beside her. "So, tell me about your childhood. You lost your mother at a young age, but surely your father didn't set out with a toddler in tow while traveling the world."

Tabitha smiled at the picture the comment invoked. "Not quite. We stayed in Boston with my grandmother, my father's mother, for the first few years. Only after I'd become fairly independent did he decide it was time to move on. You'd have liked my granny. She shared similar beliefs with you."

She watched as Hunter's face lit up at the thought. "Your grandmother was a believer? She said she loved the Lord, too?"

Tabitha nodded. "Very much. Not a night went by that she didn't tell me a story from the Bible before bed. I used to find them fascinating."

"And your father was okay with that?"

"My father had no choice in the matter. My granny loved the Lord, and she ran a tight ship. No one dared to cross her, not even my father. He was one of seven sons. Granny was the tiniest little thing, but she stood her ground. My father was the only one of her sons who refused to embrace her beliefs. Even in later years, when my papa tried to dissuade her from her teachings, she'd set him straight. She always told him he'd regret choosing his belief in evolution over her belief in creation."

"So he's heard the truth, too."

"He's heard her version of the truth. It doesn't necessarily mean it's the truth."

Hunter's face dimmed as he listened to her choice of words. "So you don't believe your granny's way to be the truth?" His earnest expression led her to believe her next few words would make a huge impact on their friendship. She didn't want to let him down but couldn't lie to him, either.

"I'm not completely sold on the theory of evolution."

"So you're open to hearing other thoughts and ideas? Have you studied the Bible or searched for the truth yourself? I can help you if you'd like."

He reached over and took hold of her hand again.

"And your 'help'—it would be completely unbiased, right?" She softened her sarcastic retort with a small smile.

"Well, maybe not entirely. But your grandmother had a few short years, while your father has had—what—well over a decade since to give you his point of view on the subject?" His devotion to the topic was endearing. "I'm just saying that while you're waiting for him to recuperate, you might want to delve into the subject a bit more deeply on your own. . .with my help." His eyes twinkled over his words. "I'll loan you my Bible. Please?"

She hesitated.

"For me?"

Still she hesitated.

"For your grandmother then. . ."

Now he'd stopped playing fair. She'd adored her grandmother and missed her dearly. Only the small hope in the back of her mind that her granny had indeed been right and now sat in her beloved Lord's presence helped take away the grief when the older woman died. That fact was something Tabitha had never admitted or verbalized to her father, but she suddenly found herself wanting to share with Hunter.

"I promise to keep an open mind."

"Good, then let me start by praying with you for your father."

Hunter clutched her hand tightly in his own. A peace and contentment descended over her that had nothing to do with his reverent words or kindness.

Chapter 5

The next morning Hunter slapped his hand against Tabitha's tent and called out for her to wake up.

"What time is it?" Tabitha's voice sounded husky from sleep, and he tried to envision what she looked like at this early hour. As groggy as she sounded, he might not find out for quite a while.

"It's time for you to be up and about. We have a lot to do today."

"I thought today was Sunday, our mandatory day of rest."

Hunter heard her rustling around inside the tent. He knew the long hours of the required day off would allow her more time to worry about her father, so he figured this would be a good chance to take her to see some of the sights in the surrounding area.

A melancholy sigh drifted out to him. "I can't believe the night has already ended. I tossed and turned, every noise alerting me to the fact that someone might be lurking outside my tent. And I worried about my father. Without him snoring away in the cot beside mine, I felt alone and vulnerable. I didn't realize how much I'd come to rely on him. He's always been there for me."

Hunter knew she'd moved onto her father's cot to sleep, since the damage to her own made it unusable. He'd taken her cot back to his camp the night before so he could rebuild it before Dr. Augustine returned. While he'd worked on the cot, Tabitha had sewn the rip in the tent, doing most of the stitching by lantern late into the night.

"I've borrowed two horses. I have something I want you to see. The excursion will only take up the morning. After we return for lunch, if Doc hasn't returned with an update, we'll ride into town and check on your father."

Tabitha finally appeared through the opening of the tent and stepped out into the early morning sunlight. A pink ribbon wound through her long blond braid and neatly formed a bow at the end. Though dark circles ringed her eyes and proved her lack of sleep, she looked pretty in a dainty floral blouse and flowing pink skirt. Since he'd only seen her in work clothes up until now, the change in her appearance took his breath away.

"You look wonderful." He'd stopped himself short of saying beautiful, not wanting to scare her off.

The color his remark put into her cheeks matched the outfit she wore and made her eyes appear even bluer, a perfect match to the blue of the early morning sky above.

"So, what do you think of my plans?" He pointed toward the two mounts that waited on the road.

"I like them, but could we switch things around and go to see my father first? I'd really like to check on him."

Hunter shook his head. "Doc said he'd stop by with a report. I don't think we should bother them until then. He would have sent for you if things looked worse during the night. Let him do his job. I bet he'll be back here before we return."

"I suppose." Tabitha led the way toward the breakfast table, her dainty boots leaving small imprints in the dust.

Hunter hadn't realized how petite she was, but now, without her work gear on, she seemed to have diminished in size. Or maybe the change reflected her insecurity with her father gone.

They ate quickly in the mostly empty kitchen area and set out on their trek. Hunter led the way, explaining about the different plants and rocks as they rode. Though Tabitha freely admitted her worry about her father, she also admitted this was a most welcome diversion from her sordid thoughts. If he'd left it to her, she'd have sat around and sulked about her father. He was glad he'd thought to busy her with sightseeing.

The day promised to be a beauty and remained cool at this early hour, a fact that Hunter had taken into consideration when planning their itinerary.

He slowed his horse and waited for Tab to come alongside him. He matched her pace as the trail widened. "Other than the obvious, was there a reason for your lack of sleep? Did you hear anyone near your tent during the night?"

"No. My imagination took over from the events of the day. I kept waiting for another rock to crash down on me or for someone to try another approach with my father gone." She rode in silence for a few minutes. "I looked over first thing, used to seeing him nearby on his cot, and it took a moment before I realized he'd fallen ill and wasn't there. The realization brought with it a most awful feeling."

"I'm sorry you're having such a hard time." He paused and thought about her comment. "How about I leave my tent flap open tonight? That might help you feel better."

Tabitha, amused, shook her head. "You'll have a bed full of lizards and other unwelcome critters if you do that. I'm sure I'll be fine. But I appreciate the offer."

"I've been in the area for a while. Usually I don't even bother with the tent. So a few critters aren't going to bother me."

Considering the matter settled, he pulled ahead.

Tabitha enjoyed watching him. Today he wore soft brown leather pants and a loose shirt that he didn't bother to tuck into his waistband. The ensemble didn't even remotely resemble the khaki pants and shirt he usually wore. His hair blew free in the breeze, and he looked completely at ease in the saddle. The overall effect gave the impression of a very savage man, one used to riding the trails. If she didn't know him better and had just run into him on the path, he would have terrified her. As it was, she knew he was kind, and his true personality was nothing like the rough image he presented. The thought made her realize she knew nothing about his past or his family, though he already knew most everything there was to know about hers. She determined to use their time together to learn more.

They rounded a large formation of sandstone, and Tabitha's audible gasp caused Hunter to turn in his saddle with a chuckle. "I thought you'd like it."

A valley opened before them, and at the bottom a beautiful winding river carved out a swath in the pink and orange landscape. The array of color against the vivid blue sky took her breath away.

"This alone is worth the ride. The beauty. . .it's like nothing I've seen before. I have no words to describe it." She fell silent.

"Yes, the beauty is without equal."

Hunter's voice sounded reverent, but when she turned to look at him, he stared at her, not the scene before them. The realization flustered her, and she began to chatter, a nervous habit. "If only I could capture the magnificence of this vision to share with my father."

"We'll bring him back as soon as he's up to it. He should be on his feet within a couple of days, and he, too, will have to take a break next week. We'll drag him out here for his own good."

"He'll love it."

"Come on. I have something else to show you."

She followed him, staying close as the trail narrowed.

"Are we safe? I've heard that Butch Cassidy and his gang ride through the area regularly." The hair stood up on the back of her neck as she belatedly remembered that little tidbit of information.

"We should be fine."

"Should be? Or will be?" she teased. For whatever reason, she felt completely safe in Hunter's care. If he wasn't worried, and she felt sure he'd never have brought her here if he had any thoughts of running into an unsafe situation, she wouldn't worry, either. Though she had to admit, the fact that he carried weapons helped her sense of security.

"I promise, while you're in my care, I'll do everything in my power to keep you safe."

She knew he meant it.

They rounded a cliff and Hunter swung down from his saddle before reaching up to assist her. His hands were strong on her waist, and she felt their warmth through the thin fabric of her skirt. He set her before him and held her a moment longer than necessary.

"Have you ever seen petroglyphs before? Or pictographs?"

Tabitha's heart picked up speed in anticipation of what Hunter was about to show her. Or maybe her struggle for air came from his close proximity only a moment before. More than likely, the effect came from a combination of both. "I've seen petroglyphs, but only pictures of them in some of our books."

He led her around the bend and pointed to the canyon wall. She caught her breath in surprise. "Oh, look at all of them! I can't believe there are so many carvings in the wall. It's amazing!"

She ran from one set of inscriptions to the next. "And look over there! Pictographs! They're fantastic. My father will never believe this. He's wanted to see them his whole life, but we didn't realize they were right here where we'd be spending our time. I thought they were farther north."

"My grandfather and I discovered this batch when we were exploring a few months back. I'm writing an article for publication, but as far as I know, nobody else knows of this specific location. The petroglyphs are all through the area." Hunter just stood and grinned at her enthusiasm. "So I guess you're glad I dragged you out here?"

She belatedly remembered her manners and hurried back to him. "Oh, Hunter, yes, thank you! Thank you so much for thinking to bring me here." She threw her arms around him and gave him an exuberant hug. He took a step backward from the force of her hug before grabbing her waist to momentarily stabilize her. Once he'd let go, she hurried back to the walls, trying to figure out what each of the carvings and pictures represented. She turned to him and caught a strange expression on his face. "Are you okay?"

Maybe she'd hurt him, or maybe he just didn't like someone invading his space in that way. Now that she thought about it, she'd been horribly forward. "I'm sorry."

"Why are you apologizing?" He snapped out of his funk and came to join her in front of the nearest etching.

"You had a funny look on your face. I thought I might have hurt you."

He sent her his charming smile. "You couldn't hurt me if you tried."

❧

As they rode back toward camp, Hunter inwardly laughed at himself. Famous last words. When she'd thrown her arms around him with such abandon, he'd enjoyed it. And he'd felt bereft when she'd pulled away. He'd meant what he'd said, that a petite person like her would never hurt him in the way she'd meant, by hugging him too hard. But for the first time ever, he realized his heart had become entangled with hers, and he'd enjoyed her brief hug far too much. All his life, after watching the family he grew up with and their self-centered ways, he'd been careful to guard his emotions and not let any woman get too close. Yet here, in just over a week, Tab had somehow slipped past his barrier and snagged a bit of his heart. He hadn't even realized, or at least he hadn't admitted it to himself, until that moment.

He'd noticed her beauty right from the start, but after she'd come at him like a wildcat that first day, he'd planned to keep his distance. For whatever reason, that distance had been breached, and here he stood, alone, in the middle of nowhere, with a very dangerous woman. One who was dangerous to him, his bachelorhood, and his future. And more important, he had a feeling she'd prove dangerous to his heart.

He'd have to keep her at arm's length, a task that would be hard with her father ill and no one else to watch over her. He'd given his word and would do his part for now, but as soon as Dr. Augustine returned and took over again as guardian for his daughter, Hunter would return his focus to the find. Tabitha's words broke into his thoughts.

"Hunter? You've been distant and silent the entire ride back. I must have hurt you in some way. Or perhaps it was my forwardness." A look of realization passed through her eyes, and she raised a delicate—and smudged—hand to her mouth. "Oh my, as I'm sure you've noticed, I'm not very wise or experienced in the ways of propriety while under the care of a gentleman, and I do believe I overstepped my bounds."

Her innocence and the way she verbalized her thoughts was refreshing. He couldn't help but smile. The women he'd grown up with would be more shocked about her voicing those very words than they would have been over the spontaneous hug, though the hug would surely have set their tongues a waggin', too.

"You did nothing of the sort. I enjoyed our time together immensely. I'm ecstatic that you found such joy in the sights I took you to see."

He didn't miss the immediate release of her breath or the relief in her light blue eyes. "Oh, good. And we'll still take my father out there next week? It would mean so much to him. To us both."

Hunter hesitated, but only for a moment. "Of course. If he's up to the trip by then, we'll ride out first thing Sunday morning."

Mentally he called himself a coward. Hadn't he just told himself that when her father returned, he'd pull a safe distance away? Then why did he find himself blurting out the surest thing that would put a smile back on her face, without any thought to his decision? Keeping his distance from her would definitely prove to be one of the harder parts of this dig.

They entered camp to see Joey hurrying their way. "You two, over here, right now."

Hunter felt like a wayward schoolboy who'd just been caught sneaking out of class for a day of fishing at the pond. Not that he'd done such a thing in his youth. Well, maybe once or twice. A grin from memories past curved his lip.

"You find something to be amusing?" Joey motioned for them to dismount.

Hunter did as he asked and hurried to assist Tabitha before Joey could get his slimy hands on her. The effort earned him a scowl from the coordinator. "Nope, I find nothing amusing here. But I did just return from a most enjoyable ride and sightseeing excursion with Miss Augustine. That's enough to put a smile on any man's face."

The comment earned him a glare from Joey and a stomp on the foot from Tabitha. A hard stomp. For such a little thing she used the heels of her boots very thoroughly. "Ow!" His teacher's raps against his knuckles paled in comparison.

Joey stalked away and picked up a bundle of papers. "If you can try to focus on the matter at hand. . ."

Hunter suddenly had a bad feeling about where this conversation would lead. He glanced at Tabitha, and she shrugged. "What's going on?"

"With Miss Augustine's father out of the picture, I must insist she leave the site and return home. A woman without a chaperone at an event such as this is most inappropriate, as you've both just demonstrated." He sent them each a piercing glare. "Didn't you realize how unscrupulous taking off for parts unknown would look?"

Hunter couldn't say he had. One glance at the stricken expression on Tab's face had him pretty sure she hadn't, either. "Tab, I'm sorry. I didn't mean to bring your reputation into question. I should have known better."

She waved away his words, her hand fluttering through the air. "No, I'm sure any thoughts about propriety should have been mine. My instructors at finishing school—before I got kicked out anyway—were very adamant on the weakness of the male species when it came to things of such a nature as this."

Joey stood speechless before them, his mouth gaping open at her comment.

Hunter began to pace, his nervous energy never allowing him to stay still for long. "No, I promised your father I'd look after you and didn't even think about how it would look to ride off alone in such a way. I truly am sorry."

She nodded her acceptance but wouldn't look him in the eye.

"In any case, Miss Augustine, I'm forced to ask you to leave. Surely you agree that it isn't proper for a woman such as yourself to remain here without the guardianship of your father. Your self-appointed guardian has made it clear he isn't up to the task."

Hunter wanted to take Joey to task for the way he'd just publicly embarrassed Tabitha. "We did nothing to harm Miss Augustine's reputation, Mr. Matthews. I'd appreciate your not insinuating anything of the sort. You're embarrassing us both."

Joey's expression became smug. "Perhaps you're embarrassing yourselves. I certainly didn't send you off alone to cause speculation amongst the men."

Hunter made a point of looking around the camp where the other competitors all went about their business, none of them paying the trio any mind at all. "The speculation seems to be all yours." He mimicked Joey's tone of voice. "Perhaps that's because you're the only one in the camp who's curious about our day?"

The man sputtered and ignored Hunter's comment. "As I said, Miss Augustine, you need to pack and leave immediately."

"What's she going to do, Matthews? Walk to the nearest train station and buy a ticket out?" He waved in the direction of the nearest town. "Or do you expect her to put all their belongings on her back and hike out? Be reasonable."

Joey huffed out a frustrated breath. "Of course I don't expect her to do those things. But I do expect her to be ready so that when the next wagon comes through, she'll be able to pull out."

Hunter decided to take a different tack. Tabitha stood in shocked silence as the men debated. He wanted to fix this for her. "Has Doc returned with an update on her father?"

"He arrived earlier this morning, not that you were around to greet him."

"Skip the *theatrics* as you call them, Matthews, and get to the point." Hunter had tired of dancing around with proprieties. He took a menacing step closer to the other man, closing the space between them.

Joey backed away from him and again focused on Tabitha. "I—I, well, he said your father would be fine, and he'd be able to return to work in the next couple of days."

"And yet you threaten Tabitha and tell her you're sending her away. Your actions are despicable, Joey, and you can be sure the people back East who are funding the dig will hear about this." He sent the man a final glare before turning and taking Tabitha by the arm. "Come, Tab. Let's get you back to camp."

As they walked away, he glanced over his shoulder. "Please make sure the horses are properly cared for."

Joey's face filled with rage. "I'm not here to do your bidding, Pierce. I'll have you remember I'm in charge of this operation."

Hunter stopped and turned around to face him. "Oh, really? I seem to remember you greeting each of us with the comment that we're to come to you if we need anything. And for now, I need you to look after the horses. You've upset Tabitha, and I need to return her to her quarters."

Without another backward glance, he led Tabitha away.

"Do you think he's the one behind the accidents?" Tabitha finally broke her silence when they were a safe distance from the man.

"I'm not sure, but I doubt it. What would he have to gain? I'd say it's more likely someone in competition with us. Regardless, we'll be extra diligent and watch out for each other."

An endeavor he found most intriguing.

Chapter 6

Two mornings later, Tab hurried to greet the wagon as it pulled up to their claim. She'd been working her regular quadrant all morning and had just taken a water break when she heard the sound of approaching horses. Dust swirled around them and made her cough, but she waved it away, eager for the first glimpse of her father.

His illness had aged him in the brief time he'd been gone. Or maybe she'd been too busy during the past couple of weeks to notice his decline. She hadn't realized how thin he'd become. His sunken eyes sought hers, but he didn't hold their contact. Instead, he busied himself with stepping down from the wagon, refusing the hands offered him.

Hunter appeared beside Tab, and she welcomed his quiet strength.

"C'mon, Papa, let's get you settled over here." She motioned toward the chair Hunter had so thoughtfully brought over the night before. "You can supervise me as I work, and we can talk and catch up."

Her father stood silently before her, contemplative as he surveyed their claim.

"Or if you'd rather, you could lie down for a bit after your trip out here. I'm sure it wasn't pleasant to be bumped around after your illness."

"I'd rather you stop fussing and leave me alone. I'll make the decisions on what I do or don't do next."

Her father's words, clipped and abrupt, cut through her.

"I–I'm sorry." She stepped back, blinking away tears. She didn't want Hunter and the other men around them to see her pain.

Hunter stepped in, saving her further humiliation by addressing the men who had wandered over to check out the new arrival. "There's nothing to see here. You can all go back to work. Dr. Augustine is fine."

The men drifted off, but Tabitha held her spot, staring at her father with confusion. Maybe the bad disposition had to do with his episode. Or maybe he'd taken medications that caused him to act in such a hurtful manner. But she knew if nothing else, the behavior was completely out of character. Maybe if she ignored it, he'd get better and things would return to the way they used to be.

"Well, if you don't need anything else, I'll return to my work." She turned her back to him and left Hunter to pick up any pieces.

Though her hands were busy, her mind wouldn't stop analyzing her father's peculiar behavior. She and her father were close, and this new side of him broke her heart. She'd always been the center of his world, and he hers. But from the moment they'd arrived here, his attitude had changed. She hesitated and rocked back onto her heels, deep in thought. Now that she considered things, he'd actually changed in the month or so before their arrival. His lack of enthusiasm began after reading a note, delivered to their door, weeks before the dig began. She'd asked him about it at the time, but he crumpled it angrily in his hand and threw it into the fireplace.

Tabitha forced her cramped muscles to stretch and stood to her feet. She nervously ran her hands over her skirt to smooth it before approaching her father. Thanks to Hunter, at least he now rested in the hardwood chair.

"Father, will you please tell me what's going on? You've not been yourself for a while now. I remember a note that was delivered to you in town just after our arrival in Utah. Did it have anything to do with the dig?"

Her father closed his eyes a moment before looking at her in exasperation. "Must you ask so many questions all the time? Can't you just leave a man alone with his thoughts?"

"You taught me to ask questions. You've always said questions are the basis of science and our reason for living. We ask questions so that we can seek an answer, which gives us purpose in life. Now you want me to stop?" She folded her arms and glared. "I don't understand you anymore. You haven't been yourself this entire dig. Please help me understand what has changed."

"I've changed. It's that simple. I think we need to pack up and go back East. It's time for me to settle down and find you a husband. You need to have a stable life and settle in one place. I'm taking a teaching job at a university." For the first time, he looked directly into her eyes. "We're pulling out and moving home. Your grandmother's house is available. As soon as we can pack up, we'll head that way."

"You can't be serious!" Tabitha hadn't expected this. "We're here. We're in the middle of something we've dreamed about for years. Please talk to me, Father. Help me to understand what has stolen your dream."

"I am serious, and I don't need to explain things to you. We're pulling out as soon as we can. I've already arranged for our passage on the train. We need to be at the station in three days."

Tabitha, for the first time ever, dug in her heels and took a stance against her father. "I'm not going."

Her father's face registered his shock. "You have to go. They aren't going to let you stay here without a male escort. It isn't safe."

Tabitha contemplated his words. He had a point. Joey had pretty much told her the same thing two days before. "Then I'll find an escort, a chaperone."

THE GREATEST FIND

She bent her knees to bring herself to his eye level and grabbed his hands, so thin and cold in her own. "Father, just help me understand. We've wanted this for so long. We've been on other explorations, and we've learned so much, but never have we been able to be in on the beginning of something this grand. You wanted that award as badly as I still do. What's happened? What's changed?"

"A lot, but I don't feel I have to go into it with you." He pulled his hands from her grasp and eased to his feet before slowly shuffling to their tent.

A sob caught in her throat. She didn't know how to break through his hard shell. He was a stranger. He even walked like an old man as he entered the canvas flap. A heavy burden pressed hard against his chest, and it broke her heart that she couldn't fix it.

Tab glanced up at the cliffs looming over their site, the place where someone had stood to roll a huge stone over the edge and had sent her father into this deep dark place. She had a sudden urge to escape the mundane work of the dig and to go to the highest place. Maybe she'd try to talk to God. Maybe He'd hear her if she got close enough to Him. She wasn't sure, but she knew she had to try.

❧

Hunter watched as Tabitha walked up the dirt road and turned at the far end, moving out of his sight as she rounded the last tent. The day promised to be hot like the others, but dark clouds lingered on the horizon. He didn't know if rain would be a refreshing, welcome respite from the heat, or if it would only make their work area a muddy mess, but as he'd inadvertently listened to Tabitha and her father talk, he felt an oppression that weighed heavier than any storm.

When Tabitha's father didn't reappear from the tent to go after her, Hunter set down his work tools with a sigh. The direction in which she'd headed led out of camp, and though he didn't know what she had in mind, he knew that without her being familiar with the terrain and area, she wasn't safe alone. He also knew that if any of the other men, especially the more unscrupulous ones, saw her leave on her own, she wouldn't be safe.

Actions like this proved her father right in that she needed to leave with him and not stick around to make such poor choices. She wouldn't be happy, but he intended to set her straight and back her father's decision for her to leave the site. The thought made him sad. The dig would be infinitely more boring without her cheery talk, feisty comebacks, and spontaneous ways. But her leaving would also be more conducive to returning his focus to the task at hand, something he should be doing at this very moment, when instead he now plodded along behind a runaway daughter whose actions seemed to constantly overrule his better judgment.

He stopped short as he realized he'd lost sight of her. His heart skipped a few beats before a shower of rock from above had him looking heavenward.

279

"Tabitha, what on earth are you thinking climbing up the bluff like that?" He decided in that instant her father had probably suffered a minor heart dysfunction from the many years of trying to keep up with his wayward daughter. How the older man managed to keep up with her as long as he had, Hunter didn't know.

"Oh—Hunter!" Her foot slipped and sent a few more rocks tumbling down his way.

He stepped backward to avoid them and shaded his eyes with his hand. She'd managed to find a sort of path that led up the bluff and apparently intended to climb it to the top.

"You startled me." She'd regained her footing and now clung to the side of the cliff. "What are you doing out here?"

"I think the question would better be asked, what are *you* doing out here?" He tucked his thumbs in his waistband, determined to talk her down. How on earth did a person go from arguing with her father to climbing a cliff that led to nothing but the heavens?

"I need to get away, to think."

She said it so simplistically, as if her need to think explained everything.

"And you can't do that from down here on the ground?" He glanced around at the vast, open desert that surrounded them. "Are there no other quiet places where you can gather your thoughts without putting your pretty little neck at risk?"

She'd continued to climb and now had reached the top. He decided his inactivity only put him at a disadvantage, so began to follow her ascent with his own.

"You think my neck is pretty? What an odd thing to say." Her voice wound over the top of the cliff, where she now sat, and drifted down to him. "I could understand 'pretty eyes' or 'pretty face,' but 'pretty little neck' doesn't really work."

He considered changing his statement, because right about now he only wanted to throttle her pretty little neck, but he waited to voice the comment until he reached the top of the treacherous climb. In hindsight, now that he was committed to the endeavor, he couldn't believe she'd kept her grip when he'd startled her moments before. It took every bit of his concentration to keep from slipping and falling. A fall like this would guarantee at the very least a broken leg when landing on the hard-packed ground below. He reached the top, pulled himself up over the edge, and lay on his back while staring up at her.

Guileless blue eyes returned his stare.

He shook his head. "That was stupid."

She nodded. "But you had to do it, didn't you?"

"I meant on your part."

"Well, that's a matter of opinion. I considered it necessary."

He pushed to his elbows. "What would make a dangerous climb like that 'necessary'? You said you wanted to think. Is there no other place—a place safe and on solid ground that doesn't entail a forty-foot drop—for you to give way to your thoughts?"

She shrugged. "I'm sure there is, but at the moment, I could only think of getting up here. I needed to be able to have complete aloneness." She sent him a sideways glare. "You can see how well that worked out."

Pulling her gaze from his, she glanced down and fiddled with her skirt. "I thought if I could get up here, maybe I'd feel closer to God and He'd hear my prayers."

Hunter dropped back to stare at the sky in frustration. "God hears your prayers wherever you are. You don't have to risk life or limb to get to Him. He's everywhere you are. A quiet prayer uttered from the safety of my chair would have been just as effective as one uttered on this bluff."

"Really?" The corner of her mouth tipped up into an alluring grin. "Now you tell me."

"Yes, really." He pushed to a sitting position and scouted out the area. At least no rattlers sunned on the platform with them. But his thoughts went in dangerous directions with Tabitha sitting so close and with them being so alone. He wondered what it would be like to kiss her, while they were alone up here without all the prying eyes that had followed their every move at camp—a temptation that showed him exactly why they needed to stay under the watchful eyes at camp.

He stood and hurried away from her and the alluring thoughts. "Look, footprints."

Though the sandstone was hard, a soft powdery dust covered the outcropping, and a path of footprints led to the edge on the eastern side.

Tabitha reached for his hand and, in a moment of triumph, he walked back to help her to her feet. A week or so earlier she would have tried to bite any hand offered to her. She rolled her eyes at his smug grin but kept his hand gripped tightly in her own.

They followed the footprints to the edge and looked down. The entire dig spread out before them, the workers looking small from this vantage point. Everyone was intent on the ground below them. Not one person looked up to see them standing there, which had worked in Tab's attacker's favor when he'd pushed the rock over and onto the tent. Hunter tightened his hold on her hand as the picture passed through his mind of what could have been.

"Your father's right, you know. You need to leave the area with him. You aren't safe here."

She caught her breath with a fast intake of air. "You don't want me here? I thought you'd offer to watch out for me, that you'd want to keep me here as badly as I want to stay."

She pulled her hand away, and he suddenly felt bereft and alone.

"I want you safe. Someone stood on this very cliff and had taken the time and forethought into getting that huge rock up here. It wasn't a spur of the moment deal, nor done on a whim. Someone wanted to hurt—or possibly even kill—you."

He crossed his arms over his chest and stared at her. "I don't want you to leave. I've grown fond of you, and I enjoy your presence, but I don't want you to stay with your life at risk."

"I want to win the plaque for my father."

Stubborn woman.

Hunter wasn't in the race for fame or fortune, though he did love the thrill of finding new bones and the challenge of touching history. He liked that his work would further the science of archaeology for others who came after them. Though he didn't understand her determination to do this for recognition only, and to win the event at all costs, he did appreciate her devotion to her father.

"Why?"

She walked away from the edge, away from the eyes that might pry at them from below if someone looked up from their digging for a momentary break. "Because I've watched him work hard his whole life, and he's never once been recognized for that. He lost some prime years to stay with me as a child. Most men would have left their child with the grandmother who wholeheartedly embraced the opportunity. But he chose to stay. He didn't want me to lose him after losing my mother."

"Then maybe this is the time for you to show him that same concern and do as he asks and leave. I'm sure he'd rather have you over some silly plaque."

She turned to face him, pushing back the blond tendrils that blew free from her braid and drifted across her face. "No. He's not leaving because he wants to. I'm sure of it. If he were, I'd go along with him. But I have a feeling he's leaving because he's being forced to go, and I won't let someone do that to him. I'll stay and fight for the find. . .for the award."

"That doesn't make sense!" Hunter again wanted to throttle her. Here she'd admitted that someone wanted them gone, someone desperate enough that he would go to the extremes of murder to get his way, yet Tab stubbornly wanted to stay and face more potential threats. "You're in danger, and you need to go."

He saw the expression of doubt pass across her features, followed by a look of fear before he realized how harsh his words sounded. She took a nervous step away from him.

"It could be you. You might be the one chasing us out. And here I've foolishly led you right out of camp and onto a desolate and dangerous place."

Hunter couldn't believe she'd think such a thing of him. "It's not me. I followed you so I could protect you."

"But how do I know that for sure? You're just as determined as everyone else to make the find."

"Right. That's why I'm up here arguing with your stubborn little self while the others continue to work below us."

She glanced at the cliff and moved farther away. "If you were to push me, my father would be devastated."

"If I wanted to push you, I'd have done it when we were standing together over there minutes ago. No one would have seen me. You're safe with me, Tabitha. Admit it." He saw the hesitation in her eyes, but she must have realized he had a point. He'd had his moment and didn't take it.

"I'm sorry. I don't know what to think or who to trust anymore. I can't even trust my father's judgment."

"You can trust me, but I still say you need to listen to your father and leave."

"He's always taught me to chase after my dreams. This is one of them. It's his dream, but it's also my dream for us. I'm not leaving."

"Are you sure? I know your father isn't making sense to you—and I can't understand his stance on this, either. But he's a great scientist, and I appreciate and respect his work. I don't agree with his thoughts on all his scholarly attitudes, especially when it comes to God, but I do know he's running scared from something, and I'm not sure you want to stick around and find out what it is."

"I'm not leaving."

She'd dug her heels in again, figuratively speaking, and he knew he couldn't pry her from her determination to stay. He reached out his hand, and after a small hesitation, she took it. "You came up here to pray. Let's do that now, together." He pulled her close and held her soft form in his arms while he said the heartfelt words to his Lord. He prayed for her decision, for her father's pain and struggle, and for their protection.

"Hunter, how do you suppose the person responsible for the boulder got it up here?"

"I've wondered that myself. I guess there's a possibility it already waited here. Maybe it fell from one of the higher bluffs."

She voiced her agreement. "There's no way someone carried or dragged it up. Unless they hoisted it?"

"Maybe, but I doubt it."

As he led her back to the ledge to begin their descent, she balked.

"C'mon. I'm not going to hurt you."

"I know. It's not that."

She glanced up at him with a new fear in her eyes and nervously licked her lip. "It's the drop. The distance looked much better from the ground, and I'm not sure now how I'll ever make it back down."

She had a point. The ledge looked nonexistent from up here, and taking the first step into thin air held little attraction for him, either.

"I tell you what. Why don't we scout around a bit and see if we can find another way. If we don't find a safer path, I'll support you and get you safely down."

They walked around the entire perimeter but found no other way off the sandstone bluff.

Hunter sat down at the edge of the cliff where they'd climbed up. "I'll go first, and I'll assist you as you come behind me. It's wider than it looks. It's all an illusion. You're going to have to trust me."

"The ledge might be an illusion, but the forty-foot drop beyond it isn't." She shuddered.

"I'll keep you safe. Just do as I say and trust me." And he'd trust God to watch over them and keep them safe in the same way. He sent up a frantic prayer that Tabitha wouldn't panic and cause a fall that would surely lead to both of their deaths.

He lowered himself over the top ridge and settled onto the firm support of the ledge. He turned and assisted Tabitha in doing the same.

Once they'd made the initial turn, they were fine. He jumped the last few feet to the ground and reached up to lift her down.

"We did it!" Her euphoria was contagious.

"We did."

"I'm sorry I suggested it might be you trying to hurt us and chase us off. I know better."

He waved away her words. "You really don't. But I'll do my best to convince you."

They walked in silence for a few minutes.

"If I'd wanted to hurt you, I could have done something the other day, too. I had the entire morning."

"I thought of that, but everyone knew the two of us were together. It would have been too dangerous. You'd have been the first suspect and would have been caught." Her smile showed him she wasn't serious, at least not anymore. If the thought had crossed her mind, and at some point it apparently had, she'd found peace with it for now.

"Hmm, good point."

They'd reached the site, and no one had missed them this time.

Tabitha touched his arm. "I'm serious about staying, too. I need you to help me. I can't do it without your support."

"We'll worry about it if your father indeed decides to leave. Maybe after he thinks things through, and after seeing your reaction to leaving, he'll change his mind."

"Maybe. But I highly doubt it." She rubbed her hands up and down her arms as goose bumps formed on her flesh.

Though the air felt warm, Hunter also felt the chill. Something was wrong, and he determined to find out what it was. He'd protect Tabitha, no matter what the cost. He'd found a treasure worth more than the dig, something he hadn't expected when he'd originally signed up.

Chapter 7

Tabitha woke early the next morning and watched her father sleep. His loud mutterings had wakened her, and she realized the term *sleep* was a stretch as there was nothing restful about the process in his case. He tossed and turned and cried out about treasure and danger. Even in his dreams he battled something unknown. Tabitha listened intently, hoping something he said would give her a clue about the cause of his recent behavior. But she could only decipher a mix of phrases that meant nothing.

When he finally returned to a more restful state, she gave up her own attempt at sleep and climbed out of bed. She stepped behind the hanging sheet they'd rigged for privacy and pulled on a fresh white blouse and tan skirt. Though the colors were practical, she'd already tired of them. She longed to wear some of her prettier clothes, but she'd left most of them behind, knowing the work out here would permanently soil them. The clothes she brought were chosen with care—light, airy fabrics that wouldn't hold the heat any more than necessary and bland colors that were easy to clean.

She laughed inwardly at that thought. Her entire wardrobe carried stains from the work site, and nothing she could imagine would prevent the arid heat from seeping through to her skin. Not for the first time, she wished for a pair of trousers like the men wore. But her father drew the line at that notion. His daughter might work on the sites in a man's world, but she'd do it while wearing the clothes of a lady.

She tried to slip quietly through the tent flap, but her father's snore turned into a waking cough and slowed her. He leaned up on his elbow.

"Tabitha? Where are you going?"

"I'm sorry I woke you, Father. I thought I'd slip out for an early breakfast and get a head start on the day."

He stared past her to gauge the slant of the rising sun. "So you can get a start on the packing, I hope?"

She sighed. "I've not changed my mind. I don't want to leave. I don't plan to leave. I want you to stay, too."

He already shook his head in denial. "No."

"Then please explain to me why. I don't understand what's changed since we arrived. If you'd share your thoughts, your concerns, maybe I'd be able to understand, but. . ." Her voice tapered off, and she held her hands helplessly out at her side as she sank down on her own cot and faced him. "Without knowing what's going on, I can't."

"There are things you don't know and don't need to know. I don't have to explain myself to you."

"But you always have before. And I'm not a child, Papa. I'm an adult. I deserve to know what's behind your departure so I can make an informed decision of my own."

"No." Her father turned away, and she knew that in his opinion the conversation had ended.

"Then I'll remain here, even if you leave."

He returned his stare to her for several long moments and then shrugged. "I won't drag you out of here against your will, but you're making a big mistake."

Tears filled her eyes at the coldness in his tone. His eyes were icy, and she felt no warmth emanating from him at all. The man before her was still a stranger. She felt more at ease and had more peace when in Hunter's company than at this moment, and since Hunter had rubbed her wrong from the moment she met him, that said a lot.

She refused to cry. "Where will you go?"

"I'll head in to town. If you need me, inquire at the general store. I'll let them know where I'll be. I have some research I can attend to until you come to your senses, which I dare to suggest won't be long. In the meantime, I'll delay our train tickets."

"Father, I fully intend to stay here until the dig is over. That could be days, or it could be weeks."

"Well, whenever that is, you know where to find me. I'll have to borrow a horse since the supply wagon isn't heading to town for several days. I'll leave most of my things and the supplies here with you."

Tabitha nodded and hurried through the tent flap to the welcoming breeze outside. The early morning sky already caused her to squint with its brilliant blue colors. And without a cloud to block it, the sun shone directly into her eyes. She lifted her hat and placed it on her head.

"Talk to Me and pray." The unbidden words carried so clearly to her that Tabitha looked around to see if Hunter stood nearby. But she stood alone. No one else moved about this early. She considered the gentle command. *"Talk to Me and pray."*

The words brought with them the urge to talk to God. The long day loomed ahead of her and would continue to pass, while her dilemma simmered deep inside. She thought of her prayer the day before with Hunter and for a moment considered returning to her cliff, but the memory that the trip down wasn't an easy one even with Hunter at her side caused her to stay put. She knew her best plan would be to place one foot in front of the other and continue making progress, both figuratively and emotionally, on what she needed to do. So instead of heading toward the cliff, she headed toward the empty tables of the dining area. The cook would begin his preparations soon, and she'd eat and get right to work. But in the meantime, she'd listen to the tiny voice and pray.

&

"Huh-uh. No way." Hunter held up his hand and interrupted her plea for assistance before she could get any more inane words past her pretty little lips. "We've already been through this. If your father says you need to leave, you need to leave. It's settled."

Tabitha sent him her most stubborn glare, and he knew he was in trouble. "It's not settled, at least not between you and me. As to my father and I, yes, you're right. He's leaving, and I'm staying. That's the only thing that's been agreed upon."

"The committee will send you packing in his tracks. You heard what Joey said the other day. The only reason he changed his mind and backed off is because we pushed, knowing your father's return was imminent. Now that he's leaving again, the situation has changed."

"Not for me it hasn't. I signed on for the dig, and they accepted me."

"As a partner to your father."

"Nowhere in my paperwork does it state that."

"But it's implied."

"Implied where?" She crossed her arms over her chest and stared him down. "I've seen no rules stating such a thing. There's no mention of women not working alone anywhere in the paperwork. And trust me, I've been through it all."

He imagined she had been. The woman was nothing if not meticulous. "But the committee will state the information on women isn't there because they've never had an issue with it. No woman has dared to step foot in their world or question their process."

"Until now."

He sighed. "Until now."

"I've already told my father, and now I'm telling you. I'm staying. I can do this with your support and backing, or I can stay without it."

Her words caused visual after visual to pass through his mind. If she stayed without her father's protection—or his—she'd be at the mercy of any of the scoundrels who filled the camp. Her reputation would be sullied, not that she seemed to care at this point. And whoever had already made attempts on her life would have free rein to try another attack. And worse, but most important to him, he didn't know if he'd ever see her again if she left, nor would he have the chance to speak further to her about the Lord.

"I'm not going to sway you on this, am I?" His weary tone gave away the fact that he hovered on the verge of giving in. The way her face lit up at the question proved she didn't miss that little fact.

"Nope." She stepped closer, hope filling her eyes for the first time. "Look. I have the book knowledge, and you have the field knowledge."

"I have book knowledge, too. I studied at the university back in St. Louis."

"Oh, I'm so sorry. I didn't mean to insult you." She tipped a grin his way. "And I've never actually studied at the university level. After my short stay at the preparatory school, my father felt it best I continue my studies with him. Regardless, if we work together, I know we'll make a good team."

Resignation battled with concern. "Then I'll head over to speak with your father, and you'd best get to work. I'll let you know what he says. If he's agreeable, we'll work the claims as a team."

She grabbed his arms in a quick hug before she caught herself and looked around. "Sorry. But thank you. You won't regret this."

Hunter was sure that in some way or another, he surely would.

❧

Two days later, Hunter found himself questioning why he'd ever made such a harebrained decision to help Tab. When she wasn't hard at work, she talked. Incessantly. When he needed to talk, she held up her hand for silence while working on inanely delicate procedures that made him want to pull his hair out. At the rate she worked, they wouldn't find anything of relevance for at least another decade.

"I don't know why you're all bent out of shape over my methods. It's not like you had someone faster to work with before I came along. You should look at everything I do as a bonus." Tabitha stood and peered at him, hands on hips, looking truly confused about his frustration.

"But the deal was you'd be an asset to my 'team,' and as it is, your work method looks like you're picking fleas out of an old hound dog. We aren't going to make progress or win any competition at this rate. If you work any slower, people will think you're taking a nap." Hunter grabbed his sledgehammer and stomped over to the farthest edge of his work area. He didn't miss the fact that she rolled her eyes and went back to her own area with a frustrated huff. She kicked an innocent rock high into the air before she settled back into place.

Hunter swung the sledgehammer up and back over his head with more force than he'd meant to use. He was thrown off balance by the sudden lightness as the head flew off the wooden end and catapulted through the air, barely missing Tabitha's bent form. She screeched and jumped to her feet after it whizzed past. They both watched in shock as it tore through her tent and landed inside with a *thud*. Her face paled of all color.

"What on earth are you trying to do?" Her shriek pierced through his ears. His head began to pound. "You could have killed me."

"The confounded thing flew off. It's not like I did it on purpose." He strode over to her tent and pulled back the flap to see that the iron had embedded itself in the dirt floor. He stepped inside, pulled it out of the ground, and picked it up, bringing it outside for his perusal.

Tabitha peered over his shoulder. "Did it wear out from use? How old is that thing anyway?"

"I bought it new for this expedition, and for the price I paid, it should have lasted for years." He turned the heavy item over in his hand and compared it to the piece of wood he still clutched in his other hand. "If that don't beat all. Look here."

He pointed to the place where the head had attached to the wood handle.

Tabitha did as he said. "Okay. What am I looking for?"

"See this streak on the wood? It's a scrape. Someone pried the head loose. This wasn't an accident." He raised his eyes and met her concerned gaze.

She contemplated his words a moment before disbelief filled her eyes. "What are you saying? Someone purposely pried it loose, just hoping this would happen? Or worse, that you'd hit me with it? What are the chances. . . ?"

"I'm serious, Tab. Someone did this on purpose."

Another cloud of concern passed over her face. "How do I know it wasn't you?"

"Right. I tampered with my own tools. I damaged one of my most important pieces of gear on purpose. I'm doing that to self-sabotage, and if I can aim at you in the process, that gives me bonus points." It was his turn to face her with hands on hips. He couldn't begin to figure how to show her the level of frustration she brought out in him. "C'mon, Tabitha, give me one good reason as to why I'd tamper with my own tools. That doesn't even begin to make sense."

She flinched. "Sorry."

He stared her down. "I could just as easily accuse you, you know. I didn't have any problems until you joined me. And you're the one so determined to get the plaque with your name on it."

"*Me?*"

Her indignant gasp shot through the air, and even with the severity of what had just happened, he battled an urge to smile.

She glared, and the color returned to her cheeks. "I think not. What would I have to gain?"

"Exactly my point to you. We're a team."

"Then let's get back to it." She stalked over to his site but tossed her final words at him from across her shoulder. "And for the record, it's my *father's* name I want to see on the plaque, not mine."

Chapter 8

Tabitha, have you seen my chisel? I had it right over here before we went for lunch." Hunter turned in a circle, a perplexed expression on his face. Three weeks into the dig, this Monday afternoon had been nothing but one slowdown after another.

After wiping her hands on her skirt, an act she regretted when she noticed the streaks of mud her sweaty hands left there, Tabitha sat back and glanced at her partner. "No, I have my own chisel. Why would I need yours?"

"I don't know." Hands on hips, he continued to glance around his work area. "I thought maybe you needed it for some reason. Hmm, this is odd. I know I left it right here when we went to eat." He turned in another circle, surveying their work areas.

Tabitha shrugged and went back to her own work. She'd found a few fossils that looked promising and didn't want to be distracted.

She could hear him tossing a few tools around and digging through his bins and boxes of equipment. The noise distracted her, and she wished he'd settle in.

When it became apparent that wasn't going to happen until he found his beloved chisel, she called out to him. "You're welcome to use mine."

"Or. . .I could use mine," he stated from right behind her.

She about jumped out of her skin. "Oh good, you found it." When he didn't answer, she turned around to look up at him. He had a funny expression on his face.

"What?" She stood. "Is something wrong? Where'd you find it?"

"Where indeed?" He continued to appraise her, something akin to doubt in his eyes.

"Hunter, I don't have time to play guessing games. What's the problem?"

He flipped the chisel over and over in his hands. "I found it in your box."

"In *my* box? Well, I surely didn't put it there. I went to lunch with you, remember? When would I have had a chance to sneak back here and tamper with your chisel?"

"You left for a few moments. . ." His voice drifted off, his meaning clear.

She reached back and ran her fingers over her hair. "I only took a trip to the. . .well, you know. . .a trip to take care of necessities. You think I faked that so I could make a side trip over here to hide your chisel where you'd find it in my box? And how would I have sneaked past the table with you sitting there? The kitchen area backs up to the cliff. Or wait, you saw my agility on the cliff the other day—maybe I climbed up that way? Did I drop off the bluff over there?"

"It does sound a bit silly when you put it that way. But I can do without the sarcasm."

"But honestly, Hunter. How do you think it feels to be accused of such a silly thing? You should know me better by now."

"I do. And I'm sorry. But you have to admit, things keep happening since we've joined forces, and that's kind of odd when nothing of the sort happened before."

"Nothing of the sort? What do you call someone pushing a rock over onto my tent? That's not exactly an everyday occurrence." Though he had a point. Since they'd become partners, strange things kept happening at regular intervals. Items went missing. Then the missing items turned up in the oddest places. The sledgehammer had been tampered with, and other items disappeared completely. Hunter once walked into his tent, and the entire thing collapsed on top of him. Though she had to admit, the bewildered expression on his face when he'd poked his head back out through the opening after flailing around inside for a few moments had sent her into gales of laughter. That didn't mean she had anything to do with it.

"So you admit, the trouble seems to come where you're concerned, not me."

"Ohh." He was back to that again. She stalked over to her side of the work site before swinging around to face him. "I'll admit no such thing. I can just as easily blame you. If you scare both my father and me off, you'll have this whole area to yourself. Maybe that's what's going on here. You know we've chosen a prime area for the find."

"If that was my intent, why did I agree to watch over you, which is the only reason your father allowed you to stay?"

She hesitated for a moment and thought that question over. "So you'd look innocent while casting blame on me, as a woman, for the odd things that keep happening."

They were at a standoff. She didn't know how she could possibly work with him a moment longer. *The man is insufferable.*

"I kept you here because I enjoy your company."

Aw. . .and he can be sweet, too. She amended her previous thought.

"And I kept you here because of the importance you said the event held for your father. Though I have to say, if that's the case, he sure has a funny way of showing it."

She couldn't dispute that. He had a valid point.

He eyed her, his face pensive. "I've wondered about something since your father left."

"What?" She walked over to settle in Hunter's chair.

"Why'd he leave you behind? If he felt so strongly about leaving, why did he give in to me so easily when I asked about you staying?"

Tabitha sent him a wry grin. "I tend to be a tad stubborn. He knew he'd face a losing battle."

Hunter let loose with a belly laugh. "That has to be the understatement of the year."

Tabitha determined that she liked the sound of Hunter's laughter. She decided she'd work extra hard to make sure she heard it often.

❧

Though it hadn't rained since Hunter's arrival at the dig, heavy clouds promised this day would be different. The oppressive humidity hung over the camp, making tempers flare. Several fights had broken out, and they could hear raised voices from across the way that signaled the start of another fiasco.

Tabitha had kept to herself, quietly focusing on the closest corner of her father's dig. She'd taken to moving from one spot to another, her randomness a complete change from the focused methodical path she'd taken when working with her father. Apparently, she found the freedom refreshing.

"Tell me something." After watching her for a while, Hunter couldn't keep silent a moment longer.

She whipped her head around, a startled expression showing how intent she'd been before he'd interrupted. "What?"

"You've changed your whole work process. Could you fill me in on your thoughts?"

"Oh. Well." She stood and shook the dust from her skirt and arms. "We've been at this for weeks and haven't gotten anywhere. I figure if I keep at it with that method, I'll never find the right area."

She glanced around at the many holes that covered the dirt in front of her and grinned over at him. "I guess I have skipped around a bit. But I'm finding some promising signs over there, so I won't move on until I've fully investigated it." She pointed at the location.

"Really? Show me."

Hunter followed her to the spot and hunkered down beside her. He was close enough that he could smell the scent of flowers emanating from her hair, a most surprising revelation. He'd found her to be all business, so this feminine attribute caught him completely off guard for a moment.

"Did you hear me?" She nudged him with her boot. "You didn't hear a word I just said. Where'd your mind disappear to?"

"Sorry. I got distracted." He felt a flush move up his neck.

"Anyway, as I said, if you look closely, the first sign of life is embedded in the ground right there."

He peered to where she pointed, and his heart leaped with excitement. "You're right! This is wonderful. Why didn't you call me over immediately?"

She looked at him warily. "I wanted to be sure. It's not like I was holding out on you or anything."

"I didn't mean. . ."

A shout from across the way interrupted their conversation. "I've found it! I discovered the first bone! I've won!"

The dismay on Tabitha's face reflected the disappointment that flooded Hunter at the man's words. He helped her to her feet, and they walked over reluctantly to see what the man had uncovered.

Hunter had to admit his first thought was that Tabitha now would return to her father and they'd head off to parts unknown, far away from him. The disappointment of that realization far overshadowed the fact that he'd not been the one to win. But as they moved closer, a certain excitement seeped through him. History had been made again, and they were close to seeing the remains of the huge creatures that had once walked the same area where they now stood.

Joey pushed through the crowd as they circled the winner's encampment. "Everyone move back. Out of the way, please. I need to get through here. Let me see what you have."

The crowd parted, and Joey took the item the man held exuberantly in his hands. He surveyed it for long moments. Everyone waited in anticipation. A *crack* of thunder had everyone jumping, so intense was their concentration on hearing what Joey would have to say.

"What is it? Can you tell?" Tabitha asked from beside Hunter. Though she stood on her toes, she couldn't begin to see over the towering heads of the men in front of them.

"No, I can't see anything. It's a small bone, but they're holding it down low, and I can't get a glimpse of it from here."

More long moments passed, and the crowd grew impatient.

"Let someone look at it who actually knows about these things," one man called out from the back.

Cheers of agreement echoed around them.

Hunter could hear frustration in Joey's muffled reply.

Thunder rolled again, this time much closer. The storm seemed to be moving fast. Black clouds filled the sky and moved rapidly their way. Tabitha moved a step closer to Hunter.

"I don't think this is going to be like the storm we saw from atop the bluff."

"I don't either." Hunter tried to mask his worry. Storms out here were vicious, and all they had for protection were flimsy tents. It wouldn't be proper for either one of them to be unchaperoned in the other's tent, so they'd have to take cover alone. With Tabitha's move toward him at the thunder's loud boom, he didn't think she'd feel safe after she left his side. He said a quick prayer for their safety and for her peace. Maybe the storm would divert.

As the storm neared, the crowd echoed the tension.

"I've got to get closer. Maybe if I see the bones, I can help identify them." Tabitha began to work her way through the throng of men, and Hunter stayed close at her heels. He wasn't taking any chances in this mob of losing her. If the bone had indeed been found, the event would be over and a lot of disappointed men would have reason to act out.

As they neared the front, they could see Joey looking at the object in his hand with consternation.

Without seeming to give thought to what she was doing, Tabitha walked right up to him. "Mr. Matthews, if you don't mind, I might be able to help identify this if you'll let me look at it."

Joey all but thrust the object into her hands. Hunter watched her face with interest as she perused the bone from all sides. She pulled it close where she peered intently at it for several more moments before sending a strange look Joey's way.

"May I speak with you in private?"

Joey nodded. He took her by the arm and led her away from the crowd.

Hunter followed.

"Mr. Pierce, the lady specifically asked to speak with me alone, if you don't mind."

"It just so happens, I do mind. I have a commitment to her father to watch over her at all times."

Tabitha waved their words away. "I don't mind Hunter staying. This isn't about him."

Joey returned his focus to her. "Then what is it about? Why didn't you just tell me the name of the bone over there? I'm sure the entire crowd is anxious to hear what we have."

"Well, that's just the problem. This bone isn't from here."

"What are you saying?" Joey's face reflected his confusion.

"I'm saying exactly what I mean. The bone isn't from here. It's a counterfeit."

Joey had the audacity to laugh. Hunter had the audacity to want to punch him in the face.

"You're surely mistaken. Why would the man have reason to pull out a fake bone?"

"Why, indeed? You'll have to ask him that question. I'd venture a guess that he wants to win, and by bringing his own bone along, he'd have a sure thing."

"Unless we have a resident expert on hand, which we do." Hunter's pride carried through his words.

"He'd have to know we'd have an expert look it over anyway," Joey spat. "I'm sure you mean well, Miss Augustine, but I'll have to take this to the committee before we can resume the dig or accuse one of our fine scientists of such a severe crime."

Tabitha shrugged. "Suit yourself." She handed the bone over without another glance. "But if you'll look at the plaster caked on the end, you'll see that I'm correct without making a fool of yourself in front of your 'committee.'"

Joey's face burned red as he saw the blob of plaster she'd pointed out to him.

"Also, the density isn't at all appropriate for such a small bone. The entire thing is wrong."

This time the crack of thunder and following strike of lightning raised the hairs on Hunter's neck. The following roar and blast of wind that followed signaled that a downpour was imminent.

"Everyone to their tents, and hurry! We aren't safe standing out here in the open." Joey hurried toward the crowd without a backward glance.

The rain swept over them, and everyone's eyes were on the bone as it began to fall apart. Tabitha's mouth quirked up at the corners as Hunter took her arm and tried to move her in the direction of their tents. "You might want to hurry up yourself and get that in a dry spot before it melts completely and you have nothing left to show the committee."

Joey's expression of fury matched that of the oncoming storm.

੩੪

Tabitha ducked into her tent and felt relief to see that the entire interior had stayed dry. She closed the flap against the wind and slipped her wet clothing up over her head. After pulling on a dry nightdress, she hung the wet objects around the tent so they wouldn't mildew. Though it was early evening, the tent had darkened considerably with the weather, and Tabitha found the need to light her oil lamp.

She found a book to study and turned to settle on her cot. A strange white envelope lay on her pillow, and her heart skipped a beat with excitement. Only Hunter would have entered her tent and thought to do something so bold. She'd been careful to hide her growing feelings for him, not sure how he'd react, but maybe he'd decided to make the first move and declare his feelings for her.

Her hands shook as she tore open the envelope, her fingers awkward with excitement. Finally, the single page slipped out, and she opened it with trembling fingers. She settled down onto the cot and leaned nearer the lantern in order to see the tiny print that covered only the top portion of the letter. Tamping down her disappointment that it was so short, she reminded herself there'd be plenty of time for Hunter to work into longer missives. She began to read the words, and her heart sank with dread.

The letter wasn't in any way Hunter's declaration of his love. Instead, she read a threat that said in no uncertain terms that Tabitha was to pull out and leave the competition or her father would face dire circumstances. She had no doubt as to the meaning of the statement. A shiver passed through her at the pure evil in the intent of the note.

She had no idea how long she sat there, but a tap on her tent made her jump, and she realized the rain had finally tapered off to a drizzle.

"Tabitha? I just wanted to check on you. Are you doing okay? The storm seems to have passed, and I've brought you a plate of dinner."

"Just a moment. I'll be right out." She heard the tremor in her own voice and knew Hunter would think it left over from the storm. She hurried to dress in a dry outfit before joining him outside. The dusky sky left just enough light for them to see each other well. The refreshing scent of new rain filled the air. She wondered how the air could smell so sweet when someone among them breathed evil into it.

One look at her face and she could tell Hunter sensed something more than a storm had upset her.

"What is it, Tab?"

She held out the paper she clutched tightly in her hand. She watched Hunter's reaction as he read. As the realization of the threat passed over his features, she knew without a doubt he'd had nothing to do with its arrival. Besides the obvious fact that they'd been together the whole time leading up to her finding it, his emotions made it clear.

"That's it, honey. You have to get out of here. I can't let you stay when we know someone has a personal vendetta against you. I can't keep you safe when I don't know who the person is who would do something like this."

"If I run, if he chases me off, he wins. I can't let him win, Hunter. My father received a note. . . . What if it was similar to this one and that's why he's been acting so strange? Are we all going to quit the dig one by one until the coward who would do this claims the prize? I won't stand for it."

Hunter stared at her a moment. "I can see where the stubborn part comes in. I don't stand a chance on convincing you to leave, do I?"

"Absolutely not. I won't be chased away."

"Then we need to take this to Joey. He's not going to be happy, especially after you pointed out the fallacy of his melting bone."

She actually giggled, which in turn mortified her. She hadn't giggled since girlhood. "At least I pointed it out in private."

Hunter tried to hide his own grin. "Yes, but I'm not sure he'll see it that way. Being bettered by anyone doesn't seem to set well with the man. But regardless, he needs to know about this."

She took the plate he'd brought her and set it inside where she'd eat it after they returned.

"Thank you for not giving up on me," she told Hunter as they walked.

"It's against my better judgment, but we'll be extra diligent. I want to be with you wherever you go. Promise me you'll not step foot out of this camp again unless I'm at your side."

"I promise." It wasn't exactly the declaration of love she'd wanted earlier, but she'd be content with his desire to protect her. With him by her side, watching her so carefully, what else could possibly go wrong?

Chapter 9

Tabitha opened her eyes and tried to see through the pressing darkness. Though the air hung silent and heavy and not a sound reached her ears, the hair on the back of her neck stood up. Something—or someone—had wakened her, and she felt sure the vague movement or brushing noise had come from the interior of her pitch-black tent.

"Hunter?"

She whispered his name into the darkness, even though she knew he'd never enter her tent without a chaperone, let alone have reason to sneak around in the dark.

A chill ran up her arms, and she hugged them tightly against her chest. If only she could see; even a dim outline of her surroundings would be helpful. Most nights, depending on the moon, she could see pretty well, but tonight, due to the clouds that still remained after the storm, she couldn't see a thing.

Hesitantly, she sat up on her cot. She cringed as the wood and canvas-shrouded apparatus squeaked in protest, the sound loud in the oppressive quiet. When she froze in place, a soft shuffling noise reached her ears, barely discernible, but there nonetheless. Her airway seemed to close off, and she felt as though she couldn't breathe.

"Who's there?" her fear-filled words rasped out from the tightness of her dry throat. "Please, tell me what you want."

Nothing. Only silence and the beating of her heart reached her ears. There wasn't any answer. Only her labored, terror-filled breathing cut through the silence. She wondered if she could have been on the verge of a nightmare when she'd awakened. Maybe the noise had filled her dreams, not her reality.

She sat motionless for a few more moments and with a sigh of relief realized that must have been exactly what had happened. Already on edge from her father's desertion, and then the storm and threat, it only made sense that she would be nervous. The unease carried over into her dreams and had in this case turned into a nightmare. She swung her legs over the side of the cot and onto the cool dirt floor.

She'd noticed that though the days were hot and arid, the nights were pleasant and at times even chilly. A breath of fresh air would do wonders to slow her beating heart and put to rest some of the fears running rampant through her.

She'd not realized how vulnerable she'd feel without her father's protective presence beside her.

She felt around for the robe she'd placed on the trunk at the end of her bed and slipped it on as she stood. Though she couldn't see, she knew the way to the entry of her tent. With only her cot and her father's, both in opposite corners across from each other, and then a trunk for each of them for clothes and personal items pushed against the ends of the beds, there wasn't a lot of furniture to weave around or worry about. She'd moved a crate of books over to his side, and now she had even more clear space to walk through.

As she reached for the canvas flap, a rough hand grasped her upper arm while the other yanked her backward and wrapped around her mouth. She screamed, but the gloved hand masked the noise. Her entire body trembled in terror.

A gravelly whisper reached her as the man murmured into her ear. "So, does *Mr.* Pierce make it a habit to sneak into your tent in the dark of night? No wonder you two seem so chummy."

Tabitha took advantage of the moment and slammed her elbow back into the man's ribs. Though he grunted in pain, he rewarded her action by tightening his grip on her upper arm. She cried out in pain. His hand pressed tighter against her mouth, too, and with the edge of his glove pressing against her nose, she could hardly breathe. She panicked. Her father couldn't lose her this way. He'd never forgive himself. Whatever the man wanted, she had to survive this attack.

"I'm going to remove my hand from your mouth, but if you so much as cry out, I'll hurt you. Do you understand?"

After her nod, he moved his hand slightly away, and she gasped in the welcome breaths of air.

She caught her breath and then hissed, "Hunter has never so much as stepped foot in my tent, other than to retrieve the top of his sledgehammer in the light of day. How dare you accuse him—or me—of anything less than stellar behavior?" She had no clue why she felt the need to clear the air at such a time, but the man's insinuation bothered her.

Again the man's grip tightened around her arm. He now held her tightly against his chest, his free arm having slipped down from her mouth to curve around her neck. Did he plan to strangle her? What could he possibly have as a reason to hurt her?

"Oh really, then why would you cry out for him in the dark?" The man's snide chuckle wrapped around her. "It sounded to me as if you expected his little midnight visit."

"You're despicable. I heard a noise, and he'd be the least of my worries. Unfortunately, it wasn't him, was it? Now I demand you tell me what you want. I want you out of my tent immediately."

He didn't answer, and a feeling of dread coursed through Tabitha. Anger boiled and made her brave. If he'd come to hurt her, surely he'd have acted immediately. Since he hadn't, his intent must be to scare her.

"I want you out of here, now. Leave my tent at once."

Again, her words only met with silence. She wanted to scream, as much in frustration as terror, though terror had the upper hand.

He leaned close, and she held her breath. "You're not safe here, and you need to leave. You've been warned." She tried not to gag as his fetid breath filled her nose.

After grabbing her by the arms, he spun her around and flung her toward the far side of the tent while he made his quick exit through the doorway.

Not wanting to take any more chances, Tabitha took advantage of the moment and called for Hunter. The sound pierced the darkness that surrounded her.

❧

Hunter flew off his cot at the sound of Tabitha's terror. He pulled on his clothes at a run and reached her tent as neighboring men poured out of theirs. Tripping over the corner rope, he stumbled and caught himself before hurrying around to the front.

"Tabitha, I'm here."

His heart skipped a few beats when she didn't answer, but after a few moments, she pulled the flap open and hurried into his arms.

"It's all right, you're safe. What happened? Did you have a nightmare?"

She pulled away from his embrace, wrapped her arms around her midsection, and seemed to be in shock. At his question, she snapped out of whatever stupor she'd been in and shook her head. "No."

A tear trickled down her porcelain cheek, and she was paler than ever in the overcast moonlight. "Someone came into my tent." Her voice caught in a sob.

"Oh, honey." Hunter pulled her close, not caring what the others thought at the moment. They were well chaperoned. "Are you hurt? Did he. . . ?"

Already she shook her head in answer. "He only grabbed me and whispered in my ear. He said. . .he said. . .I've been warned and I need to leave." Another sob stopped her words. She reached up and mindlessly rubbed her upper arm.

Someone brought a lantern over and set it on the chair beside them. Hunter set her away from him and pushed up her sleeve. Several red welts covered her upper arms. Anger coursed through him. Only the most cowardly of cowards would sneak into a lone woman's sleeping quarters and threaten her in the dark of night.

He leaned close. "Did he hurt you anywhere else?"

"No." Her voice came out as a whisper, a far cry from the strong voice of the woman he'd met on the first day at the dig.

How dare the man take away her confidence and security.

"Will you be okay for a few minutes? I need to look around."

When she nodded, he glanced around at the crowd of men and motioned for Jason to come forward and sit with her. "Stay close and don't let anyone near her."

Jason nodded, his eyes heavy with concern. As Hunter walked away, he heard Jason offer to pray with Tabitha, and though he didn't hear her reply, the older man's prayer immediately filled the air.

The other men drifted off, and Hunter scoured the area around the tent. He found no sign of anyone lurking around, though he hadn't expected the culprit to wait for him. He'd brought the lantern along and saw a dark shadow of a figure walking toward him.

Lifting the lantern, he called ahead, "Who's out there?"

"It's me, Mr. Pierce, Joey Matthews. Will you kindly stop bellowing?" Joey's voice, though always put out, sounded more stressed than usual. "What's going on over here?"

"Someone sneaked into Miss Augustine's tent and threatened her."

Joey had reached the circle of light and stopped short of it. Did he have something to hide? Hunter watched carefully for any signs of something being out of order.

"This is exactly why she needs to leave."

"Interesting. Those are more or less the words her intruder stated."

"Are you accusing me?"

Hunter stepped closer and lifted the lantern so he could see Joey's face. "I don't know. Should I be?"

Joey squinted into the brightness. "Get that thing out of my face."

Hunter lowered the lantern a bit but didn't move away. "You haven't answered my question. Do you know anything about the intruder or what happened in her tent tonight?"

Joey wouldn't look him in the eye. "I don't know what you're talking about, but if someone told her to leave, they have more sense than she does. She needs to heed the warning and go."

"That sounds like a threat to me. Where were you when everyone else came running? I find it interesting that you're arriving now, after the fact."

"That's none of your business. I don't have to answer to you." Joey glared. "And you'd do well to mind your own business."

Hunter turned his back on the man and ignored his last words. He walked back to Tabitha and relieved Jason of his guard duty. The man muttered something about keeping her in his prayers and hobbled back toward his site.

"You need to go inside and try to get some more sleep."

"How can I do that? I'm sure I'll not sleep a wink now that I've been accosted."

She had a point. Hunter surveyed her site and then his. "I tell you what. I'll sit outside here and doze in my chair. Nothing will get past me. We'll sort this out in the morning."

He helped her to her feet and gave her a gentle shove in the direction of her tent. "Secure it tightly after you go inside. You'll be fine."

If Hunter had to stay awake the rest of the night, he'd make sure of it.

⁊

Morning came quicker than Tabitha wanted, but she'd been able to sleep in sporadic stretches. When she stepped out from her tent, she was surprised to see several gaps where tents were missing from various sites.

"They packed up during the night and moved out at first light," Hunter called over to her. He sat on a crate outside his own tent and worked on his broken sledgehammer. "It seems as though someone's threatening the other archaeologists, too."

While Tabitha supposed she should feel relief at Hunter's words, she only felt a pang of apprehension. What was going on?

"Is Mr. Matthews going to do something about this? It seems it's his place to make sure the process is carried out with integrity."

Hunter walked toward her and propped his foot up on a box. "I'm not sure. You'd think so, but he's not spoken to anyone, nor have I seen him today."

A thin sheen of dust had coated the chair, and she stooped to wipe it off. "The rain sure didn't make a difference in the dryness around here."

"No, it usually doesn't." Hunter grinned. "The rain soaks into the ground, and an hour later there's no sign it ever happened."

"I guess it's a good thing since we need to continue working. Digging in mud would surely cause problems."

"How are you feeling today? Do you have any lasting effects from last night?"

"Such as?" She was sore. Her arm hurt. She'd had nightmare after nightmare. But she doubted Hunter really cared to hear all that.

"How's your arm?"

"Sore."

"Did you sleep?"

"A bit." She grinned.

"You find something about my questions amusing."

The comment was more statement than question. "I didn't figure you'd be interested in such detail."

"I'd not have asked if I wasn't interested. I don't waste words."

"I've noticed."

They returned to their companionable silence. The camp came alive as other scientists emerged from their tents and headed over to the eating area. Neither made an attempt to join them until Tabitha shot to her feet.

"I have an idea."

Hunter stood next to her, watching the diners in the next section, and folded his arms. "What's that?"

"Well, if we're all being threatened one by one, and someone is determined to chase us off from reaching our dream and being part of this history-making event, why don't we all band together as a group?"

"The idea has merit. How do you propose we go about this?"

Appreciation of her suggestion filled Hunter's eyes, and Tabitha felt her heart skip a beat.

"Well, for starters, we can join the men eating over there and see what we come up with together."

"You amaze me, Tabitha Augustine. Most women would have left long ago, but you're figuring out a battle plan. I'm proud of you."

"Thanks." Tabitha turned away so Hunter couldn't see the effect his words had on her heart. A higher compliment, she couldn't imagine.

ॐ

Hunter watched in amazement as Tabitha united the remaining men into a watch group. Over the past few weeks, she had evolved from a harsh but insecure woman to a gentle and independent one. The men had gone from resenting her to pretending she didn't exist to embracing her and her ideas.

Though he respected her desire to stay and her determination to see this through, he knew it would be best for her to return to her father's care and to leave the dangerous situation they now found themselves in.

Convincing her would be the hard part. He contemplated how to approach her with his thought as they worked. After dinner, Tabitha excused herself for a bit and went into her tent.

He'd missed his chance. The evening stretched before him, and he wished Tab would come out and enjoy the summer sunset with him. Though the bluffs blocked their view of the actual event, the sky would light up with glorious colors as the fiery ball dipped low beyond the horizon. Hunter's next thought was to wonder where the previous crazy thought had come from. He blamed it on his lack of sleep. He'd never needed anyone else in his life before and didn't need anyone now. He and the good Lord had done just fine without throwing in a woman's interfering ways, especially a woman who hadn't embraced the Lord in the same way as he had.

He waited a bit to see if she'd return, but when she didn't, he headed over to her tent, knowing he needed to tell her how he felt. As soon as he arrived, he rethought his idea, deciding it could wait.

Just as he turned to walk away, he heard her quiet voice. "Oh no."

A moment's hesitation and then, "This can't be."

Her anguish was palpable.

"Tab? What is it?" His heart pounded at the thought that someone had again attacked her in her tent, under his watch. He fought the urge to burst into the tent uninvited.

"Hunter. . ." Her voice tapered off as she stepped outside. Her tears again flowed freely. "I needed to go through my father's trunk, and I found this note. I can't believe what he's done."

She held it out, and his eyes widened in question. He wondered how he'd originally missed the fact that she was such a delicate and dainty woman. And at times like this, her vulnerability completely overshadowed her academic role.

"Read it. Please." She pushed a stray blond strand of hair behind her ear.

Hunter took the proffered piece of paper and glanced at it. As he skimmed the first few words, he slowed down and began to read more carefully. "It's a statement of some kind."

"Yes."

"I'm not sure I understand."

"My father apparently gave up his chance for the win for a very large sum of money."

"Why would he do this?" Hunter searched for an explanation. "Someone must have been very confident in your father's skills to offer such an amount to get rid of him."

"Well, besides the recognition and hoopla for the actual find, you know there'll be more to it than that. The winner will assist with the actual dig and will surely be offered worldwide opportunities to speak of the experience. The long-term financial effect could be far-reaching."

"Hmm. I've not thought it through that much. I just enjoy the quest. And I enjoy touching history."

"But it won't end there for you or anyone else who wins."

"I'm starting to realize that."

The situation increased his concern for her safety, but he decided that instead of rushing to approach her about leaving, he'd be better off praying about the whole situation. "What do you plan to do?"

"I have no choice. I'll leave first thing in the morning and go into town to talk this over with my father. I plan to return by nightfall or the day after tomorrow at the latest."

Hunter felt relief at her words. He'd pray she would see the practicality of staying in town with her father and that this turn of events would show her the need to turn her life over to God. He couldn't imagine going through life without the guidance his faith offered him, but especially in times like this, he desired and was drawn close to the One who watched over him.

He realized how lonely Tabitha must be with neither her earthly father nor the heavenly Father to lean on. He prayed that God would wrap her in His protection as she traveled and that no more dangerous events would threaten her safety while she was away from him. He knew he'd offer to accompany her on the trek because no treasure or find was more important than her safety. But he also knew that with her stubborn streak, the offer would most likely be declined. He couldn't force her to take him along. Instead, he would continue to trust and pray for her safety.

Chapter 10

Tab arranged for a ride into town on the supply wagon and glanced around at the landscape as they entered Vernal. Horse-drawn wagons hurried along both sides of the street, people bustled about, and all the activity felt foreign after her stay at the dig site. The trip to town had been uneventful, but the more they'd traveled, the more she realized how gritty she felt and how much a part of her life the grubby feeling had become. Now, as she watched the womenfolk walk from store to store in all their finery, she suddenly realized she had one goal more important than that of talking to her father. She wanted—no, she needed—to find the closest hotel where she could reserve a room and have a hot bath. For this one day she'd feel clean and dress in the frilly, feminine dress she'd brought along.

The wagon master assisted her to the ground in front of the general store and handed her the satchel he'd lifted from behind the seat. After procuring directions from the shopkeeper to the lone hotel, she walked briskly toward the worn building. The town's noise filled her ears, and she hoped the hotel would be a nice buffer from the chaos that filled the streets and walkways outside.

Though its door stood open to the elements, she let out a sigh of relief at the muffled quiet that surrounded her as she walked into the posh setting. Thick carpet covered the floor, and floral wall covering gave the entry area a cozy feel. The woman behind the desk sent her a warm smile, and Tabitha hurried over to the counter.

"What can I do for you?" The middle-aged woman motioned for her to set her satchel down.

Tabitha did so with relief. "I need a room and hopefully a hot bath."

"We can take care of that. How many nights will you be staying?"

"Just this one. Could you tell me if my father has checked into this establishment? His name is Peter Augustine."

The woman's face lit up as she registered Tabitha's comment. "You're Dr. Augustine's daughter? Oh, we're so glad to have you here. Peter has told me all about you." She hurried around the long counter, and Tabitha found herself in a tight embrace from the older woman.

"So you do know of him?" Tabitha knew her comment was redundant, and with the woman's obvious familiarity with Tab's father, speaking of him by his first name, she surely knew of him.

"Oh my, yes." The woman actually blushed. "Peter has stayed here from the first moment he stepped foot in town two weeks ago. He's been very worried and, as a matter of fact, planned to leave first thing tomorrow to travel out and check up on you."

"Well, now that I'm here, he won't need to take the trip. I'm glad we didn't cross paths and miss each other." Tabitha found herself warming to the woman.

"Oh my, where are my manners? My name is Bitsy. Bitsy Barnes. I'm going to set you up in one of our most comfortable rooms, and I'll have your bath drawn immediately. As soon as I have that taken care of, I'll notify your father of your arrival. He's going to be so happy to know you're here safe and sound."

Not after he finds out why I've come. Tabitha kept her thoughts to herself, nodded her agreement, and followed Bitsy up the carpeted stairway and down a long hall. They stopped outside a room at the far end while Bitsy worked a key into the lock.

"You'll have a corner room and views of two different streets down below." Bitsy hurried over to the window and pulled back the curtains. A soft breeze blew through the room. "Your father's room is just across the hall, but he's not in at the moment. He'll be back shortly for dinner, and you two can catch up then. I'll tell him to meet you down in the dining room, that is, if that suits you."

"Yes, thank you. That will be fine."

"I'm sorry. I tend to be a tad bossy. You be sure to tell me if I'm overstepping."

This time Tabitha smiled. She could grow to like Bitsy and wondered if her father had finally met his match. "I'll be sure to do just that, but for now I'm fine with all that you've suggested."

"Then I'll leave you to your bath." Bitsy motioned for her assistant to bring the tub in. "I'll send some water up immediately. Enjoy."

Tabitha surely would. The thought of feeling clean, if only for a day, drew her like no other.

&

Clean and freshly dressed, Tabitha hurried down to dinner. She'd twisted her hair into an elaborate style that complimented her light blue dress. As she reached the entrance to the dining room, she hesitated, seeking out the table where her father waited. It didn't take long to find him. His face lit up at the sight of her, and Tabitha hurried over to him as he stood.

"You look beautiful," her father said after giving her a quick hug. He pulled out the padded chair opposite him for her, and she sat down. "I'm so glad you've finally come to your senses and decided to join me here."

Tabitha couldn't believe how heavenly a proper chair felt. The rough-hewn seats at the tables on the dig site were incredibly hard and uncomfortable, almost as uncomfortable as Tabitha felt at her father's words.

"I've not come to stay. I'm only here for the night. I'll catch the supply wagon back to the site tomorrow at daybreak."

She didn't miss the disappointment that swept across his face. She felt bad that her words caused a sudden rift to return between them that moments earlier had been gone.

A young girl hurried over to take their order. Her father suggested the daily special, and Tabitha nodded her agreement. Their server hurried off toward the kitchen where savory scents wafted through the door.

Tabitha found herself wishing they could enjoy the meal before she got to the point of her visit, but she knew her father was never one to mince words and didn't like others to do so, either.

She glanced down at her distorted reflection in the silverware and tried to figure out the wording of what she needed to ask. There was no good way to ask someone why they'd sold out on their dreams.

"I found a note in the tent." She glanced up at her father, and he returned her look, perplexed.

"A note? And this note caused you to take a day's trip into town? What note?"

She stayed silent and watched as several emotions crossed his face. Confusion. Awareness. Dismay. He began to shake his head in denial, even as she spoke.

"Please don't speak of this."

"Father, the note offered you a large sum of money for pulling out of the dig! Why would you ever consider doing such a thing? This has never been about the money for us."

Suddenly her father's face held all the emotion of a poker player. A well-practiced poker player. "You shouldn't have read the note, and I'll not explain my actions to you."

Tabitha slapped her hand down on the tabletop, causing several people to look their way. She hurried to control her own emotions before returning her eyes to her father. "You've shut me out ever since we've arrived. It's because of that note, isn't it? You dragged me all the way out here and never even intended for us to stay. Why?"

He wilted before her eyes. "I didn't come out here intending to quit. I've wanted this for a long time. You know that. But after I started to get the threats and things escalated, I decided that for both of our good, it would be best if we accepted the money and left."

"But *we* didn't accept the money, Papa, *you* did. I knew nothing about it. Don't you think for my own safety the least you could have done was tell me

309

what I faced? Did you not think I had any interest in this?"

"I thought you'd leave with me, and after you refused, I figured if I pulled out, the mishaps would stop because no one would take you seriously."

"Well, the mishaps haven't stopped. If anything, they've escalated." Tabitha forced herself to stop there, without detail. It wouldn't do any good to get her father more riled up. He'd forbid her to return, and that was a chance she couldn't take. "I feel safe for now, and Hunter is watching over me, just as he promised, but others have been forced out. You should have confided in me and trusted that I could be a part of your decision. I miss you."

"I miss you, too, but this decision was mine alone to make and didn't concern you. I don't think you need to continue the work out there after this, either. We're set financially and can go back East and settle down. You can focus on finding a husband—if it's not already too late. I've made a mistake in dragging you around all these years, and we need to remedy that."

Tabitha shot to her feet. "There's nothing to remedy. I've enjoyed our life and wouldn't change a thing. And it's been my decision along with yours. If you want to make such a decision for yourself, I know I can't change your mind. But I will be returning to the dig, and I will see this through to the end. I will not sit by while a manipulative criminal chases everyone away in the name of money." Tabitha spun on her heels and hurried from the room, ignoring her father's call from behind.

Bitsy stood behind the counter, her face creased with concern. "Oh dear. I'd hoped your visit would be a good one and we could perhaps get to know each other a bit better."

Tabitha slowed and let go of some of her anger. "Maybe another time. For now, if you don't mind, I'll have my dinner in my room." She needed to be alone to figure out her next move and couldn't return to the dig site fast enough.

᪥

"He didn't have any good reason for selling out?" Hunter's concern after her return the next day lifted the first layer of sadness her father's harsh reaction had brought on. He watched as her face registered surprise that he'd care. He stood outside her tent, arms crossed at his chest, feeling very ferocious and protective.

Tabitha shook her head. "Not any reason I consider good enough. He said the money would allow us to move back East and settle down. He wants me to find a. . ." She allowed her voice to trail off as a charming flush settled over her features. "Never mind."

"Find a what?" Hunter loved to tease Tab when she set herself up in such a way.

Tabitha looked at the bluff and refused to meet his eyes. "A husband. All right? He wants me to find a husband."

Suddenly Hunter didn't feel so cocky. The notion of Tabitha taking a husband, with said husband not being him, didn't sit too well.

She glanced back at him and this time stared straight into his eyes. "But I'm not interested."

He had a momentary panic that she'd read his thoughts. "Not interested?"

"I've met plenty of men," she continued, "and not one has ever caught my eye in such a way that'd I'd choose to spend the rest of my life settled down and stuck in one place with him."

Hunter, feeling brave, moved a step closer. "Not a one? No potential husband has ever turned your head? Not even me?" He had no idea where those words had come from.

"Oh stop. You're only trying to make me blush. I've no need for another male in my life. My father's quite enough to handle, thank you very much."

"Well, I hate to be the one to inform you—oh, not really, I rather enjoy being the one to inform you—but you're already blushing. And whoever said marriage meant you'd have to settle down? I can promise you that if you were to marry me, we'd be anything but settled."

"Hunter, if that's a proposal, it's the worst one I've ever heard."

He now wondered if she'd heard a lot of them. He had to admit that by being constantly surrounded by men with the life she led, he'd be a fool to believe no other male had ever noticed her quiet beauty, let alone asked for her hand in marriage. She probably left a trail of more broken hearts in ports throughout the world than any sailor he'd ever met. The thought saddened him. He didn't want to be one of many in a long line of Tabitha-caused broken hearts.

Tabitha stared at him more closely. "You were joking, weren't you?"

"Would it be so awful if I were serious? You're a beautiful woman, Tab, and I've come to enjoy your company."

"Thank you." Hunter had to lean in to hear her quiet words. "No one's ever told me that before."

"I mean it. Though I never thought I'd say them back when we met. You didn't come across as the same woman you are now."

Tilting her head, Tabitha considered his statement. "I believe you're right. I am different now. With my father away, a new side of me has emerged. And I have to admit, I kind of like the Tabitha I've become."

❧

"I like the Tabitha you've become, too. And I liked the Tabitha you were. Don't leave her behind." Hunter's grin charmed her.

Hunter continued to hold her attention as he searched for his next words. "You know you don't have to be alone anymore, either, right? Even with your father gone?"

"Is this another marriage proposal?" Tabitha laughed. The thought actually intrigued her, and she'd found herself fantasizing of late about what life would be like with Hunter as her husband. She knew there would never be a dull moment, for one thing. But this was a perfect example of how she had changed now that her father no longer stood around to censor her thoughts with his constant focus on work or how she should believe and act.

Never before had she even considered marriage, let alone had her thoughts run wild with dreams of marriage to a certain man. Now that they'd had this conversation, she realized she was lonely and only a husband would fill the void in her desire for a life companion. Her father's company was nice, but he tended to lecture and teach. They had no give and take, nor a friendship of any sort. She longed for a friend—and more—and Hunter was the friend she wanted. Her life would be incredibly empty after they went their separate ways, a situation she didn't even want to think about.

She realized as her mind drifted and pondered her future, Hunter was answering her question about marriage, which she first thought she'd thrown out in jest, but now realized was a true desire of her heart.

"Not exactly a marriage proposal. I guess you'd say it was more of a 'you have a heavenly Father just waiting for you to acknowledge Him' proposal."

Tabitha felt a mixture of emotions at his comment. Embarrassment that she'd misread him. Disappointment that he apparently didn't share her dreams about a shared marriage in their near future. And frustration and irritation that he never gave up and once again pushed her toward God. That frustration made her words come out more harshly than she intended.

"Hunter, if you want to believe, it's a choice you're free to make. But as I've told you before, I'm not ready to make a decision about something like that. Someday, when life slows down, I'll research all angles thoroughly, but until then, I have too many scholastic pursuits that override my desire to worry about studies of the unknown."

"But they're not unknown." Hunter let out an exasperated breath. "The Bible is very clear."

"And reputable scholars will refute you with the fact that the Bible is fiction."

"The Bible is absolutely *not* fiction." A vein at the side of Hunter's neck now throbbed with his intensity. "I'll not remain here and listen to you say such a thing. You can disagree with my stance and beliefs, but I'll not stand by while you blaspheme the Word."

"Hunter, don't be angry," Tabitha softened her voice. "I only said there are scholars who would argue with you. I didn't say I was one of them. You need to give me leniency and time. I've told you, my father taught me early on to believe only what could be seen and proven, not the things that cannot be seen and cannot be proven. I have agreed to be open, but you keep pushing your beliefs at me."

"I've pushed nothing. I've only spoken the truth. Hebrews 11:1 states, 'Now faith is the substance of things hoped for, the evidence of things not seen.' This is completely opposite of what your father has taught you. Maybe you need to expand your horizons and realize there's more out there than what your father has wanted you to see. I sure don't see him standing here beside you fighting for what's right. If you don't want to listen to me, you have that choice." Hunter stated his words carefully. "But, Tabitha, sometimes your time runs out, and it's too late to make a decision about Christ. You have someone after you out here. You can't deny that. If this person, even under my watchful eye, catches either one of us by surprise and something happens to you, it will be too late. And I'll have that on my soul for the rest of my life."

With that last comment, he turned and walked away toward his camp.

Tabitha stomped her foot and growled with frustration. His words repeated over and over in her mind. She wasn't a child to take only her father's teachings to heart and no others, but he had taught her to use her own mind to make decisions and not just take someone else's words for granted. But was that what she'd done? In all honesty, she had to wonder.

Tired from her long day, she stepped into her tent and prepared for bed. She pulled a nightgown over her head and slipped under her cool sheet. She'd analyze things as she waited for sleep to claim her. She had a feeling that even as tired as she was, sleep would prove to be elusive. Hunter's words had struck a chord deep inside, and though she didn't want to think poorly of her father, she had to admit that though he stated one thing—that she needed to be free to search out her own truth—her father did have a way of guiding her to his truth and thoughts and beliefs.

"I don't see how God has anything to do with my disappointments or my father's choice to sell out," she muttered into the darkness. Her granny's face floated through her consciousness, and Tabitha had such a sudden homesickness for the woman, it cut her to the core. She missed her. And she realized the best thing she could do to feel close to her granny would be to read the Bible that was so dear to the woman's heart. She'd promised Hunter she'd read it but had let her reading time go of late with all that had gone on. Since her whirlwind thoughts kept sleep at bay, she sat up and reached over to light her lamp. She pulled the Bible from her trunk and opened it to the verse Hunter had quoted. As she read, another sense of peace passed through her, just as it had when Hunter had prayed. With the turmoil that had been at the forefront of her mind for the past few days, that unexplainable emotion alone showed she was on the right track.

❧

Hunter saw Tabitha's lantern come on and hurried over to her tent. "Tab? Is everything okay?"

"I'm fine, Hunter. I couldn't sleep so am doing a bit of research." Tabitha's calm voice through the fabric of her tent brought him a measure of peace.

"All right. I just wanted to be sure." He stood silently, hoping she'd say she needed to talk. Those words never came.

The camp was mostly quiet at this hour, the majority of men sleeping after a hard day of digging. He grinned at the snores that carried to him on the night breeze. Such a sound must constantly remind Tabitha that she lived in a man's world. He could hear muffled voices here and there as a few night owls sat around a fire. A lone man walked toward the end of the road where the outhouse sat silhouetted under the full moon. Dark fluffy clouds momentarily obscured the illuminating orb, only to move quickly by, allowing light to reach back over the camp.

"Thank you for checking on me." She hesitated a moment. "And thank you for caring."

"I'll always care, Tab." His hand reached for the cloth that separated them, but he didn't allow himself to make contact. "I don't want you upset with me, but I have to share what I consider to be most dear to my heart. I'll try not to push so hard in the future."

Her sweet sigh carried through the night air and brought another smile to Hunter's lips. "Don't hold back from me, Hunter. I want to know your heart."

"Well, if you're sure." Silence filled a few more moments. "I'll be off to my tent then. Call if you need me."

"I will. G'night."

"Good night."

She's not angry at me. The thought filled him with more relief than it should. He'd tried not to care, not in the way his heart had begun to long for. Without a shared faith, he couldn't move further into a relationship with the woman he now knew he loved.

He only wished he could better share what his faith meant to him and the peace in all situations he drew from the knowledge that there was more at work in his life than random happenings that were out of his control. With his concern for Tabitha the past few weeks, he'd grown away from that security. If only the woman he loved shared his beliefs, he'd be able to pray with her consistently and things wouldn't feel as out of control as they now did.

He could remedy his own lack of action by getting back to the Word and focusing more on prayer. His first prayer would be for Tabitha to understand. His second would be for her safety. She might not be open to God at the moment, but his faith alone would fill the gap, and he'd pray for her until he could convince her of God's love and direction for her life.

If Tabitha would only acknowledge God, she could use her trust of Him to carry her through this dangerous and confusing time. Instead, she leaned on her own understanding, and he had no way to comfort her. Her quest overruled the urgency of her finding God. Hunter's hate of riches and prestige flared, taking him by surprise. Her father should have stayed, and he should be the one to worry about and watch over her. Instead, he'd gone for the money and left her behind.

Hunter had grown up with everything he could ever want, but until his good friend told him about the Lord, he never felt truly happy. Now, after learning the truth of what life was really about and what he needed to focus on, he preferred to live without excess money. Tab's father's decision to throw everything he'd lived for away—to give up his dreams for a bit of money—reinforced that thought.

Money might not be the cause of all evil, but he could see how the love of money did indeed allow evil to carry on.

Chapter 11

Tabitha pushed herself up from her cot early the next morning after lifting the heavy Bible off her chest. She'd apparently gone to sleep in the wee hours after reading too many of the pages. Instead of feeling tired, though, she felt refreshed. The words the book contained brought a gentle quiet to her restless heart, and she now knew what she had to do.

She hurried to dress so she could find Hunter and share her thoughts. He'd be happy to hear that she'd followed through on her promise to stay open to God's Word and her spirit felt renewed from her reading.

"Good morning, Hunter!" She hurried to where he squatted over a box at his site, making him jump at her sudden arrival. "Sorry."

She couldn't hide her giggle at his reaction, and a slow grin filled his features as he stood to look down at her.

"Good morning." He wiped the dust from his hands onto an old rag before stuffing it back into his pocket. "You seem to be in a good mood today. What's the occasion?"

"A woman has to have a reason to be in a good mood?" Tabitha surveyed his site, putting her plan into motion as they bantered about with small talk. At a lull in their conversation, she said, "I have an idea."

"Ah, so here comes the reason. I knew there was a catch."

His smile caused her heart to skip a beat. He really was a handsome man. "Um. . ." She couldn't remember what they were talking about. His nearness suddenly did strange things to her mind. Her thoughts scattered in all directions. "What were we talking about?"

"I believe you were getting ready to tell me how you planned to stage my day." His warm laughter filled her heart. She wanted to hear the sound again and again. This phase of their relationship surely beat the first few weeks when they always found themselves at each other's throat.

Tab sighed. "I'm not about to 'stage your day.' I merely have a new direction I think we should go. . . ."

"We?"

She felt the flush cover her cheeks as she stumbled over her own words. She'd been watching his hair blow in the wind. Her mind again drifted to thoughts of their future, a future he obviously wanted to tease her about but that her mind wanted to grab on to with all the possibilities.

"Oh, uh, we, as in, the team, you and I. The dig team, that is. Where we both work together to find those elusive bones." She huffed. "Oh bother! I can't seem to think."

Hunter leaned against his shovel and stared at her in a most disarming way. The forward movement brought his face nearer her own, and she caught her breath as his warm brown eyes drifted down to her mouth. She glanced at his full lips and irrationally wished he'd kissed her while they were up on the bluff. Though she wasn't as wise to the ways of the world as she knew many other women must be, she did know Hunter had come close to kissing her while they sat in that remote place. And she also knew that with him being the respectful man that he was in such a private place, he'd never dishonor her by kissing her here, in full view of the entire camp.

"I think you were about to plan our day." After another long, measured glance, he abruptly stood up straight and walked a few feet away, putting space between them.

Tabitha decided it would be more fun to show him what she'd planned. She hurried to the crate farthest away from his tent, the one that rested against the rock wall. She rummaged around inside it and triumphantly pulled out what she'd been looking for.

"Tab. . .what are you doing?" Hunter looked perplexed.

She hurried over to the place where Hunter had blown out the hole in the wall. "Help me out here."

Hunter let loose a strangled sound and hurried to her side. "What are you thinking? Give me that."

He pulled the dynamite gently from her hands. "This stuff is very sensitive and dangerous." After setting it aside, he pulled her by the hands and led her over to sit on a different crate from the one she'd found the dynamite in. "Now tell me what you're thinking."

"I can't sit here any longer and sift through miniscule amounts of dust. I want to find the bones. I want to show my father we can win this and that there's more to life than money. I want. . ." Much to her embarrassment, her voice cracked and tears spilled from her eyes. "I want my life to be as it was."

Hunter pulled her into his warm embrace, not seeming to care what the others around them might think. "I know, sweetheart. This hasn't exactly been the experience I expected it to be, either." He caressed her back, the movement the most wonderful sensation she'd ever felt.

"I'm sorry. I know what you mean. I've been nothing but trouble to you." Her words and sobs were muffled by his shirtfront.

"Nah, that's not what I meant at all. Look at me." He gently lifted her chin, forcing her to look into his eyes. "The distraction of you is the most wonderful thing I've ever found on a dig."

"Really?" Her heart began to beat double time again at his words, but the look in his eyes made her want to swoon. Only the knowledge that a swoon would pull her out of this moment held her together.

"Really." His voice had dropped to a husky whisper. He dropped his hand from her chin and took her hands in both of his. "Listen, Tabitha. I know things haven't been easy. And I know this experience hasn't been what you expected. But I'm here to help you through it. We are going to get through it. I promise."

She could do nothing at the moment except nod.

"I'm sure your father had a reason for his decision, and I'm sorry it hurt you, but we can move forward as you've planned, and we can make the most of things as they are." His fingers absently caressed the back of her hands. "What do you think?"

She couldn't actually think much at all past the fact that he held her hands so securely with his and that his caresses muddled every intelligent thought in her head. "I, uh, I think you're right."

Those words were certainly less than intelligent. She cringed and rolled her eyes. Hunter let loose another heartfelt laugh, and she felt her mouth quirk up in response.

"I hate money."

Hunter pulled her to her feet. "So do I, Tab, so do I."

❧

Tabitha led him over to the rock wall and pointed to the dynamite he'd carefully set aside. "Let's do it."

"Excuse me?"

"The dynamite. Let's blow through this rock and see what's hiding behind it."

Hunter cocked his hand to his ear. "I'm sorry. One more time, please? I'm afraid I must not be hearing very well this morning. I do believe that you, Miss Scratch-the-surface-off-the-dirt-below-us, just suggested that we blast our way through the precious bluff that protects the ancient secrets of the past."

"Yes, well, the previous blast of dynamite from your early days here surely did damage your hearing if you can't follow the simple and direct words I'm saying. But I did suggest just such a thing. I'm tired of playing it safe."

He watched in amazement as the prim and proper strait-laced woman from a few weeks before stood before him and spun in a circle with her arms spread wide toward the heavens. The smile on her face as she tilted it skyward with eyes closed in a moment of pure abandonment had him smiling in response. She was breathtakingly beautiful.

As she stopped her spinning and stood and surveyed him with a goofy grin on her face, he stepped toward her.

"Tab?"

"What?"

"Let's blow this mountain."

"Yes, let's."

They hurried to the wall of sandstone, and Hunter showed her how to place the dynamite for the best blast and least amount of damage to the underlying fossils. He then sent her across to her own site—though they'd taken down the rope that had previously outlined their separate spaces—where she could watch in safety. He ran to join her as the blast rocked their area. He pulled her into a protective embrace as dust and small fragments of rock fell around them.

This time, instead of berating him as she had the last time he'd used this method, she threw back her head and laughed with merriment as the men stationed near their site stumbled from their tents while attempting to force their legs into their clothing.

"I'm so sorry," she laughed into her hand, not sounding the least bit sorry at all.

The other men must have realized the same thing, because instead of grumping about the abrupt wake-up, they exchanged amused smiles as they watched Tabitha's uninhibited glee.

"C'mon, let's see what we've uncovered." Tabitha tugged at Hunter's hand and led him toward the wall. As they neared the freshly blown spot, she dropped his hand and hurried forward to inspect the area they'd uncovered.

Jason walked up and hooked his fingers through his suspenders. "I don't know what you been doin' to that girl, but whatever it is, keep it up." He shook his head in a way that had his wild gray hair flying. "She's a balm to my heart when she lets loose like this."

"I don't know that I did anything to change her," Hunter defended with a shake of his head. He turned and grinned at the old man. "But if I ever figure out the secret, I'll surely use it again."

"Oh, I think you know the secret." Jason looked at him with knowing eyes. "The woman is in love."

"Now wait just a minute." Hunter glanced around to make sure no one else heard the man's crazy words. "It's nothing like that, I'm sure. I think she just needed to get a breather from her father's overbearing ways, and I'm the one nearby she's found to be a safe place."

"Mm-hmm. If you say so." Jason sent him another knowing look and turned to walk away. "Just make sure you don't bungle things up for the rest of us. We're enjoying her fun-loving nature and can't wait to see what she has in store for us next."

Hunter watched the man walk away and shook his head. Who'd have thought him to be such a romantic? He returned his attention to Tabitha, who now brushed the last of the dust away and turned to him with dismay.

"There aren't any bones."

"Really? Well then, let's get busy and blow some more of this bluff out of our way."

☙

Tabitha stepped backward as more rock sailed her way. Tiny pieces fell around her, but she wasn't concerned. Hunter's skill enabled him to set the blast in such a way as not to put them in a harmful situation. So far their more aggressive approach hadn't moved their search forward. As Tabitha waited for the dust to die down, a sharp pain pierced her upper arm, and she cried out in response.

"Ah." She ducked her head and fell to her knees, clutching her arm tightly with her other hand. She gasped for breath and laid her head down on her upper legs as the burning pain intensified. She rasped out the first name that came to mind. "Hunter."

When he didn't appear at her side, she forced her head up and tried to see him through her tears. "Oh, Hunter. It hurts. I need you." Her words were barely a whisper, and she knew there was no way he could hear her.

A piece of rock must have ricocheted off the cliffs and nicked her arm. Her head spun as she tried to see the damage. Blood coated the torn sleeve of her blouse and spread to soak into the fabric across her chest, the sight causing her stomach to turn in horror.

"Tabitha!" Hunter's voice carried to her from far away. "Sweetheart, what happened?"

She heard footsteps pound the ground and could hear his voice, but it seemed to come from far away. No words came forth as she tried to answer. She heard the anguish as he yelled for help, his tone one she'd never heard before, just before everything went hazy.

"Tabitha. Please, honey, answer me."

Pain continued to shoot through Tab's arm, and she fought consciousness. Though she felt his gentle, rhythmic caress on her hand, she refused to do as he asked. It hurt too much. She'd rather go back to that dark place.

He pushed her hair from her face as he told everyone to move away and give her some space. Grumblings showed the men didn't want to leave, but their footfalls receded.

She gave in to the haziness and drifted away.

☙

"Tabitha, c'mon. You need to wake up." Hunter didn't care who heard the emotion in his voice. "Come on, please. I need you to wake up. I need you. Tabby, please."

"Hunter. Shush. I'm not a cat."

Hunter sat back on his heels and thanked God she'd finally responded. Even though her voice sounded disgruntled and the barb was aimed in his direction, he hadn't ever heard more wonderful words in his entire life.

"How do you feel?"

"Like the entire mountain collapsed on one small spot of my arm. It's throbbing, but not as much as before."

She'd not yet opened her eyes. He worried that she'd also taken a blow to the head—perhaps they'd overlooked it in all the chaos.

He felt the panic well up and tried to control the shaking of his voice. "Tabitha, can you see? Open your eyes."

"I got hit in the arm by a rock, Hunter, not in the head." She turned and blinked at him, her blue eyes staring up at him with reproach.

"You were shot, Tab. You weren't struck by a rock."

He watched her glance around, taking in the fact that she rested on her cot in her tent. "But how. . . ?"

"I'd guess from the trajectory—based on the path from which the bullet entered and exited your arm and how you were standing when shot—that the coward once again stood up on the bluff. The same place where he pushed the boulder down."

She let her eyes drift closed. "I wish we'd blown him clean off the face of the cliff with our dynamite."

"Tabitha!"

Hunter found it encouraging that she had the ability to smirk through her pain, even if she didn't reopen her eyes.

"Well, maybe not clean off the face, but maybe backward enough so he'd feel a bit of the pain I'm feeling right about now."

"We gave you some medicine to help. Isn't it working?" Hunter couldn't stand it if she felt severe pain.

"It's helping some. I feel much better than I did." She opened her eyes and glanced at him again. "How long have I been out?"

"A few hours."

"Oh."

He fussed with the sheet that covered her.

"I feel much better than I did a few hours ago then."

The doctor pushed his way through the opening of the tent. Jason stood from where he'd been keeping watch so no one would talk about improprieties. Hunter started to argue when the doctor motioned him out, too.

"I hear our patient has finally come around." When Hunter hesitated at the tent's opening, the doctor motioned him forward. "I'll fill you in as soon as I have a look at her. She's going to be fine, Hunter."

"Doc, if it's all the same to you, I'd like for Hunter to stay."

Hunter's heart danced at Tabitha's words. She wanted him to stay. He just about busted a button on his shirt over the pride her words evoked.

"Very well, but stay back."

Hunter moved to the end of the cot and placed a reassuring hand upon Tabitha's foot. It felt delicate through the thin fabric of her sheet.

The doctor examined Tabitha's eyes and then pulled the bandages from her wound. Hunter had been so upset when the attack happened that he'd focused on keeping Tabitha awake more than on what the doctor had discovered. Now he felt his anger burst forth at the ugly wound that sliced down her arm.

"Ouch!" Tabitha jerked and her foot slipped away from Hunter's hand.

"I'm sorry," Doc said with remorse, momentarily releasing his grip on her arm. "Did I hit a tender spot? I'm trying to keep my hand away from the sore area. Maybe we missed something?"

"No, you're doing fine. Hunter just about squeezed the life out of my foot, though."

"Sorry." Hunter flinched. "But I hadn't seen the wound before now. I want to get my hands around the man's neck who did this to you."

"Spoken like a true man of God." Tabitha smirked.

Hunter shook his head at her amusement. "So maybe that isn't exactly the response God would want from me, but I'm only human. I know I need to turn the anger over to Him, but I'd give about anything right now to help Him in doling out punishment."

"He won't need help from what you've told me. Don't let bitterness creep in on my account, Hunter."

"Yes, ma'am." He waited for her to open her eyes and meet his. "Tab. You know you need to leave now. The shooter might not miss next time. Remember what we talked about the other night? That sometimes things happen and it's too late to make things right with God? This almost became that time."

"I know, Hunter, and I've given it a lot of thought since then. I want to talk more about it. But if you send me away, that talk will never happen."

She had his attention with that comment, he had to admit.

"And I doubt the rough trip would be good for me in my condition, right, Doc?"

"Don't pull me into your squabble," Doc stated without missing a step of his examination. He'd tended to her wound and now wrapped a fresh piece of cloth around her arm. "I'd say Tabitha would be the best judge of her ability to travel."

"And I judge that the trip would be too difficult for me at this time," Tabitha insisted. Her stubbornness had reached a new level.

"The pain will be intense for at least the next few days and will still be annoying you for quite a while thereafter. I'll leave some more medications in case the pain intensifies over the next day or so."

Though Hunter knew she'd feel the pain of the gunshot for the next few weeks, he hardly thought it would keep her from traveling the day trip to town. He raised an eyebrow at her to convey his thought. She averted her eyes, suddenly intent on watching the doctor pack up his bag to leave.

"As always, send someone for me if the pain becomes unbearable or if you feel the wound is becoming infected." Doc turned and sent Hunter a pointed look. "Don't let her tell you otherwise. If you think she's in pain, send for me."

"I'm sitting right here, you know." Tabitha made her annoyance clear.

Doc continued as if she hadn't spoken. "Now if you'll step outside, I'll explain what you need to do the next couple of days to keep the wound clean."

Jason slipped inside while Hunter finished up with Doc. When Hunter reentered her tent, Jason remained stoically near the opening.

"I don't need a caretaker, Hunter. I've been enough of a nuisance to last you both a lifetime. If you'll just leave me alone, I'm sure I'll sleep until morning."

"Not a chance," Hunter replied. "We're both going to sit right here. We'll take turns sleeping if it makes you feel better. The only way you'll get us away from you will be a trip to town at dawn."

"Not a chance." Tabitha mimicked his words.

They were at a standoff, and Hunter motioned for Jason to take the other cot for the first round of sleep. After he settled, Hunter took his place in the chair near the door. Men had been stationed around the dig site to stand watch, each within sight of the next. It wasn't likely anyone would breach that protective line, but Hunter knew he wouldn't sleep well until Tabitha was safely entrusted into her father's care.

"Tabitha, you need to think of the rest of us here. The men won't sleep now that you've been shot. They're having to trade off guard duty." He studied her petite form under the sheet. "You've lost weight since coming here."

If Tabitha could shoot him down with her glare, she would. He ignored her expression.

"Your skirts are so cumbersome that you can't move quickly. You're exhausted. The shooter might not miss next time."

"*If* there's a next time. I don't intend for there to be."

"Did you intend to be shot this time?"

She didn't answer.

"Of course not. You didn't expect it in the least. But even our being prepared won't help. This person is determined. I'm scared for your safety."

Still she remained silent, but hurt permeated her eyes.

His voice softened. "There hasn't been a sign of one fossil or bone. The men are getting weary and tempers are short. As we near the prize, the stakes are getting higher and the price is getting bigger. Your life isn't worth losing over a dinosaur bone, Tab."

"So you want me to sell out like my father." Her voice, devoid of emotion, sounded flat with disappointment.

"No, Tab. I just want you to live."

Chapter 12

A week later, Tab awakened at sunup after another restless night to begin an early day's work in a promising area of their plot. She moved quietly so as not to rouse Hunter when she passed his tent. Judging by his surly mood of late, an extra allotment of sleep would do him good. He'd become worse than a protective mother bear with her cubs.

Her stomach growled in reaction to the enticing aroma of fresh biscuits that wafted over from the dining area, but she tamped down the hunger and forced herself to take advantage of the early morning quiet while she could. Several of the other miners that were left had taken Hunter's lead in blasting through the sturdy sandstone, and the blasts from the cliffs throughout the day were enough to put her already fragile nerves over the edge. She knew Hunter would hustle her over to eat as soon as his feet touched the hard-packed dirt from his cot. He seemed to think a full stomach equated a full recovery, and from his actions he possibly even thought a solid meal would serve as an armor of protection against another bullet attack.

While recuperating she'd stubbornly—according to Hunter—sat on the ground and continued to work a small area she could reach without exerting herself. Meanwhile, her irritable partner concentrated on blasting rock from the equally stubborn—again according to Hunter—wall of rock before them. The effort it took to blow things up seemed to fill a void he had inside. But apparently, in between blasts he still felt it his duty to keep a steady commentary on where all the other annoying situations they'd run up against throughout this dig rated next to her innate refusal to see reason.

She'd found a few fossils the night before and could hardly sleep with the excitement that she finally might be getting close to the find that would end the competition and put Hunter out of his protective misery.

The sound of a rider arriving had her on her feet and shading her eyes from the bright morning sun with her good hand. Too early for the regular supply wagon, she watched as the man slowed and hopped down at the far end of the road. As several other miners staggered out of their tents, she dusted her hand on her skirt and hurried over to see what brought the visitor to the camp at such an early hour.

When the stranger smiled at her and swept his hat from his head, she stopped in surprise. "I have a note for you, ma'am. I was told to deliver it at dawn." He bent the brim of his hat back and forth in his hands. "I figured it must be pretty serious and important for the gentleman to pay me what he did and to want it brought to you so promptly."

"How. . . ?" Tab cleared her throat, which seemed to have closed, whether from the dry morning air or concern, she didn't know. "How do you know it's for me?"

"Well, ma'am," he furrowed his brow in concern, "since you're the only woman here waiting for a letter, I figured I made a pretty good guess." He suddenly stopped fiddling with his hat and reached up to pull a crisp note from his pocket. "Tabitha Augustine. . .is that you?"

She nodded, her heart now battling to join the tightness in her throat. Immediately, she knew something terribly wrong must have happened to her father.

The rider swung back onto his horse and turned to leave as quickly as he'd come.

A few of the more curious miners stood and stared, waiting to see what the fuss was about. Not wanting them to see her reaction if the news didn't bode well, she pushed her way through the crowd and hurried to the privacy of her tent.

Once inside, she tore open the thin paper and read the words scribbled sloppily across the single page. "No, not my Papa. . ."

Tab stared for a long moment at the evil missive clutched tightly in her hands.

A *thump* against her tent made her jump. "Tabitha? What's all the fuss about? Jason came for me and said you needed me."

Leave it to Jason to feel the need to go for Hunter. She'd have preferred a few more moments alone before having to share the awful news the note contained.

She slowly exited the tent and looked up at Hunter, where her telltale heart paused in its panic and skipped a few beats at the concern written across his handsome face. He took her by the arm and led her to a chair, and his concern grew more evident when she didn't balk at his chivalry.

"The note. It's about my father. A threat." The emotionless voice that escaped from her mouth surprised her. "My father's in danger. I'm to take the next coach from the area and head home. If I do as instructed, my father will stay safe. If I don't, he'll lose the small fortune he won for quitting. . .and. . ." She stared at the ragged holes in the cliff, holes that matched the ones in her heart.

Hunter dropped to his knees and took both of her cold hands in his, careful not to jostle her hurt arm. "And what, Tab? He'll lose the fortune and what else?"

The gentleness in his cajoling words forced her eyes to look into his. They were dark with concern. "And. . .if I don't go immediately, he'll also lose his life."

❦

Hunter couldn't stand the raw fear he saw in Tabitha's eyes. "Let me pray for you, Tab. It's going to be all right."

She nodded and continued to cling to his hands as he said the soothing words that had the potential to calm her heart.

"I want that peace you have, Hunter. Tell me how. What do I need to do?"

"You have to have faith. You have to believe. God will get you through this."

Her eyes searched his, her fright tearing at his very being. "I don't know how."

"Yes, you do. We've been talking about this for weeks. You've been reading the Bible, right? You need to turn the situation over to God and know that He will bring good out of it. Place your trust in Jesus. Only then will you have peace."

"I have. I prayed the other night that the Lord would lead me, and I told Him I wanted Him to be in charge of all I do. The bullet showed me how fragile life can be. But if He's there, why don't I feel Him? I only feel fear."

"That's to be expected. This is a scary situation. But your faith can carry you through. You have to do as the note instructs. You have to go on faith."

"But how? I don't even know what that means. Help me understand!" Tears of panic gathered in Tabitha's eyes.

"You have faith that if you go to your father as the note instructs, the sender will keep your father from harm, correct?"

"Yes." Tabitha nodded.

Hunter wanted to pull her into his arms and promise he'd make things right. Something he had no business doing. Instead, he focused on his explanation. "You can't know for sure that by obeying the instructions, his captor will keep him safe, but you have to have faith that if you do as you're told, he'll be left alone, do you agree?"

Again she nodded, and one lone tear made a path through the dust on her cheek.

"That's faith, Tab. And you have to believe with the same faith that God will provide for you if you do as the note says. You have no choice but to leave. The supply wagon will be here soon, and you need to be aboard when it pulls back out."

❦

Tab stared at him, though she knew he spoke the truth. He seemed much too eager to be rid of her and hadn't said a thing about accompanying her to town. If he cared as much as he let on, he'd want to be by her side while facing her father's captors, right? It only made sense. But instead, he seemed all too ready to have her on her way. Her suspicion about his motives had her pulling her hands from his gentle grasp. She pushed away the thoughts of faith they'd discussed and instead lashed out at him in the only way she knew—with her words.

"You're on the side of whoever is against me. Why else would you encourage me to give up after all your talk about my father doing the same? You made it clear what you thought of his decision, yet now after I get a mysterious note from a complete stranger, you're more than ready to send me on my way. How do we know this note is legitimate? Maybe it's just a cruel joke."

A shadow of hurt passed across Hunter's face, but she pushed aside her guilt. If he truly was behind the events and note, he most definitely was a good actor. It all felt so confusing.

"Your father made his decision for a price. This is different. Your father is in danger. As I said before, you have no choice. I don't see that you're giving up. You're being blackmailed. Would you really risk your father's safety out of stubborn pride?"

"I can't believe you just said that." She spat the words at him. "How do I know this isn't a ruse to get me off the dig? Look around you. How many others have been chased off? Yet here you stand, untouched."

"I'm not alone. There are a few others. But unless I miss my guess, there will be others threatened once you leave. I'm sure I'll eventually be one of them." He frowned. "This is why I have to stay. You've put up a good fight, but it's past time for you to go. You should have left with your father. If you had, you wouldn't have a bullet hole in your arm right now."

"That sounds suspiciously like a threat. A belated threat."

"How can you say that? I've made my feelings for you very clear. I care about you. I want you safe. Why is that so bad? Can't you even trust me?"

"At this point, I don't feel I can trust anyone. Someone is determined and wants to find those bones."

Hunter yanked off his hat and shoved his hands through his hair in frustration. "We *all* want to find the bones, but not all of us would resort to threats and bribes in order to do so. To have you think so little of me after our time together is inexcusable. And while we're on the subject, for all I know, you and your father could be in cahoots together with this as an outlandish scheme to throw the rest of us off."

"That's preposterous—with our stellar reputations? What would be the point?" Tabitha gasped, and the sound cut sharply through the heated air. "If that's what you think, then I have nothing more to say to you."

She watched for his reaction, and her heart broke a little as he spun around and stalked off in the opposite direction. As soon as the words escaped her mouth, she'd known she shouldn't have said them. But before she could call them back or retrieve them, he'd lashed out at her with his own accusation. And she had to admit, neither one had a reason to trust the other. She really didn't know all that much about him. Now that she thought about it, any attempt to dig too deeply into his background had met with a quick change of topic.

The sound of his open tent flap blowing in the wind caught her attention. He'd taken the liberty to enter her tent on several occasions, yet she'd not once entered his. A small scorpion hovered near the opening. Her approach sent it scuttling inside. As if they moved of their own volition, her feet led her over to the flap, and she peered inside. The area, as sparsely furnished as hers, beckoned to her. She knew she couldn't leave the creature inside, so she hesitantly stepped into the tent. She grabbed a shovel near the doorway and scooped up the offensive critter, tossing him out the entry. The motion dislodged a stack of papers on the nearest crate, and she bent to pick them up. Guilt filled her as she sneaked a peek at the contents, but dismay soon pushed the emotion away.

Several minutes later, she held in her hand proof that he was an active participant and heir to a huge business back East and that he came from a wealthy family. Everything he'd said he stood for had been a lie. While he talked of his hatred of money, he'd failed to trust her with the fact that he was an heir to a fortune.

&.

Tab waited for Hunter to return then slapped the evidence of his deception into his hands.

"You hate riches and the love of money, yet interestingly enough, according to these documents I just found, you're rich beyond measure." Anger had her gasping for her words. "And to think my father trusted you. I trusted you! To the point I left my father in town and came back here to you! He considered me to be under your protection. How could you do this to me?"

Hunter's expression darkened, and she took a step backward, away from the wrath that slipped across his features.

"And why were you going through my things? You had no right to snoop. You were supposed to be packing to leave."

"Oh, I'll leave all right, as soon as I turn you in to the man in charge. If you would deceive me about your wealth, I'm sure you're capable of deceiving us all these past few weeks. I'm sure Mr. Matthews will be most interested to hear what I have to tell him." She sent him another glare. "To think that you, the man I've come to care about, were the one behind the attacks, the sabotage, and the other incidents. How could I be so foolish?"

"The only thing you're being foolish about is to think such things about me. I thought better of you."

"You thought better of me! How can you say that? I've been forthright with you in every area we've talked about. I didn't hide behind a facade or hide my past. Why wouldn't I think you were behind all the other cowardly attempts to clear the competition out of your way?" She turned her back to him and hurried toward her tent. She stopped suddenly and swung around, blinking back her tears. "All your explanations about God, about faith. . .I believed them. And I let go, and I believed in you. . . ." Her words broke off again. "How could you?"

She saw devastation, pain, and dismay reflected in his eyes, but his voice was steady as he answered her. "It's all true."

"Yes, thanks for that." At least he admitted the truth when confronted. As much as she hated to admit it, she needed to leave—for her father's sake. Though with Hunter pretty much confessing to everything, surely the bogus note wouldn't matter anymore. But nothing made the past month worth what they'd all gone through. The excitement was gone. The recognition, the thrill of the find, and the ability to choose their own future and have money to cover all their plans dimmed in view of what she'd just learned.

Despondent and angry, she turned to go. Her heart broke more with every step she took away from the man she thought could do no wrong. The man she only now admitted she'd fallen in love with.

༄

Hunter sank to his knees and began to pray. Nothing he'd said had come out the way he'd intended, and apparently she'd taken his words the wrong way. He'd only meant that his teachings about God's love were all true. Not her accusations. He had no idea how she'd translated his negligence to mention he came from a wealthy background to a confession of guilt in the other situations.

He'd really botched things this time. His wealth, always a thorn in his side, had taken on new dimensions this time. Why hadn't he just come out and opened up to Tabitha about his background and the life he'd endured because of his parents' obsession with money?

"The money always came first with my parents." His words were quiet, but they carried across the early morning air and stopped Tabitha in her tracks. "Just as your father turned his back on you and the dig for a price, no price was ever too high for my parents when it came to turning their back on me. I didn't want to watch you go through the pain that life caused me."

Though she didn't acknowledge him, she stood silent, listening. He whispered another quick prayer for God's guidance. "I'm exactly the man you thought I was, not who you think I am right now. I've done nothing to harm you or anyone else around us."

She turned to look at him, her eyes full of questions.

He stood to face her and moved forward a few steps. "I'm ashamed of my family, of what they stand for. Nothing will stand in their way when they want something. My grandfather made his fortune in mining, and at my earliest opportunity, I moved out here to live with him. He thrives on discovery and adventure, just like me. My family, on the other hand, only thrives on spending my grandfather's funds. And if they were here, I'd not think twice before suspecting them of a deed such as the one you suspect me of, setting up an elaborate ruse so I could bring in this find alone. But I promise you I'm nothing like them." He raised his hands and then dropped them, not knowing what else to say.

"If that's so, why didn't you trust me enough to confide in me? I've shared so much with you. How do I know this isn't more of your deception?"

"My past is my past. I don't consider my family relevant to the here and now. I saw no reason to burden you with things that can't be changed. It wasn't that I didn't trust you enough to share. I just didn't think the story worthy to be shared. I've forgiven my family, but I've moved on. I have a different life now. Unfortunately, my family won't let me go so easily. They had those papers delivered to me here at the site, hoping to entice me back to the family fold."

Tabitha hesitated a moment longer, then shook her head as if to clear it. "I don't know what to think anymore. I don't feel I can trust my own decisions. I'll send for Joey, and we'll let him sort this out."

Hunter's heart fell at her words. Regardless of whether she believed him or not, she'd shut down, and from the look of things, there was no way she'd let her emotions loose for him again.

"I love you, Tabitha." The words were too quiet for her to hear, which he thought best. He felt a gentle nudging to go after her, but he ignored it. He'd only make things worse, and there was no reason to scare her further by chasing her like a desperate man. He paced back and forth in frustration before kicking a large stone with all the venom and frustration he could muster. Instead of the action bringing him release, though, it brought him a searing pain that spread through to his ankle.

"Argh!" The shout of pain went unanswered from any of the men in the nearby tents, and Hunter realized more of the men must have cleared out during the night. He remained alone in his isolated little world.

Footsteps pounded on the packed dirt road, and Hunter peered through his haze of pain to see Tabitha hurrying his way, her feet throwing tufts of dust up in her wake. "What is it? Have you been harmed? Or is this another ruse to let you have your way?"

When he didn't answer, she stepped closer and stared at him. "Oh."

Apparently the fact that his face contorted in pain clued her in to his dilemma.

He grimaced. "I kicked that rock, and it kicked back harder."

Tabitha glanced at the protruding stone he'd dislodged with his anger. "Well, it might have kicked back, but you cracked it into two pieces. Let's hope it didn't do the same to your foot bone. Here, let me help you stand."

"No!" He pushed her hands away. Her eyes reflected the hurt his rejection caused. "I don't mean no to your help, I only mean, no, don't help me stand right now. Let the pain pass first."

"Then it might really be broken. Let me take a look."

"Not yet. Just let me sit a few minutes." He could feel the sweat bead across his forehead from the stress of holding his tongue. He wanted to let loose with some of the choice words that would have flown out in his younger days. Never had he felt such pain.

"I don't understand." Tabitha drifted over to the upturned rock. "Sandstone is tough, but not so porous as to cause this much pain. What on earth did you kick?" She picked up the innocent-looking stone in her hand.

"A boulder from the feel of it. Just add it to the list of not-so-smart things I've done of late." He gasped. Though the pain had dissipated a bit, the few remaining daggers reverberated up his leg in a most vicious way.

"Are you going to be all right?"

He glanced up as she asked the question. Her tone almost had a laughing quality to it. Surely she wouldn't be callous enough to find humor in the situation. "I'm sure I will be in time." He didn't mask the grumble of frustration.

A short giggle escaped through her clenched lips.

He looked at her in surprise and saw the shock pass over her features.

"I'm so sorry." She looked conflicted as she tried to tamp down her mirth.

If he hadn't been in such pain, he'd find it amusing to watch her try to control her emotions as the laughter defied her and bubbled out.

"This isn't funny at all. I'm not sure what's gotten into me." More horrified giggles. "Oh my!"

Hunter, amid his best efforts not to do so, found himself joining in. "'Oh my' is right. Not one thing has gone our way during this entire operation. You've been shot, almost crushed by a boulder, accosted in the dark. I might have just broken my foot, but of my own accord. We do make a pair, don't we?"

Tabitha's expression immediately changed, all traces of humor gone. Her voice became a whisper. "We do."

"Tab—"

"Hunter—"

She sank to her knees beside him. "You go first."

"I just wanted to say I'm sorry for everything that's happened." He reached over to pull her hand into his before hurrying to add, "Not that I'm taking credit for any of it, mind you."

"And I wanted to say I'm sorry I doubted you. I know the man you are inside, and I know in my heart you'd never be able to harm anyone or to deceive others in such a way. I have no excuse for my behavior."

He nodded. "We're both worn out."

"Which means if it's neither of us doing this, someone who means harm to us and my father is still out there. And I still need to leave. Do you think you can stand now?"

"Give me another moment or two, and we'll see. Right now I'm content to sit right where we are." He raised his eyebrows up and down and tightened his grip on her hand.

"Hunter!" Tabitha pulled her hand from his and stood, picking up the broken stone and inspecting it again. "You have me wondering if you're really hurt at all."

"You have my word. I wouldn't fake something like this. I'm definitely hurt." He tugged at her skirt. "Maybe a kiss would make it feel better."

Tabitha narrowed her eyes at him, but the corner of her mouth quirked up and her blue eyes sparkled.

"Or then again, maybe not. From the looks of things, you'd tramp the injured appendage on your way over, just to verify that I'm telling the truth."

"I would at that." She tossed the stone back and forth from one hand to another before laying it next to the other half, then dislodged the other half from where it was embedded into the packed earth. Her hair fell to form a frame around her face, though she'd pulled it back before she'd exited her tent. The emotion of the morning, along with her tendency to run her fingers through it in frustration, allowed tendrils to come loose. Her rapt attention on the rock enabled him to continue the long perusal.

"Hunter. . ." She began to dig into the ground with her bare hands. She glanced at him with sparkling eyes. "Hunter!" Her breathless voice pulled his attention from where it had lingered while appreciating her pretty profile.

"What?" he absently responded.

"I've found it. The first bone. I'm sure."

"This better not be an attempt to get me to prove my injured foot's ability. . . ." Even as he said the words, he ignored them and made an effort to stand. "Argh." He groaned again.

Since Tabitha didn't even glance his way at his moan of pain, he knew she meant business. He tamped down the pain and crawled over to her side.

She sat back on her heels. "I've done it. *We've* done it. I've never been so happy to see anyone give way to their anger in my life! If you hadn't kicked that rock. . ." She glanced up at him, and the wonder and excitement in her eyes made everything in the past month worthwhile. "We did it."

"Indeed we have." He pulled her close into his embrace, and this time she didn't pull away. Nor did she push him away. "We make a wonderful team."

He leaned toward her, and she closed her eyes, parting her lips as she moved to meet him halfway. He gently brushed his mouth against hers, and they lingered for a moment. When she opened her eyes to look into his, love reflected from their depths.

"You know what we need to do now?" she whispered, reaching up to push a wayward strand of his hair away from his face.

He had several ideas. The first one had to do with trying for another one of her sweet kisses, and the last one ended with thoughts of speaking their wedding vows. He ought to propose first, he guessed.

She tugged away from his grasp and hopped to her feet, brimming with excitement. "We need to get the site coordinator over here to verify the find and record this into the records. Don't go anywhere—I'll be right back."

With a hurt foot, he mused, he couldn't go anywhere. Least of all, as it appeared, to the altar anytime soon.

Chapter 13

Tab hurried away from Hunter and all the conflicting emotions he brought out in her. When she'd walked a safe distance, she slowed to contemplate the past hour. Her euphoria dimmed as doubt once more consumed her. Had Hunter really hurt his foot? Or was he such a good actor that he'd again conned her into believing something that wasn't true?

But they'd found a bone! That was the important thing for now. Unless . . .her steps slowed again. . .unless he denied her part in the find and took the credit for himself. Surely he wouldn't stoop so low. Her heart skipped a beat. The bone had been found on his claim, his work area. She hated the doubt she felt and suddenly longed for her father. He'd know where to place his trust.

"Have faith." A quiet nudging in her spirit sounded as clearly as if someone stood beside her and whispered into her ear. She glanced around, suddenly aware of the unusual quiet of the camp. By this time things were usually bustling as the men got busy with their work, and dynamite blasts routinely filled the air. Instead, an eerie silence hung over the area, and not one person moved anywhere that Tabitha could see. Jason and the other miners had disappeared from sight. Dark storm clouds hung over the horizon, slowly moving their way.

She hurried her steps. She had to find someone, anyone, other than Hunter. If he were indeed fooling her, she didn't want to be alone with him. The men sometimes went into town on Friday and Saturday nights, but it wasn't usual for them not to return late in the night. If things were this silent on a Saturday morning, she had to assume more of the men had abandoned their claims due to more threats. While their tents remained behind, she noticed that most sites had been cleared of equipment. She knew Jason had to be nearby with the other men she'd seen earlier, but with the early hour, they'd most likely headed back to bed. She'd feel silly if she yelled and brought them running—again—unnecessarily.

A chill passed up Tabitha's back, and she froze in her spot. Hunter was aware that at the moment only she knew about the bone they'd found. She could be in danger if he was the person determined to win at all costs. On the other hand, if it wasn't Hunter who had chased everyone off, she could be in the path of the true villain.

The true villain. . . The words moved across her mind, and she realized with clarity that if she truly felt Hunter were the villain, she wouldn't have had that thought. *Oh Lord, what am I to do? Who do I trust? I feel so alone.*

Again she looked around, feeling as if each tent hid a possible attacker behind it. She needed to get back to Hunter. Together they could figure their way out of this. But with his injury, he'd not be much help if someone confronted them.

"Return to Hunter." A sense of calm settled over her as she felt the guidance in answer to her prayers. She wasn't alone. Hunter was her refuge.

Another thought occurred to her. They hadn't announced their find, so even if someone appeared, they could conceal the bone until help arrived. As it stood, they'd be as safe as possible with that piece of information hidden.

She turned and hurried back toward Hunter's site. She heard voices as she rounded the kitchen tent and darted over to the tent's cover to see whom Hunter spoke with. The two men stood between Hunter's tent and her own, but their voices carried clearly to where she hid.

No, Hunter, don't say it! Of course her silent warning went unheeded. She listened as Hunter told Joey Matthews they'd found the bone, and then he clarified that Tabitha herself had actually found it.

Tabitha felt a peace descend as she realized Hunter hadn't double-crossed her and even went as far as giving her full credit for the find, even though it had been found on his claim. This confirmed what she felt the Lord had told her.

She stepped forward into the company of the men. "Good morning, Mr. Matthews. I'm glad Hunter caught your attention, since I hadn't been able to find you."

Only after her greeting did she notice that Hunter's face had suddenly gone from enthusiastic to wary. And only after she stepped closer did she notice the small gun that Joey clutched in his hand, a gun he aimed directly at Hunter's chest.

"And a good morning to you, too, Miss Augustine." Joey's syrupy smile turned Tabitha's stomach. "You've arrived back just in time. Just in time to save me the trouble of hunting you down, anyway."

His laughter told of a man who had come unhinged.

"Have you shown this bone to anyone else? Or have you told anyone about it?" He turned the gun on Tabitha, and Hunter's face went pale.

Hunter shook his head to silence Tabitha. "Don't be pulling Tabitha into this, Matthews. And since you don't know for sure who all knows about the find, you'd best not do anything rash with either of us."

Joey looked around, and his laughter filled the air. "Right. And with so many witnesses around, there are a lot of prospects whom you could have told."

"But you don't know for sure," Hunter bluffed. "You don't even know for sure when we found the bone. Help could be on the way as we speak."

A touch of doubt crossed Joey's features. "Well then. I guess I'll have to take Tabitha along with me, just to be on the safe side."

"Take her with you where?" Hunter tried to stand, but his foot gave out and he sank back down, his face blanching with pain. "There's no reason for you to take her anywhere." He sagged with resignation. "Listen, leave us alone. You take the bone. Take the credit if you think you can get away with it. I don't care anymore, and I know Tabitha will agree. This isn't worth the trouble it's brought us."

The man obviously wasn't thinking clearly and would never get by with such a stunt, but Tabitha nodded her approval. Joey shook his head. "I can't take the chance you'll change your mind by the time someone else arrives."

ðŸ

Hunter had begun to pray the moment he saw Joey's gun, and he hadn't stopped since. If only he'd pushed harder for Tabitha to understand about God. He felt a measure of peace that she understood about salvation and had truly turned her heart over to God, but more time and talks would have let him know without a doubt. Though he'd never liked Joey, for the first time he realized just how unstable the man seemed to be.

Tabitha was in jeopardy, and Hunter had no way to defend her. He didn't know how to help. He sent up a plea for intervention. He'd made a mess of things, starting with his omission to Tabitha about his family and ending here, a stubborn holdout when even the hardiest of men seemed to have had the sense to get out while the getting was good.

Again he pushed to his feet, but the pain sent him staggering. He didn't think the foot was broken, but he'd definitely bruised it well. He looked around, but nothing lay within reach for him to use as a crutch.

"Joey, please. We'll sign a statement, a legal affidavit that you're the rightful winner of the contest. Whatever you want us to do. Just please"—he sent a look to Tabitha that he hoped would convey how he felt—"let Tabitha stay with me."

"You've had her eye since she stepped foot here. You think I'm going to hand her over when she's finally mine?" Joey spat. "She's mine, you hear me?"

"I'll *never* be yours, *Mr.* Matthews. I'll die before I let you touch me."

"Don't tempt me, *Miss* Augustine," he hissed. "As I see it, you don't have much choice but to go with me. By the time I'm done with you, you'll be begging for my protection and security."

Tabitha shook her head in terror and backed away. Joey grabbed her roughly by the arm. Hunter lunged forward, disregarding the pain that shot through his foot. But he came up short when the foot gave out, and he found himself flat on his face. Pulling himself along, he inched toward them, but Joey continued to move away, dragging Tabitha along.

Joey stopped long enough to point the gun Hunter's way. Hunter refused to close his eyes, and instead he stared Joey down.

"Lucky for you I don't have more ammunition. With only four bullets left, I'm not inclined to waste any on you. I think the elements and your injury will hurry along your demise. If not, I'll take care of you when I return. Alone."

Hunter sent a message of reassurance to Tab, but it didn't take away the panic in her eyes. Somehow he'd find a way to rescue her, *before* the deranged man harmed her. He continued to send up pleas to God. He knew there were others somewhere nearby. Joey apparently thought otherwise.

"On second thought," Joey stopped and lifted his gun Hunter's way. "I think I will risk one bullet and take one shot."

Hunter stared him down and watched as Joey pulled the trigger. Tabitha screamed, and he felt the bullet graze the side of his head. A mix of blood and sweat dripped into his eyes, but he wiped it away and watched as Joey yanked Tabitha around the tent and out of his sight. The man was insane. And, thank heavens, a lousy shot. The bullet had barely scratched the surface of Hunter's skin. Like any minor head wound, the bleeding had already slowed after a momentary trickle. He fought the urge to laugh in his enemy's face. He knew the action would only fuel the crazy man's fire. An angry rumble of thunder sounded to the west, and with the scent of rain heavy in the air, he lowered his head in defeat.

God, please help me. There has to be a way. You can do a miracle on my foot. He gingerly tested it, but the pain shot through as intense as ever. *Then send someone, God, please. Please bring Tabitha to safety. If nothing else, let her come to know You before she comes to harm.*

He pulled himself along the ground toward his tent, determined to get his guns. He stopped when he heard what sounded like hoofbeats in the distance. *No, God, please! If Joey leaves by horseback, I'll never be able to catch them. Not in this condition.*

After listening a moment longer, he realized the hoofbeats were nearing the camp, not going away from it. He looked around for cover. He wouldn't make it to the tent in time. If Joey had decided to use up any more of his bullets, he'd make sure he wasn't an easy target. He pulled his body along the ground and swung behind Tabitha's tent just as the first raindrop fell.

"Hello there!" A familiar voice called out, and Hunter's heart leaped with gratitude at God's quick answer to his prayer.

"Over here, behind your tent."

Hunter had never been so glad to see anyone in his life, especially since his rescuer turned out to be Tabitha's father. Dr. Augustine rounded the canvas side, and alarm filled his features.

"What on earth has happened to you?" He leaned down and hoisted Hunter o his feet, or foot in this case.

Balancing against the surprisingly strong older man, Hunter half hopped vhile Dr. Augustine half carried him over to his beloved chair.

"Joey Matthews happened to me. He's the one behind the threats and the langer, and now he has Tabitha."

"Which direction did they go?"

Hunter pointed.

"Were they on foot?"

"I believe so. The only horse I heard turned out to be yours. You're the an-wer to my prayers."

"Well now, I don't know about that, but I do know I'm going to rescue my laughter."

"In all due respect, sir, do you think that's a good idea? You've barely had ime to recuperate from your heart ailment."

Tabitha's father pulled himself to his full height. "I'm plenty young enough o take care of my daughter's captor. But with both of us on their trail, he surely von't have a chance to better us."

"But my foot. . ."

Hunter watched as the man walked into the tent and returned with a valking stick. "Carry this along. You'll ride the horse, and I'll walk alongside. We're going to get my daughter."

Gingerly, Hunter put pressure on his wounded foot, relieved that the walk-ng stick sufficiently diverted the pain.

Jason stumbled out of his tent. "What's going on? I thought I heard a gun-shot but saw the dark clouds when I looked. I figured it was thunder."

"Joey Matthews has Tabitha. Round up any of the remaining men and fol-ow us." Hunter continued to move as he talked. He swung up on the horse and, after the older man retrieved Hunter's weapons from his tent, motioned Dr. Augustine in the direction he'd last seen Tabitha as she'd been dragged along by Joey.

❧

Terror didn't begin to cover the emotion Tabitha felt at being alone with Joey. Though he wasn't a big man, he still towered over her by several inches. Not to mention the fact that she knew he carried a gun. A gun he'd already shot her with once. And the gun he'd just used to shoot Hunter in the head.

"You've all ruined this for me. It's your own fault you're in this situation."

His words angered her. "Our fault? We came and did what was expected of us. You're the one who misused your power."

"I'm always the one who has to set things up on these digs. I do all the preliminary work and oversee everything. Yet it's the scientists and archaeologists who get all the praise and credit and acclaim. This time, though, will be different. This time the credit will be mine, even if I have to dispose of you, Hunter, and even your father when the poor man arrives to check on you. Most of the others took their warnings to heart and cleared out. Even your own father listened, but you"—he used the butt of the gun to push his hat up away from his eyes—"you had to stick around with your sweetheart."

She started to interrupt that Hunter wasn't her "sweetheart," but when she contemplated his words, she realized Joey correctly summarized their relationship.

She had no idea if Hunter had survived. She'd only had time to see a trickle of blood, and then Hunter's head dipped down to rest on his arms. Joey had jerked her around before she could assure herself of his safety. But she had a small inkling of hope since Joey had just mentioned his *future* intent to kill them all. Then again, who could trust the words of a madman? Though she'd uttered a few awkward prayers so far, for the first time ever, she felt a strong inner desire to pray. *Please, God, hear my prayer and keep watch over Hunter until help comes. Please help us find our way out of this situation, a situation all my worldly knowledge added up together can't fix.*

Continuously she said her silent prayers, and peace descended upon her. God had been there for them so far, and she felt sure in her heart He'd continue to be there for them as this all played out. How He'd intervene, she had no idea. But she knew deep inside that even if worst came to worst, she'd have a place in heaven next to her dear grandmother. That thought alone lifted her spirits. Hunter, bless him, had brought her to this realization and knowledge. She reassured herself that the peace of knowing Jesus surpassed all fear she'd felt moments before. Whatever her future held, she had peace in knowing she wasn't alone and that God walked along beside her.

"You're finding humor in this situation?"

Joey's voice, full of contempt, interrupted her musings. Tabitha realized a small bubble of laughter had passed over her lips. Though she knew she wasn't out of jeopardy, she had faith everything would be okay. God was watching out for her.

Her mouth curved up into a smile as she looked Joey full in the eyes for the first time since they'd left camp. "Not humor, Joey, but peace. God has given me the most incredible peace."

Chapter 14

Hunter led the way and followed the markings in the dust where Tabitha had dragged her feet. She'd done a good job of leaving a trail, if the rain cooperated and didn't wash the remnants away. As usual, the rain had stopped after a quick drizzle passed over them. The humidity remained, and thunder continued to rumble above. A few bolts of lightning caused him concern for their safety now that they were without the protection of the bluffs.

They'd taken a moment to grab some other weapons, which included sticks of dynamite. But he had no idea how they'd get close enough to do much good before alerting Joey of their presence. Their gun wouldn't do much good as long as Joey had Tabitha as a shield.

After hearing a noise to the west, Hunter turned his head in that direction and tensed as a cloud of dust moved their way.

"What is that, a dust storm?" he asked, eyes squinted against the dimness brought on by the storm.

"Nope. It's reinforcements." Dr. Augustine didn't even try to hide the delight in his voice. "I rounded 'em up before I left town. Some of the men filled me in last night about the latest threats. Most of them decided at the last moment to carry out what they could, while leaving the tents behind for later. I reminded them my Tabitha had also remained behind. They couldn't remember if they'd seen you all at the impromptu meeting. This morning, at sunup, I reminded them of all the sweet things my daughter had done for them throughout the past month and asked if any of them would want her loss of life on their conscience."

He glanced at the oncoming stampede and sent Hunter a grin. "Apparently, they decided they didn't."

Another cloud of dust from the south showed that Jason had succeeded in rounding up some other men who had stayed in the camp and the extra horses.

"Yeehaw!" Hunter spurred the horse on, though he made sure his cry of glee was a soft one. No way would he alert Joey to the oncoming mass of angry scientists. No telling what he'd do. Besides, he wanted to personally see the look on the man's sorry face when he registered the wronged men had all banded together against him, as they should have from the start.

The riders pulled up short, towing along an extra mount that hastily found its way to Dr. Augustine's side.

Jason's grim smile preceded his words. "I brought 'im along for Miss Augustine, but apparently you can use him more."

"You all sure are a sight for sore eyes." Hunter slapped Jason on the back. "Thanks for coming to help us. Joey has about half an hour on us, but they're on foot, so we should catch up in no time."

"We're mighty glad to help." Jason spoke for them all, but the other men nodded their agreement. "It's a sad day to find out our trusted overseer has betrayed the position he's been given and is behind all the threats. And to think he's sunk so low as to kidnap Tabitha. There's never a finer lady to walk the earth if you ask me. We've been braggin' to her father each time we met up in town. We're happy to help."

Each man muttered his own thought as to what should be done to the renegade site coordinator when they caught up with him. They wanted to be sure and punish him for taking Tabitha away from them.

Hunter didn't bother to point out that the majority of them had silently abandoned Tabitha and him the night before without an apparent backward glance. But they'd come back today to bring Joey to justice. That's all that mattered now. He swung his own horse around and began to trail the prints at a much faster pace now that Dr. Augustine had his own mount.

❧

Tabitha pretended to stumble again, digging her boots into the ground as deeply as she could, which earned her another hard jerk from Joey. Her arm would be bruised and swollen tomorrow, if tomorrow ever came.

"Can we stop a moment? I'm thirsty, and I need to rest."

"We'll rest soon enough. See that cliff up ahead? That's as far as we're going."

Suddenly her desire to rest came second to her desire to stay alive and on the move. If they stopped, she had no idea what would happen. The few things she could think of didn't make her feel like reaching that destination anytime soon.

She felt much safer out here, in the open, where Hunter could see her if he found a way to reach her—if he was even alive. The thought brought tears to her eyes. If Hunter had died from the gunshot, there would be no rescue. She pushed the upsetting notion away. She feigned a faint, which earned her another jerk.

"If you continue to yank on me in such a way, you're going to pull my arm right out of the socket."

Joey snickered. "If you'd stop dawdling, I wouldn't need to urge you on."

"I can't help it if the weather and upset is causing me to swoon. I'm sure my fainting would dampen your plans a bit. Surely you want me to remain alert for the afternoon of terrors you have planned."

"Not necessarily." Joey shrugged. "I'll follow through on my plans whether you're alert or unconscious. It makes no matter to me." He leered over at her. "Though I must admit, having you awake will make my plans more fun."

Tabitha felt sick to her stomach. They approached the cliffs, and the queasiness intensified with every step nearer they took.

"There. In that little alcove to our right, that's where I'll take you."

In her mind, his words could mean either of two things, neither of them pleasant. Did he intend to have his way with her before he killed her? Or did he mean to kill her outright? She felt pretty sure he planned to go with the first horrible scenario that had come to her. The thought made bile rise up into her throat.

With sudden clarity of thought, she pushed her hat from her head and let it drop to the ground as they diverted from their previous path and headed for the bluffs. Joey, focused as he was on where they were going, didn't even notice.

She couldn't hold her silence a moment longer. "What do you have planned for me?"

He turned to her with glazed eyes. "You'll find out soon enough."

Tabitha decided to make the decision for herself. "What you won't do is lay a hand upon me."

Digging her feet into the ground for what she figured would be the last time, she refused to move a step farther.

"Is that right? I seem to have the gun, and you seem to be defenseless. Common sense says you'd be prudent to stay quiet and do exactly as I say."

Tabitha let out a sardonic laugh. "The ironic thing about that is that common sense has never been one of my stronger attributes. Ask anyone who knows me. It seems that book knowledge, even when it comes easy for a person, doesn't assure that a person will have the slightest hint of common sense."

He jammed the gun into her side, and she forced herself not to react. "You have three bullets left. One more for me, one more for Hunter, and one for anyone else who might come to find out what's happened to us. I don't think you'll waste one on maiming me for a thrill."

"You're more trouble than you're worth. I'm going to enjoy putting this bullet into you at close range."

Tabitha stood tall. "Then please do it quickly and put us both out of our misery. I don't want to spend another moment in your company, and if death is what it takes to avoid that, I'll gladly embrace it."

Raw fury took over Joey's countenance. "You'll not rush me into anything. I'm making the decisions now, remember? You might not have come to me willingly, but you'll go out only after I've gotten what I want from you."

He threw her to the ground and grabbed a handful of her tan skirt. She

343

fought him with all she was worth.

"You will not win!" she screamed. "Not in this. I can't stop you from killing me, but you will not lay a hand upon me before doing so."

A hard slap across the face was her reward for standing up to him.

She spit at him and laughed. She wanted to provoke him enough to make him shoot her. She knew she couldn't get away, but she could ensure he sent her on to Glory before defiling her body in such a disgusting way. She would die first. She had to.

He again grabbed her skirts, and again she fought him off. Her arm throbbed where the bullet had entered, but she couldn't take time to worry about that. Besides, the pain kept her more focused on her mission.

Another hard slap had her seeing stars. She smiled. Soon it would all be over. Joey screamed his outrage at her contempt, but before he could lay another hand upon her, a horse seemingly appeared from out of nowhere and jumped over them at full speed. Hunter leaped from the saddle midair and landed full force on Joey. He didn't stop punching him until her father pulled the enraged man aside.

"That's enough, son."

Hunter stood with fists clenched, breathing hard, unaware that in his fury he balanced on one foot while obliviously babying the other. Dried blood on his temple showed the remnant of his run-in with Joey's gun. His filthy shirt, torn in several places, hung from his shoulders. Tabitha had never seen a more beautiful sight in her life.

She only tore her eyes away from him when her father bent down and pulled her into his arms. "Are you all right? Did he hurt you?"

"I'll be fine now." As her emotions died down, her body began to shake with shock. She watched as the men removed the gun from Joey, draped him over a horse, and secured the crazed man face down.

Only after being assured the man could do her no more harm did she feel safe enough to throw her arms around her father. "Oh, Papa. I'm so glad you're here."

"I'm sorry I wasn't here already. I never should have left you. Can you find it in your heart to forgive me for my actions?"

She pulled away and searched his eyes. "Your safety and spiritual life are more important to me than anything else."

He looked confused.

"I talked to God, Papa, and I've turned my life over to Him. I felt a peace like I can't describe throughout this whole ordeal. I know it sounds crazy to you and I know where you stand in your beliefs, but will you promise me you'll listen later when things settle down and we have a chance to talk? Will you keep an open mind to my words and let me have my say?"

A thoughtful expression crossed his face. "I would, but. . ." He glanced at Hunter and smiled. "Hunter asked if I'd pray with him on the way out here. I knew I needed the faith and determination he has. He said he only had that because of his faith and belief in God. I've spent my time in town well. I've attended church with Bitsy, and we've had a lot of talks about faith and salvation during the past three weeks. Hunter only had the few moments to share, but his faith solidified my new understanding. All that said, I'm working on making my peace with God."

"Oh, Papa! That's the best news I've heard in a long time."

"Well, Jesus has certainly been my greatest find." Her father laughed out loud. "The journey for riches—the big 'find' we've searched for all these years—has been unfulfilling and left a void. But this latest find—Jesus and all He has to offer us—well, with that realization, I know my adventure of seeking to grow closer to Him will prove to be a greater joy than all my former quests combined. I'm glad you'll be on the journey with me."

"Always, Papa. As you stated so eloquently, the journey to grow closer to Christ will indeed be our greatest find."

Epilogue

Hunter smiled with gratitude as he and Tabitha stepped forward to accept the plaque from the Statford Museum curators. Then, in unison, they turned to hand it over to her father. Dr. Augustine stepped up and smiled when he saw all three of their names engraved upon it.

"We're blessed to have you join us on such a special day." Hunter addressed the small crowd gathered for the occasion. "As you know, we'll be starting the actual excavation next week, and we'd be honored to have each one of you, those who stuck things out when the going got rough, to join us in the work laid out before us."

His announcement was welcomed by cheers.

"You'll be paid nicely for your time by the museum, unlike the free month you 'donated' not too long ago."

Chuckles—and more cheers—rang out around them.

Hunter turned to Tab, who looked radiant in a long, white silk gown. She'd decorated her hair with tiny flowers for the occasion. Her blue eyes sparkled as they met his. "And Tab, I can't imagine a bigger challenge than working with you."

"Amen!" several voices called out from the crowd. Tabitha sent them a playful glare before turning her sweet smile his way.

He continued his spiel. "I want you by my side—forever."

"Get on with the important part!" Jason's voice rose above the others. "You think we came all this way to watch you get an award or to watch your sappy interlude with Tabitha?"

This time it was Hunter's turn to quiet the rowdy crowd with a look. He turned to the preacher behind them.

The man stepped forward and said the words that joined Hunter's and Tabitha's lives into one. Hunter didn't wait for the final proclamation before pulling a startled Tabitha against him for a long, slow kiss. She returned the kiss with passion, apparently forgetting that anyone other than the two of them existed. Only after her father cleared his throat rather loudly did Tabitha seem to remember their guests. Mortified, she glanced at the crowd. Hunter followed her gaze and noticed there wasn't a dry eye in the bunch.

The crusty old miners and scholarly scientists all had different excuses for their softhearted reactions. "I seem to have gotten some dust in my eye."

"I've been under the weather ever since that last storm roared through. My eyes have been watering ever since."

"Oh right, the storm that only brought a few drops of rain?" *Snort.* "Of course."

"That rock chipped that one day and flew up to nick my eye. I must have irritated it again standing out here in this hot sun."

Tabitha couldn't hold back her laughter as she listened to their ruminations. "Seems all sorts of ailments have fallen upon our workers; we'd best go easy on them in the future."

"Seems so." Hunter pulled her close again as the crowd dispersed and went their separate ways. "But for now, the only future I'm concerned about is the one we're about to begin together."

He surprised her by swinging her off her feet and up into his arms. Her father appeared with a horse and wagon in front of the makeshift stage where they'd received their plaque and held their wedding ceremony. "Your chariot awaits."

After carrying her down the stairs, Hunter deposited her gently on the wooden bench seat before climbing up to join her. He lifted the reins and nodded to the men who'd stopped to watch their retreat. "We'll see you all soon."

Hunter watched the look that Tabitha and her father exchanged. Though they'd see him later in town, she suddenly leaned down and gave the man a teary hug. Bitsy, standing at Tabitha's father's side, received a hug of her own.

They waved good-bye and were on their way. Tabitha snuggled close against his side.

"Well, Tab, I have to ask. Was the dig everything you hoped it to be?"

Tabitha threw her head back and let her laugh carry on the wind. "Everything and more, as I'm sure you know. The greatest find: Jesus. The most fun find: the bone." The expression in her eyes softened as her mouth tipped up in the spontaneous grin he found so endearing. "And the most unexpected find: you."

He leaned down and kissed her. "Here's to many more finds in our future."

"Amen to that," she agreed. "Our adventures have just begun."

A Letter to Our Readers

Dear Readers:

In order that we might better contribute to your reading enjoyment, we would appreciate you taking a few minutes to respond to the following questions. When completed, please return to the following: Fiction Editor, Barbour Publishing, Inc., P.O. Box 719, Uhrichsville, OH 44683.

1. Did you enjoy reading *Salt Lake Dreams* by Paige Winship Dooly?
   ❏ Very much. I would like to see more books like this.
   ❏ Moderately—I would have enjoyed it more if _____

   _____

   _____

2. What influenced your decision to purchase this book?
   (Check those that apply.)
   ❏ Cover   ❏ Back cover copy   ❏ Title   ❏ Price
   ❏ Friends   ❏ Publicity   ❏ Other

3. Which story was your favorite?
   ❏ *The Petticoat Doctor*   ❏ *Carousel Dreams*
   ❏ *The Greatest Find*

4. Please check your age range:
   ❏ Under 18   ❏ 18–24   ❏ 25–34
   ❏ 35–45   ❏ 46–55   ❏ Over 55

5. How many hours per week do you read? _____

Name _____

Occupation _____

Address _____

City_____ State_____ Zip_____

E-mail _____

RODEO HEARTS

THREE-IN-ONE-COLLECTION

Rose Kinsey's father's will demands she return to the family ranch in Nebraska and learn to run it or else lose the entire inheritance to Bane Jacobs—the man charged with teacher her the ropes. When injured bull rider Will Martin comes under nurse Dina Spark's care, she'll have to decide whether to trust God or to run from the change of falling in love with the overworked and overwhelmed head of the dysfunctional family.

Contemporary, paperback, 352 pages, 5⅜" x 8"